SBS
SPECIAL BOAT SQUADRON

SBS
SPECIAL BOAT SQUADRON

IAIN GALE

HEAD
of ZEUS

An Aries Book

First published in the UK in 2022 by Head of Zeus
This paperback edition first published in 2023 by Head of Zeus,
part of Bloomsbury Publishing Plc

9 7 5 3 1 2 4 6 8

A catalogue record for this book is available from the British Library.

ISBN (PB): 9781801101332
ISBN (E): 9781801101349

Cover design: Ben Prior

Printed and bound in Great Britain by
CPI Group (UK) Ltd, Croydon CRO 4YY

Head of Zeus Ltd
5–8 Hardwick Street
London EC1R 4RG

WWW.HEADOFZEUS.COM

In memory of
Bruce Dingwall 1959–2021

1

There is something eerily unsettling about the inside of a submarine at any time. But at 11.30 in the evening, with your stomach churning with terror of what the coming hours might hold and your mouth full of a half-eaten ham sandwich, it becomes particularly unpleasant.

Sergeant Jim Hunter pushed away the remains of his supper and gazed in wonder at one of the men in his landing party. Jenkins had already devoured two of the grease-laden slabs of white bread and tinned ham that the Royal Navy seemed to be able to conjure up at such moments and had just snatched a third from a plate of them in the centre of the table and crammed it whole into his mouth. Hunter shook his head.

'You never cease to amaze me, Corporal Jenkins. We're about to go ashore into enemy territory, to conduct an operation behind the lines, and all you can think about is your stomach.'

Jenkins, sweating profusely as they all were in the cramped space, spoke through the sandwich, spraying the wooden table and the three men seated at it, with wet bread and pieces of half-chewed ham: 'Well, Sarge, it's a shame to waste them, isn't it? You've got to admit, you never know when you might get another one.'

It was true enough, thought Hunter, lighting a cigarette, permitted when, as now, the submarine was on the surface. They had no idea when they might eat again. Or even if any of them would live to see another dawn. He inhaled deeply, savouring the smoke. Bugger the sandwich, this would be his last cigarette for days. None allowed in the field. Too dangerous. He looked around at his five companions. Noticed their nervous habits: the things that all men did as they prepared to go into battle. They all had their own means of remaining calm; of maintaining sanity. The insistent tug at the sideburn; the repeated, sometimes frenzied twiddling of thumbs; the light drumming of fingers on the tabletop; the almost imperceptible whistling under the breath. And, inevitably, in one corner of the room, the apparent calm of the slumbering man. In this case a bearded British Army officer.

Hunter hated this moment. It was neither one thing nor another. You were neither able to relax, nor were you in action. It was just a ghastly limbo in which the mind filled with the horrors of what might be. He looked at his watch. Felt again the familiar hollowness in the pit of his stomach. Spoke out loud: 'Christ, how long now?'

The sleeping officer opened one eye and closed it, smiling.

Hunter gazed at him, marvelling at his appearance. Lieutenant Peter Woods was remarkable for the neatness of his dress, which consisted of a neatly pressed battledress tunic, trousers with razor-sharp creases, gleaming puttees and heavy boots, all topped off with a turquoise cravat.

'Dandy' Woods, as the men knew him, was just that. But he was also, as Hunter knew too well, one of the finest officers in the SBS: the Special Boat Squadron. Furnished with men selected from across the British Army and the Royal Marines for their endurance, their quick-wittedness and their fighting ability, the SBS was just one of the new elite forces that had been created to carry Churchill's war into the heartland of enemy-occupied Europe. Until such time as the Allies were able to take on Hitler with a major invasion.

Recruited from the Gordon Highlanders in 1941, just a year ago, Woods had previously served in France, being one of the few men to escape from the debacle of the 51st Highland Division at St Valery. Commando training at Achnacarry had followed and then he had been with Layforce on Crete. That's where Hunter had first seen him. And what a bloody shambles that had been. Now, at twenty-six, two years older than Hunter, Woods was a hardened veteran. They both were. And that, he knew, was the reason that they had both ended up here. Poised to jump off a submarine and go sneaking behind enemy lines on some godforsaken Greek island.

He looked round at Jenkins, who had begun to eat a fourth sandwich. Hunter shook his head again. 'Good God, when the hell do we go?'

Woods opened his eyes and looked at Hunter. 'Soon enough, Hunter. Soon enough. Patience is a virtue, and all that.'

Woods closed his eyes again and pondered the word. Truth be told, there was little that was patient about Jim Hunter, thought Woods. And damned little that was virtuous. But he trusted Hunter. Would trust him with his life. Had done. Even if it was damned nigh impossible to get to know him. To get beneath his skin. Jim Hunter was an enigma. Famously hard to befriend. Not cold. Just defensive. A man who guarded his secrets. Whatever they might be. And Woods was determined to be the one who would unravel him. First though they had a mission.

Hunter spoke again: 'For Christ's sake. Let's just get on with it. When do we go?'

As if in answer there was a tap on the steel door of the anteroom and a heavily bearded young naval officer stuck his head into the room. 'Alright, chaps. Time to go.'

As one the six men leapt to their feet. Gone now was the officer's pretence of sleep.

As they made their way up the steel steps towards the conning tower, they were joined by another two men, both unmistakably Greek. Hunter knew them from the ops briefing and smiled as they saw him. One of them did not return his gaze but the other man shot him a smile.

In silence now, they climbed the iron ladder up inside the tower and, reaching the top, emerged into the balmy night. The vessel lay three-quarters of a mile off the coast of the island of Rhodes. The sea was perfectly calm and, as planned, there was no moon.

Taking a last, long drag, Hunter flicked his cigarette into the sea. Four two-man collapsible canoes lay along the casing in readiness. Woods nodded to another, younger British officer, who led the way along the casing, to the farthest two canoes, followed by two marines and one of the Greeks. Then he gave a second nod to Hunter, and the four of them climbed into the remaining two canoes, into which they had already loaded their stores and weapons.

They had left Beirut four days ago and the decadent luxuries of Lebanon were now a distant dream.

On paper, their mission was simple. Though Hunter knew as well as anyone that no 'op' was ever simple.

Sitting in the canoe, waiting to go, Hunter went through it once more in his mind.

Once ashore, they were to split into two parties. Woods, one of the Greeks, Jenkins and himself would head south for Kalathos, close to the east coast port of Lindos. The others – Lieutenant Roy Percival, two marines and the other Greek – would make for Maritsa, near the town of Kremasti, in the north. Both parties would lay timed bombs on as many enemy aircraft as they could find and leave the remainder to explode in stores and supply dumps. Then they would all head for the shore. The submarine would be back to pick them up and it would be plain sailing down to Alexandria. That, at least, was the plan.

At a given signal, almost in unison, the four little boats slipped off the casing of the submarine and into the dark waters of the Mediterranean.

They paddled hard, yet all the time increasingly conscious of the noise, as they grew closer to the shore.

Unlike on other raids, this night they were not looking out for any flashed torchlight signals. All of them were well aware that they were not going to meet any friends here. If they saw any lights, it would probably mean trouble. Twice Hunter saw a light, but guessing from the looming silhouette outline of the high mountains that was now so clear, despite there being no moon, he presumed it to be a car's headlamps or some electric house light being switched on and off.

Gradually they neared the shore and then, quite suddenly,

they could see the surf on the beach and hear the waves as they lapped at the land. One by one the little canoes grounded on the hard shingle and sand. Hunter braced himself for the sudden bump and then heaved himself out of the aperture, landing his feet on the beach in time with Jenkins, before the two men dragged their boat up on to dry land.

Down the beach the other three canoe teams were doing the same, before foraging in the boats for their kit. Each man carried a canvas bag of grenades, a haversack of rations for five days, a full water bottle, a belt with two pouches of spare ammunition and, most importantly, a Sten gun, fitted with a silencer.

Having strapped on the ammunition and slung the two sacks and the submachine gun across his body, Hunter looked up and saw Woods approaching them. 'Sarn't Hunter, Jenkins, find Zombanakis. We've got to move fast.'

He turned to Percival. 'Roy, we'll split here. All good with the plan?'

'Khushi.'

Percival turned to his party: 'B' Party.

'Phillips, Barry, find Lieutenant Pitridis. We're off.'

Silently, they made their way away from the beach by two separate paths, each group led by a Greek, both of whom were local men. Percival's lot got the smiling officer. 'A' Party – Hunter, Jenkins and Woods – were left with the taciturn foot soldier, whose name was Zombanakis.

Their targets lay directly across the island and Hunter was well aware that it would be a gruelling journey.

On the first night, all the time in silence, they made only three miles through the dense undergrowth of hard, spiny scrub. From the cliffs which rose high above the coast, they touched on inland vineyards, groves of cypresses and fragrant orange trees. They laid up at dawn, around 0600, in a cave and, after sleeping for most of the day, taking turns, with one man on 'stag', doing sentry duty, they began to move again, only when night came down, towards 2230.

They made five miles on the second night. Their guide seemed to know his stuff, for they encountered none of the enemy and, apparently, remained on course.

Halfway through their rest during the second day, however, around 1400, just as he was drifting off to sleep, Hunter woke to the sound of raised voices and saw Woods and their Greek guide locked in what appeared to be an animated conversation. He pushed himself up on his elbow and strained to hear what they were saying. It was clear that neither man was happy and, after a few more minutes, Zombanakis walked off a few yards down the mountain. Woods walked slowly back to Hunter, shaking his head, his face a mask of fury. He was rubbing at his temples. 'Christ all bloody mighty.'

'Sir?'

'He's just told me that he has no idea where we are. No idea at all. Not a bloody clue. He's a native, for God's sake. How can he not know where we are? I lost his thread I was so bloody furious. Your Greek's better than mine, Hunter.'

'Sir.'

'Have a word with him. Find out what the bloody problem is.'

Hunter got up and walked across to the Greek. It didn't take him long to understand completely what was wrong. The man was frozen with terror. He reported back to Woods. 'Cold feet, sir.'

'Sorry? What?'

'He's bloody terrified. He's realised what he's done by helping us and thinks that if he's caught his family will all be shot.'

'He's too bloody right. But he knew that before he volunteered.'

'Well now he wants to "unvolunteer". He's had enough, he says. Wants to jack it in.'

Woods shook his head. 'Well he can't. Tell him that. It's too bloody late for that. He can't just resign. He'll get us all killed. Never mind his bloody family. He can get us to the aerodrome and then he's welcome to take to the hills. You tell him that. I've done with him.'

Hunter turned and walked slowly back to Zombanakis. He smiled at the Greek and spoke quietly. 'Listen, my friend. There is nothing I can do for you now. Believe me. But if you don't help us, many men will die. Not just us, but many other men, because we were unable to carry out our mission. Not just British, but Greeks too. Your countrymen will die. What you do now will help to save your country. That's why we're here. We have come to help you. Of course you're worried about your family. We all would be. But you must see that there is more to this than that. This is a time to make sacrifices. To take risks. Unless we do that, all of us, then your country will never be rid of the Nazi scourge.'

Hunter spat on the ground and slapped his thigh. Then he pulled out a flask from his pocket, opened it and then offered it to Zombanakis, who took a long draught of the fiery raki, before handing it back to him. Hunter put it to his own lips and drank an equal measure. They passed the flask two more times, and when they had finished, Hunter spoke again: 'That is what we want. Your help against the Nazi scum. Your help to free your people. That is what we all want. Please help us. Then you are welcome to go back to your family. That's all we ask.'

The Greek slapped Hunter on the back, smiled, nodded, and walked away.

Of course, Hunter knew in his heart that Zombanakis was right. The Italians might be in *de facto* control of the island, but the Germans were ruthless with the families of anyone who aided the British. Hunter walked back to Woods. 'It's done. He won't be any trouble. He'll help us.'

It must have been close on 2100 when Hunter awoke. Lying there, under the emerging stars, as their first day became their second night, lost in the singing of the cicadas and the heady scent of a nearby orange grove, he found his mind wandering. Thinking about the extraordinary journey that had brought him here.

He had, of course, like so many of them, joined up at the outbreak. When Chamberlain's voice had come over the radio in the small Soho pub where he had been working at the time, he'd been out of the door like a shot. The Black Watch had been the obvious choice. He had given it some thought. His mother's family were Scots and he recalled as a very young boy seeing photographs of uncles in tam-o'-shanters and kilts. Well, family or not, it was as good as any mob and Hunter soon took to it, assimilating easily with the men from Perth and Fife who filled its ranks. He had boxed at school and quickly excelled at inter-regimental matches, much to the amusement and pride of his Scottish comrades.

His training had still been going on when 1st Battalion

had gone into the bag at St Valery, almost to a man; 2nd Battalion had been out in Palestine then and Hunter had joined them in July 1940, a replacement for recent fever casualties, in Aden.

Then they had been sent to a horrible little place called Jibuti, in British Somaliland. That had been his baptism of fire. A bayonet charge downhill to rout the Italians. It had earned him his first stripe.

Leave in Cairo had introduced him to everything the Orient had to offer, from shishas, to a minor dose of the clap, and by the time they sailed for Crete in the winter of '40, he was a corporal.

The first few months had been idyllic. He had improved his Greek and managed to take long walks in the hills, getting to know the country and its people.

And then, Armageddon. May '41. The German invasion of Crete.

At first the stupid buggers had dropped from the skies in their thousands – and been massacred. But once they had got hold of a couple of airfields and landed their mountain troops on the island, well then Hunter knew that he and all the 38,000 other British and Commonwealth troops in the garrison were all but done for.

His battalion had defended Heraklion airfield heroically, until they had been overwhelmed and outgunned. Most had got off with the navy. But Hunter hadn't made it out with the others. He'd found himself caught up in the retreat south. That was when he'd first bumped into the commandos. Brigadier 'Bob' Laycock's mob – 'Layforce'. So he'd fought with them, all the way down to Sphakia and eventually got off – by the skin of his teeth – on a fishing boat to Alexandria.

He'd rejoined his battalion for leave at Zahle, in the Bekaa, in Lebanon. The 'city of wine and poetry' they called it and that had suited him just fine.

And that was when he'd been 'found'.

It turned out that, after Crete, Bob Laycock had put in a recommendation that Hunter might be suitable for one of the new special forces units that were forming. Hunter's CO had agreed and that was that. He had recalled, too late, how back in '39 barely a week into his basic training, a kindly old lag at Catterick had told him: 'You don't volunteer for anything in this army, son. Not never.'

Hunter had asked, 'Why's that, Corp?'

'Because, my lad, them that volunteers don't hardly ever come back.'

Well, it had all been out of his hands. He'd been volunteered. No question of refusing. And no more Black Watch. And, with that, he was Sergeant Hunter of the Special Boat Squadron.

That had been last September. A year ago. And now, here he was, listening to the cicadas again, surrounded by the enemy and getting ever closer to another date with destiny.

Suddenly, Hunter's meandering thoughts were interrupted by a noise: the crunch of footfall on twig. Gently, instinctively, he reached for his Sten. Then a voice – Peter Woods: 'Sorry, couldn't sleep.'

Jenkins was on stag.

'This is a rum do, Hunter. I hope to God Roy's alright.'

Hunter raised himself up on an elbow. 'I think he's got a better chance than us. His guide seemed more clued up than our chap from the off. And he was an officer.'

Woods smiled. 'Greek officer. Doesn't count for much.' He thought for a moment. Here perhaps was a rare chance to get something out of Hunter. 'Though, now you come to mention it, you know that it's you who should be out there, Hunter, leading that patrol. I really don't understand why you keep refusing a commission.'

Hunter, sitting up now, scratched at his head and shrugged. 'Can't say, really, sir. Just doesn't seem like me. Responsibility. Not sure I could handle it, sir, if you see what I mean.'

Woods shook his head. Same old response. But still a chance to push the point. 'It's our loss, I'd say. You might give it some thought, when we get back.'

The third day took them five more miles into the island. The 'job' had been set for the fourth night and by the time the sun rose on the fourth day Hunter too had tired of the Greek. As they moved, the man had cussed at every twist and turn of the path. By night he sat alone and grew increasingly morose. It was unsettling. Almost as if he was waiting for something to happen. It occurred to Hunter, as it had to Woods, that Zombanakis might have betrayed them, but then why would the enemy have waited so long? Perhaps his family was being held hostage. Who knew? Hunter prayed for the fourth night to come and eventually, after what seemed like an eternity, it did.

The airfield at Calato was their objective and they had spent the day hiding out in the mountainside, which overlooked the valley where it lay. Tree-lined slopes framed the area, although close to the airfield itself, the enemy troops who had first occupied the area had cut down swathes of cypress and olive trees to give a better view around the perimeter. Nevertheless, the valley still held its age-old appearance of bucolic charm, as vineyards crawled up the lower slopes, dotted with a few, now abandoned, whitewashed farmhouses.

Throughout the day Jenkins, Woods and Hunter had gazed intently at the target from their hidden vantage point, noting again and again the positions of all the buildings and, importantly, those of the bombers themselves, until both were imprinted on their minds. They had also noted the frequency of the movements of the perimeter guards, perhaps two dozen of them, although local knowledge had already given them the details. Thankfully these seemed to be correct.

At around five o'clock in the afternoon, much to the relief of the two others, Woods ordered Zombanakis to make himself scarce. His original instruction had been to send the Greek back to the RV with any spare stores, but in view of the man's behaviour, Woods had decided to let him do what he pleased. The man thanked him and without a word to the other two men, sped off, faster than he had moved on any day on their march, back over the way they had gone. A couple of hours after he had gone and as night was falling, the rest of them edged down the hillside towards a dried-up riverbed, whose crusted banks were high enough to ensure that they would be concealed from the view of the aerodrome. The night came in very fast and as it did the rain began. Very soon it was pelting down, soaking them to the skin. Bloody unpleasant, thought Hunter, but a real help to their not being detected.

After about an hour, Woods crept towards the far side of the riverbed and peered over the top, through the grass towards the airfield. He signalled to Hunter who joined him. There, around two hundred yards away from them, in the dim yellow light of one of the camp's tall streetlamps, stood a Savoia-Marchetti bomber and beside it stood an Italian sentry. To its right stood two more bombers, but thankfully no more guards. Woods motioned to Hunter with his hand indicating that in fifteen minutes the man was due to move off. Sure enough, as Hunter's watch read midnight, the soldier walked away towards the guardroom, on his regular round.

Woods crept up and out of the ditch then at a crouch, ran – head down – towards the aircraft. Hunter followed five yards behind and behind him at the same distance came Jenkins. Reaching the first bomber, Woods slipped the heavy haversack from around his neck and pulled out two of the precious bombs. He laid one on the wing and attached the other to the front of the aircraft, close to the engine. Hunter, reaching the second plane, did exactly the same, as they had rehearsed time and again back in Egypt, and then moved on to his second target. With Woods to his left and Jenkins on the right, he crossed an anti-tank ditch and slipped over a strip of low barbed wire, emerging on to a rough stone pathway that ran between several wooden accommodation buildings and the main area of the landing strip.

Suddenly, directly in front of him, an Italian sentry walked out from between two buildings, buttoning up his trouser flies. That hadn't been in the script. Not wanting trouble, Hunter dodged into the shadows beneath the eaves of a building and flattened himself against it, holding his breath. The man paused for a moment and then took his time to extract a packet of cigarettes from his breast pocket and lit it before taking a long drag. Hunter prayed for silence and the sentry looked straight in his direction. And then he was gone.

Hunter let out his breath and, after waiting for a few seconds, padded on again, down the path. Veering off to his right, as he remembered from Woods's sketch map, he found the officer. He had located the petrol dump and, wearing a beaming smile, was dotting it with the remaining bombs from his haversack. Hunter followed suit, but kept a couple of the bombs back. Then, moving as carefully as they had come, the two men made their way back towards the riverbed. As they reached the bombers, Hunter headed quickly left, much to Woods's alarm. Quickly, he placed the two bombs on the wheels of one of the Savoia-Marchettis and ran back towards the officer who hissed at him as they ran on: 'You bloody fool. You'll get us all killed.'

Hunter grinned, panting: 'Just making sure of it, sir.'

Ahead of them they saw Jenkins, his head down, heading for the same place.

Reaching the edge, they hurled themselves into the ditch and just as they did so, the first bomb exploded. The night sky was suddenly lit by an intense red-yellow glow. Two more bombs went off, followed by the cacophony of the others laid on the planes by Hunter. He grinned at Woods. 'Bloody hell, sir. We did it.'

Woods smiled back and then looked back to the airfield. It was a scene of blind panic as the guards ran in all directions, some towards the fires; others, in terror, away from them.

More bombs were exploding now in a glorious symphony of destruction. The ones in the fuel dump, Hunter reckoned. And as the fires began to spread to other parts of the camp, so they took hold in ammo dumps and petrol lorries and most impressively among the bombs destined for the planes, one of which exploded with a huge roar, obliterating a neighbouring barrack hut and sending wood and debris and huge chunks of burning metal high into the night sky.

The more courageous of the Italian guards were manning searchlights now, sweeping their yellow-white beams across the surrounding hillsides, searching in vain for the saboteurs.

The three men crouched in their riverbed until, giving silent signal, Woods indicated that they should move. They crept from the rear lip of the trench and crawling, disappeared into the undergrowth of the hillside. After they had gone a hundred yards, Woods raised himself into a crouch and began to run. The searchlights were arcing across another area as he did so and, followed by the others, he was soon lost behind another fold in the landscape.

With the crump of the last explosions growing quieter as they moved away from the airfield, they heard a new noise cut through the night. The distinct sound of automatic weapon fire came from the north-west, answered quickly by the unmistakable rattle of a Thompson submachine gun. Again they heard it. And then silence. Hunter looked at his watch. It was approaching three in the morning. He stared at Woods and found a mirror of his own ashen gaze. Both men knew that it could mean one of two things. Either B Party had been taken prisoner, or they were now all dead.

They said nothing and carried on moving as fast as they could over the difficult terrain, in the direction of the rendezvous. But when they reached it, as both had predicted, they found no one. Jenkins spoke for them all. 'Bugger it.'

Woods spoke: 'That's it then. We're done for.'

'They won't talk, sir.'

Woods shook his head. 'I'm not so sure. The Greek might and I'm not certain of Zombanakis. Not with the SS on hand.'

'Let's just hope they're dead then, sir.'

Woods looked at him. Christ, he thought, Hunter really

was a strange one. Wished them dead? Nobody wanted that. It was true though he supposed. It wasn't that Hunter was callous exactly, just matter-of-fact. He paused. 'Yes. You're right. Let's hope they are. For our own sakes.'

Although their instinct now was to make as fast as they could for the coast and the hope of deliverance, they had one more task. At first light, leaving Jenkins at the RV, Woods and Hunter climbed back across the hills to a pre-marked vantage point high above the airfield. Woods took a pair of field glasses from his sack and scoured the area below them. Across the airstrip the wreckage of the burnt-out planes lay like so many dead birds. So many black, useless piles of steel. Around the site he could make out the ruins of the ammo and petrol dumps. Smiling, he handed the glasses to Hunter. 'Well, what d'you make of that?'

Hunter scanned the charred camp. 'Yes, I would say we'd done our job, sir. Wouldn't you?'

As he watched, a transport aircraft came into land on a runway that had been cleared of debris. As they watched an Italian officer emerged, a general judging from the amount of brass on his uniform.

Woods spoke. 'Come to tally up his losses. Poor bugger.'

'Il Duce's not going to like this at all.'

Woods took back the field glass and swung his gaze away from the airfield, further along the plain where more activity caught his eye. He swore to himself. He could see lorries, transports, moving with some speed along one of the major roads. He passed them back to Hunter.

'Now we're in trouble. Look at that lot.'

Hunter took the glasses and, focusing them once more, looked towards Woods's pointing finger. He saw the trucks.

And knew that they would be filled with Italian troops. And perhaps Germans too. He counted twelve, sixteen, maybe more.

'Christ, sir. We'd better get weaving.'

Moving swiftly away from their vantage point and down the hill, they reached the RV and collected Jenkins before making for the coast and the point that had been chosen with some care, from which they would be able to look out for their means of escape.

Woods spoke softly: 'We know they know we're here somewhere. God knows what happened to Roy's lot, but if any of them are still alive, and not POWs, we can't have them running into the enemy. They'll have to come through the pass that runs into that valley.' He shook his head. 'We've got to warn Percival.'

Hunter looked at him, momentarily incredulous. 'What do you suggest, sir? We can't go back and we can't move down the valley. We'd just be captured ourselves.'

Woods mulled it over. The man had a point. 'You're right. Like you said, Hunter, let's just hope they didn't make it.'

They moved off again, away from the enemy and away from whatever might be left of B Party and by early the following day had reached the lying-up area, from where they could observe the beach below.

Jenkins was on point, leading the way, moving cautiously through the undergrowth. Suddenly he stopped and dropped flat to the ground. The others followed suit. Jenkins waved an arm, urging them to stay down.

Peering through the long grass, breathing deeply the scent of the wild grasses and rich earthy soil, Hunter managed to catch sight of what had startled Jenkins. Up ahead of them, perhaps six hundred yards away, advancing steadily through the scrub, right in the direction of their objective, were two dozen Italian soldiers, their arms levelled and at the ready. And more worryingly, they were accompanied by five Greek civilians. Woods crept forward to Jenkins and tapped him on the ankle, making him turn round, then indicated that they should move off up the hillside to their left.

They ran at a crouch, as fast as they could, and eventually stopped higher up the mountain, on a sort of ledge cut into the hillside, behind which lay what appeared to be an ancient well. They lay there for some time, not daring to peer down at the enemy moving below, but all the time hearing voices and becoming increasingly aware of the danger.

They heard a command being given in Italian and then another, more staccato, and – this time – in German.

A second party had appeared now; Germans in their distinctive *feldgrau* uniforms, Schmeisser machine-pistols slung over their shoulders. They were moving in what was clearly a pincer movement, intended to take anyone who might be hiding in the exact position of their lying-up area.

At once it became clear to Hunter what had happened. One of B Party, or more likely one of the guides, must have spoken. Perhaps Zombanakis's fears had been right. Perhaps he had returned to find his family held hostage. Perhaps he had been tortured. They would probably never know. And right now, lying here, awaiting at any moment the bullet or the bayonet, it was of no importance.

For what seemed like much more than the two hours it actually was, they lay as still as they possibly could, acutely aware that the slightest movement might alert either of the two search parties to their presence.

No more than ten or eleven feet below their ledge, the Italian party was now combing the undergrowth, their keenness to succeed and impress their German masters all too evident from the growing noise and urgency of their shouts. Luckily, however, they confined their searching to the slopes below the three men. Perhaps, thought Hunter, they could not conceive that their prey might have managed to climb so high and so fast. Never, ever, he smiled, underestimate your enemy. It had been one of the first tenets drummed into him by the instructors at special training school.

From time to time they took it in turns to peer over the lip of the ledge and report back. As Hunter took his turn, his eye was drawn away from their pursuers towards the sea beyond and a small boat making its way along the coast from the direction of Lindos. Unable to use field glasses, for fear of reflection, he peered at it and eventually decided that it was an Italian motor torpedo boat. He could just discern a group of men gathered on deck and surmised that they might be about to make landfall. He shinned back from the edge and whispered to Woods, 'Italian MTB, sir. Looks like they're landing. Reckon that's our Carley boats in the bag.'

Together the two men moved up to the lip. The boat had disappeared, but after a few minutes, as they watched, she came into view again, this time towing the distinct black shapes of their three landing craft.

Woods swore: 'Damn.'

Quick-witted, Woods was able to grasp their situation in a moment. And it was not good. Their rations had almost run out. And now they were effectively cut off from any submarine that might be sent to collect them. They were surrounded by the enemy, who in all probability were also in possession of any stretch of beach that might have allowed them to be picked up. Their friends in B Party were either dead or POWs and they were running dangerously low on ammunition. All that they had, apart from what they carried, were the life jackets and signal torches that they'd had the foresight to conceal in a cave on the beach. Although it occurred to him that even these might have been discovered by the enemy. Hunter, he knew, would also have summed up the severity of their position.

To both men there was now only one option open. They would have to resume the initiative.

Hunter turned to Woods. 'Sir, do you think we might be best to try to make our way down to the beach?'

The officer nodded. 'Yes, my thoughts too. It's the only way now. Otherwise we're just waiting here till they find us. And I don't want to think about what happens next. We'll go at nightfall.'

As the dusk came down, they made ready for the journey down to the beach. Anything that might hamper them was left behind, including their haversacks. Hunter put a grenade into each of his breast pockets and his last few clips of ammunition into the pockets of his shorts. He made sure that his water bottle and pistol in holster were secured to his belt and his fighting knife in its scabbard, strapped to his left leg.

When it had become sufficiently dark, they began to edge down the slope. Small dots of light, either from campfires or cigarettes, alerted them to the positions of the enemy sentries and, moving slowly, they were able to weave a path to avoid them. It was hard going and certainly not the path that any of them would have chosen, even if it had still been daylight. But there was no alternative if they were to avoid the sentries. Their route took them deep into an ancient olive grove where the ground became rocky, with small anthills and dozens of unseen tree roots. Their progress was agonisingly slow and it took them a good four hours to cover ground that in daylight would have taken half the time.

They had made it to perhaps halfway to the beach when there was a stifled cry from Jenkins, who had been bringing up the rear. Spinning round, Hunter saw the man lying on the ground, writhing in agony. His first reaction was that he had been shot, but he had heard no riddle crack. Crouching, he and Woods moved back towards him.

'My leg, sir. My bloody ankle. Went over on that mound.'

He was gripping the limb tightly and only released his hands when Woods went to look.

His foot was lying at an unusual angle to the leg and it was clear at once that he had broken his ankle. Woods shook his head. 'Christ. I don't bloody believe it. Can you stand?'

'Don't know, sir. I'll try.'

Jenkins, helped by the others, attempted to get to his feet, but the moment he attempted to put any weight on the injured leg, he winced in pain. 'Sorry, sir. It's useless. I'm done.'

They laid him back down in the grass.

As Jenkins stared at his ruined ankle, Woods drew Hunter to one side. 'He's right, Sarn't – it is useless. He can't come with us.'

Hunter nodded. 'Yes, sir. I know that.'

There was a pause, then Woods spoke, quiet and expressionless: 'We'll just have to leave him here.'

'They'll get him, sir. You know what that'll mean.'

'And so does he, Sarn't. We'll leave him a pistol and two rounds. He can take the decision as to how he does it. That's the decent thing to do, wouldn't you say? He can either use them both on the enemy, or save one for himself. He knows the drill.'

Hunter nodded. Woods was right. It was the only thing to do, aside from shooting Jenkins themselves. And both men knew that neither of them was going to volunteer to do that.

Woods went over and briefed Jenkins, although there was no need. All of them had always been well aware of the potential dangers. Jenkins nodded and took the pistol from the officer. Hunter went over to him. 'Cheerio, Jenkins. See you in Cairo I expect.'

'Yes. Sure of it. I'll stand you a beer at Groppi's.'

'Not if I can help it. I'm paying.'

Jenkins smiled. 'Righto, Hunter. I'll hold you to it.'

They moved off fast and quickly put thoughts of Jenkins behind them.

The route down the hillside to the beach grew increasingly steep and perilous as they went but at last they were close enough to hear the sea. Cautiously, they slipped down the final few feet to the beach and found the cave where on arrival they had hidden lifebelts and a signal torch. Grabbing this and two of the belts they began to climb back up the hill in search of cover.

In their desperation to get to the cave, they had lost track of time and the dawn was now coming up fast. They were perhaps halfway back to Jenkins' position when they heard voices from above. Shouts in Italian. They froze and dropped to the ground.

Clearly one of the search parties had got between them and their helpless comrade. Perhaps, thought Hunter, they were still looking for members of the other landing party.

The chattering continued. Evidently their pursuers had decided to halt where they were.

Woods looked at Hunter and raised his eyes heavenwards. Their safe area had just shrunk from small to almost non-existent. The two men lay down in the long grass and pressed their forms against the earth in an attempt to camouflage the outline of their bodies. They had been there for around three hours when the Italians moved off. Woods looked up slowly and then dropped down. Whispered: 'There's an overhang about forty yards up the hill. If we can get in there we stand a much better chance of not being seen. We won't move down to the beach till dusk.'

Hunter nodded. He too had noticed the overhanging rock. The morning sunlight was now upon them and it was their only hope.

After waiting for the Italian voices to die away, the two men crawled slowly up the hillside, their lifebelts strapped to their belts. At length they reached the shelter of the rock and tucked themselves inside the small gap with seconds to spare before the Italians appeared again below them. Hunter counted fifty of them, moving methodically across the brush and rocks. Ten minutes later he watched as one of them peeled away to relieve himself, close to their position, before sitting down on a rock to light a cigarette. He was no more than twenty yards away. Clearly his absence had not been noticed by his commanding officer, for the man sat on his rock for a good twenty minutes, smoking another cigarette, before moving off. After he had gone the two men sat very still in their hideout for, Hunter guessed, around another three hours.

It was almost midday now and the sun was at its hottest. Hunter's mouth was parched. His limbs too were beginning to seize up, contorted as they were in their cramped quarters.

Suddenly, there was a series of shots from above them, followed by furious shouting. Then silence. The searchers had found Jenkins.

The two men looked away from each other into nothingness and Hunter took the opportunity of the noise to stretch his painful limbs and manoeuvre himself into a slightly more comfortable position.

And so they waited. Two, three, five, seven hours passed with excruciating slowness. Hunter licked his lips, dry and cracked from lack of water, and squeezed the final tiny drops from his long-empty bottle, allowing each one to linger for a moment on his swollen tongue.

Finally, as dusk enveloped the hillside, Woods raised his hand to signal the 'off'.

Slowly, being conscious that to move too fast might bring on a cramp in their limbs that could mean disaster, each man slowly stretched out legs and arms before crawling out of the little cave.

The night was unexpectedly cold and Hunter shivered as they began to make their way downhill towards the beach. Both men now knew that they had a narrow window of opportunity before the sentries on night patrol would take their posts. As they neared the sea again there was no sign of the enemy and Hunter scarcely dared to breathe lest the slightest noise might bring down a hail of bullets from an unseen observer.

After half an hour they set foot upon the sand and quickly made for the cave where the torch and belts had been hidden. The rest of the kit was still there, undiscovered, which was surely a good sign. Woods looked at his watch and signed to Hunter with his hand. Fifteen. He would have a go at signalling to any rescue vessel in fifteen minutes.

It seemed like forever, but at length Woods moved to the mouth of the cave, switched on the torch and flashed it up and down and on and off in the prearranged signal pattern.

Hunter went after him and strained his eyes for any sign of a reply from the water. Woods flashed the sign a second time and Hunter froze. Surely, that had been a light. He spoke in a whisper: 'Sir, over there. One o'clock. D'you see it?'

'Where? Are you sure?'

'Not certain, but... Look. There.'

He pointed and both men looked hard in the direction of his finger.

But there was nothing. Hunter looked away. 'Sorry, sir. I could have sworn.'

Woods said nothing. Perhaps Hunter was right. He flashed the torch again.

But another twenty minutes passed, with no sign of any reply.

Half an hour. Woods flashed again. Surely, thought Hunter. Surely now they must see them? There had to be a boat out there, waiting for them. Didn't there? If not then...

Suddenly Woods gasped. 'There, Hunter. Did you see that. There. At two o'clock. Look, man. D'you see?'

Hunter looked intently towards the horizon and, through the darkness saw what might just have been the glimmer of a light.

'Yes, sir. A light. It's a light. Just there.'

Woods was sure of it now. He flashed the signal again, and then a third time. And now both men could see the light being flashed back at them. Hope at last.

Woods began to signal a message. 'Folboats gone. Swimming to you. Come in.'

Both men reached for their Mae West life jackets and, after putting them over their heads, began to inflate them. Then, taking with them just the essentials, they left the cave.

Hunter glanced back up the hillside, expecting to see a search party waiting for them. But there was no one to be seen. They padded across the sand towards the sea and waded in until they were neck-deep in the surprisingly cold water and the waves began to pull them out to sea. After a while they began to swim, in the general direction of the light. Woods had kept his signal torch, fastening it around his wrist with a cord, and whenever they made out a flash from the rescue ship, he flashed out their call sign in return.

The sea was dead calm, but for some reason, Hunter found that swimming was almost impossible. Wondering why, he realised that they were simply exhausted. They had not eaten for the past day and no water had passed their lips for over twenty-four hours.

Woods too was shivering now and his hands had started to go numb. He prayed that neither of them would pass out before the ship reached them. He had no idea how far they had swum or rather floated, but turning to look back at the beach, he realised that it was some distance. Perhaps a mile or more.

Suddenly there was a rumble, like thunder. Hunter tried to shout to Woods, 'Engines, sir.'

But he wasn't sure whether the officer had heard. Or indeed, if he was still conscious, for the signal torch had stopped flashing.

He tried to paddle over to Woods and found him semi-comatose. He shook his shoulder. 'Sir, engines.'

Woods started awake. 'What? Engines. Are you sure?'

They could both hear it now. A ship. But then, as quickly as it had come, the noise went. Hunter was instantly overwhelmed by disappointment and despair.

Woods yelled, 'Christ almighty!'

Hunter grasped him. 'Come on, sir. They're just circling. Coming about. They haven't gone. They know we're here. We know that.'

'Yes. You're right. Just circling. That's it. Coming about. That's right.'

For minutes that seemed like an hour, in which Woods drifted in and out of consciousness, they waited. And waited.

And then, with a huge roar of water, like some God-given miracle monster rising from the deep, as Hunter watched, the periscope, conning tower and black metal hull of HMS *Traveller* broke the surface of the water to their left.

Within minutes they were aboard the submarine, pulled up the hull by the strong, gentle hands of men with English voices.

2

'What is it, exactly, you're trying to tell me, Sergeant Hunter?'

Hunter stared at the man opposite him across the desk and wondered quite how this somewhat jowly, rubicund major in the Intelligence Corps had not yet managed to understand his meaning.

With Woods beside him, Hunter had been sitting in the major's office for the last fifteen minutes and his patience was wearing thin. Over his head a rusty fan whirred slowly with an annoying hum, its pathetic breeze incapable of alleviating the oppressive heat. The 'office' had until a year ago been the junior housekeeper's quarters of a shabby Edwardian hotel on the Sharia Khedive Ismail.

Now, commandeered by the army, it had been transformed into a busy debriefing room in British Intelligence Head-quarters and, thought Hunter, it was clear that its current occupant would clearly have much preferred to have been anywhere else but here.

Taking his time, Hunter spoke the words again, in a slow, measured voice: 'What I'm trying to tell you, sir, is that the mission was a total fuck-up. A shambles. A bloody Horlicks. Call it what you like.'

The major started and stared at the other man in the room. 'Lieutenant Woods. Did you hear that? Will you stand for that? It's rank insubordination. Put this man on a charge.'

Woods shook his head. 'No can do, sir, I'm afraid.'

'What?'

'Can't do that, sir. I am really sorry – but I can't.'

The major's already red face began to deepen in colour now and he pressed his palms into the leather of his desktop. Finally he managed to speak, barely audible through his rage. 'Why the devil not?'

Peter Woods smiled at him, then began: 'Because, sir, I'm afraid that I agree with him. The whole op was an utter fuck-up. From its shambolic beginning to its ghastly, bloody end. In fact, if you ask me, it's a bloody miracle we came back at all. Two hours that sub was in those waters. Two bloody hours. And they really should have left us and scarpered. The minute we get on board she's depth charged. Bloody brave to hang around, if you ask me. We owe those matelots our lives. No one else. Without them we would all be dead, sir. Not just Jenkins. So you see... that's why I won't put Sarn't Hunter on a charge, sir. D'you see?'

Five minutes later, as the two men were walking away from Intelligence HQ, Hunter turned to Woods. 'Christ, sir, I thought for a moment I'd gone too far.'

Woods was smiling. 'Don't worry. He's powerless, and he knows it. You can bet that he won't be sitting there behind that desk for long. That man's long overdue a front-line post. Once he slims down a bit of course. And I know someone who can make both of those things happen. But that's not our concern right now. You were right, Hunter.'

Woods looked at him and smiled. 'Quite right about the op. And right to speak up too.'

'Thanks, sir. Felt that I may have overstepped the mark.'

'No. You said exactly what any officer worth his salt would have said.'

The word hit home. 'Sir?'

'I won't tell you again, Jim. You must be commissioned.'

Hunter opened his mouth to speak, but Woods put up his hand, determined not to let the moment pass.

'No, don't protest. I've heard it all before. You and I both know it, Jim. Your time's finally come. You're too good a man to waste.'

They had been heading east, along the main street, in the direction of Groppi's. But suddenly, Woods took a sharp right turn and Hunter went with him, and before long the streets became less familiar. As far as Hunter could tell, they were heading not into the centre of town, but to the south and Garden City. After a short while they turned into Sharia Kasr el Aini.

'Where are we going, sir? Groppi's is the other way, isn't it?'

'I'm well aware of that. Don't worry, we'll go to Groppi's soon enough. We've both earnt a beer. First though, Sarn't Hunter, we have another, rather more important rendezvous to keep.'

Just over an hour later the two men emerged again into the bright light of midday Cairo from a discreetly anonymous block of flats on Sharia Tolombat. It had all happened so fast that Hunter's head was still reeling. Woods had waved him off the street, past the salutes of the two red-capped military police sentries, into the gloomy interior of the modern apartment block, which quickly proved to be 'Grey Pillars', GHQ, British Army in Egypt. Needless to say, Hunter had never before set foot within its hallowed walls.

The place bore all the hallmarks of a hasty conversion to suit its new purpose. There were seemingly endless flights of concrete stairs and once on the second floor, the two men made their way past innumerable boarded-up doorways and ragged holes punched through walls to create open offices. Everywhere were signposts bearing mysterious initials, acronyms that Hunter presumed must have meant something to the people who worked there. Men and women in various variations of khaki and tropical uniforms bustled past them, purposefully hurrying away on vital errands. It bore a resemblance, he thought, to a huge department store, an Egyptian Derry and Toms, in which the staff vastly outnumbered the shoppers.

At length they reached their destination. Woods knocked on an unmarked wooden door and they entered a small, overheated office, which had clearly and rather badly, been converted from a kitchen. A brief conversation followed, between Woods and a lean, moustachioed brigadier, in immaculate tropical kit, who bore a long scar on his left cheek and struggled with a stammer. He greeted Woods by his Christian name and was clearly an old friend.

Woods motioned Hunter towards the window. 'Shan't be long, old chap. Just wait over there. See what's going on in the street. Just need to acquaint Brigadier Miles with the facts.'

Hunter did as he was told and moved to the window, which looked directly down on to the street. He watched as a small drama played out before him in which a pretty, well-dressed Arab girl was arguing with a young Egyptian. Clearly it was a matter of the heart and as she began to remonstrate the young man's face grew more and more serious.

At length she turned on her heel and walked away, leaving the boy to gaze after her until she had disappeared in the crowd. Just another everyday tragedy. War or no war, love prevailed. The others had stopped talking now and Hunter turned back to them. Woods smiled at him and motioned him to join them.

The brigadier was writing something on headed paper. Moving closer to the desk, Hunter tried to read it, upside down, but after a while he gave up on what, even the right way up, was an illegible scrawl. Eventually, the brigadier signed it and then rang a little silver hand bell on his desk. A woman entered, a uniformed warrant officer in the Women's Royal Navy, the WRNS – presumably his secretary – and brusquely whipped the letter away. She returned a few minutes later bearing the original and three meticulously written copies, which she gave to the brigadier before leaving.

The brigadier turned to Hunter and held out one of the copies.

'There you are, Mister Hunter. Field commission. If anyone questions it just refer them to me. Now go and find yourself some pips. Oh, and congratulations.'

★ ★ ★

Finding a set of lieutenant's shoulder pips proved rather more difficult in Cairo than the brigadier had suggested, but eventually, after a lucky scrounge from a friendly, if predictably expensive quartermaster sergeant, Hunter managed to get to work with a needle and thread. Now, an hour later, he was just finishing the job, sitting on his metal bed in the small shared NCOs' quarter of the British barracks situated in the Citadel, high up on a hill above the centre of Cairo. He looked admiringly at his handiwork, and was holding it up when the door flew open and Woods entered, in a flap.

'Ah, there you are, Mister Hunter. Finished? Good. Come on. We're late.'

Groppi's at that time was one of the very few smart cafés in Cairo open to all ranks. The high prices, however, tended to put off the ORs and so its usual clientele was a coterie of well-heeled British and Allied officers and their ladies.

Although there were two branches of the famous restaurant, when Woods spoke of Groppi's, Hunter knew that he meant not the small establishment on Midan Soliman Pasha, but the other, somewhat grander one over on Sharia Adly Pasha – 'Groppi's Garden' – opposite the exclusive Continental Hotel, which was the preferred haunt of the smarter side of Cairo's British set. There were others here too: displaced Europeans, French, Spaniards, Greeks, the inevitable Armenians and a couple of sad maharajahs. A well-spoken, well-dressed newly made-up British lieutenant, such as Hunter, was an easy fit in the eclectic mix.

The garden was always crammed with people, some in couples, others on their own and clearly looking for some companionship. In other words, thought Hunter, it was a high-class pick-up joint. And in fact, he had often found it most rewarding.

With their hair neatly slicked down, service shirts and shorts sharply creased, atop rolled khaki socks and suede 'desert boots', Woods and Hunter entered the courtyard, which reeked of roasting coffee and baking pastries. They were instantly accosted by one of the nattily uniformed waiters and shown to a table, where they settled down beside the flowering creepers and bougainvillea. As night began to fall, strings of brightly coloured fairy lights were switched on making the place look, Hunter had always thought, like a cross between a fairground and the 'palm court' of some tired British seaside hotel. He had loved it the first time he had come here, back in '41 in the evacuation from the Crete debacle, and the attraction never faded. The waiter brought two large beers, so cold that the glasses were frosted with condensation.

Pleased with himself at having at last triumphed with Hunter's commission, Woods raised his glass. 'Here's to you, Lieutenant Hunter. Though I have to say I never thought I'd see the day. Well done, Jim.'

'Thank you, sir.'

Woods frowned. 'Eh? You should know better, Jim. Never "sir" to me. You're one of us now. Jolly useful in Cairo too, having those pips. You can go to Shepheard's now and the Turf. No end of fun. I'll introduce you. Show you around, so to speak.'

It was true, thought Hunter. Rank brought privilege. But it also brought responsibility and that was something he had always, instinctively, avoided. Throughout his twenty-four years, from school to the workplace, to the army, Hunter had made it his business never to be in the right place at the right time. He had ensured that his demeanour and his attitude made him very easy to ignore. At school – a toweringly Gothic edifice, run on unforgivingly Spartan lines up in Scotland, where his mother's side had been sent for decades, he had deliberately flunked exams, from Latin to Maths. Although a natural leader, he had suppressed his instincts on rugby field and cricket pitch and had instead taken to solitary sports – boxing and fencing, at which he had allowed himself to excel.

Later, at work in London, he had kept to the shadows, moving from casual job to casual job, being careful not to volunteer or to show too much enthusiasm. Promotion had never been an option.

Somehow, despite a natural talent, for two gloriously hedonistic decades, Hunter had cleverly managed to evade responsibility, but now, at last, here in the most unlikely of places, it had caught up with him.

Of course being a sergeant had had its own level of responsibility, but there was something different about being an officer. About commanding. Something final. It was your order on which your men would move, he thought, would fight, and, without doubt, would die.

The evening passed quickly. It seemed as if Woods had summoned every passing officer he knew over to join them and of course, on hearing Hunter's news, all of them had pleaded to buy him a beer. Thus it was that shortly after ten that evening that the two officers stumbled back to their quarters.

★★★

By the following morning the reality of Hunter's sudden promotion had soaked in. There was all the official business and paperwork associated with his passage from NCO to officer. But Hunter had always been good at admin and, even though slowed down by a slight hangover, he quickly found himself with a few days of leave.

He had been to Cairo before and knew parts of it well. But then he had been a junior NCO and a sergeant. Now he was an officer and there were certain no-go areas for someone of his rank, the most obvious being the Berka, the notorious red-light district that abounded with prostitutes and outrageous pornographic shows. He had, naturally, as any inquisitive young man would have done, visited it on earlier Cairo trips. Now it was out of bounds. Anyway, why pay for something when as an officer he could expect to get it for nothing?

For now there were new and previously inaccessible places to explore.

It was the habit of most officers to lunch at the Gezira Club after tennis or a swim and Woods introduced Hunter to this easy way of life. The evening started late for most officers, after work finished, at around seven or eight. Those not 'dining in' would be out for dinner at one of the 'French' restaurants and those who did not fancy a nightclub would inevitably end up in one of the hotel bars.

Thus it was that, four days after his evening with Woods, Hunter found himself after dinner, drinking alone in the bar at Shepheard's Hotel. He'd had a disappointing date with a rather plain girl from the South African Women's Auxiliary

Army Service, the WAASes, who were known to be game for a lark. But the evening had not gone well.

He had been fixed up by Woods and his girl with a friend of hers. The cabaret of the restaurant at the Continental had been laughably bad, though his date had hardly smiled. In fact, she had proved to lack conversation in equal measure to her looks and so after a drink, they had soon gone their separate ways.

For two hours Hunter had wandered disconsolate through the crowded streets, jostling between couples, arm in arm and groups of drunken soldiers, along with numerous civilians.

Finally, turning a corner, he saw the familiar front façade of Shepheard's and headed towards it. Once inside, reconciling himself to the fact that this evening he would be sleeping alone, he ordered a beer and was just about to take a drink when a British officer sat down at his table. Hunter looked across at him.

He was not wearing army uniform, but Royal Navy tropical dress. Hunter took in his rank. A commander, in his early thirties, Hunter guessed. Lean and chisel-jawed, with neatly cut dark brown hair and piercing blue eyes. He began to speak, but Hunter beat him to it: 'Sorry, sir, do I know you? Have we met?'

'No, Lieutenant. We most certainly have not.' He spoke with the unmistakable, clipped accent of the English public schoolboy.

Hunter smiled, taking the man for a 'nancy boy'. Well, he would soon dispel any notions he might have.

'Could I possibly ask then why you might have sat down at my table?'

The commander smiled. 'Of course, Lieutenant. I do apologise. Fact is, we need to talk, old man.'

'Sorry, sir?'

'Talk. Need to. You and I.'

Hunter put down his beer. 'Do we? Are you quite sure about that, sir?'

'Quite sure, Lieutenant... Hunter, isn't it?'

How the devil could the man know his name? 'Yes, sir.'

Hunter waited for the officer to introduce himself, but he made no attempt to do so. Clearly the commander, whoever he was, had done his homework. Taking a drink from his beer, Hunter cast an eye about the room, looking for anyone who might have come in with him. At length his eye rested on one man standing in a shadowy corner, away from the hanging lights. Another naval officer, observing them both from the bar. That would be him. The escort. Just in case. Hunter put down his glass. Decided to be cooperative – in the extreme.

'Righto, sir. Just let me know how I can help.'

The commander nodded and set down his Martini. 'Well, this is it. The word is, Lieutenant, that you're somewhat disaffected with the handling of the war. Your war, that is. Would you say that might be the case?'

Hunter shrugged. 'The word? Whose word? Sorry, sir.'

'Less of the sir, Lieutenant.'

But still no name, thought Hunter. He decided to play it straight. 'Is that so, sir?'

The commander ignored his comment. 'That was some stunt you pulled off on Rhodes.'

'You know about that?'

'Of course I do, old chap. It's my business to know about

39

these things. Splendid bit of work. You certainly deserve those new pips.'

Hunter said nothing but, slightly incredulous, took a draught of beer as the commander sipped his Martini. Finally, Hunter spoke: 'It was a shambles, sir.'

'Yes. I know that too.'

'You do?'

'I told you, Mister Hunter, I know about these things. I make it my business. It's what I do.' He snapped his fingers at the waiter and ordered another Martini.

'And make sure it's shaken. You know how I like them. And one for my friend.'

Hunter shook his head but the commander nodded and the waiter nodded back.

As the man went off to fix the drinks, the commander spoke again: 'Your friend Captain Woods suggested that you might be interested in joining a little scheme I'm putting together.'

'Sir?'

'Well, it's strictly hush-hush at the moment of course. He just thought it might interest you.'

'What exactly is it, sir? This "scheme". Can you say?'

The man cast a glance across at his companion who was still standing at the bar sipping at a bright green cocktail. The commander nodded and the officer wandered over to join them.

'Allow me to present Lieutenant Vickery. My second in command, if you will.'

The officer put out his hand. 'Good to meet you, Hunter.'

'Sir.'

As Vickery sat down with them, the commander began to speak: 'Well, here's the thing. For some time now we've believed that we've been missing a trick. Every time the Jerries carry out a raid on one of our positions, every time they take an HQ, they send in a special unit which, well, clears it out.'

'Sir?'

'Basically, this special unit goes in with the raiders and makes a beeline for the HQ building and the admin offices where it blows any safes it finds and sweeps up any intelligence that looks of interest before skedaddling.' He paused and then smiled at Hunter. 'Well, Lieutenant, I intend to do the same.'

Hunter thought for a moment. 'A new special force? You intend to lead it yourself, sir?'

The commander shook his head. 'No, no, old chap. I'm far too old for that. That role will be down to someone rather younger and fitter than me. Captain Woods is keen to join us and he thought that perhaps you...' He shrugged.

Hunter paused and took a long drink. He wiped his lips and looked at the commander. 'How many of us would there be, sir?'

'Hard to say as yet. It'll be a totally cross-service unit, you understand. Navy, army, marines. There will be an intensive training course, but we're only approaching men with real experience and specialist skills.'

'Are you quite sure that I'm the right man for the job?'

The commander smiled again. 'Oh yes. Quite sure, Lieutenant. In actual fact you fit the bill so well you might well have been the blueprint for it.'

This time it was Hunter who laughed. 'But I don't know how to blow a safe.'

'But we have a man who does. Besides, you have other talents. You can speak German, yes?'

'Yes, sir. But...'

'And Greek?'

'A little. Mainly classical though.'

'And most importantly of all, you are – I believe – quite used to keeping company with all varieties of lowlifes and rogues?' He grinned. 'Correct?'

Hunter stared at him, nonplussed. The commander spoke again: 'Correct?'

'Yes, sir. I suppose so. Correct.'

'Good. It would seem that all that time skulking in that sordid Soho bar might have finally paid off then, Mister Hunter.'

'You appear to have done your homework, sir.'

'I make it my business to do my homework, as you put it.'

'Can I ask what it will be called, sir? This new unit?'

'We don't have a name yet and even if we did, Hunter, do you suppose for one moment I would tell you?'

'Well, if I'm to join it, sir, I think I'd better know what it's called.'

'Then you are interested?'

'I didn't say that, sir. Just asking the name.'

The commander turned to Vickery and smiled. 'Said that he was smart, Tony, didn't they. They were right.'

He turned back to Hunter. 'OK. No name yet but you will be part of Special Service Brigade. Commandos, just as you are now. You and Woods. You will be part of a small unit that will accompany any front-line commando attack on any enemy installation to capture intelligence before the enemy have any chance to destroy it.'

'Will it work?'

'Oh it'll work alright, Lieutenant. You're going to make it work.'

'Without intending to be facetious sir, how do you know that?'

'Because the Nazis already have such a unit. And it works bloody well. Too bloody well. I won't beat about the bush, Hunter, the Jerries are ahead of us. Miles ahead as a matter of fact. Their technology is vastly superior to ours and if we are going to win this damned war, we must ensure that we are one step ahead of them. At present it's the other way around. The enemy have the initiative. And we're suffering... Badly.'

He lit a cigarette and rolled it around in his fingers. 'Did you see the headline in the *Times* yesterday?'

'Headline, sir?'

'The cruiser.'

'Oh that poor ship. With all hands. Yes, a terrible loss.'

'Yes, quite terrible. Well that was down to Nazi ingenuity. New type of bomb. That's what we have to stop.'

'But I'm not trained, sir. Yes I can blow things up, destroy installations, wreck no end of kit. But ask me to crack a safe or find a secret dossier. We... I'm not sure, sir.'

'Oh, you'll be trained. Highly trained. By the time they've finished with you you'll know everything there is about getting into enemy installations, locating and taking secret material... and getting out alive. You'll be... you'll be...'

Vickery chimed in, 'You'll be no more than a bunch of bloody burglars.'

The commander smiled at him. 'Oh very good, Tony. Very droll.'

He stared at Hunter. 'You in then?'

'Who else knows about this new unit, sir?'

'It's hush-hush. Top brass only. In fact if you really want

to know, even the top brass don't know a thing about it. It's strictly "need to know".'

'I thought the high command knew about everything that was going on. I mean to say, surely, sir, we're all on the same side aren't we?'

The commander inclined his head. 'Of course we are. Although sometimes, Hunter, if you must know, I truly wonder if we are. The fact is that with matters like this, we must have a degree of... independence. Security... confidentiality. Call it what you will. That's where the secrecy comes in.'

'How do I know that it won't be just as badly run as the last mess? How do I know we might not just be abandoned?'

The commander let out a breath and shook his head. 'Good God, you really have lost faith in command, haven't you, Hunter? And that's precisely why you're here. We're offering you a chance to work on your own. You won't be depending on the usual support. You'll be part of our support. And believe me, when you're a part of us, we will never let you down.'

'I wish that I could, sir.'

'Could what, man?'

'Believe you.'

There was a cold silence. Then, quite suddenly, without warning, the commander got to his feet. Clearly the interview was over. Smiling, Vickery strolled across to the bar and paid for the drinks.

The commander looked hard at Hunter, who was now standing opposite him. After a few moments he spoke, very quietly. 'Well, there it is. That's what's on the table. Take it or leave it. I might well be lying to you. I might be getting you into your worst nightmare. Anything could happen to you.

Unimaginably horrible things.' He paused. 'What choice do you have? Either you believe me and you join us and help us to shorten the war, win the war and save God knows how many lives, or you stay with the mob you're in now and pray that what happened to you on Rhodes doesn't happen again. It's your choice, Hunter. Us or them.'

Hunter said nothing, but looked at the bottom of his glass.

The commander spoke: 'So. Are you with us?'

Hunter looked up at him and smiled. 'It would appear that I am.'

3

An hour later Hunter was already beginning to question what he had done. But there could be no going back now. He had given the commander his word and was due to report in the morning to an address written on the back of a packet of cigarettes that Vickery had passed to him in the bar. That was all that he knew. Something inside him, though, was silently excited. Surely here was the chance he had wanted. The chance to really make a difference. The chance to make the killing count for something. The chance to save lives. The chance to matter.

He sipped at his beer and from his vantage point at a shadowy corner table, looked around the room.

Groppi's was alive with chatter and laughter. Most distinctly, the unmistakable, irrepressible laughter of young women. Instantly, it undid the darkness in Hunter's mind and took him for a moment back to other times. To London and to Soho and to another smoke- and noise-filled, crowded bar, bursting with laughter. From a gramophone player at the end of the bar came the sound of a recording by Harry Roy. Hunter knew the lyrics well.

Hunter took a long drink from the cool beer in his hand and

listened as the gramophone wailed on with the unmistakable sound of Cole Porter's *Night and Day*.

Quite suddenly, a female voice from behind him cut through the music and chatter with the distinctive clipped and polished tones of the English Home Counties, talking about the surprising potency of cheap music.

Hunter smiled and put a hand to his head, shaking it in disbelief. There was no need to look round. He recognised it instantly: low, feminine, effortlessly seductive, emphatically in charge. The reference to Noël Coward confirmed it and, rising to his feet, he turned to see a familiar face.

A young woman in her early twenties, plucked eyebrows above an aquiline nose and high cheekbones, her skin showing just the hint of a slight tan from the Egyptian sun, her exquisite lips defined by a cupid's bow of harsh bright red and those eyes – sapphire blue, flashing and filled with mischief. He would have known her anywhere: the unforgettable, unmistakable, always unpredictable Lara Heatherly.

She grinned at him. 'Good God, Jimmy Hunter, and you're wearing pips.'

Hunter looked down at his right shoulder. Nodded. 'Good God, Lara, so I am.' He glanced at the other shoulder. 'Four of them, to be precise.'

The girl let out a huge guffaw. 'Christ Almighty. "Lieutenant bloody Hunter". I never thought I'd see the day.'

'Nor I, Lara, as you know. But, well, I held them off for as long as I could. But you know how it is.'

He was an officer now and, if he was going to wear those bloody pips he was damned well going to make the most of it. Rank was a powerful aphrodisiac. It might have been true that all the nice girls loved a soldier, but Hunter knew that the really nasty ones preferred officers. He was surprised to see Lara here, in Cairo. And, he had to admit to himself, pleased. It was almost as if his reflective mood had conjured her up from the smoke, like some genie from a bottle. Lara Heatherly. They'd had a brief, painfully passionate liaison in London, three years ago. Perhaps it would happen again?

She spoke, breaking his reverie and as she did so, he realised that she too, was in uniform.

'Well, Jimmy, didn't you hear? I said how long does a gal have to stand around here before someone buys her a drink?'

'I'm so sorry, Lara.' He clicked his fingers at a waiter and ordered what he remembered to be her preferred drink. 'Campari and soda, please. And I'll have another of these.'

Lara smiled at him. 'I somehow knew you'd end up here. I just knew it. And you may remember, I'm never wrong. Chaps like you always end up in places like this.'

He laughed. 'Well done, dear Lara. Of course, you're always right. Always were. I see you've joined up too.'

She posed, twisting her body to show off her uniform. 'Well we all have to do our bit, don't we?'

'Who are you with?'

'Oh, nothing special, darling. I'm just a secretary to a dear old general.'

'Well done, Lara. I'm sure he's very lucky to have you.'

'Careful, darling. You always were a shameless flatterer, Jimmy.'

She flashed him an electric smile and in an instant he was transported back to London, to a basement off Greek Street and to someone's party, late into the early hours. Smoke rings, jazz on the gramophone and Lara kicking off her shoes to dance, her long arms twined around his neck. He clicked back to the present. She was talking to him again: 'I said, what are you up to? Christ, Jimmy, are you listening at all?'

'Yes, of course I am. Just had something on my mind.'

'Or someone, no doubt. So, what are you up to?'

Hunter shrugged. 'Can't say really. You know how it is. Careless talk and all that.'

She raised an eyebrow. 'Oh, I say. I really do say. How t'rifically exciting. You old fox. You're a spook aren't you? SOE. They're all over the place here. The waiter's probably one of them. Out to catch Jerry agents masquerading as British officers.'

'No Lara, not really a "spook". But I just can't say.'

'Oh, I know all about that anyway. My general's a "mister big" in all that sort of thing.'

'He is?'

'Oh yes. But I shouldn't be telling you that should I? Though of course if you're one of them too, well then I suppose it's alright, sort of. Isn't it?'

'Yes, I suppose it is. Sort of.'

'I say, are you with Stirling's lot? SAS? Out in the desert, "biffing the boche". They're frightfully brave, don't you think? Well of course you do, if you're one of them. Are you? Oh God. There I go again.' She rapped herself on the knuckles. 'Message to brain: "Mustn't ask questions". Careless talk and all that. You see. I told you. I'm utterly useless. A genuine security risk.'

She laughed and smiled at him. He didn't believe her for a minute. One thing that Lara Heatherly was not was useless. Or stupid. If she was working for SOE or SIS or some other bunch of letters he didn't know about, then you could be sure that it was not just as a secretary to 'a dear old general'.

Perhaps she was working for his new employers? Now that was a strange thought.

Unless, of course, she was lying about the whole thing. Perhaps it was a fantasy. Or perhaps she was an enemy agent. No, that was too absurd. Lara Heatherly a Nazi spy?

He realised that he hadn't noticed that Lara had put her hand around his waist and was now swaying to the music, which had changed to another Cole Porter song: 'You'd be so Easy to Love'.

She sang a line of it, then whispered in his ear, 'Isn't this lovely, Jimmy? Us being here, together I mean. How lucky we are.'

He was thunderstruck. Lara? Really?

She rested her head on his shoulder and, as she did so, he saw a British officer approaching them. The newcomer spoke: 'Lara, darling. How wonderful. What can I get you? And who's this?'

The man, a captain, lean and athletic in build, with a high forehead, looked at Hunter with a mixture of contempt, suspicion and envy.

Lara had straightened up and let go of Hunter's waist.

'This is Jimmy Hunter, Xan. Jimmy, have you met dear Xan? Xan Fielding, Lieutenant Hunter. There you are.'

Hunter had heard of Fielding. Of course he had. He was well known among the special forces for his work as an SOE agent. Along with Paddy Leigh Fermor. Hunter was familiar with their work. Leigh Fermor, who had famously walked his way around the Balkans and Greece before the war, living in Athens and Romania. Joining up he'd become an officer in the Irish Guards and fought in Crete before joining Special Operations. He had since run operations in Crete and had apparently helped hundreds of the men left behind after the evacuation to escape. God knew what else he had been up to, but in SOE it seemed that anything was possible. Hunter wondered whether Fielding too might be mixed up in his own new mob.

Fielding smiled at Lara and spoke, bubbling over with the unbridled enthusiasm of the English public schoolboy. 'I say, Lara. What are you doing here? You're in luck. There's a bit of a "do" on at Tara this evening. The princess is throwing a party. Everyone's going to be there. I'm off there now. Why don't you come?'

He had heard of Tara too. It was the villa on Gezira island in the middle of the city that had quickly become the focus for the British 'smart set'. It was crammed full of SOE. Basil Moss, another SOE man, had rented it from some Egyptian and filled it with his friends, their pets and countless hangers-on. Some Polish countess held court there. Whatever its owners had originally called it, the villa now took its new name from the palace of the High Kings of Ireland. Reports of the parties and balls held at Tara had already become almost legendary. It was, thought Hunter, as if all the bright young things who had haunted the London he had known in the years between the wars, now equally excited and terrified by the violence and destruction around them, had found their new spiritual home in the unlikely setting of Cairo.

Clearly, Fielding's invitation was intended for Lara alone. And Hunter was taken aback when she looked at him for approval.

'Jimmy? What do you think? Should we go? Might be fun.' She squeezed his arm.

Suddenly, it appeared they had become a couple. A 'we'.

Hunter thought for a moment. While he was intrigued by the prospect of seeing the villa, he had also been thrown by Lara's sudden, unexpected advances and had not yet decided what he should do about her. He decided on caution.

'Perhaps not, Lara. Not this evening.'

She smiled at him, knowingly. Then, gently taking her hand from his arm turned to Fielding. 'Well, I'm up for it. Come on then, Xan. To Tara! Jimmy, perhaps we could try again tomorrow?'

Unthinking, Hunter nodded and she smiled back at him and leant over to give him a kiss, full on the lips. As she did so he smelt her perfume again.

'That's settled then, darling. Tomorrow it is.'

Darling? Where had that come from? Hunter felt Fielding's eyes narrowing as he waited to watch his response.

'Yes. Of course, Lara… See you tomorrow.'

'Here? Dinner? I'll meet you here at eight.'

Before he could reply, she had smiled and kissed him again.

'Till tomorrow, Jimmy. Promise me you'll be a good boy till then.'

And then she was gone, clutching the arm of Xan Fielding, off into the Cairo night.

Hunter's mind was reeling.

Seeking something different, he made his way through the narrow Cairo streets towards the poor side of town, far away from the jazz bars and the socialites. At length, he found what he was looking for. Joe's was as run-down a bar as any wandering soldier could have hoped for. Tucked away in a corner of the Burqua, it was a mass of khaki uniforms and packed with drunken squaddies and NCOs. Hunter could not see a single other officer among them.

He pushed his way through to the bar, ignoring the glances as some of the less drunken men recognised a lieutenant in their midst. At length managed to get there and, catching the barman's eye ordered a beer. He drank it down quickly, keen now to lose himself in the press of uniforms. Keen too to banish the worries that were increasingly haunting his mind. He wanted a justification for his new and still-unwanted promotion. He wanted an explanation for Lara's sudden passion. Perhaps he should after all have gone with her to Tara. At least he wouldn't have been alone. For here, in this packed bar, with men pressing from all sides, he had once again begun to feel alone. He knew it all too well, the gnawing loneliness that always took him when he found himself without company at this time of night. The loneliness that had been his life since childhood.

It had not, he thought, been the death of his parents that had affected him so much – he had hardly seen them as a child, banished to that Scottish boarding school, while his mother had accompanied his archaeologist father on trips to Greece and the Middle East. Of course their unexpected loss in a road accident here in Egypt almost ten years ago now had been a terrible shock, but the fact that he was already used to the concept of being alone had made it easier to bear.

Since then though, to his surprise, their absence had begun to affect him more and more and now Hunter's loneliness hung about him like a shroud, and as the evening drew on it seemed, as so often it did, to weigh ever heavier on his shoulders.

There were, in his experience, only two things that lightened that weight: sex and alcohol. And when, on occasion, the former was not available, or as tonight had been somewhat confusing, the latter inevitably took over.

Hunter caught the barman's eye again and ordered another drink, feeling his mood lighten as he did so.

He looked around the bar. It was typical of its type, with a polished zinc bar top, and behind the barman glass shelves boasting a dazzling array of bottles, including twenty famous malt whiskies and premium British brands, most of which, he guessed, contained alcohol that bore little or no relation to their purported contents. The whole thing was finished off with a red velvet pelmet over the shelves, hung with tassels, and black and white photographs of half-naked women, while at either end of the bar stood several stuffed camels and three large hashish pipes.

He peered at his fellow drinkers. They were a mixed lot, typical of the British Army in North Africa. He listened out for the accents: Scousers, Geordies, Scots, Welsh and Irish along with a smattering of New Zealanders.

He began to take stock of his own situation and was beginning to think that perhaps he might at last have found somewhere where he could find some sort of happiness, when without warning, his right elbow was knocked violently, sending the beer flying from his hand, drenching the man standing to his right.

Instinctively, Hunter turned to his left towards the man who had knocked him, but it was already too late, for as he did so the soldier crumpled to the floor, felled by a huge punch from some unseen hand. At the same time Hunter felt a hand on his shoulder, as the man behind him, now covered in beer, went to hit him. As he did so Hunter heard the man behind him shout, 'Mick, no, don't. He's a bloody officer. Oh, fuck it.'

Then the punch connected and Hunter fell backwards into a group of soldiers. Shaking his head to clear it he stood up and stared at his assailant who was glowering back at him, his fist still clenched.

He was a big man, bigger certainly than Hunter, but Hunter knew that his weight and height would not always work to his advantage and that they could be used against him. For an instant Hunter considered the possibility of not reacting, but despite the entreaties of his mates, the man looked ready to have another go. There was nothing for it. Hunter made to punch him with his left fist and the man flailed his own fist towards him.

But before it connected, Hunter had ducked and shot out his powerful right fist to hit the man a full blow in the solar plexus.

The big man grabbed at his stomach and his knees gave way. But, as he did so, Hunter was hit from behind by a man's shoulder crashing into him and pushing against the bar. He swung round and saw a smaller man, a sergeant, coming at him, his fist raised. Hunter clenched his own right fist and, raising his arm quickly, blocked the man's jab, before hitting him with a swinging uppercut from his left arm that connected with his chin. The man hardly blinked, but let fly with another haymaker, which hit Hunter in the chest. Before he could respond, Hunter was being pulled round by the first man he had hit, who had now risen from the ground and was swaying groggily.

Before he could get another punch in, Hunter jabbed out a short rabbit punch and connected hard with his nose.

Spurting blood, the man went down and this time he did not get back up. Hunter moved fast now. Turning back to where the sergeant had been, he saw the man had now gone, his place taken by a ferocious four-man fist-fight. Pushing down on the bar, Hunter pulled up his body and clambered onto the bar top before jumping down beside the cowering Egyptian barman. As he did so, a beer glass flew over his head and smashed against the row of bottles that lined the shelves at the back of the mirrored bar, bringing them down and smashing the mirror behind them.

From his right came a voice: 'Oh dear. That's bad luck, sir. And seven years of it too.'

Hunter looked to his right, in the direction of the voice, and found a soldier staring at him. It was the sergeant who had hit him. He didn't seem as if he wanted to do it again. He spoke in a gentle, Scottish accent: 'If you don't mind me saying so, that was a bloody good thump you gave me, sir. You'll have done that before, I reckon.'

'You reckon right then. You too, Sarn't, if I'm not mistaken.'

'Thank you, sir. Yes, I'm not afraid to handle myself.' He smiled. 'Now, sir, if you want my advice, you'd be best to get out of here before the redcaps arrive.'

'Thank you, Sarn't, I'll take your advice.'

Hunter raised himself up till his eyes were level with the bar top and peered into the room at a chaotic mêlée of thumping fists and flying objects. He quickly ducked down. 'Looks like I might have to fight my way out.'

'Two might have a better chance than one, sir, would you say?'

Hunter nodded. 'Agree. If you're quite ready to go, Sarn't. If I really can't tempt you to another one, Sarn't... your name?'

'Name's Knox, sir. James Knox, 1st Black Watch, but call me Jack, and thank you, no, sir. I think they're about to call time.'

There was a flurry of noise as, on his words, the door of the bar flew open and a twelve-man squad of red-capped military police charged in, bowling over half a dozen of the brawling drunks nearest the door.

Hunter indicated to Knox to follow him and the two men trotted fast, bent over, along the rear of the bar, away from the cowering barman. Hunter had spotted a door leading from the bar into the kitchens and reaching this he pushed it open and headed through, followed by Knox. It swung shut behind them and, as it did so, both men stood up. Knox smiled. 'Nice one, sir.'

'My pleasure, Sergeant. Now let's get out of here.'

They headed for the kitchen door and stepped out into the night, being careful to shut it behind them. Knox, seeing a large industrial-sized metal dustbin, pushed it towards the door, helped by Hunter, until they had blocked it off. Then together they ran down the alleyway and emerged on to the main road. They looked at each other and both smiled.

Hunter spoke first: 'Well, goodnight, Sarn't.'

'Goodnight, sir. See you again.'

'Not around here in a hurry, if I can help it, you won't.'

Knox laughed and nodded. 'Too right, sir. Goodnight.'

They split up and headed off in different directions, just as the MPS began to load their drunken, protesting prisoners on to two lorries parked outside the bar. Hunter didn't dare look back, but keeping his head down, walked off until he was lost in the crowd.

★★★

The following morning, having managed to decipher the spidery scrawl of handwriting on the cigarette packet that he had found thankfully was still in his pocket, Hunter was standing outside a building in Garden City, on Sharia Rustum. Rustum Buildings was a slightly shabby concrete block of purpose-built modern flats, all with iron balconies, not far from GHQ at 'Grey Pillars'.

The handwritten note had directed him simply to: *Go up staircase to first floor, room 7.*

He entered past the two red-capped sentries, who noticing his pips, snapped up a salute which, unused to being an officer, he returned rather belatedly. The place was not the usual hive of activity, but seemed deathly silent in comparison to GHQ. There were far fewer people and all of them were going about their work in silence. Hunter walked to the staircase and after climbing it arrived on the first floor. It wasn't hard to find the door of what had obviously previously been flat 7. He paused to gather his thoughts and then knocked. It was opened immediately by a stunningly pretty young WRN as neatly turned out as if she might have been in Whitehall.

She smiled at him then noticed his black eye. 'Oh. Oh dear. I say that looks nasty. You here to see "V"?'

'Who? Yes, I suppose I must be.'

'He's in there. On a call. You'll have to wait.'

He looked around for a seat, but there were none, save for the one in which the WRN now sat herself, behind her tidy little desk.

There was another knock at the door. She tut-tutted and got up to answer it. To Hunter's surprise the newcomer was the sergeant from the previous evening and for a moment he wondered whether they had been caught.

'Hello again, Sergeant. What a coincidence.'

Knox looked as nonplussed as Hunter. 'Good morning, sir. Didn't think I'd have the pleasure of your company again quite so soon.'

There was a loud cough from the inner office. The WRN had sat down again and was filing her nails. She spoke without looking up. 'He'll see you now. Just go in.'

Hunter opened the door into what had previously been the apartment's master bedroom. On one wall were a large framed photograph of the king alongside a smaller photograph of a Royal Navy corvette. On another hung an unintelligible timetable, with handwritten notes scrawled across it, and a huge map of the Mediterranean and Aegean.

In the centre of the room, in a leather-covered club chair, at what looked like a George II partner's desk, with his back to a huge picture window, sat 'V', the man who had previously been Lieutenant Vickery. Now however, he had been transformed and was wearing a lieutenant commander's insignia. He was dressed in an immaculately pressed naval officer's white shirt and shorts.

'Ah, Hunter, there you are. And the redoubtable Sarn't Knox. Do come in, both of you. Take a seat.'

They sat down in the offered dining chairs opposite Vickery, who carried on speaking: 'You need to meet your 2IC, Hunter. Sergeant James Knox.'

He smiled. 'In fact, I believe that you two might already be acquainted. Am I right?'

Hunter wondered how the devil he could have known that. 'Let's just say, we've met socially.'

Knox smiled at him and nodded. 'You could say that, sir. Good to see you.'

'Yes, Sarn't Knox. Good to see you again too. Didn't know you were part of our mob.'

'Couldn't resist it, sir. I just seemed to be the right man for the job.'

Vickery smiled. 'Sergeant Knox comes to us highly recommended... As an expert safe-cracker.'

Knox laughed. 'Five years in Barlinnie jail can't tell any lies, eh, sir?'

'Quite so, Knox. He's really very good, Hunter. Invaluable. And a good man in a tight spot too, I believe.'

'Oh I can vouch for that, personally, sir.'

Vickery looked at him closely. 'How's the eye this morning?'

'Surprisingly painful actually, sir.'

'You want to avoid that sort of thing. You can never be quite sure who's watching, can you?'

Hunter nodded. 'It would appear not, sir.'

Vickery looked down at his notes. 'We're sending you to Athilt.'

'Sir?'

'Don't worry, its nothing unpleasant. Well, not too unpleasant. It's a training camp, near Haifa, on the coast. Most of the place is filled with SBS chappies. You'll find Captain Woods is already there. He left this morning. And the other men you'll be working with. You two are the last two recruits. Well done both of you.'

He looked down at his desk. There was a pause before Vickery looked up again, 'Any questions?'

Hunter looked at him. 'Yes, sir, as a matter of fact I do have a question. When might we go into action? I mean if we're so important, then surely we need to be in the field as soon as possible. The commander himself said that thousands of lives were being lost needlessly every day. Surely we need to stop that?'

'Of course we do, but all in good time, Hunter. All in good time.'

'But I've already been trained. When I joined the commandos. Trained bloody well and damned hard too. What else is there to learn?'

'Oh, you'd be surprised, old chap. You've all got a lot more to learn before we let you loose on a mission. You too, Sergeant. Don't worry. As soon as you're ready we'll know it. And what's more so will you. No point in going off half-cocked. We want you to be able to deal with anything they throw at you. You'll thank us in the end.'

He looked at his watch. 'Right. You'd better go and get your kit together.'

Hunter frowned. 'Sir?'

'Well, your plane leaves in an hour. Goodbye and the best of luck.'

Hunter nodded. Well that put paid to his date with Lara. He wondered how it might have gone. Too late now. He supposed that he should get some sort of word to her and wondered if the pretty WRN in the office might help.

Vickery coughed, loudly, and the bedroom door was opened by the WRN, who showed them back into the anteroom. Knox opened the door and was already halfway into the corridor when Hunter turned to the WRN, ready to ask her if she might possibly get a message to a Miss Heatherly. But she spoke first, smiling at him disarmingly. 'Better get that eye looked at, Lieutenant. You don't really want to go into action looking like that, do you?'

Hunter returned her smile. 'Depends what sort of action you mean, doesn't it?'

Stupid thing to say. He cursed himself. Too late now for the message anyway.

The WRN smiled and looked away, going back to filing her nails. 'Goodbye, Lieutenant Hunter. Do close the door behind you.'

4

Hunter came round slowly from unconsciousness and, with some difficulty, opened his swollen eyes. The room was black, save for the light from a single, bare light bulb that hung suspended from the ceiling, almost directly above his head. Seeing it, he quickly realised with a sickening clarity that it was not, after all, a dream. He shivered, partly from fear and partly on account of the fact that he was utterly naked and very, very cold.

He tried to move but found that he was tied to a wooden chair by his wrists and ankles. In that instant memory returned and, with it, the pain. He winced. His body felt as if he had been ruthlessly beaten, perhaps for hours. There did not seem to be a single area of his body that had not been attacked. His head throbbed with pain and his eyes felt puffy, as if he had been punched repeatedly. His body was coated in sweat but rubbing his forearm against his thigh he felt a thicker liquid and supposed that it must be blood. His blood. He tried to flex his fingers and toes and found to his surprise that nothing appeared to be broken.

He tried to concentrate. To focus his mind on the facts and away from the pain. Tried to recall how he had got here. How the men who had done this to him had managed to get him into this position. Surely, he thought, he must have fought. But he was unable to remember anything.

He panicked and struggled but that only made the ropes cut into his wrists and ankles.

The door of the room opened suddenly, flooding the room with white light and swinging back against the wall with a thud and from the periphery of his vision, he was aware of someone entering the room. The door closed and the room was again only lit from the single bulb. A man, no it sounded like two men, were standing behind him. He struggled again, determined to turn to see them. But it was no use. He could hear them speaking now, in German. He strained to make out what it was they were saying, but they spoke too softly for him to make out anything more than the occasional word.

'Dead... want him alive... let him suffer... Plans... slowly.'

Every word filled him with a new horror.

One of the men appeared before him. Straining to see, he focused on a tall man in unmistakable Nazi uniform. Black tunic, trimmed in silver with a double lightning flash on the collar and the ribbon of the Iron Cross on the left breast pocket. SS political wing. A torturer. A thug. Not that he needed to be told that. The man was holding something in both hands. Something shiny, and before Hunter could see what it was it became all too evident. He was hit full in the face by a torrent of water, thrown with force from the bucket in the man's hands.

The sudden shock made him gasp and he pulled his body away from the flood. In doing so he unsettled the chair, which toppled backwards and landed on the stone floor. Luckily Hunter managed instinctively to stop his head hitting the floor with maximum force. But the crash instantly renewed the pain in his limbs and back. He was aware of the other man, similarly dressed to his colleague. Standing over his face. Could smell the leather and polish of the black jackboot. Waited for the heel to kick him in the face or grind into his skull and eyes.

The two men were talking now. Of course he could not hear what they were saying. Nor did he want to. Hunter had gone beyond caring. They spoke together for what seemed to be an interminable time, during which Hunter's body went from being red hot with agony to freezing cold.

The man walked across to Hunter and drew a long SS knife from its sheath on his belt. Hunter shivered and tried to close his eyes to its blade but so puffy and swollen were they that he found it hard to do so. He saw the double-edged straight blade glint blue steel in the cold light from the solitary bulb and waited, sickened, for the inevitable cut, wherever it might hit home. Tried to brace his body for the shock. But instead, the man used the knife to slit the rope that held his hands.

Christ in heaven, thought Hunter. What now? What had they in mind for him now? What new horror was this? Dozens of ghastly thoughts raced across his mind. The full panoply of the medieval torturer: fingernails being extracted, limbs being snapped like twigs, knees bored through, digits lopped off, slowly, eyes being gouged out, fingers being severed, castration. He felt utterly vulnerable and realised that there was absolutely nothing now that he could do about it. He was, he knew, going to suffer unbelievable pain. There was no option. No way out and as it sunk in the thought simply made him more determined not to tell them what they demanded to know.

With slow and deliberate steps, his jackboot heels echoing around the walls, the man walked away from him and Hunter, lying naked and foetus-like on the cold stone floor, instinctively began to try to move. New pain surged through his limbs, as he asked them, begged them to move again. He brought his hands together and gripped them tightly against each other, pushing strength into his weary arms. Feeling his strained biceps swell with what power he could muster. Feeling too the anger rise within him. And then he waited.

The two men stood at the other side of the room and watched him. He could feel their eyes boring into him, urging him to crack. This was the psychological way of breaking through. Of breaking him. They were allowing him to become even more afraid. Urging him to panic. To explore his worst fears and delve into their deepest darkest imagery. Playing with his mind. Well he wasn't going to be played with. They had done what they had to do and, he knew, they had worse to do. But he was finished with them.

From now on he would be a dead man. He would will his body to feel no pain. Whatever happened. No pain. He tried to remember the techniques he had been taught in training. How to resist torture. You count in your head, he thought. Yes that was it, you count very, very slowly and that just somehow cuts out everything else that's going on. That's what he would do. He would count slowly. Very, very slowly. He prayed to God that it would work.

After what he thought might have been a few minutes one of the men walked over to him. He closed his eyes and waited for the kick that would herald the next awful tortures. But nothing came. He was aware of the man's presence as he stood over him. But there was no kick. No punch. Instead he felt a hand on his shoulder and then another hand gently grasping his own. Helping him up and into the chair.

What was this now? he wondered. Was this the clever mind work they had warned him about in the training camp? When they fooled you into thinking they had finished. When they calmed you down so that your resolve on which you had worked so hard was instantly broken and when the pain began again it was as if it was all happening for the first time? Or worse. Was that what this was?

He heard a voice, but was at first unable to make out the words. He was sure it was German but his scrambled brain would not translate. Could not make the connection. And then he realised that the man was speaking in English. Another trick. He opened his eyes and looked at the man. Read his lips and was suddenly able to understand. 'You see, as I said. I am most terribly sorry. It's all part of the process. You do understand, don't you, old man? Just a part of the training programme. In fact in our opinion it's the most important part. I have to say you did rather well.'

Hunter stared at him. After a while he managed to speak: 'Bastard. You, you... bastard.'

He spat the words from his blistered lips. The man spoke again: 'Quite, well. Yes. Yes, they all say that. It is a thankless task, this, but someone's got to do it, old man. You do understand.'

Hunter tried to express what he felt: 'Understand? You almost fucking killed me you bastard. And fucking stop calling me "old man". Shit.'

He had tried to stand up, but his legs were too weak and he merely slid to the floor.

'Captain Rodney here will help you, old chap. Jolly well

done. There's no way any Jerry interrogator could break you, Hunter. Good effort. Very well done.'

Hunter grimaced. 'Good effort'? It was like school sports day. Good bloody effort. For a moment he considered taking a swing at the man, but realised that he would fail and thought the better of it.

The other man, Captain Rodney, helped him up and slowly guided and half dragged him across to the room's wooden door, which he noticed, with amusement, wasn't locked. Outside he found himself in a small anteroom made of mud bricks. It smelt of stale sweat and damp. With difficulty, leaning his arm against a wall, Hunter managed to stand up on his own. He noticed his uniform, pressed and smelling fresh, hanging up above a wooden bench on which his boots and cap had been placed with precision. The man indicated a shower apparatus on the right.

'You can wash there, Hunter. Take your time. Call out if you need anything. Then get yourself dressed. Debrief in an hour. Oh and see and get some scoff before that if you can keep it down. You know where the canteen is, don't you.'

He sat down on the bench and watched as the man in Nazi uniform left the room and closed the door behind him. Hunter sat down on the bench, suddenly dizzy. Christ, his head was reeling. A few minutes ago he had been ready to die an agonising, slow death. Ready to die for his country, his king and all of that. Prepared for the very worst. He had really believed it all. Suddenly he felt very angry. Massively angry that he had fallen for it and that they could have done it. And then within moments the anger was replaced with a surge of relief. Real relief and joy at being alive. And at it all being a game. That's what it all was. A great game wasn't it?

All this. The unit. The war. A bloody great game. A game that no one could win.

He shook his head and tried to grasp at reality. After a few strange minutes he started to understand what had happened and, willing himself to his feet walked into the shower. It was a primitive affair, but to Hunter it might as well have been in a suite at the Dorchester.

He stood beneath the tepid water for much longer than he usually did, luxuriating in its touch on his fractured skin. Looking down he could see the blood from his wounds mixing with the water as it ran into the uncovered hole that was the drain. Gradually the water ran clear. He turned off the shower and after grabbing the towel that lay on the bench, dried himself with care, trying not to disturb newly forming scabs.

He dressed with equal care, pulling on his bush shirt, shorts, socks and boots. Found his belt and beside it a small parcel of the personal effects they had taken off him: wallet, cigarettes, lighter, watch, a pile of coins and most importantly, the old St Christopher medal given to him by his nanny the day he had started school.

He winced occasionally when a movement caused a sudden twinge of pain. God, they had done their job well. He had been convinced that his end had come and of the horrible fate that awaited him. The relief he felt now was quite unparalleled. He had never felt so liberated. And so very, very thankful to be alive.

Hunter walked out into the brightness of the day and blinked. It was no trick. He was exactly where he had been, however many days ago it had been when they had taken him. Here, in the training camp at Athlit. As he stood there, slowly adjusting to the daylight, a man passed him by and waved. 'Morning, Jim. Been away?'

He recognised him as one of the SBS officers, Jack Cartwright.

'Yes. You might say that, Jack. I have been away.'

He had been away, alright. Away to somewhere that he never ever wanted to visit again. It had all happened so fast. One moment he had been walking away in the night from the officers' mess tent, off to have a quick fag. The next he had felt a sharp blow and then blackness. He had woken up in that darkened room, stark naked. And then it had begun.

He had been brought here, with a few others from Cairo immediately after his leave had expired. They had arrived by motor launch, in the middle of the night. But after a couple of whiskies the captain had told him where they were headed.

Athilt, in Palestine, some eight miles south of Haifa. A newly built training camp. They would be the first to use it. And now they had been here for the last eight weeks, since the first of April, a date that some of them found highly amusing, given the perilous and anonymous nature of their mission.

To refer to Athilt camp as being 'built' was, of course, something of a misnomer, as it was almost all under canvas. Beyond the camp lay barren hills, dotted with a few spots of green desert flora. The few exceptions to the tents that formed the camp were a group of white-painted mud-brick buildings that clustered together and were known collectively as the 'admin block'. No one was quite sure what they were all there for. Well now at least Hunter knew. It was in one of those that he had been held and interrogated. He wondered for just how long. It was of no matter now. He was out. But how much time had he lost?

He walked towards the tent lines, keen to get back to his own little sanctuary. Back to some semblance of normality. The sky as usual was a brilliant azure blue above the sand and in it hung the sun, a dazzling yellow disc.

To his left lay the sea, its blueness a mirror image of the sky, save for the waves that agitated its surface and broke against the strip of bright yellow sand.

The location for the camp had been chosen by the new overall commander of the reformed SBS, the new Special Boat Service, George, Earl Jellicoe, who had taken over the project when poor David Stirling had been captured by the Germans in the Western Desert. And in Hunter's opinion at least, the location for the new camp had been chosen with more than a dollop of unbridled romanticism.

The camp lay above the dunes of Athilt Bay, in the shadow of the Carmel Hills, where a long stretch of golden sands came to an end at the base of the walls of a Crusader castle, the Chateau Pelerin.

Pelerin had been a stronghold of the Knights Templar, and Hunter – more than anyone else in the camp – was privy to the details of its history. By an extraordinary coincidence, his father, a distinguished archaeologist, had made a special study of the castle and had come here on an excavation back in the early 1930s.

Built by the Templars seven hundred years ago, Pelerin had been abandoned to the Muslims in 1290 but had stood there ever since, a splendid, slightly crumbling, ruinous reminder of another conflict and another age when a very different band of warrior brothers had taken arms against what they had seen as the evil oppressor.

What, he wondered, would the Templars make of him and his comrades today as they trained in the shadow of their fortress. Certainly, some of their ways of waging war were very different: the machine gun and the bomb. But others, particularly those favoured by today's crusading warriors, had not changed, would never change: the knife, the fist, the handkerchief knotted tight around a stone and pulled tight around the throat, the swift silent sudden presence in the night that brought death in the shadows. These, he thought, would surely all have been familiar to the Templar Knights.

He gazed up at the yellowing battlements and felt a strange sense of belonging. For the castle was also a connection to his parents and that was important to Hunter. There were precious few of those. Every time he looked at it he thought of his father, working there, kneeling in the dirt, sifting the sands of the past, searching for history, and it deepened the mystery of his parents' death that had haunted him ever since.

He supposed that mystery and uncertainty had always followed him. That it was somehow appropriate that he should now himself be involved in covert operations.

He had gradually found out more about his new unit. They were under the overall command of the SBS but in theory he had been told by Vickery, they were authorised to operate independently.

It was all a bit confusing. But it meant that in the field they were their own men. Answerable to no one, but at the same time the reverse of the coin meant that they would be the first to be abandoned. What it really meant was that no one was going to take responsibility for them.

It was suitable too that they would only be known by a number: XXXI Commando. That was it. They were neither army nor navy. Neither fish nor fowl as he saw it in his mind. They were a Frankenstein's monster of a unit.

They had been accepted by the bigger unit, the SBS. That was made up of some 250 men. Men who had come down here from commando units in Syria, Persia and Kabrit. They fought and bickered all the time, their inter-unit rivalry constantly coming to the fore. The Persian group, under Fitzroy Maclean, in particular stood out as being all 'spit and polish'. It was made up almost entirely of guards and cavalry officers; perfect caricatures of upper-class soldiering. All shiny brass and Blanco. That wasn't to say that they were bad soldiers. On the contrary, these men were all born fighters, just aching for a scrap.

But Hunter had learnt to leave them to it. His own unit was half the size of the main body and seemed less inclined to get into a fight. God knew there were enough Germans around to kill without knocking seven bells out of your own side.

Some, of course had come from another unit of the Special Boat Squadron. A real bunch of mavericks, who for the last two years had been raiding the Italian coast. Hunter had worked with them before. As usual the divide between what they did and what he had been engaged in these last two months was cloudy. But now Hunter felt that he might just be where he belonged. Here, with a real bunch of misfits and miscreants, he somehow at last felt that he fitted in.

He was surprised at the scale of his new unit. It was much larger than he had envisaged, as well as being diverse in its mix of the services.

XXXI Commando comprised three detachments each of between twenty and thirty men. A total of eighty men.

First there was 32 Troop (Royal Marine), the smallest, made up of two officers, both of them captains, and twenty marines. Then there was 34 (Royal Navy) Troop consisting of a lieutenant commander, three lieutenants and three sub lieutenants, along with twenty men.

The largest unit though was his own, 33 (Army) Troop, under Woods, with under him three ten-man sections, each one commanded by a lieutenant. One was under Hunter, another led by a homicidal Dane and the third by a Coldstream officer. Plus there was an HQ staff, wittily described by the naval unit as 'base barnacles'.

All the men were volunteers, vetted by their individual troop commanders and ultimately by Vickery and the commander. And this, he thought, with amusement, was the crack force that was going to shorten the war.

Feeling incredibly weary, Hunter finally found his tent and, opening the flap, entered, lay down slowly on his bed and stared up at the faded green canvas of the roof. He lit a cigarette and blew a smoke ring up into the void. The room was sparsely furnished with merely a bed and a small bamboo table. The bed was hard and had a paillasse mattress but as he pushed his aching body into it, it might have been a soft bed of feathers. He stretched out his legs and flexed his fingers, blowing another smoke ring.

Eight weeks he had been here under canvas. Eight weeks of training.

All of them had, of course, already been through the basic commando courses, from street fighting and handling explosives, detonations and enemy booby traps to uniform, badge and vehicle recognition. They had brushed up on all of these. But the big stuff, the new stuff was, as Vickery had said, what they were really here for.

They had trained in parachute jumping at an RAF base on Mount Carmel. First in a landing harness on to crash mats, then learning how to fit through the tiny trapdoor using a section of fuselage on the ground. Finally they had jumped from a cage hung below a huge metal framework. Seven hundred feet up.

Then there was boat-craft, out on the sea, learning to handle the sort of small caiques that they would be sailing in. There would be naval ratings sailing them for the most part, but each of them had to know what to do if the crew were shot up.

They had an intensive course in how to recognise different enemy documents. How to tell an inconsequential requisition letter from a vital piece of intelligence.

They learnt too about the care of prisoners and how to make a body search. Most importantly they were taught how to recover material from an enemy HQ, where to look for valuable material, how to pick a lock and how to blow a safe without destroying the contents. How to slip a lock and break a window silently. How to prise open windows. How to photograph documents and replace them as if they had not been disturbed.

And finally, as it now appeared, they had learnt about escaping from custody and how to behave as a prisoner of war and, as they had not been warned and he had recently learnt, under interrogation.

He seemed to have hardly touched the mattress when the flap to his tent opened and an officer's face peered in. 'Hunter. Debrief now. Follow me.'

He pushed himself up, extinguished the cigarette under the heel of his boot and followed the man outside.

The debrief was held in the same simple white-painted adobe building from which he had emerged after his interrogation. He entered it with some trepidation, not entirely sure as to whether they might try something else. Another trick to test his resolve. But nothing happened. He walked past the shower room and through the doorway into the room where he had been tortured. It was transformed. A window had now appeared in what he had presumed to be a blank wall and through it the bright sunshine was playing across a battered green-painted metal desk at which an officer was seated.

Hunter was surprised not to be met by one of his interrogators, but instead by Lieutenant Commander Vickery.

'Sir, I didn't expect to see you here.'

'Always expect the unexpected, eh Hunter? Well here we are. Well done. You made it.'

'So it would seem, sir.'

'So it would seem, Hunter. I'm afraid I don't intend to apologise for your treatment. We need to make these things as realistic as possible... without going too far, of course.'

'Yes, sir. Of course. Without going too far. That really wouldn't do.'

Vickery ignored his sarcasm and continued, 'You'll be pleased to know that that last test marks the end of your training for the unit. You're in. Well done.'

Hunter smiled at him. Could he really believe this man?

There had been no hint of the last test, until it had happened. What if...

'Really, sir? Are you quite sure? You've nothing else in mind for me? I mean, no one else is going to kidnap me? Half kill me?'

Vickery laughed. 'No, no, no. Of course not, Hunter. That's it. You can believe me. You've made the grade. One thing, I must ask you not to reveal, however, is the final test. To anyone. It is vital, as you will appreciate, that it should come to each of you as a complete surprise. Otherwise it is a waste of our time and of yours. You are not, as you may have guessed, the last man in the unit to complete these tests.'

Hunter gave a barely perceptible grin. Oh no, he wasn't the last man. Far from it. There must, he thought, be at least a dozen who hadn't yet completed the course.

'Of course, sir, I wouldn't dream of letting the cat out of the bag. You can rely on me.'

Of course he wouldn't tell the others. That would defeat the purpose. But also, more than that, he wanted each of them to go through what he had just gone through. Wanted all of them to experience the sheer terror of believing you were finished, ruined, worse than dead. If he was going to go through that then they bloody well would too. And serve them right for joining this godforsaken mob anyway.

Vickery smiled again. 'Knew that I could count on you, Hunter. Good man. Why don't you go and take a few hours' rest. You've been through a bit of an ordeal.'

'Thank you, sir. I'll do that.'

Hunter turned and left the room. *A bit of an ordeal, he thought. I should bloody say so.*

Outside the colour of the sea was changing from blue to green, as the sunlight caught it. He turned away from the beach and walked a few hundred yards closer to the castle. On a grassy bank below the ramparts wild flowers had bloomed and were filling the air with their scent. He could hear the shouts of a hand-to-hand combat class further down the beach and the noises of animal aggression made a jarring contrast to the sweet fragrance of the flowers.

He headed to the canteen – a large, gazebo-like tent in the lee of the castle – and had just entered when a man walked up to him.

'Christ, sir, what the hell happened to you?'

It was Knox.

'What? Ah, hello, Knox. Um. Nothing really, why?'

'Well, it's just that you look like shite, if you don't mind my saying so, sir.'

'Really?'

It suddenly occurred to him that his face might be battered and bruised almost beyond recognition.

'Oh, just a bit of a barney I got into.'

'Bit of a barney? Must have been some stramash, sir. And you can handle yourself better than most. Where was it?'

Hunter thought fast. 'Back in Cairo. Had forty-eight hours' leave. I took a wrong turning.'

Knox let out a whistle. 'I'll say you did, sir. Straight into a brick wall by the look of it. You want to get that seen to. Go to the MO, sir.'

'Don't need the MO. It'll heal. But thanks for your concern, Knox. I'm off to get some scoff.'

'You'll be here for the end-of-term party, sir, won't you? Should be some bash. Better than ENSA, I reckon.'

Hunter laughed at the reference. 'What? Don't tell me you're going to give us your drag act, Knox.'

'Oh aye. Suspenders and all the rest. No me. Never. But you can be sure one of the guys from that Persian mob will get hisself up in a frock. They're all like that.'

Hunter laughed again. 'I'll be there, Knox. Wouldn't miss it for the world. When is it again? Remind me.'

'Tomorrow, sir. Christ, you have been away haven't you. Don't you even know what day it is?'

'Evidently not. Why don't you tell me that too, Knox.'

'It's Thursday, sir. Must have been one hell of a leave. Must run, sir. Need to see a man about a fighting knife.'

And he was gone.

Thursday, thought Hunter. Christ, he had been out of his mind locked in that bloody cell for two days. And whatever Vickery had said about the others not having finished, clearly they all had. He realised that if Knox had noticed it, then he must look really bad. He touched his cheek and winced. Of course it would heal. No point in seeing the MO. Besides, there was a party to think about.

5

Cairo seemed incredibly crowded and busy to Hunter after his eight weeks spent in the glorious isolation and fresh sea air and wild flowers of Athlit. The surfaces of the filthy streets were powder-dry and the passing military vehicles, of which there seemed to him to be many more than before, kicked up great plumes of khaki dust that hung suspended in the breathless air. Holding a handkerchief close against his face, Hunter walked alongside Woods and was relieved when at last they reached Garden City and the steps of Rustum Buildings.

They walked in, returning the snapped salutes from the MPs at the door and climbed now with a new confidence up the steps to the first floor. Woods looked at his watch and knocked at the door of flat 7, which was opened by the same pretty young WRN. She shook her head at them and smirked. 'Oh, hello, it's you again. I'm afraid you're a little late. "V" doesn't like late you know. This way.'

She admitted them to the inner office. Hunter was not surprised to see Vickery, seated at his leather-topped desk in his club chair, looking as if he hadn't moved since their last meeting here. The room was unchanged too. There was only one noticeable difference. Vickery was not alone.

Behind him, seated in another similarly incongruous chair, more suited to White's or Boodle's, sat a British Army major, wearing the ubiquitous uniform of an 8th Army cavalry officer: brown cavalry twill trousers, a white shirt topped off with a paisley-patterned silk cravat and a V-necked khaki pullover.

Both men were smoking cigarettes.

Vickery looked up at Hunter and Woods briefly, then down to his watch and then back up at them. 'Ah, Captain Woods, Lieutenant Hunter. You're late, gentlemen. Do remember: in the military, punctuality is not a luxury, it's a given.'

Hunter felt as if he was back in the headmaster's study at Fettes.

Vickery managed a queasy smile. 'Sit down, won't you.'

He motioned them to a pair of Victorian dining chairs positioned in front of his desk and as soon as they were seated, opened the square silver cigarette box that was lying on the desk and offered it to them. 'Cigarette? Sullivan and Powell Egyptians. Had ten cases flown in yesterday.'

The two men each reached for one of the oval cigarettes. Hunter lit them both.

'How did you find your training? You both look remarkably well on it.'

Woods spoke: 'It was, er… Well it was, interesting, sir.'

Hunter stared at Vickery. "Looking remarkably well". That hardly summed it up. He presumed that his bruises were now no longer visible. He said, 'It was harrowing, sir, but no less than I would have expected.'

Vickery, who was quite clearly not really listening to them, spoke again: 'Ah yes. Of course. Very good. Well, as it happens, you completed the course just in time.'

Woods asked, 'Just in time? In time for what?'

'We've got a mission for you. Rather a good one, actually.'

Hunter muttered, 'That'll make a change.'

'Yes, Hunter, I dare say it will. And if you manage to pull it off, it really will make a hell of a change.'

The army officer smiled and took a long drag from his cigarette. 'Right, David?'

'Right.'

'We're calling it Operation Inkspot. As you are aware Woods, your troop, 33 AU, will be attached to 8 Commando. Jellicoe's mob. We've just redesignated them all SBS so it's a much bigger force now. We're sending in two troops of them. No prizes as to what they'll be doing. We need to get back control of Crete, or at least to put all enemy planes on the island out of action. Crete is the key. There are three main air bases.'

He stood up and moved over to the map and, picking up a stick, used it as a pointer. 'Tymbaki here, in the south, Heraklion, here on the north coast and Kastelli Kissamou, over here in the west of the island. That is the task of 8 Commando. They'll hide up for a few days before they go in and do their damnedest to blow all three to blazes. Which will give you the time you need.'

'Time, sir?'

'Time, Woods. Your own task is rather different. You will RV with one of our SOE agents in the hills and with him as your guide, head for Heraklion airstrip. Once there you will infiltrate the base and retrieve a vital piece of British military intelligence, which was left on the island when we lost it to the Germans in May '41. Our SOE man on Crete tells us that his intelligence sources suggest that the Germans have not yet discovered it. Which is a bit of luck isn't it? Apparently it was missed by their intelligence officer *Obersturmbannführer* Otto Skorzeny when he cleared the bases with his "intelligence commandos" last May. Which is somewhat ironic, as the boss got his own idea of putting you lot together when he found out about Skorzeny's mob. Funny eh?'

Woods smiled. 'Very funny, sir.'

Hunter shook his head. 'Hilarious.'

Vickery ignored the comment. 'Of course, we've asked the SOE chappie to get hold of it himself but he's asked for assistance. Says he's there for the long haul and if he gets caught his number's up. Which is utterly understandable. So his refusal makes it the ideal first mission for you lot.'

Hunter muttered, 'Because we're expendable.'

Woods looked at him and shook his head.

Vickery continued, 'Also, there is something else that makes your job more than vital.'

'Sir?'

'I don't know how much you've heard about what we intend to do. I mean how we intend to win the war.'

Woods nodded his head. 'A fair bit, sir.'

'Which is?'

'Well of course all the chat at present is about what's going to happen in the desert. I mean everyone knows there's going to be an offensive. It's just about when it happens, sir, isn't it?'

Vickery nodded. 'Yes, of course, it's common knowledge, apart from the timing of Monty's big push. But what do you know of the bigger picture?'

'Well, there's been quite a lot of talk about the bigger plan being the invasion of Italy. The chat is that we're going to go up through Sicily. Most people reckon that if Rome falls then

Berlin will follow. Of course, sir, I presume that either that might be the real plan or it might all be a grand deception. I mean that's the sort of thing we do, isn't it?'

Vickery nodded. 'True. That's just the sort of thing we do.'

He strolled back to his desk and sat down, taking another cigarette from the silver box and lighting it, before continuing, 'Well, Woods. You're right and then you're wrong. It's no secret that Monty's going to push Rommel out of the desert. We outnumber him and it's all been planned to the last detail and I have no doubt he'll do it. Which as you say leaves us with the next move. That's where you come in. The documents on Crete contain details of ideas that came out of a conference a while ago.'

'Sir?'

'Early in '41 there were talks in Washington.'

'Before the USA entered the war? Before Pearl Harbor?'

'Exactly. Long before. March last year. It was clear even back then that the US would eventually be sucked into this bloody war and it was obvious that we needed to make contingency plans. That was the first Allied agreement – ABC-1. The actual plan was given the overall name "Rainbow".'

'Christ! I mean, sir, I wouldn't have guessed at anything like that.'

'I wouldn't have expected you to. Neither would I, to be honest. It was agreed that out of all the Axis powers, Germany was the strongest and needed to be attacked first. It was to be called Operation Gymnast and was ultra-top secret. You're the most junior officers ever to have heard about it.'

Hunter and Woods exchanged glances.

'The Yanks want us to go all out for an attack on France and I dare say that's what will happen. But not before we've had a go at the underbelly. We need to go in from the south. The details were put together back in April last year, as it became very clear that Greece would fall. We knew that we had to come back and attack the Third Reich and one way of doing that was through the Med. It's Churchill's baby. First we take North Africa in a combined assault with the Yanks and then we move up through Sicily and Italy. Those papers contain details of the initial high-level discussions of our method, timing and potential numbers involved. Ordnance, hardware. The lot.'

Hunter whistled. 'Good grief.'

'Yes, as you say. Good grief. But there's something else. The papers we need you to get out don't just give the breakdown of our plans. They make it crystal clear that when we do fight back Italy will take precedence over Greece. Italy will be the focus of our first and most decisive attack, via Sicily, rather than Greece and the Balkans.

'If the Germans find out it will jeopardise our entire strategy. More than that. Their intelligence chaps are no fools. They're sure to realise that if they tell the Greeks what they've found it will destroy our position in Central Europe. It's absolutely vital that the Greeks believe that we're going in through the Balkans.'

'Why so, sir? If I may ask.'

Vickery pointed to the army officer, who for a while had said nothing at all.

'This is Major Wallace. He's the political assistant to the British Liaison Officer, Greece, the BLO. He's been dealing with the Greek resistance. All three parts of it. Although perhaps I'd be better to allow him tell you about it himself. David?'

The army officer leaned forward in his chair, extinguished his cigarette and looked at Woods and Hunter.

'Good morning, gentlemen. I don't know how much you chaps know about our Greek friends, but basically here's the gen. You see their resistance is made up of three quite different groups and they're all plotting and planning who is going to rule Greece when we've won this bloody war. They call themselves the ELAS, EDES and EKKA. I must say, they've been doing a pretty good job together with us thus far, but the differences between them are starting to get a bit out of hand.'

'Differences, sir?'

'Basically the EDES are Nationalist and Republican. They're led by an eccentric and highly dangerous ex-army officer called Napoleon Zervas. The ELAS, the military wing of EAM are Communists, the largest of the groups controlled by the KKE, the Greek Communist party. The EKKA are actually National Socialists.

'ELAS think that EKKA are in our pockets, that they're bourgeois Anglophiles, and they despise them for it. They've all been persuaded to collaborate up to now because they think that their unholy alliance is only for a limited time. They truly believe that it won't be long before we come across the Aegean and sweep up through the Peloponnese to liberate Greece.

'It is my belief, based on everything I've seen and heard in the last few months, that if the Greeks learn that we don't intend to do any such thing, but instead are going to head for Rome, it will result very quickly in no less than a civil war. And a very bloody one at that. The Jerries would love it. It's just the sort of thing their own spooks do all too bloody well: getting one faction of the enemy to take out another.

In fact it looks very much as if when the war does end the Communists will prevail and then the country will erupt in civil war. But we can't allow that to happen until we have beaten the Jerries. Is that clear so far?'

Woods and Hunter nodded and Woods spoke: 'Yes, sir, I think so. I get the whole thing about the different groups and the fact that we need to unite them and that to do that they can't possibly know that we're actually going to be invading Europe up through Italy, not Greece.'

'Yes. That's it. Very good.'

'So what do we do, sir? To make sure they don't find out?'

'What we have to do is stall for time. We need the Greeks – all of them – to believe that the Balkans is still our goal. I'm here in Cairo with my own boss – the British Liaison Officer – and members from each of the three main Greek resistance groups. In fact the moment I leave you I'm off to sit round a table with them and try, if we can, to encourage them to keep working together. But we know that just a lot of talk won't be enough. The Greeks like to see things happening. They like proof. They need proof that we won't let them down.'

He paused. 'So, to do that, to give them proof of our commitment, we're sending missions by SBS commandos into Crete and Rhodes. These will have a double purpose. Firstly, in real terms, they will consolidate our hold on the Aegean islands, in preparation for the invasion of Sicily. Secondly though they will persuade the Greeks that we really are in earnest. That we really are going to liberate their country first and ensure the stability of the regime.'

Hunter spoke: 'So, we're using the Greeks, sir. And we're duping them.'

'Yes, that's exactly what we're doing. There's no room for

moral sentiment in modern warfare, Lieutenant. You should know that.'

Hunter shook his head. 'I know that, sir, as well as anyone. It just seems a pity that we can't be honest with them. Seems to me that when we do push up through Italy and abandon the Greeks, the Jerries will have a field day.'

'We are not "abandoning the Greeks" as you put it. We're merely reapportioning our strengths.'

'Whatever you want to call it, sir.'

Woods glanced at Hunter and nodded. 'It's very clever, sir. Still not entirely clear where we fit in.'

'It's simple. Just make sure that we get that missing intelligence off Crete. It details in no small way that our initial plans are to move into Italy, rather than Greece. If the Germans work out how important it is and leak it to the Greeks then all hell will break loose. If we lose it, the war will almost certainly go on for many more years and many, many thousands more will die.'

Vickery spoke: 'So, Woods, you see the importance of your task?'

'Yes, sir. Quite.'

'And the fact that absolute secrecy must be maintained.'

'Absolutely, sir.'

'Don't be flippant, Lieutenant Hunter. There is one more thing. The Foreign Office, our Foreign Office, have no idea that we have been working with the Communists. They simply want us, the Brits that is, to back the King of Greece in taking back his throne. They don't realise how unpopular he is. But if they find out that we're tied up with the Communists then you can bet that they'll try to persuade Winnie himself to shut down the entire operation. Even though he's the one who ordered us to ignore the Greek resistance politics in the first place.'

Hunter shook his head. 'Christ. I had no idea.'

'No one does. So be bloody careful who you talk to and what you say. Best of luck to you both. Just be sure to remember how important your mission is.'

Vickery pushed a hand bell on his desk and the pretty WRN opened the door. Clearly, they were now meant to leave. They stood up and were about to do so when Vickery spoke again: 'Oh yes, I almost forgot. You go in three days' time.' He reached into the drawer of his desk and produced a brown envelope, which he handed to Woods. 'There you are. Everything you need to know is in there. Once you've read it and memorised it, burn it. And make sure that you do that, will you? Well, that's it, gentlemen. Goodbye.'

They left the building and, once they were out of earshot of the redcap sentries, Hunter gave a whistle. 'Christ all bloody mighty. What the hell was that all about?'

Woods smiled at him. 'That, my dear boy, was what the Secret Service do. That's what that was all about. That is why you and I are sleeping in caves and fighting in the hills and why chaps like Lieutenant Commander fucking Vickery are ordering cases of posh fags from St James's and sleeping in silk sheets.'

'Poor bloody Greeks.'

'No point in thinking that. We've just got to get on with the bloody job. Three days? Christ. Better make the most of them.'

'Yes, we'd better. What do you suggest we do?'

'Well, I'm meant to be meeting that old flame of yours, Lara Heatherly. We had a rather jolly time the other night. I really think she's fallen for me. Lovely girl. Well, you would know, of course.'

Hunter paused for a moment. 'Did you? Yes, she is… Lovely, that is.'

Woods looked at him. He was grinning.

'Good Lord. You're still smitten, aren't you? Well I never.'

Hunter said nothing. He had not thought about Lara before bumping into her at Groppi's. But now he realised, to his surprise, that Woods was right. He did still feel something.

Woods was still smiling. He spoke again: 'Well, if I'd known, old man, perhaps I wouldn't have become involved.'

Hunter looked at him. 'Are you? Involved?'

'Depends what you mean by involved I suppose. As I said, we had rather a jolly time the other night. If you know what I mean.'

He smiled. Hunter stared at him.

Woods spoke again: 'I say, old man. You're jealous!'

'Perhaps I am. After all, she was my girl before she ever met you.'

'Well, now she's my girl, old man.'

Hunter shook his head and smiled. 'Oh, I don't think so, *old man*. She'll never be your girl.'

'Well, we'll just have to see about that shan't we. Let's allow her to decide.'

'My mind's made up, Woods. Like it or not.'

'Actually, Hunter, I don't much like it. But let's not let that ruin a perfectly good evening. God knows we may not see another for a long time.'

Both men fell silent, lost in their thoughts. Woods spoke

first: 'I say. How very stupid of me. I totally forgot to tell you. We've been invited to a party.'

Hunter looked up, not entirely interested in the news. 'No, you didn't tell me. Whose party? Where is it?'

'Need you ask? There is only one real place for parties in Cairo, isn't there? We're off to Tara, old man.'

That the party was in full swing by the time they got there was instantly evident from the moment they crossed Gezira island and entered Sharia Abou El Feda. The shrill staccato bleat of clarinets hit them first, wailing out Gershwin into the warm Cairo evening.

Tara was a sea of light, with every lamp in every room blazing and every shutter thrown open to the night. Above their heads it seemed that dozens of men and women, most of them in uniform, were hanging out of the windows, perched on the windowsills, their brimming glasses spilling their contents into the street below. Hunter and Woods walked into the marble entrance hall of the villa and up the wide steps, which led to the *piano nobile*. Couples of all permutations were draped everywhere, chatting, kissing, mostly drinking. Woods turned to Hunter. 'Here we go. Good luck. Remember, Hunter, I'm on the lookout for Lara. Let me know if you see her. If I'm not back in three days send out a search party.'

And with that he was gone.

Hunter grabbed a cocktail from a passing waiter and plunged into the throng.

In a far corner of the library, by an open window, he caught sight of Xan Fielding. The young officer was locked in conversation with another British officer whom he thought he recognised from Athilt as SBS or SAS, expounding his theories about how the Greeks would end up after the war and what they should be doing about it now. Before it was all too late.

Hunter drew close and listened.

'You see the problem is, you just don't know the Greeks. You may be as good as you like at all the sabotage stuff. But if you don't know how the Greeks think, then you're lost. We need the Greeks. They're the one weapon we have that the Germans never will have. The problem is knowing which bloody lot of them to trust. That's where we can help you.'

Hunter walked away.

In the ballroom, at a baby grand piano being played by an Armenian in a dinner jacket and a fez, the ever-exuberant Paddy Leigh Fermor was holding court, performing his celebrated party piece of singing 'It's a Long Way to Tipperary' in French. As Hunter joined the crowd around the piano, a small man beside him in Australian RAF uniform tapped him on the arm. 'You just wait, mate. When they ask for an encore he'll do it in Arabic. I've seen him do it before. Bloody nuts.'

Hunter was surprised. He had presumed that Leigh Fermor would already be on Crete, awaiting their arrival. To see him at a party at Tara was a shock. A girl standing beside them, with a Rita Hayworth hairstyle and a figure to match, turned to the Aussie. 'Oh give him a break, love. The poor darling's making the most of his last night. They're dropping him back into Crete tomorrow.'

So here was their SOE liaison officer. This half-cut, multi-lingual boulevardier.

And so much, thought Hunter, for all their blessed secrecy. If the walls had ears, as the posters said, then all Cairo must by now know Leigh Fermor's clandestine movements.

Hunter downed the cocktail in one. Much to his regret, it turned out to be a white lady, which he loathed, and he decided to try to find a beer. But before he could do so a waiter handed him a glass of champagne. He was attempting to hand it back when, from out of nowhere, Lara appeared in front of him, shimmering in a long pink evening dress, and draped herself across his body, winding one of her legs around his.

'Darling, Jimmy. Didn't think I'd see you again.'

Her sparkling eyes pierced his thoughts. He knew what was coming.

'You stood me up, you rotten bugger. Where on earth did you go?'

'Look, Lara. I can explain.'

'Really?'

'Really.'

'Well then, go on. Explain.'

Hunter shrugged. 'Well, actually, it's not that simple. You see, I'm afraid I... can't really say. But I'm really, really sorry. I just couldn't do anything about it, Lara, darling. You understand. Orders.'

Lara laughed. 'Orders? Of course it was bloody orders. You see, my dear, dear Jimmy. I told you that you were a spook. I knew all along.'

Hunter shook his head. 'I am not a spook.'

'Well, whatever you are, darling, you bloody well stood me up.'

'I know. And I'm sorry. I really am. What else can I do?'

'I'll tell you what you can do. You can prove it. Prove to me that you're really sorry.'

He looked into her eyes as she spoke again, smiling, and he knew he was forgiven.

She whispered, 'Let's go, darling, shall we? My apartment?'

He looked down at her. 'Do you really mean that, or are you just drunk?'

She shook her head, smiled again, and pouted at him. 'You silly, silly man. I'm both actually. But mostly I think I'm drunk. Of course I mean it. Oh God, really… Come on, Jimmy. Can't you see? Stop being a tease. Let's go. I really can't wait for you any longer.'

He stared at her, unable to believe that he had been forgiven, and suddenly in his mind they were back in London. In that lovely, incredible summer.

Lara wobbled to stand up straight and, as he reached to put his arm around her shoulders, Hunter glimpsed behind her head, framed in the doorway, the figure of Peter Woods. He was looking directly at Hunter, his face a mask of surprise and bewilderment. Woods walked towards them and, as he approached, Hunter made sure that he could see quite clearly that his arm was on her shoulders and hers on his neck. He made sure that he spoke first: 'Peter, there you are. Lara and I were just chatting about you.'

'Really? Didn't look like that to me. It rather looked as if you were chatting about something else. As if you were about to leave. Together.'

'Really, Peter? How very clever of you. That's exactly what we were doing.'

Lara seemed quite suddenly to snap out of her romantic mood. 'Jimmy, darling. Do be careful. No one wants to fall out. Least of all over me.'

Woods was bristling with anger. 'Hunter. I thought that I had made myself clear. She's spoken for. Why don't you just back off? Don't you know when you're beaten?'

Hunter had seen Woods like this before. On Rhodes. He stepped away. 'Perhaps that's just it, Peter. I don't know when I'm beaten. When to admit defeat. And neither do you.'

Woods shook his head. 'Why don't we just go outside?'

'What?'

'We could just go outside and settle this properly. Once and for all.'

'Don't be ridiculous. You're acting like children. Both of you,' Lara shouted.

Hunter shook his head. 'I don't think that's the answer. I'm not backing down, Peter. And you had better not try it on again.'

It was too much for Woods, who took a swing at Hunter, who again stepped back, this time into a passing waiter. The blow connected with the air and hit no one. But it unsettled Woods, who fell against the piano.

'Fuck.'

Hunter tried to help him up, but Woods shook him off.

'Don't touch me.'

Woods took another swing and this time hit Hunter hard in the chest, sending him back into another waiter who was unfortunately carrying a full tray of drinks, which crashed to the floor. Leigh Fermor stopped his recital, which he was now attempting in Arabic, and yelled at them, 'Oh please. I'm trying to sing.' Then, seeing Woods circling Hunter he launched himself over the top of the piano towards them. 'A fight. Now that's more like it.'

Hunter moved quickly, dodging through the crowd, away from Woods and the growing mêlée as fast as he could go. Somehow, he made it to the top of the staircase where, much to his surprise, he collided with the naval commander who had recruited him. The man was out of uniform, dressed in a beautifully cut dinner jacket that proclaimed Savile Row.

'Lieutenant Hunter. I say. You seem to be in a bit of a hurry.'

'Hello, sir. What are you doing here? Yes I am. Bit of a problem with a girl.'

The commander smiled at him. 'Looking for somewhere to hide?'

Hunter nodded.

The man beckoned him to a door cleverly disguised as a bookcase and pushing it open, revealing a billiard room laid out as another bar. An Armenian waiter greeted them, as the commander shut the door, 'Drinks, sirs?'

The commander spoke: 'Yes, another of these and the same for my friend. They'll never find you in here. Now. The girl. Let me guess... Lara Heatherly.'

'What? How did you know about her?'

The officer laughed. 'When will you realise, we know everything about you, Hunter?'

Hunter thought fast. Realised that the eve of a mission was no time to proclaim an attachment. 'In that case you'll know that I'm not involved with Lara.'

The man laughed. 'Oh, but you are, Hunter. Believe me, you are.'

'You don't know what you're talking about.'

'I'm just giving you a bit of advice. I would stay away from her.'

'But why? Don't tell me you're keen on her too?'

'Keen on her? Me? Good God no. Not my type. Far too bluestocking.'

'So what is the problem with Lara, sir?'

'She's trouble, Hunter.'

'Yes I know that. She always has been.'

'No. I don't mean like that. She works for SIS.'

'Oh I know that too.'

'No you don't. She works for a very different branch of SIS than we do. She's trying to get you to talk.'

'She'll have some bloody chance, after all that bloody interrogation training.'

'I'm not joking. They want to know what you're doing and they want to know all about the Greeks.'

Hunter shook his head. 'Are you by any chance drunk, sir?'

The commander pointed to the door from behind which rose the noise of a fight.

'No, not yet. But I do intend to be quite soon.'

'Well it's lucky that I met you then, sir. I have a problem.'

The commander looked serious. 'Problem?'

'With the mission. With Crete.'

'Problem? Oh, I shouldn't worry about it at all. Piece of cake. You lot are more highly trained than the winner of the St Leger. Wish I was coming with you in a way. But someone's got to man the desk while you lot get covered in glory. It's quite brilliant, what you're doing. First class.'

The man was in his element, waxing lyrical about the role of the new unit. How it was going to 'revolutionise warfare' as they knew it.

'You see what we've done, Hunter – and this is what's really clever – is to pitch you somewhere between a spy and a saboteur. You're not a real spy like the spooks at SIS and you're not just a saboteur like SOE. Well that's not to say that SBS aren't also saboteurs, but they're in and out. SOE well, they're in, and they're staying in. For the long term. But they're definitely in the business of sabotage.'

'Are you listening at all, sir?'

'Of course I am.'

'Then listen to me, please. I really don't think I can go on the mission.'

The commander smiled and shook his head. 'I'm sorry, I don't quite understand, Hunter. What's up. Are you ill? Are you unfit?'

'No, sir.'

'Then what?'

'I'm putting in a request to be relieved from the mission.'

'Sorry? What do you mean?'

'You heard what I said, sir. I want to be stood down.'

'You're drunk. I'm not sure I understand you, Hunter. What the devil are you talking about?'

'Incompatibility, sir. I can't go into action with Captain Woods. You saw him down there. Once he gets like that he's beyond either reason or logic.'

'Then it's Woods who needs to be stood down.'

'No, sir, it's the trigger that's the problem and I'm the trigger. You saw it, sir. We have… personal differences. If he gets into one of his red moods then God knows what'll happen.'

'Personal differences be damned. There's no option to stand down I'm afraid. Particularly over something as immaterial as a girl. You're the best man for the job – and you're trained to do it. Plus the fact you've already been briefed. Besides you were hand-picked. You were on Crete when the Jerries invaded. You know your way around the place. Plus the fact that you survived that bloody fiasco on Rhodes didn't you? That was the test.'

There was a pause as Hunter tried to assimilate the bombshell. 'That bloody mess was a test?'

'Of course it was. You didn't think it was an actual mission did you?'

'But a man was killed. Several men. We all almost died.'

'Collateral damage. But you made it back alive, didn't you, and that's exactly what they told us would happen. That you and Woods would make it back. And they were right.'

'Who? What? Who told you? You are drunk. That's nonsense. I was selected for this unit because of my skills and my attitude.'

The commander took a sip from the cocktail glass in front of him. 'Yes, in a way you were. But we'd had our eyes on you for a long time, Hunter. You were promoted. But we had to be sure that you would behave the way we had thought you would.'

Hunter said nothing at first, but gritted his teeth. He had been used. Just as they were using the poor bloody Greeks. 'You're outrageous. All of you.'

'We're fighting a war, Hunter. We do what it takes.'

'I won't go. I… I refuse.'

'Can't refuse, I'm afraid. You've no choice, old man.'

'But if I do refuse to go?'

'In that case you'll be court-martialled and ruined. And there'll be a scandal. We'll think of something suitably sordid. Rest assured. We're good at that.'

Hunter was silent. The waiter appeared with more drinks.

The commander drained his glass, grabbed a fresh one and pushed the other cocktail glass into Hunter's hand. 'Don't sulk. Here, try one of these. Best Martinis in Cairo. Recipe perfected at Shepheard's, by a friend of mine, the bartender,

Joe. Well you know how hard it is to get the good stuff here, don't you? Awful bloody hangovers. So Joe, dear fellow, has come up with a real winner. Try it.'

Hunter took a long drink and then paused, allowing the exquisite mixture to trickle down his throat. 'That's extraordinary, sir.'

'Yes, isn't it. Who would have thought that one little change could make such a difference? Six parts forty-two-per-cent-proof vodka to one part vermouth. And a fresh black olive. That's it. Oh and, vitally important, it has to be shaken, with ice. Never stirred. Any further questions?'

He took another drink and shook his head before speaking again: 'Actually, sir, I do have just one question for you. Can you tell me who *exactly* it is I'm working for?'

'Why, you're working for us, of course.'

'Yes, I see that, but who's my actual CO?'

'Oh, I see. What you're actually asking me is who was it who gave you the job?'

'Yes that's exactly what I mean. That's it. You see all I want to know is, who I can blame when it all goes wrong. When everything falls apart. Whose name do I curse when the Gestapo and the SS are squeezing the information out of me inch by inch? Who exactly do I tell to go to hell?'

The commander smiled. 'Oh. Me I suppose.'

'And, with all due respect, sir, may I ask who you are?'

The commander smiled at him and took another sip from his Martini, before replying, 'The name is Fleming. Ian Fleming.'

6

They had left the camp at Athilt a day ago, slipping away shortly before midnight in a convoy of four five-tonners bound for Alexandria, and had travelled down on the old coast road through Port Said. The first leg of the journey was just under two hundred miles to Port Said and it took them a good five hours. Sitting alongside the driver Hunter felt sorry for the men of his troop in the back as they felt every bump and rock on the road. This, Hunter knew, was the hardest part of the journey. There would be little sleep for any of them.

There were forty men in all on the operation. Larger than usual for a raiding force, but then, in effect, he realised, there were actually two raids taking place. The main commando force of twenty-nine men consisted of three sections of Royal Marines under Captain Sandy Wilson, a genial, soft-spoken Scot, whose family had an estate in the Highlands.

Hunter and Woods's own raiding force, the so-called 'intelligence commandos', was composed of just ten of them. Of course, Hunter had not really had a chance to get to know all of them well. He was sure though that each of them would be good to have around when they went into action.

All had initially been selected by Vickery and Fleming, with the final say-so being given to Woods and himself. There had been more of them in the bunch who had gone through Athlit. But some had been weeded out and others had left of their own volition, as the training had intensified and become more brutal and demanding. Those who were left were, he thought, probably among the fittest, best-trained and most intelligent fighting men this war had yet produced. He wondered how many would survive the coming days.

There was Jack Knox, of course, the Glasgow safe-cracker. Hunter watched him as he puffed on a woodbine and knew that he now had a definite bond with him, an instinctive thing. He felt an affinity too with his corporal, Lennie Russell, a weasel-faced petty criminal from the East End of London, known to his mates as 'Squirrel'.

Russell had worked for a while as a barman in Soho and he and Hunter had soon discovered that they shared common ground in their memories of that long-distant nirvana of poets, painters and pimps. There was little too that Russell didn't know about mixing a cocktail and he was equally good at making things disappear. Put down your wallet for the briefest moment and you could be sure that minutes later 'Squirrel', grinning, would produce it from his pocket. He was also the wise-cracker of the section. There was always one of them and quick-witted Russell had a gag for every situation.

Russell's wit was rivalled by that of the lance corporal, Bryn Fletcher, a curly-haired Welshman from Merthyr Tydfil. Fletcher was a career soldier. Having enlisted in the Royal Welch Fusiliers as a boy of seventeen, he had managed to survive Dunkirk, just. His battalion had been almost wiped out, losing 780 men. Just three officers and eighty men had made it to the beaches.

Fletcher had been promoted to sergeant, only to be broken down to corporal after a particularly rowdy night on the town in Colchester.

The problem was that Fletcher exuded charm. He could freeze you with his smile and oozed a smooth self-assurance that the ladies seemed all too ready to lap up. Although that might also have had something to do with the fact that Fletcher's mates knew him as 'Todger' Fletcher. In fact he had lost his second stripe after a fight with a woman's husband in the street while on leave in Cardiff. Though why anyone would have considered fighting Fletcher was beyond Hunter. He had also played in the second line of the scrum for the army and had scored when they beat the Royal Navy 14:3 at Twickenham in 1937. To top it off the man was a fine singer and his baritone could often be heard belting out a heady combination of bawdy rugby songs and Methodist hymns.

Both Russell and Fletcher had been selected from existing commando units. Russell had served in France and been in the raids on Vaagso and Lofoten in 3 Commando. At Vaagso he had personally brought out a complete copy of the German Naval Code, along with three prisoners. The experience had also toughened him up and given him reactions that were razor-sharp. On the downside it had also left him with a degree of mental trauma. But both Woods and Hunter reckoned the one was worth the other.

Fletcher, after surviving Dunkirk, had been involved in Operation Ambassador, the bungled 1940 raid on Guernsey. Like Hunter, he had seen first-hand what happened when things went wrong.

Hunter also had much in common with Dave (Chalky) White, an ex-Scots Guardsman. Like Fletcher and Russell, he had been selected for the commandos, back at the start of the war. White had been on Crete before, back in '41, in Layforce under Colonel Bob Laycock, and had proven himself then during the retreat, when he had met Hunter in the pass at Babali Hani, both of them split up from their units. That had been a day. Hand-to-hand fighting that took both sides back to the Middle Ages. Hunter had himself watched White kill two German mountain troops with nothing but rocks and his bare hands. That wasn't something you ever forgot.

Then there was Brian Miller, a six-foot-six, red-haired ex-policeman from Bristol, who spoke in a broad Somerset accent and punctuated his sentences with unintelligible words. Miller was blessed with the ability to sniff out trouble at a thousand paces. He literally had a nose for it. His colleagues had said he could smell a criminal halfway down the street. Woods and Hunter reckoned he was now able to do the same with a Nazi. Miller was the eyes and ears of the unit. First in, last out.

Sid Phelps, a motor mechanic from Croydon, had lost his wife and two young children in the London Blitz. He had been away at a camp with the TA and arrived home to find the local shelter destroyed and all those in it dead. Now he just wanted 'to take as many of the bastards with me before I go too' as he had told Hunter in his cups one evening, at Athilt. Phelps was a genius signaller. What 'Sparky' Phelps didn't know about comms wasn't worth knowing. He was good at Morse and was constantly learning about codes and ciphers.

But in real terms, the only thing that Sid had left now

apart from his elderly parents, was his dog, Sally, a racing greyhound who lived with his mum and dad in Pinner and who before the war had won at Catford and White City. He carried one of her racing collars in his kitbag along with a photo of his family.

And lastly there were a pair of unlikely misfit boffins: Duffy and Martin.

Bill Duffy had been studying at Cambridge for a degree in chemistry when war had broken out. He had enlisted and had immediately been transferred to the Intelligence Corps. Duffy was no less than a genius, a natural academic who, in any other times, would have been a Fellow of All Souls, proving some unlikely theorem, but who was now the unit's explosives man. However, despite his public school and university background, the army was also certain that Duffy had absolutely no officer potential. He simply wasn't cut out to lead. But what he did have was a huge and brilliant mind and, having been a rowing blue at Cambridge, a physique to match. If anyone seemed to have been cut out for the new unit, it was Bill Duffy.

Harry Martin was a small, wiry Belfast-born accountant with an extraordinary mathematical brain, a truly photographic memory and an unerring eye for detail. Martin had been living in Glasgow on a fast trajectory accounting career and had been a territorial soldier with 3rd Argylls when the balloon had gone up. The army had quickly transferred him to 1st Battalion and made him a quartermaster sergeant and his stores had been the best run in the Western Desert. But on Crete in May '41, Martin had been one of those men of the Allied rearguard who had saved the day. Low on ammunition, food and water and utterly exhausted, he and his comrades – drawn by chance from units of Aussies, Kiwis, and Indians, as well as Brits – had had to think on their feet as they were hunted down by Kampfgruppe Wittmann's ruthless mountain troops. They had slipped away from them at Megala and then managed to hold them back at Stilos, Babali Hani and Sin Kares. Finally, south of Imbros, they had fought them for as long as they could. Martin had been one of the lucky few to get in a boat.

It had all been down to the regular NCOs and among them, QSM Martin had shown beyond any doubt what he could do in the field. With rifle ammo exhausted, grenade throwing had quickly become his speciality. He had already been, needless to say, a brilliant fast bowler. It helped. Cricket was a religion to Martin. He could tell you, if asked, exactly how many matches had been won, lost or drawn in England's international cricket tests between 1925 and 1939. He could also tell you that Wally Hammond had set the record for highest individual test innings at 336. But that it was overtaken by Len Hutton's 364 against Australia in 1938. And, chillingly, he could also have told you, straight-faced, what the odds had been on his survival the last time he had been on Crete. And he might have added that this time he was going to make damned sure they were better.

All things considered, thought Hunter, they were as diverse a group of soldiers as you would ever have hoped to find in any section of the British Army. And their diversity was matched by their unique individual skills. There was something quite special about every one of them. But there were two things that united them. Firstly, their physique, stamina and discipline were faultless. And secondly, they were all trained killers. Several of them, Russell and Martin in particular, might not have looked capable of hurting anyone, but they had all proved, in training as much as in the action they had seen in the past two years, that when called upon to do so, they looked more than a match in combat for any of Hitler's men.

Hunter and the driver were in the cab, his section was in the second of four trucks each with a lieutenant and seven to nine men, while in the lead went a jeep containing the two captains: Wilson and Woods.

Taking a single break, the little convoy stopped at Port Said at around 5.30 in the morning and Hunter watched as the modern port came into view, a jumble of flat-topped buildings, minarets and spires against the curve of the coastline. Embarking again just after 6am, they passed Lake Manzala and rattled the next two hundred miles to Alexandria along the slightly better, newer coastal road, which often seemed to have nothing to do with the coast at all.

They appeared to Hunter to be driving across an enormous beach with hardly a soul to be seen and the sea at times unbelievably distant. Despite the bumpy ride, Hunter slept intermittently, waking at one point to see the islands of Lake Burullus, before they touched the edge of the old town of Rosetta, rattling through the narrow streets in the lee of its extraordinary Ottoman buildings.

As they headed south-west and grew closer to Alex, groves of date palms, thick and lush – the trees laden with fruit – lined the road. And beside them lay vast carpets of wild flowers, white, orange and red.

Finally the rooftops of Alex came in sight and Hunter strained to try to pick out something recognisable from the old town. As he did so his driver yelled through to the men from the front, 'Alex, boys. Here we are, you lucky lot. Welcome to Alexandria.'

Hunter looked at his watch. It was approaching 11.30am. They had been travelling for twelve hours.

Alexandria was a very, very different place to Cairo. Indeed, thought Hunter, it might as well have been in a different country. If Cairo was at its heart still profoundly a city of Islam, then Alex was the very opposite: essentially a metropolitan Mediterranean playground for the rich, set on the coast and facing towards Europe. It had a distinctly Greek character to it, tinged with the heady flavours, scents and smells of the Levant. Its 'white collar' workers, clerks, managers, restaurateurs were Greek to a man. Its manual workers, mostly Arab and Egyptian Muslims, were universally consigned to at best a second-class status.

The old city had not suffered too much from enemy action. The German bombers had tended to concentrate their destructive attention on the commercial port, the docks, which lay to the west of the town. A few bombs had landed in the older areas and rubble and clearly un-archaeological ruins testified to the might of the Luftwaffe. But for all its survival, Hunter detected a distinct air of shabbiness that had clearly not been brought on by the war. And where Cairo preserved an air of antiquity and even of grace, Alexandria's past was hidden beneath the ground. On the surface it was all about show. To the newcomer the city presented a façade of opulence, from the Cecil Hotel to the Royal Alexandria Yacht Club. But after a few days the illusion was dispelled and it became clear that there was no real substance to it. It occurred to Hunter that some sort of deceit, from espionage to the fragile veneer of social climbing, was rampant throughout this godforsaken country, not merely confined to the hallowed halls of GHQ and Rustum Buildings.

Another deceptive thing about Alex was the extreme vulnerability of the place. Despite appearing to possess an air of normality, Alexandria was actually almost the front line. Only in June this year the episode of what had become known as 'the flap' had caused widespread panic as Rommel's panzers had borne down with lightning speed on Alexandria. They had smashed through at Mersa Matruh and before anyone knew it were terrifyingly close.

There was a widespread burning of files in the British offices of the city. The panic had quickly spread to Cairo and they called 1st July Ash Wednesday due to the amount of incinerating of documents that took place. But at the eleventh hour the line had been held and Monty's 8th Army had stopped the enemy at a little station halt called El Alamein, about a hundred miles west of Alex.

And now it seemed that Monty had turned the tables and was about to push Rommel back.

The big push was coming but defeating Rommel in Egypt and Libya and clearing the Western Desert was only the start.

Hunter and his men were laying the groundwork for the next stage. That was why they were here, bumping uncomfortably through the desert, heading for Alexandria's old town.

As they entered the same seedy townships that defined any north African town, Hunter looked out from the lorry and saw dozens of British Army trucks in groups around the road. At first he wondered how so many transport vehicles might be there. The thought had just crossed his mind when, as they reached the entrance to the city, the column came to a halt.

He turned to the driver. 'What now?'

'Bloody jam, sir. Nothing I can do about it. Just traffic. Never seen the like.'

'But why so bloody much? Christ, at this rate we'll be late for the RV.'

'Sorry, sir. Just my job. Can't be helped.'

'Well I'm going to see what the hell's going on.'

Hunter opened the door and jumped down onto the dirt road. He lit a cigarette and walked a few yards in front of the column. Sure enough there was a traffic jam. Vehicles, military and civilian, were locked in the narrow streets.

He was walking back up the road, towards his truck, when he noticed another group of trucks parked up a little distance away and surrounded by a fence. He walked towards them and, as he grew near, saw the armed sentry. He waited, as he had been trained to do, until the man's back was turned and hared through the fence. Once inside the perimeter it was easy to hide among the vehicles. Something wasn't right, he thought. There was something very strange about these trucks. He ducked down and examined the wheels. They seemed to be fine, but on closer inspection he saw that they were fixed in place.

He moved to the rear of one of them and gently lifted the canvas tail flap. What he saw made him gasp. Instead of the inside of a truck he was looking at the rear of a Crusader tank. The whole thing had been carefully camouflaged with a dummy bonnet and windscreen to make it seem from all angles as if it were a truck. The device was brilliantly simple.

It didn't take long for Hunter to realise that he had stumbled on something much bigger than a few camouflaged tanks. This must be the build-up for Monty's offensive. There had been rumours of a huge number of tanks and transport being seen entering Egypt. And then nothing more had been heard of them. Here was the answer. He prayed that no enemy spy would have as easy a time as he'd had in getting in.

He waited behind another of the fake trucks, close to the gate, until the sentry paused to light a cigarette and then slipped silently back through the fence and once outside walked casually away in full view, from the vehicle park towards his own trucks. His discovery made him doubt for a moment, quite what in his present life was genuine and what false.

Woods was leaning out of the window of his truck. 'Christ, Jim, where the hell have you been?'

'Just having a fag; interesting place this. Full of kit.'

Hunter swung himself back up into the passenger seat of his truck just as the column began to move off, a red-capped British military policeman having uncorked the jam.

Changing gear, the driver smiled at him. 'You called that a bit close, sir; thought we'd have to leave you behind.'

'No chance. Did you think I'd miss the party?'

Hunter watched the leafy suburban villas slip by, each one of them a model of ersatz neo-classicism, each one of them with the same manicured lawn and large American car in the wide, gravelled drive.

The denizens of Cairo might still continue to choose to decamp here during the hot summer months, when the air of the capital became stiflingly warm. But the city held no attraction at all for Hunter.

Of course he had been brought up on tales of its past glories. His father had filled his head with tales of its founding by Alexander the Great. It had been the greatest city on earth before being outdone by Rome. The Romans had ruled it, then the Persians, the Ottomans and the French before the British had taken it, not once but twice.

Here Ptolemy had set up his lighthouse and established his great library. Here Queen Cleopatra had entertained Mark Antony and Caesar. In recent years it had proved attractive to other royalty, including the British. But now it looked to Hunter like any other opulently sordid Mediterranean resort, tired and lacking in any redeeming virtue.

They rattled on, through the city towards the western docks. The centre of the city had been blocked off and they were pushed along the coast past the opulent hotels and the apartment blocks.

Many of the inhabitants had moved out at the time of the flap but a few remained and, as the little convoy rolled past the tall blocks, Hunter glimpsed a few of them as they settled down to lunch overlooking the Mediterranean as if the world was just going about its day-to-day business. It all seemed a million miles away from what they were about to do. They were going to go deep into enemy territory and chance their lives in a mission on which might hang the fate of so many and indeed the outcome of the war. But rather than unsettling, he found it strangely calming. Slowly the landscape of the city began to change and after a few more blocks they left the smart apartment blocks and old Levantine houses behind and rattled into the industrial area, which housed the western docks.

Everywhere around them in this part of the city lay the evidence of war. There were the shattered hulks of bombed ships. Beside them the broken and twisted cranes and haulage gear. They drove past a railway, the steel rails of the railway sidings, twisted and ripped from the ground as if some petulant giant child had pulled them from the ground. Craters littered the road and the tumbled bricks of what had been warehouses and factories lay in piles. The port was still operating though and nearing it he could see a number of ships being loaded. There were fishing boats too, tying up as the crew prepared to unload their catch as generations had done before.

There was, of course, no need for silence or subterfuge yet and once the trucks had reached the quayside, the men debussed in good spirits, cracking jokes at each other's expense and displaying all the cocky bravado of nervous professionals about to go into action.

But as Hunter's men looked around themselves, taking in the scene of devastation, they were quickly jolted back to the reality of the war.

And, as they moved off towards the two caiques that were to take the raiding party the four hundred miles to Crete, they did so in relative silence.

One by one they moved aboard and instinctively began to stow away their kit below. And Hunter went with them.

Their two craft stood out among all the ramshackle trawlers and battered merchant ships. There was a gleaming motor torpedo boat, which looked ready to go, and further down the quay the blue-grey eminence of a Royal Navy frigate.

The caique on which Wilson's thirty marines were now embarking was larger than their own and indeed one of the largest caiques Peter Woods had yet seen. About forty-five feet long and weighing he reckoned around twenty tons. It was Woods's first experience of one of the boats of the newly commissioned, and somewhat grandly named 'Levant

Schooner Flotilla'. He had been told all about it in Cairo, first by Vickery and then briefed about it again at Athlit.

The 'Flotilla' was the brainchild of some eccentric young nutcase, named Seligman, the son of a society novelist who had sailed around the world in a fishing boat with a small crew, his teenage wife and a piano for company. Apparently his military service to date had been on minesweepers and piloting Russian merchantmen through the Baltic blockade. He was just the man to find the ships that would be necessary for the sort of covert operations that Fleming, Jellicoe and the others had in mind. So now, typically of the quirks of fortune that this life-changing war brought with it, young Mister Seligman was a lieutenant commander in the Royal Navy and had under his command an entire flotilla of twelve newly converted gunboats. A regular pirate fleet, two of whose finest men of war had been commandeered for the raid on Crete.

Woods, who had grown up sailing his father's motor launch on the Norfolk Broads, examined the marines' caique with interest. AHS 31 *Tewfik* had just one central mast, with one large, lateen sail and two similar, smaller headsails. She was what the Greeks called a tricanderi, a double-ended gaff-rigged cutter, with canvas bulwarks laced to sheer poles either side down two-thirds of her length. She had no wheelhouse, just a tiller. There was, he noted with approval, a large Oerlikon 20mm anti-tank gun mounted in the bow. There were also two 50-calibre Browning machine guns in her waist and in the stern a pair of Vickers .303 machine guns. She was a formidable vessel indeed and he thought should be able to put up a reasonable fight against a German torpedo boat.

He walked over to his own caique and looked at it in comparison. Though smaller than Wilson's, AHS23 *Rosetta* was still of a good size. Like the other boat, she had the same lateen rigged configuration of mast and sails and no wheelhouse, but she was fitted only with a similarly lethal Oerlikon cannon and two .303 Vickers guns, amidships. She would do the job.

He noticed that there were four crewmen on the boat. They were uniformed in blue or white shirts and white shorts and all had heavy beards. A couple of them wore light-blue painted tin hats and one, the captain, an officer's cap. These were clearly the men who had been recruited by Seligman from the Royal Navy. Volunteers wanting something rather more exciting than working below decks on a destroyer.

Woods caught Hunter's eye and beckoned him across, then together they walked up to the captain, a lean, bearded, heavily tanned man in his late thirties whose wide smile revealed an appalling set of teeth.

'Captain Woods. And this is Lieutenant Hunter.'

'Ah yes. Good morning, gentlemen. Dick Gorringe. I'm in charge of this little beauty. Do make yourselves comfortable. It would seem that we can look forward to three days on the water together.'

7

Once the men had got their personal kitbags loaded Hunter gave them a shout. 'Right ho, let's get the rest of this kit on board. All of you lend a hand and then we'll get some scran.'

They moved to the fourth truck and, flipping up the canvas flap, lowered the tailboard. Inside lay a small arsenal and a pile of wooden packing cases.

Two of the men clambered up into the back of the truck and began to unbuckle the canvas bindings and hand the guns and boxes down to the others. Hunter watched as it began to empty. There were two boxes of provisions, dry and wet, and a case of drink containing beer, bottles of the local wine and retsina, along with a bottle of ouzo. There were also two cases of water, and a small field stove with two canisters of fuel. Then several coils of rope followed by spades and pickaxes and a radio receiver and transmitter. The guns were impressive. Two Bren guns, nine Stens, a bag containing pistols, Webleys and Enfields, and a captured German MG34 and a couple of captured Schmeisser machine-pistols. There were two cases of grenades, unprimed, and their primers. There was also a case marked 'TNT'. That would be Bill Duffy's baby. Then there was all the ammo for the various weapons, including – amazingly – an entire case of belts for the MG34 that he had earmarked for Fletcher. Hunter wondered how someone had engineered that.

Unsurprisingly, it took all the men, Woods and Hunter included, a good hour and a half to get everything squared away. The marines had been working similarly hard further along the quay and had just finished.

Hunter turned to Russell. The ex-barman always seemed happy to act as mess steward, come cook.

'Squirrel, see if you can find everyone some scran. Eggs, bacon, that sort of stuff. We'll need something inside us before the off.'

'On it, boss.'

Woods was looking over the vessel. 'She's not in bad shape. She should get us there.'

Hunter smiled. 'And back, I hope.'

It took Russell just half an hour to produce a stack of egg and bacon rolls for all of them, and he was careful not to forget the ship's captain and the three crewmen.

The big, newly fitted, 90 horsepower Leyland engine started up and Woods noticed that it was significantly quieter than any of the usual, run-of-the-mill Greek fishing boats on which he had travelled, which used old Bolinder diesel engines. It had clearly been changed to at least allow them some form of surprise. That would have been Seligman's doing. Perhaps too, he supposed, it might be faster. Using the sails was effective, and of course they were silent. But speed was the thing and the engine would be the powerhouse of the boat. That would be helpful, especially should they ever be attempting to outrun an enemy torpedo boat.

Once they were at sea Woods called the men together. They sat wherever they could on the deck, some with their thin backsides hanging off the side rails, over the sea. Woods began, 'Well, I dare say you've all been speculating as to where we're headed, so I think I had better put you out of your misery.' Of course, he knew that most of them had already worked out their destination and he didn't have to guess what their reaction might be when it was confirmed.

Nevertheless, he paused for effect. 'Gentlemen, we're going to Crete.'

An audible groan rippled around the assembled other ranks. Someone said, 'Not again.'

Woods heard someone else mutter, 'Knew it. I bleedin' well knew it.'

Another joker, Private White, quipped, 'Back again, sir. Oh what luck.'

Woods smiled. 'Yes, I'm afraid so, Chalky, here you go again. Of course some of you haven't yet had a chance to sample the delights of this fine island. Others have and you know all too well what happened here. But this time we're going to do some real damage. In fact Captain Wilson and his matelots are going to do so much damage here that the Jerries won't be able to use a single square foot of their airfields. And that's why it's so vital.'

'Why, sir?'

'Because, Russell, our little raid is just the start of something much bigger. The invasion of North Africa.'

Someone wolf-whistled.

'Thank you. Yes indeed you might whistle, Knox. The invasion of North Africa. And you all know what that means. What comes next? The invasion of Sicily, Italy, and then the big push north. The liberation of Europe.'

There was more chattering. Woods knew when to put an end to it.

'Alright, pipe down. That's enough. So that's the big plan. Now you know the reasons behind this little jaunt. But our job is different. As you might have guessed, you've all been selected because of your unusual, or should I say your unique abilities.'

A ripple of laughter echoed round the deck. Someone said, 'What's yours then, sir?'

'Very funny. I'll stand any man a beer, who can come up with the best answer. As I was saying, you've all been chosen for your unique skills. You know the basic idea behind what we do. It's our job to get in there when the marines do their job and zero in on any intel that might prove useful. What we're after is something really important. When we pulled out of Crete last May we left something behind.'

Someone muttered, just loud enough to be heard, 'Too bloody right we did. Two thousand men dead and 12,000 POWs.'

'Yes, Phelps, that's true and some of you saw it happen. But look at it from a positive perspective. We did actually manage to get 12,000 off.'

He paused, reflecting for a moment. 'Yes. Anyway, now we're back and we've got a job to do. And... as I was saying, when we pulled out last year we unfortunately left an important piece of intelligence. According to our chaps on the island and the spooks back home it looks as if the Germans might not have found it. That's what we've got to find and bring away.'

A voice spoke up: 'May I ask what it is, sir? This important piece of intel?'

'You may, Russell. And I'll tell you. It's a complete summary of our plans for the liberation of Europe. What our basic plan is. Where we attack in Tunisia and Algeria, who and what with and where next we hit the Nazis, once we've taken the godforsaken place.'

'Blimey. How the bloody hell did we manage to leave that behind?'

'All too easily, I suspect, in the chaos that happened back then. I suppose those in charge just forgot about it.'

'Well, they forgot about everything else, didn't they?'

'Alright, Fletcher. Whatever happened and however it happened is not really important to us. What is important is to find this bloody thing before the enemy does.'

'How do we know what we're looking for, sir? If we find it?'

'Yes, I was coming to that. It's a sheaf of papers. Typical War Office style. Brown paper, rubber stamps, that sort of thing. The codename is Gymnast. Got that?'

They murmured their assent. 'And anything that's marked BIGOT. Alright?'

Russell spoke. 'Why bigot, sir?'

'It's one of Winnie's acronyms, Russell. British Invasion of German Occupied Territory.'

'Do we know where it might be, sir?'

'Yes. Fortunately, we do have a few clues. There are basically three places where it might have been hidden, well, "filed". Two of them on Heraklion airfield. We're going to split into two or three groups and try all of them. Now there is one other vitally important point. I have just told you all about the contents of the intel; largely as to identify it you might necessarily need to know what it contains. You all now know that we intend to attack up through Sicily and Italy. What I mean to say is that we don't intend to launch the second front up through Greece. It is of absolute importance that you should keep that knowledge to yourself. Don't tell your wives or your children. Don't tell your sweethearts or mistresses. Don't tell the other chaps on Wilson's boat and above all, when you get back to Cairo don't tell anyone at all. Not even that old tart in the bloody Burqua, Fletcher. Got that?'

The men nodded and grunted their assent.

'But as far as you're all concerned, what matters is what we do in the next few days on the island. Got it?'

The voyage, Gorringe had happily confirmed, was longer than usual for the caique. It was going to take them three days.

Woods and Hunter had known that. But the others had not and some of them, Hunter knew, were not used to a prolonged sea voyage. But they were tough enough. Patient enough. The trouble was that time out of action was time to think and too much thinking, thought Hunter, never did any soldier any good.

The other boat, containing Wilson and his marines, had parted company with them when they were five hours out of Alexandria. They were going to land in a different part of the Cretan coast. This had been planned from the start. Not only would it make the initial landing party smaller, but it would ultimately split German attention and give each team a better chance of survival.

The first day was quiet enough and not marked with any incident. They had struck out north-west from Alexandria, directly towards Crete, Captain Gorringe's plan being to get them from point A to point B as fast as possible. The Royal Navy proudly maintained its presence in the Med and, during the day at least, German vessels feared being spotted by enemies that might blow them out of the water. But that was not to say that there was no German presence and the crew were on constant alert.

At one point they spotted another large caique-like vessel in the distance and binoculars revealed that it was flying a German naval ensign. But it showed no interest in them, clearly having bigger fish to fry, or perhaps being keen to avoid an encounter with the Royal Navy.

The crew had modified their dress on leaving port, appearing now, complete with their beards and moustaches, more like the crew of a Greek fishing caique. The guns too had been cleverly camouflaged with canvas covers on to which had been sewn fishing nets, but which could be stripped away at a moment's notice.

The greatest immediate threat came from *Rosetta* being spotted from the air by one of the German and Italian planes that scoured the Aegean and the eastern Mediterranean. It was therefore vital that Hunter's men should remain below decks for most of the day. Naturally, they took it in turns to emerge for a breath of fresh air and to stretch their limbs. But only two by two. A few items of civilian dress were kept by the cabin door for the purpose, just in case they should encounter an enemy plane or boat while on deck.

The confinement below wasn't ideal for two of the men. White and Miller were both prone to seasickness and this voyage was no exception. The Libyan Sea might have been as calm as a millpond thus far, but the big, shovel-handed Guardsman and the ex-policeman had been suffering badly. Every time the two big men came on deck there was only one thing either of them wanted to do and Hunter watched Miller now, hanging over the side, and felt for his misery.

Below decks, with the portholes kept open, most of the men passed the time in sleeping, reading or playing cards. One of them, Bill Duffy, the Cambridge chemist turned demolitionist, was content to spend hours drawing portraits of his fellow raiders. These were not the sort of amusing, sometimes ribald, caricatures by talented amateur army artists that enlivened the walls of so many officers' and sergeants messes, but something rather more original. Duffy's small, exquisite pencil drawings were nothing less than beautiful. With a single line he had the ability to capture the very essence of a face. And the men were more than happy to pose for him. It gave a purpose to their sitting still, and was made all the more worthwhile by the anticipation of the outcome. He had not as yet drawn either Hunter or Woods, though both men were looking forward to being asked.

Hunter stood on deck during his allotted rest time, staring out to sea. The Aegean was a peerless lake of azure that met the cerulean of the cloudless sky at a softly watery horizon of grey, which was all that now remained in view of the coast of Egypt. The crew were mostly silent as they went about their work and Captain Gorringe stood at the wheel, a commanding presence, in touch with his craft and the charmed world it inhabited. A nautical chart was always at his hand, held down upon a bleached wooden deck table by an old and corroded brass compass.

The abiding noise, above the lapping of the water as it was cut by the prow, was the gentle whine of the newly installed diesel engine.

One of the men, Fletcher, the lothario, lay elongated on the foredeck, stripped to the waist, wearing a pair of American-issue sunglasses. It was an idyllic scene, sybaritic almost, and – had he not been aware of the armoury stored below or the nature of their mission – Hunter would have, for a moment, probably forgotten about the war.

As it was, he slipped carelessly back into the tales of his boyhood. To tales of Jason and Ulysses, of Theseus and Perseus. Myths of heroic derring-do battling hideous, hydra-headed monsters. Tales that had become encapsulated in a print of Ulysses mocking Polyphemus the Cyclops, after a painting by Turner, which had entranced his youthful imagination from the moment that his father had hung it in the nursery. The image lived in his mind. The figure of the great classical hero, standing triumphant on the deck of his ship, cloaked and helmeted beneath a crimson banner, raising his arm in victory, brandishing the flaming torch with which he has just blinded the Cyclops as his loyal companions cheer him on.

Hunter still carried with him, as he had always done these last eight years, a battered and well-read copy of Rouse's *Gods, Heroes and Men of Ancient Greece* that he had plucked from the school library before he had left that sad old place forever, at the age of seventeen, never to return.

That was how he saw himself and his men now. As

adventurers, battling against evil demigods, searching for a talisman, a modern-day golden fleece.

On the second day, at around two o'clock in the afternoon, when White and Woods were up on deck, the caique was buzzed by a low-flying German spotter plane. Gorringe yelled down into the cabin.

'Hun plane coming in. Don't panic, it's just a spotter. But make sure you all keep your heads down.'

The little plane, a Fieseler Storch, probably based on Crete, circled the caique several times and the crew waved enthusiastically at its pilot, impressively embracing their characters of Greek fishermen. After a few minutes he flew off, although it was, of course, impossible to know whether or not he had seen through their disguise.

From now on, though, Woods felt exposed and was acutely aware that at any moment sudden and unseen death might return from the air and obliterate his little command. He shivered at the thought and at how such a simple, single action could, in a split second, cause so much destruction. For Woods was not quite the man he appeared. He had carefully shaped a veneer of cold distance and efficiency over the past three years. He knew that if it crumbled so too would he. Everything he had seen since France in 1940 had taken its toll. The carnage of the Blitzkrieg, French civilians lying dead on the roads of Normandy. The hopelessness of St Valery and his incredible luck in getting away when so many others hadn't. And then Crete, where it all seemed to happen again. Another shambles, another miraculous escape. Just how many lives did he have left, he wondered?

Woods looked down at his hands and saw his right forefinger and index finger twitching. It happened from time to time. When he overthought situations. As he was doing now. He tried to snap out of it. Think of something else. The girl in Cairo. Lara. But he wondered if he was capable of affection any more. Had he lost everything he had once had?

His fingers were still twitching. He looked out to sea, the endless sea, and thought of home. His parents' home in Norfolk and his father telling him how to tie a knot, or bring a boat into a mooring. And at once, he was calm again.

Hunter's second turn on deck came at sunset and as he watched the sun sink in the sea that evening, it was for him no longer just the last sun he would see setting before they reached the island, it had become the sun of Ulysses, its golden face slashed by ribbons of vibrant pink cloud, and he longed for the moment that he might hold his torch aloft and proclaim his victory.

The third and final day brought another, rather more serious challenge. Woods and Fletcher were on deck at the time. They saw it first as a speck on the horizon, far off to the east, coming fast from the Turkish coast. Its speed was what troubled them most and Gorringe was quick to realise what it was. He snapped at them, 'German MTB. Heading straight for us.'

The crew erupted into action, making sure that the camouflage covers on the guns were still in place. Woods shouted into the cabin, 'German MTB. Closing fast. We may have to engage. Grab a weapon, make sure it's loaded and keep your heads down. If they get a shot inside the hold this whole thing could go up.'

There was frantic action below decks and then, silence.

They waited and watched. Gorringe kept his eye on the approaching boat. 'Still coming. Get ready. I'll talk to the captain. Don't worry, my mother's Greek. We're going to have to take them out. Agreed, Woods?'

Woods nodded. 'Agreed. There's nothing else for it.'

'My crew will man the cannon and the MGs. There's no time to get the covers off – we'll just fire through them. They're all loaded and ready to go.'

Hunter took charge below decks. 'Russell, Martin, White, Knox. You stay below at a porthole each. Use the Brens and the MG34. Get them up just out of sight. Miller, Phelps, Duffy. You're with me. Stay near the door. When it kicks off two of you – Miller and Phelps – get up there with a Sten gun. Duffy, you and me will follow. Understood?'

The men nodded.

'Right, get to it.'

There was frenzied action and then stillness. The boat could be seen quite clearly now. An officer in German naval uniform holding a megaphone was standing at the prow, flanked by two Kriegsmarine with Schmeissers. As they closed in he put the megaphone to his mouth and spoke in fluent English: 'Stop your engines. Heave to. We will come aboard.'

Gorringe looked at him and shrugged his shoulders. The German tried again in English and the captain shook his head. Then the German spoke in Greek. Gorringe smiled and nodded at him and cut the engines.

Hunter peered up at the German boat from below decks.

He saw one of the new Spandau machine guns, a full ammo belt protruding from its side, mounted on a tripod on the foredeck, a gunner crouching behind it. That made four men. Then another man moved from behind the wheelhouse and Hunter could just make out the muzzle of another Spandau. So there must be six of them. They could handle that. Surprise was the key.

All was silence now, save for the thrum of the MTB's own engines. The German boat was almost on them now and as she slid alongside, her turbines ran down until they could all hear the sloshing of her wake. One of the German ratings threw out ropes towards Gorringe's crew, who grabbed at them and attached them to the cleats on *Rosetta*'s deck.

Christ, thought Hunter, this was going to be a close thing.

He looked down at his men, watching their reactions. Knox looked cool enough, cradling a Bren gun in his arms and next to him Russell did the same. Martin had taken the German machine gun and it lay ready with a belt of ammo already fed in. Just in front of him the two big men, Miller and Duffy, were pressing themselves as hard as they could against the wall, as if they were trying to make themselves somehow smaller. Phelps, opposite him, was staring directly into his face with wide eyes. The man looked terrified and he was sweating. Hunter mouthed at him, 'Alright, Phelps?'

He nodded and Hunter looked away. That was all they needed now. Why the hell hadn't it come out in training? Too late now.

Up on deck, the German officer was speaking again. In Greek: 'We are coming aboard.' One of the men with the Schmeissers stepped nimbly from his own boat on to the deck of the *Rosetta* and moved quickly so that his back was to the mast and he had a view of the foredeck. The German officer followed him and walked up to Gorringe before speaking again in Greek: 'Papers? Who are you? Where are you bound?'

They were the last words he would ever utter. Gorringe made to get his papers from beneath the chart on the wooden table but instead his finger gently squeezed the trigger of his Webley, which instantly spat flame through the paper. The bullet hit the young officer point-blank in the chest and exited, making a mess of his back, embedding itself in the German vessel's wheelhouse. He sank to the deck. As he did so, the two Brens and the MG34 opened up from the portholes straight into the hull and deck of the German vessel, ripping away the wood and steel to leave three great, gaping holes. The boat lurched at the impact, unsettling the men on deck and at that moment two Royal Navy crew on the *Rosetta*'s deck let loose with the concealed Oerlikon cannon and the port side Vickers machine gun. The cannon was trained on the forward Spandau gun and its fire tore into its barrel and stock and ripped apart its gunner in a spray of blood, his body crashing to the deck. The arc of fire of the Vickers took in both the remaining man with the Schmeisser and the two men standing by the rear Spandau.

The British crewmen let rip with a belt of bullets that tore through the three men who crumpled onto the deck, one of them falling into the sea. The German beside the mast was the last to die, shot by Hunter as he emerged from the cabin, but not before he had let off a burst from the Schmeisser, which hit one of the British crewmen in the lower leg. It was all over in seconds, leaving them with a momentary deafness from the gunfire and the penetrating stench, a mix of hot metal, gunpowder and blood.

The others were all up on the deck now, but as it had transpired there had been no need for their support, save for Hunter's.

Hunter searched the deck for Phelps and to his relief saw that he was standing with the others and not, as he had worried, crouched in a terrified funk.

Gorringe took command. 'Right, we need to send this lot to the bottom before that spotter plane comes back again.'

He looked at his stricken crewman, who was lying on the deck clutching his leg. 'Woods, you've got a medic with you, haven't you? Can you get him to help young Forbes there?'

Woods nodded and summoned Martin, who apart from being the man with an eye for detail, was also the medical asset of the little party. He had qualified on a battlefield aid course while a QMS with the Argylls and carried his small canvas 'doctor's bag' with him at all times.

As Martin attended to the wounded seaman, Hunter spoke to Gorringe: 'What do you suggest we use to sink her, sir? Two grenades in the engine room should do the trick, don't you think?'

'Yes, I'd say so. No need for anything more elaborate. You want to keep your big stuff, don't you. Your chaps below did a pretty good job on the hull. She won't last long.'

Hunter found Duffy. 'I've got a demolition job for you. Nothing too exciting, I'm afraid. Just need to sink the bastard. Use grenades. I should think the engine room would work best.'

Duffy shook his head. 'No, sir. I'll just blow the ammo stores. But we'd better untie first or she'll take us with her.'

Hunter nodded. 'You're the expert. I'll leave it to you.'

He turned to Fletcher and Miller. 'You two, better get rid

of those bodies. Over the side. But tie something heavy to them. We'll need to weigh them down. We don't want corpses bobbing around alerting the enemy.'

The two men set about their unpleasant task, securing the dead rating's Spandau to him by its sling before rolling him off the side of the deck and into the water, where he quickly sank. To the German officer they tied a heavy piece of metal that the gunfire had part ripped from the boat's deck and heaved his body over the side.

They climbed aboard the German vessel followed by Hunter who moved cautiously aft. He was right to be careful: one of the men lying on the deck was not dead and as Hunter approached he turned, with a gun in his hand. He was stopped dead with a burst from Hunter's Sten gun. Fletcher and Miller moved the four German dead down into the small cabin and battened the door before returning with Hunter to the AHS 23 *Rosetta*.

Meanwhile, Duffy had been hard at work. He had found the Germans' pile of ammunition in the hold and had carefully arranged a dozen stick grenades around the boxes so that when each of them exploded it was sure to create a much bigger explosion, ensuring that the whole lot would go up. Then, satisfied with his work, he took two Mills bomb grenades from his pockets and inserted a primer into each of them. He then took a piece of twine from another pocket and cut two lengths, each of them around ten yards long. With great care he knotted each piece of twine around the circular pin of one of the grenades. He then placed each of the Mills bombs into holes that he had made within the piles of boxes, positioning another ammunition box over the top of the hole. Then he climbed out of the hold, up on to the deck, slowly playing out the two lengths of twine, as he went. Taking care not to tighten either of the strands, Duffy stepped from the deck of the German boat on to that of the *Rosetta*.

He turned to Hunter. 'Job done, sir. All we have to do is sail away from her like the clappers and, when we're a good thirty yards away, up she goes. Boom!'

'Well done. Let's hope it works.'

'Oh it'll work, sir. We had just better make bloody sure that we're going fast enough when it does.'

Woods and Gorringe were giving the final instructions to finish up before they blew the German caique. The two naval crewmen were swabbing the decks of blood, while Russell had been detailed to bring down the German naval ensigns from the mast and the stern flagpole of the enemy boat. He delivered both of them to Hunter. 'Enemy flags, sir. What shall we do with them?'

'Better give them to Captain Gorringe, I suppose. Spoils of war. They'll look good on the walls of his ward room.'

Hunter walked over to Gorringe and presented him with the two flags, neatly folded. 'How's your crewman?'

'Oh, he'll live. Nasty wound though, two bullets in the lower leg, another in his foot. I suspect that's the end of his war.'

'You might have to leave him on the island. The resistance fighters, the *andartes*, have their own doctors. Proper doctors, I mean. Poor chap.'

'Well, let's just see what your man can do for him. I'd far rather get him back to Alex with us, after you've finished your business.'

The plan was to hide the caique on the south coast of Crete while the raiders were doing 'their business' as Gorringe referred to it. Special camouflage netting cloths in varying shades ranging from grey to the yellow grey that prevailed around the Aegean had been created by some very talented creative types from SOE based in Beirut, which had the extraordinary effect of masking the ship's outline and making it blend into the scenery to look exactly like a rocky part of the cliff face. It hadn't yet been used in an active operation and Gorringe was more than a little apprehensive. Although he would never have admitted as much.

'My demolition man has rigged a bomb. It's on two lines tied to detonators made from Mills bombs. Once we get to within forty yards of her the pins will pull then we've got another five seconds before she blows. We'll have to push the engine to get this old girl to move as fast as she can. Need to get up some speed.'

Gorringe raised his eyes. 'I can push her to about eight knots. That's about it.'

'Whatever you can manage, sir. It'll have to do. Those five seconds will probably take us out another ten or fifteen yards. That should be safe enough.'

The decks were clean of blood now and there was no human debris to suggest anything had taken place. All that remained to do was to untie from the German boat and then go like blazes. And then, as Duffy had put it: 'Boom!'

Woods and Hunter ordered all of the men apart from Duffy and Martin to go below. He watched as Gorringe started up the engine and waited until it was turning over nicely before signalling to his two crewmen.

They untied the German boat from *Rosetta*'s cleats and almost immediately, Gorringe pushed down on the throttle. Gently at first and then gradually stronger, until *Rosetta* began to move away from the enemy boat. Duffy, a tin hat on his head and wearing a battledress top and gloves, had found himself a seat on the aft deck and was holding one of his strings of twine. Seated beside him, Martin, similarly attired, had hold of the other. Duffy had placed each of the loops over the end of a wooden boat-hook and these he and Martin were now using as spindles, allowing the twine to play out as if they were running a salmon on a line. Gorringe began to gather speed and the caique sped away from the German boat until she was making about seven knots.

The twine was running fast now and before the two men knew it snapped taut. Then it held for a moment as it strained against the pins of the now distant Mills bombs, buried in the enemy ship's hold, and then suddenly, both lines of twine came away, as if a huge salmon had at last managed to escape a fishing fly.

Hunter and Woods had also been given tin helmets by the crew and they watched in fascination and apprehension as the inevitable unfolded. They were around forty yards distant from the German boat now and, as Gorringe urged more speed from *Rosetta*, the caique managed to pull away another five yards. Then ten. Gorringe kept going, waiting. Yelled out to all of them, 'Take cover. Tin hats, everyone on deck. Cover your heads.'

The two unhurt crewmen crouched down on deck, as did Hunter and Woods, while Duffy and Martin took cover behind the central mast.

As they reached a further fifteen yards away from the enemy there was a small explosion from the vessel, followed by another and then, with an almighty crash, the whole thing went up.

The hull of the boat was sent twenty feet up into the air and exploded in a mass of timber and metal and body parts. None of the men on *Rosetta* saw the blast, as all were sheltering. But all of them felt it. Gorringe, though looking away from it, had stayed at the wheel, pushing the old caique to the limit of her endurance. Then, as if in slow motion, the debris began to come down, crashing into the waters behind them and narrowly avoiding *Rosetta*'s stern.

Woods looked up. The German boat had split into three main parts. Fore, aft and centre. The for'ard part was sinking fast – what was left of it – and the rear, with the mangled gun mounting attached, was also going under. The central part, where the engines had been, amazingly had still retained the twisted metal frame of the wheelhouse and the lower portion of the great mast. It was all burning, but such was the intensity of the blaze that there seemed to be little smoke to attract enemy planes. Woods gazed at the wreckage in horror. A horror that intensified when he fancied he had caught sight of a leg and then half a torso. Then the central section too began to sink, hissing into the sea as the waters extinguished the flames and as she went, oil and air made the water around her into a ghastly, boiling whirlpool coloured a deep red by the blood of six dead men.

Following Woods's gaze to focus on the vanishing ship, Hunter's thoughts returned once again to the Greek myths. To Scylla and Charybdis, the two sea monsters that lay in wait on either side of a narrow strait. Mostly he thought of Charybdis, the monstrous mouth that sucked in huge volumes of water and belched them out as a gigantic whirlpool, which swallowed up unwary ships. Aeneas had just managed to escape death in the churning whirlpool and

Jason had only survived when guided through the strait by Thetis.

Ulysses too had steered away from the Charybdis, only to lose six men to Scylla. Six men. He was suddenly chilled by the strange coincidence that there had been six Germans on the enemy boat.

As a boy, the man-eating whirlpool had lived in his mind. He had woken too often from sleep in terror of the irresistible vortex, sucking him in, as it had almost done to his hero Ulysses. And here it was, as it seemed, in reality, right in front of him, sucking down the mangled bodies of the German sailors and their doomed boat. He shuddered and stared, spellbound at the last, dying moments of their caique. Watched as her fractured mast and ruined wheelhouse slid down into the maelstrom, which gave a final froth of bubbles and a last eerie hiss and an almost animal groan, before closing over the wreckage.

And then, where there had been a German boat, there was now hardly anything to be seen, save a few pieces of floating wreckage, most of which had been strewn around the centre of the blast, for a diameter of around fifty yards. The enemy boat had simply disappeared and the surface of the Libyan Sea was flat and silent, as if nothing had ever happened.

Hunter leant over the side and fished out an upturned German helmet. He shook the water from it and placed it on the deck before turning to Gorringe. 'She's gone, sir. Very quick, wasn't it.'

'Damned quick. Faster than I'd thought, Lieutenant. Let's just hope that what's left doesn't arouse the curiosity of any enemy spotter planes. Thank God most of it's gone under. It only just missed us. Too bloody close for my liking.'

Hunter grinned. 'Yes, sir. I thought it might be rather a close thing.'

After the explosions had stopped, the men had quickly come up on to the deck and were all watching now, and cheering. Woods joined them. 'Everyone alright?'

They shouted and shook their heads, smiling. Only White quipped, 'Oh, I'd be tickety-boo, sir, if I wasn't feeling so bloody rough.'

That got another laugh. Hunter turned to Duffy. 'Well done, Duffy. With the bang.'

Duffy smiled at him. 'Think that I might have overdone it a bit, Mister Hunter. Don't you?'

8

Their caique moved on, leaving the few remaining pieces of still-smouldering debris from the vanished German vessel far behind it and making good time. By eleven o'clock that evening the *Rosetta* was within four miles of their objective.

It felt, all too frustratingly, for Hunter, as if they were almost there. Just about within touching distance. But this, he knew, was the most dangerous time of all. The moment when any raiding party was at its most vulnerable. Hunter looked around the deck and watched as the crew scoured the watery horizon for further enemy vessels and the skies for more spotter planes or fighters.

The moon had risen and the night was bright. Far brighter than Hunter felt was good for them. Before them the distinct silhouette of Crete, with its unmistakable mountains stood in sharp outline against the sky. Surely, he reasoned, not wanting to believe it, if they were able to see the island so clearly, they themselves would be equally evident to anyone looking out to sea. Of course it was nonsense, but at that moment it seemed all too horribly real.

They were supposed to be heading for the small headland of Cape Kochinoxos, in the south of the island, next to which was a cove with a secluded stretch of beach. Gorringe had spotted a couple of prominent landmarks on the coast, which were all that he needed to guide him in. As he positioned himself for the long run into the island, for an uncomfortable few minutes they found themselves sailing along the coast, as if taking part in a regatta. If any unfriendly eyes happened to be looking to the south from the cliffs, this would be their moment. According to their intelligence, there was a German post almost a mile away to the west and another just over a mile to the east.

They edged ever closer to the coast and, as they did so the two unwounded crewmen, each armed with a pair of binoculars, moved forward to look towards their destination. To find the tiny light from a flashing torch that would guide them in to safety.

Woods was alongside Hunter now, himself with a pair of glasses trained on the beach.

'Nothing yet?'

'No. Not a glimmer. Christ, Hunter, I hope they're alright.'

Beside Woods, from his position behind the wheel, Gorringe flashed another signal and waited.

Both men stared into the low mist, which lay above the sea and below the rising mountains of the Cretan landscape. Still nothing.

Woods turned away and walked towards the prow of the vessel. There was no point in all of them watching. It just made the waiting harder.

He peered over the side of the boat and into the mist-covered water, but could not resist being drawn back up to the coastline. In the distance he could just make out the line of surf around the cliffs and the beach.

Gorringe, aware of the danger they were in, at last took the decision to head inshore. Gently, he turned the caique and headed for the rendezvous. As he did so, he ordered one of the crew to move to the prow and hang over the side to watch out for rocks.

Woods and Hunter, along with the other crew member, were now straining to catch a sign of the signal light. Still the night yielded nothing. As they edged ever closer to the coast the man on the prow watch began to call back, whenever he saw a possible rock, and Gorringe adjusted course accordingly. It was a painstaking process and, as Gorringe had cut the engines to half speed, they were now travelling slower than ever.

And then, without warning, Hunter saw it. Just faintly, a twinkle of light. But it was unmistakable. He spoke quietly to Woods: 'Sir. Look. There,' and pointed into the enveloping darkness. Woods tried to follow his pointing arm.

'God, yes you're right.'

He moved to Gorringe, at the wheel. 'Captain. We've found them.'

Gorringe and the crewman looked in the direction Woods was indicating. The captain smiled. 'Yes. Well spotted. That'll be them. If it's not the Jerries.'

He didn't alter the speed, kept the engines slow, but he was able at least to settle on a course making directly for the light, which could now clearly be seen to be flashing. On and off. On and off.

With news of the signal, the men had begun to come to life, excited that at last they were nearing their objective. Hunter stuck his head below decks. 'Quieten down, all of you. We don't want to blow it now. We'll be ashore soon enough. Phelps, get yourself up here.'

Phelps clambered up through the cabin door. He looked ashen. 'Sir?'

'Watch that light, Phelps. They'll be trying to send the code word in Morse. You know what it is?'

'Yes, sir. Course I do. Will do.'

Together they stared at the torch flashes and eventually began to discern a rhythm to them. At length, Phelps spoke. He was smiling. 'Think I've got it, sir. Comet. Yes, that's it. Comet. That's correct, sir. It's them.'

Hunter breathed a sigh of relief. There was, he knew, very little chance that the Germans would have intercepted their coded messages relating to the code word to get them into the beach. He found Woods, who was standing next to Gorringe.

'We've got it, sir. It's Comet. The code word in Morse. It all looks sound.'

'That's good. One less worry.'

Gorringe nodded. 'Now let's just get ourselves in there.'

Hunter continued to stare towards the flashing light and, as they neared the coast things began to become clearer. He was able to see shapes moving around. Men moving on what looked like a little beach. A strand of sand, overhung and enclosed by cliffs. It would have been invisible from the hills above and unless you were a native of the place it might have gone entirely unnoticed. The men who believed themselves to now be the new masters of Crete could not have guessed of its existence. He tried to make out the number of men on the beach. Three, no there were four of them. More now.

The flashlight was growing larger with every yard they made through the water. Hunter shouted into the cabin, 'Right. Everyone up on deck. Grab your kit. We'll get that ashore first, then land the supplies.' The cabin and deck began to buzz with action as the men stretched their taut, unused bodies and found their equipment. Packs and bags and belts that had lain discarded these past three days were hastily grabbed and strapped on. At the last minute, and with a few exceptions, items of appropriated civilian clothing were exchanged for uniform.

When they had got to within forty yards of the shore Gorringe stopped the engines. There was a strange silence in which the loudest sound was the lapping of the water at the keel, interspersed with a hushed muttering from the men, and then Gorringe ordered his crew to lower a boat.

They slowly let down a wooden dinghy into the water and secured it to the caique with one end of a towline. Then one of the crew climbed down into the little boat. Gorringe turned to Woods. 'Can you spare one of your men, Captain, as an escort and to lay the towline?'

Woods nodded. 'Who do you suggest, Hunter?'

'I'll send Martin. He's got good sea legs.'

Martin climbed down to join the crewman and slowly the little craft pulled away to the shore, the crewman rowing. Harry Martin sat in the stern, Sten gun slung on his shoulder, playing out a towline.

Within seconds Gorringe had joined the other crew member and was lowering a second boat into the water. It dropped on to the surface and Gorringe motioned to Woods. 'Captain Woods, we're ready for the first of your lot. Four men in the boat then we'll send the kit over and then the last four of you.'

Woods nodded. 'Hunter, I'll take the first party. You and

the others can get the kit up and send it across. We'll unload. Then you follow.'

'Right, sir.'

Woods and Knox directed three of the men – Phelps, Duffy and Martin – into the dinghy and within a few minutes they were on their way to the shore, being pulled across as a shuttle on the tow rope.

Hunter turned to Miller, White and Russell, all of whom were now assembled on deck. 'Alright, boys, weapons off and let's get all this kit shifted.'

The usual groans followed, but it didn't take the four men long to move the boxes up from the hold and on to the deck. By the time they had managed it, the little boat that had taken Woods and the others to the shore had arrived back, empty, at the side of the caique. Gorringe and his remaining crewman helped with lowering the precious cargo into the dinghy. Passing everything to each other down a little rope ladder, they loaded it with the ammunition, explosives, stores and finally the weapons.

One of the most unusual and precious pieces of kit was the miniature camera that had been given to Hunter by Vickery on their final briefing and which had been passed on to Martin, the record keeper and 'accountant' of the team. Hunter found this slightly ironic as with Martin a camera really wasn't necessary. The man was blessed with what was known as a 'photographic memory'. He could read and file away documents and retrieve them at a moment's notice from the archive of his mind.

Once it was all aboard the crewman gave a sharp tug on the towline and almost miraculously, the boat began to move away, on its own, towards the beach. They waited and watched. On the shore Hunter could see several distinct groups of men now. Woods and his little party formed clearer outlines as they waited for the dinghy to arrive, while closer to the sea and it seemed standing in it, were other, big shapes. Men heaving and pulling on the towline and with every effort bringing the boat closer to the shore. These would be the andartes, eager to get the job done. Still he kept an eye on the cliff top, his gaze darting hither and thither, in search of the enemy. Expecting the worst.

Gorringe was watching him. 'Oh yes, they're out there alright, the bad guys. That's for sure. But what matters now, Hunter, is that they can't see us.'

'Am I that obvious?'

Gorringe nodded. 'Yes. It's understandable. And I know I'd rather have my job than yours. You don't know what you're headed into. You've seen what my life involves. That… what happened today. That was the most excitement I've seen in weeks.

'But you'll be fine. You've got a good team there, Lieutenant. Believe me, and I've seen a few. And these are good. And this lot on the island here – the Greeks and the Brits – they're not too bad either.'

He gestured at the men in the water and on the shore who had now stopped heaving on the line and were dragging the boat on to the shore and unloading the stores and equipment.

'Well, I know some of them well enough. The andartes. They're a good bunch. Do anything for you. Almost.'

He smiled. 'Bandits, cutthroats and gypsies, all of them.'

Hunter laughed. 'Well in that case they should get on perfectly with my men.'

The boat was coming back now, empty once again. Hunter turned to the captain. 'Thank you, sir. You've been a fine host. Will you be alright here?'

'As right as I'll be anywhere. This place is safer than most and with these clever nets of ours making us look like another rock, we can just lie unseen for a few days. No need to go ashore either. We've all that we need. We'll see you when you're done.'

Hunter nodded and then saw that the boat had returned. He called to the others and, once they had collected all of their individual kit, the three of them climbed down the rope ladder into it and settled themselves on to the seats. Hardly had they sat down, than the dinghy began to move, being pulled, through the sea and through the night, towards the beach. It was a matter of moments before they were there, and their boat was being manhandled from the water by the men he had watched earlier.

It was with no little sense of achievement that Hunter finally stepped ashore and, as he did, he was instantly caught up in the unmistakable, sweet smell of wild thyme. A smell that told him at once, that he could not be anywhere else other than back on the island. The overpowering, wonderfully pungent scent brought back with it memories of another time. Of hard days clambering over the Cretan hills, before the German invasion. Of gloriously sunny afternoons in little villages when, after leading his section on an exercise they would 'lose themselves' among the seemingly limitless hospitality (and endless ouzo) of the locals.

But it brought other memories too. Dark memories of chaos and panic and wide-eyed men who had lost all semblance of order and discipline and reason. The planned withdrawal of

British and Commonwealth forces that had all too quickly turned in to a rout. He thought of those men now. So many dead. Thousands taken into captivity. Where were they now?

Hunter and the other two had hardly stepped ashore before they found themselves enveloped by the Greeks, gabbling away, trying to make themselves heard. They were all clapped on the back and helped up towards the cliffs, as the Greeks grabbed every item that had been landed on the beach and proceeded to drag the cases up a path that snaked up into the hills.

Hunter was aware of a dozen dark faces smiling toothless grins beneath full moustaches and in most cases above even fuller beards. They wore a bewildering variety of clothes, from heavy shirts and sleeveless pullovers to shorts, overalls, hobnailed boots with ancient puttees and black, knee-high riding boots. Most sported some items of military clothing, from army-issue berets and battledress tops, to in one case an utterly incongruous ceremonial busby of black fur. Many had bandoliers of bullets draped over one or both shoulders. The only unifying factor appeared to be their smell. Clearly none of them had washed for days, possibly weeks, and all of them had been eating garlic and drinking retsina. Their stench mixed with that of the island to create a heady fragrance.

Russell turned to him. 'Bloody hell, sir. What the hell's this lot?'

'This lot, Russell, is the flower of Cretan manhood. They're andartes. And what they lack in poise and refinement they more than make up for in grit, bravery and utter hatred of the Nazis.'

White chimed in: 'Well, I ain't never seen the like.'

'Or smelt it more likely,' added Miller.

Hunter could see that Woods and his group had had a similar encounter with the locals and that they were now making their way with them up the little path, which led away from the beach.

Hunter was about to head in the same direction when one of the andartes approached him, a heavy-set, dark-skinned man with a huge beard and deep, gloriously untrimmed moustache. On his head he wore a curious turban and over his army-issue bush shirt a goatskin waistcoat. A pair of battledress trousers tucked into black riding boots completed the look, which was set off with two full bandoliers of ammunition, one slung diagonally over each shoulder. Hunter prepared to use his Greek, although he knew from experience on the island that he might not immediately grasp the meaning, such was the Cretan dialect. When the man did speak, however, he was utterly dumbfounded.

'Quite a tremendous job, wouldn't you say? Absolutely first class.'

The apparition spoke in a voice that Hunter had not heard for some time. And then in quite different surroundings. The unique, unmistakable patois that was not to be heard from anyone other than an officer in His Majesty's Foot Guards. He stopped in his tracks. 'Sorry. I mean. Yes. They've done very well, haven't they. I mean you. Us.'

'You all have, old chap. Absolutely splendid effort. Never seen anything like it.'

Hunter looked at him. 'I'm sorry. Do I know you?'

'No, can't say I believe we've ever met. Unless in White's. Are you a member?'

'Er, no, can't say that I am.'

The man extended a grimy hand. 'No worry. Ffinch is the name. Mungo Ffinch. Two F's.' He laughed. 'People don't think it matters. But it bloody does. It's my name you know. That bloody matters, don't it? How'd you like it if someone called you... What is your name?'

'Hunter, Jim Hunter...' He added, 'Lieutenant.'

'Oh yes. Sorry. Captain Ffinch. But call me Mungo. But I mean how would you like it if people started to call you Mister 'Unter? Mm? I can tell you, you'd be bloody furious.'

'Yes I suppose I would be.'

'Well there you are. Ffinch. Two F's.'

'I'll remember that.'

'You meant to be meeting Paddy?'

'Yes. That's the plan.'

'You'll have to push inland.'

'Yes, I thought I might.'

From the crowd of andartes, another bearded figure broke away and grabbed Captain Ffinch by the shoulder, yelling something at him in Greek. Hunter struggled to make it out. Ffinch clapped the other man on the back and turned to Hunter. 'We should go now. Leave your captain to disguise his boat and get away from him before the Germans suspect anything. Come on. Follow me.'

Together, they followed the andartes on to the path and Hunter saw that they had fastened the heavier cases containing the explosives, ammunition and stores on to the backs of half a dozen pack mules. He looked about and thankfully managed to do a head count of all of his men, along with Woods, who was deep in conversation with one of the andartes, who appeared to be offering to buy or barter his Sten gun from him.

When they had reached a track at the top of the cliff the party split up. Most of the andartes headed off to the east but before they went Hunter watched, with Woods, as Ffinch gave one of them – the leader he presumed – a small, heavy canvas bag, before kissing the man on both cheeks and bidding him farewell. Ffinch came over to them.

'Gold sovereigns. Just paying them off. They were brought to help unload the kit and just in case there was any trouble. We don't need them now.'

Hunter supposed that he was right. They were better off without the extra men. He was confident in his team. Well, Phelps had had a slight wobble on the boat, but it had come to nothing. Still, there was something biting away at him. This was his show. His unit. His patrol. His men. But now Woods had command. In fact he thought, Woods need not have come with them at all. Should not. But he was desperate to get in. It irked Hunter somewhat that his command had in a way been usurped, particularly given what had happened with Lara back in Cairo. Despite what Woods had said to him and the show of camaraderie, he still detected a certain tension and he wondered whether Woods's presence on the raid was also at least in part a gesture that somehow he considered himself in control too of her affections. But he had made nothing of it. Would not. Now there was work to be done.

The initial order for Hunter and his patrol was to head inland to RV with Paddy Leigh Fermor. This, Hunter knew, would be the easiest part. Approach marches tended to be boring affairs, even through the heady countryside of Crete.

It had been suggested at one point that Leigh Fermor himself might meet the *Rosetta* on the coast, but this plan had been quashed by Vickery. It was just too dangerous to risk so many valuable operatives in one place at once. If the Germans did spot the boat then why offer them the whole network on a plate? Besides, the walk inland would give Hunter's men a chance to feel more at home on the island. Most of the men – Duffy, Phelps, Miller, Fletcher and Russell – had never set foot on Crete before, although to match them, White and Martin were both more than capable of swapping anecdotes with Hunter about the horror and chaos they had seen on the island back in May '41. Though Fletcher, of course, would always have it in an argument that there was nothing to rival Dunkirk for the sort of fighting retreats that the Brits and their allies seemed to have gone in for in the last few years. Thank God, thought Hunter, that most of them still had a sense of humour.

Hunter thought that he knew the island well. Probably, apart perhaps for Woods, the best out of all in their party. It was not yet two years ago that he had first come here, with the Black Watch, but it seemed like an eternity and a very, very different world. Then, before the fighting had started, when they were still busy fortifying the island, he had walked for hour after hour in the hills. Had got to know some of the locals. To see and sample some of their ways, their habits, their lifestyle. They were a hard people, but hugely generous to those whom they liked and trusted. He wondered how much that trust had been changed in a year and a half of German occupation. He had heard terrible tales of atrocities against the civilian population – shootings, hostages, reprisals, torture and worse – and wasn't sure whether or not to believe them.

Estimates suggested that there were now somewhere around 20,000 Germans on the island. In real terms the Nazis were everywhere. Hitler and his generals were now calling it 'Festung Kreta' – 'Fortress Crete'.

There were, he had been told, still some of the Brits left who had, literally, missed the boat in '41. And there were more British officers on the island besides Leigh Fermor. Well, that much was true, as was to be seen from the extraordinary and colourful Captain Ffinch.

Hunter hadn't seen Leigh Fermor since that night in Cairo and he wondered if he had been told who was leading the little party from the new intelligence commando. In a way there was bound to be tension between his lot and SOE. They had a bit of an overlap and he wondered whether Leigh Fermor and his like might not resent the new force. He supposed that they might even see it as a criticism that Leigh Fermor and his SOE chums were not doing enough.

But he realised that now was not the time to worry about such things. If that was how it was then it was just too bad. He would deal with it. Yet it niggled. He recalled what Vickery had said to him. It was really not his concern. None of his business. All he had to do was get the job done. But what then about when the job involved working alongside not one but two mavericks? One – Woods – was a friend and also his superior, but equally Woods was his rival over Lara and might turn against him at any minute; the other man was an unknown quantity, as celebrated for his heroics as he was for his outrageous behaviour.

Leigh Fermor's current HQ (he moved around regularly to avoid detection) was up in the mountains, above the little village of Kastamonitsa. There was a cave there apparently, which was the perfect hideout for their operation at Heraklion. It would take them a good three days to get there by foot.

Wilson's men, in three patrols of twelve, had taken more direct routes to their objectives and planned to lay up directly above them, one at Heraklion, the other at Tymbaki. They had left a third patrol with the 'dump' of their own supplies above the beach as a useful source of resupply and emergency base.

If the principal two raids went well and there was still time in the schedule arranged with their transport, then another raid on Kastelli airstrip would be a bonus. That at least was Wilson's plan.

Hunter, Woods and the men of the new unit spent the first night after the landing with Ffinch and the remaining two andartes under the stars in a high ravine up in the hills above the sea, filled with bright pink, sweet-scented oleander bushes, still in bloom. Ffinch now properly introduced the two andartes to them.

'Captain Woods, Lieutenant Hunter. I don't think I properly introduced you to Andros. Andros is one of our best agents. He's only eighteen but he's been working with us since the island fell.'

The boy was unusually clean-shaven and had a baby face, but his eyes told of a deep sadness and bitterness. Andros smiled at them and shook both of their hands before turning away to get back to his work.

Ffinch spoke more quietly for a moment. 'Lovely chap. His entire family was murdered by the Germans last year in reprisal for the shooting of three Germans. His father was implicated. They strung the old man up in the village square and shot his wife and two daughters in front of him before they kicked away the chair. Andros saw it all and managed to escape into the hills. That's where we found him, with Bourdzalis's band. He's part of our mob now. Ah, here's Grigori.'

He turned to the older of the two andartes, a darker-skinned man whom Hunter reckoned must be in his late thirties, with a well-trimmed beard and dark, almost black hair. Ffinch introduced them as before and Grigori shook their hands, but he did not smile. He merely stared at them long and hard with deep brown eyes, before turning away.

Ffinch spoke again: 'It's an equally sad tale, if rather more intriguing. Grigori comes from that little village down in the valley. He's married and has three children and a pretty wife, ten years his junior. Earlier this year he helped three downed British airmen escape from the Germans and got them off the island. Since then he hasn't dared to return to his home or his village, in case he's been found out. To all intents, he doesn't exist. In fact in his village they posted his name on a wall. He's been officially pronounced "dead". That's just so that his family won't be targeted by the enemy. Even his wife believes that he's perished and we're doing what we can to keep up the illusion. And to keep her alive. That's what hurts him the most. He lives for the day when the Germans are ejected from his homeland and he can finally return to his house and hold her and his children in his arms again. Until then his only purpose in life is to kill all the Germans he can. And, as he says, he's a dead man. How can they possibly catch him, if he doesn't exist?'

Hunter and Woods watched in admiration, as the two Greeks busied themselves about the important job of making supper. They killed a sheep and opened bottles of wine, retsina and ouzo. It was a quiet meal that morning, during which each man seemed to be lost in his own thoughts. The party was strictly to move only at night, so as the dawn broke, they found what sleep they could, while each of the men took it in turns to stand watch.

First though there was the morning's glass of raki to drink. Ffinch explained that it was a Cretan custom, although Hunter had not come across it. It was meant to clear the head. Hunter drank his glass down and tried to sleep but so 'clear' was his head, that he found it hard.

He slept fitfully, his dreams haunted by images of Andros's dead family and was only too happy to take his own turn on stag, using the time to gaze at his new surroundings, while all the time keeping an eye out for the smallest hint of danger. He need not have worried. Soon the place was thronging with visitors, andartes mostly, from various bands on the islands. All seemed to know Ffinch and greeted him as one might a distant cousin.

On the first evening they climbed higher and deeper into the hills and reached Skoinia where they spent another day resting. They moved on again after dusk had fallen, passing through a number of small villages as they went. As they approached the first of these Ffinch spoke to Hunter: 'Woods tells me you speak German.'

'It's passable, but hardly perfect.'

'Passable is fine, old boy. We have a little trick here, to

stop the villagers coming out and spotting that a band of desperadoes is passing through. Wouldn't be good for security. We impersonate the Hun.'

'You do? Really?'

'Oh, yes, we've got quite good at it. Look now, here comes a village and the doors are open.' He turned to Woods and spoke to both officers: 'Now. Watch me and then join in if you like, in your finest "*mal Deutsch*"! You'll be astonished at what happens.'

As they approached the village, none of the men making any effort to reduce the noise level, it seemed that every dog in the area had started to bark at once.

As they entered Ffinch barked out commands. '*Marsch! Los, Los!*'

The two andartes joined in confident, if Greek-tinged German: '*Marsch!*'

'*Deutschland uber alles.*'

'*Straffe England.*'

Some of the men made an effort. German-speaker Harry Martin's attempt brought the broad tones of Northern Ireland to the Horst Wessel song, creating something between an Irish folk ballad and an excerpt from comic opera.

'*Die Fahne hoch! Die Reihen fest geschlossen!*
SA marschiert mit ruhig festem Schritt.'

Fletcher harmonised, humming in a powerful Welsh baritone.

Hunter laughed and joined them:

'*Marsch, Marsch. Jawohl miene herren.*'

Ffinch smiled and nodded his approval and as he did so, the doors and windows swiftly began to close until, when they found themselves halfway through the place, not a single one was open. The dogs though continued to stare at them and to bark their chorus of disapproval. Finally, as they exited the village Ffinch struck up a rousing chorus of 'Lili Marleen', in the original German, which they all joined in, Woods included, heartily placing the emphasis on the '*einsts*'.

For one ghastly moment Miller, who had sung the song in the face of the *Afrika Korps*, throughout the Western Desert, from Sidi Barrani to Tobruk, belted out half a verse in English, but he soon realised his blunder and managed to change hurriedly into a sort of ersatz German.

Not a door in the village opened. It was, thought Hunter, one of the most bizarre episodes in which he had ever taken part. Almost as soon as they had left the village they stopped and carried on in relative silence. But it served to create a curious bond between the commandos and the andartes, who now grinned at them as if they had all managed to pass some curious initiation test.

The party walked on through olive groves and under the rising forms of the ilex and cypress trees and eventually, as the dawn rose on another day, they arrived at the little hillside village of Kastamonitsa.

Ffinch said nonchalantly, 'We have to be a little quieter here. There's a German military hospital in the village.'

Woods looked at him incredulously. Surely they were walking right into the lion's den? 'What? You can't really be serious?'

'Oh yes, it's easily the best way to stay inconspicuous. Here among the sick Huns. We just have to hide for a day. Best keep your heads down, though. They do have the occasional passing sentry. Just for show, in case the local SS pass through.'

And so they found themselves taking refuge in the upper attic storeys of two whitewashed houses, opposite each other, but which belonged to the same family of another of the andartes, Kimon Zographakis, a sour-faced, bitter young man, whose younger brother had recently been shot by the Germans.

Hunter and Woods were billeted in one house, along with Phelps, Duffy and Martin. Ffinch and Sergeant Knox were in the other house, with Russell, Miller, White and Fletcher. The two Greeks blended into the village and found their own modest billets among the friendly villagers, taking with them the now unburdened pack mules. All of the boxes of supplies were taken up into the two attics and all the men made good use of their time under shelter to sort out their kit and get themselves in good order. And as they did so, Kimon's two pretty sisters along with his mother and 'baby' brother (who was actually seventeen) came and went, bearing wine and olives and flatbreads and goat's cheese and small cups of strong sweet black coffee.

From time to time the party inadvertently looked down from the windows and once Hunter saw a passing German, his rifle slung, gazing from house to house, and he quickly ducked back into the shadows of the eaves.

Hunter was pleased and somewhat surprised to find that they had actually been given beds with sheets and pillows to sleep in and, gratefully, he settled down for a good rest.

★★★

They slept soundly that afternoon and into the evening, but on rising he discovered that he had been bitten head to foot by fleas. Desperately trying not to scratch, he approached one of Kimon's sisters and asked her in Greek to whom the bed belonged.

She smiled at him. 'Oh it's mine, your honour. Your friend is in my sister's bed.' She smiled again. 'We are very happy for you to have them. You need to rest to fight the Germans.'

Hunter murmured a grateful thanks and walked over to Woods, noticing that he too was clandestinely scratching at his side.

'Good sleep, Peter?'

Woods smiled at him. 'Best I've had these past few days. Rather an itchy mattress, though.'

He scratched at his leg, this time. While Hunter scratched at his own head and neck.

'Yes, I'm the same. Our lovely beds belong to Kimon's sisters, apparently.'

'Yes, apparently so. Very kind of them, don't you think?'

'Very generous. And so kind of them to give us both a small present or two to take away with us.'

Woods smiled at him and laughed.

Then, as the sun sank below the horizon, it was time to leave the Zographakis household. Kimon's mother wailed and implored them all to come back soon. And the daughters too looked genuinely sad to see them all go, although they were obviously keen to regain the comfort of their flea-infested beds.

With Ffinch leading the way, with Kimon as a further escort from Kastamonitsa, and under the cloudless moon lighting their way, they left the little village behind them and after a while reached the foot of the mountains. Here Kimon bade them a surly farewell and they carried on led by Ffinch, climbing up over the hard shale rocks up an almost non-existent goat track for what seemed like forever, but was in reality no more than three and a half hours. Higher and higher they went. Hunter paused for breath and looked down the mountain towards the distant village down a black gorge, lit up in the moonlight.

They were on a ridge now and Russell turned to Hunter. 'Blimey, boss. How much further d'you think it is?'

'Yes, it is quite hard going, isn't it.'

Martin chimed in: 'Can't be much further though, can it? Really, sir?'

The ridge continued for another mile, and they kept walking until Ffinch called them to a halt with a wave of his hand, and found Woods and Hunter. 'We're almost there, but I don't think we should travel any further in the dark. It's a little treacherous if you don't know the terrain. We'll tether the mules and get some kip.'

Woods spoke: 'Are you quite sure that's safe?'

Ffinch raised his hand, brushing away the worry. 'Oh, Jerry won't trouble us up here. In fact, he's never been up here. Whatever his sacred Mountain Troops might boast about. We're higher than any of their bloody edelweiss.'

He posted just one sentry, in the first instance Andros. They gave the mules to Andros who took them off to a group of ilex trees, then they all looked around for somewhere to sleep. Away from the track the ground was covered with lush vegetation and following Captain Ffinch's example and that of one of the Greeks not on watch, the men each found their own spot, with a rock for a pillow, and were soon drifting in and out of consciousness.

Dawn was just an hour and a half later, at around four, and it came up with a gentle glow, which gave an almost magical air to the landscape that greeted Hunter's slowly opening eyes. They were indeed, as Ffinch had said, very, very high up the mountain, but he had imagined that they had climbed to the top of the island and what instantly astonished him was that there were even higher mountains rising above them, in every direction, their white peaks crowned with snow.

The slow, growing dawn transformed the landscape minute by changing minute, as they watched and Hunter caught sight of several of the men as, awestruck, they took in the panorama.

Ffinch started them all up, but this morning without the customary raki. This was clearly not the time for that. Despite its restorative powers, they needed all their wits about them. For the rest of the journey was as dangerous as any Hunter and Woods had ever attempted. Slowly, they continued in nervous single file along the top of the ridge, which it seemed was gradually becoming narrower and narrower until Hunter wondered where it might eventually end. He did not have long to wait to find out. After about just under an hour of perilous ridge walking, Ffinch signalled them all to stop.

Hunter watched as Ffinch and Andros made their way to the edge of the ridge and then, to his horror, disappeared from view as they began to descend down what looked like a sheer, vertical cliff face. He found Woods. 'Christ, Peter, old "Eff Eff" wasn't bloody joking about the danger.'

It was their new name for the eccentric captain. Woods

raised his eyebrows. 'Yes, I must say, I'm rather glad we didn't attempt this in the dark.'

One by one, with their weapons securely strapped to their backs, the men approached the top of the cliff face and then slid and skidded their way down the rock. Ahead of them, they could see Andros and Grigori, leading their laden mules, which incredibly seemed to be more sure-footed on this crazy incline than on flat ground. Looking down, as he slid over the rocks, Hunter saw that his destination was a ledge, wide enough to take three men abreast, but which, he guessed, could not be seen from below and, cleverly, would look merely as if it were part of the cliff above.

At last he reached it, brushing himself down and checking to see if his slither down the rocks had caused any rips in his clothing. All was fine, although Miller had torn the leg of his trousers and Phelps the sleeve of his tunic. There were no casualties, save a couple of minor abrasions to Fletcher's hand and Martin's ankle.

Ffinch was there to meet them. 'Here we are, gentlemen, at last.'

He pointed to a cave, barely discernible in the gloom, a few yards above them surrounded by towering crags and groups of tall ilex trees.

'Chez Paddy. Come on.'

They followed him and as they reached the mouth of the cave were greeted by the unmistakable, imposing figure of Captain Patrick Leigh Fermor, of the Special Operations Executive. Paddy was somewhat leaner and more battle-hardened than Hunter remembered him from that last time in Cairo, but it was probably on account of the new context in which he now saw him and might also have had something to do with his dress. Leigh Fermor seemed to have dressed for a leading role in a budget production of *The Desert Song*, or perhaps an amateur repertory performance of *Ali Baba*.

He wore a voluminous white shirt and over it a sleeveless embroidered jacket. His trousers were a pair of cavalry officer's whipcord jodhpurs, tucked neatly into tall black riding boots. The whole ensemble was completed with a wide burgundy-coloured cummerbund into which he had stuck a pearl-handled colt revolver and a dagger with a damascened silver handle. He looked like a pirate king. He smiled broadly and extended his arms. 'Welcome, all of you. So wonderful to see you.'

Ffinch slapped him on the cheek, in the Cretan manner of greeting, and was rewarded with one in return. Together, thought Hunter, the two of them made a perfect pair.

'Paddy, allow me to introduce Captain Peter Woods and Lieutenant Jim Hunter and their men.'

Leigh Fermor looked at both of them, then alighted on Hunter. 'Don't I know you? I do.'

'Yes, we met in Cairo. At Tara.'

Leigh Fermor squinted at him. 'Oh yes. You're that fellow in the fight. What a glorious night that was.' He looked at Woods. 'I say. You're the other chap, aren't you? Weren't you two fighting over a girl? That's a bit rum isn't it? Sending you both off here. Together I mean?' He laughed. Neither Woods nor Hunter said anything. 'Anyway. Not our problem. Miles away from all that. I do presume you are talking to one another?'

Woods laughed. 'Not a problem at all, Captain.' He shot Hunter a smile. 'Is it, Jim? We're the very best of friends.'

'That's good and it's Paddy, please. I'm Paddy to everyone.

You'll find that we're very informal here. Now come and meet our host.'

Leigh Fermor ushered the two of them inside the cave, which was tiny, perhaps eight feet square by six in height. There was just room for the three of them plus its owner. A blanket of leaves and ferns covered the floor. Ahead of them an old man in peasant clothing was seated before a rock fireplace. On his head he wore a traditional Cretan fringed turban and an embroidered waistcoat and a pair of baggy 'crap catchers'. And all of his clothes, apart from his white shirt, were black. He looked at them as they entered, flashing them a toothless grin. Leigh Fermor introduced him: 'This is Siphoyannis. The finest goatherd in Crete and one of my very best friends.' He turned to the old man and spoke in perfect, fluent Greek, with a hint of Cretan dialect: 'Aren't you, my friend. You are my very good friend.'

The man smiled and nodded.

'It's the perfect place. There is a clear stream for washing and drinking. I can see for miles and am the first to know of the approach of any enemy patrols. I am supplied with food, olive oil, cigarettes, wine and raki by my friends in the villages. What could possibly be better?'

And so, the four officers sat outside the cave, the trees offering shelter from the wind. More raki was drunk and Leigh Fermor explained to them some of the ways of Cretan society. Much was already familiar to Hunter but he happily sat back and listened attentively and let the raki do its work. He was just thinking how lucky he was to be there when Leigh Fermor dropped his bombshell.

'Of course I won't myself be coming with you, Woods.'

The remark took both Woods and Hunter completely by surprise. Woods spoke: 'You won't?'

'No, I'm afraid that "head office" in Cairo sees it as just too risky. Apparently I'm too great an asset and they seem to like another plan I've come up with. So I'm afraid I'll be otherwise engaged. But don't worry, Captain Ffinch will be your eyes and ears, along of course with Andros and Grigori.'

Leigh Fermor moved along the ridge towards the group of British and Greeks, who had poured themselves mugs of raki and were chatting together among the trees and exchanging cigarettes.

'Mungo, a moment if you will.'

Ffinch detached himself from the group and walked towards them. 'Paddy?'

'I've told Captain Woods and Lieutenant Hunter that I'm not able to go with them to Heraklion. But I'm sure you'll oblige.'

'Only too happy to, Paddy.'

'And you'll take Grigori with you?'

'Of course.'

He turned to Woods and Hunter. 'Of course I'll talk you through everything I know. Mungo and Grigori will guide you in. How does that sound?'

Woods nodded. 'I'm sure we can work with that.'

Leigh Fermor nodded. 'Good. That's that settled then. Now let's get down to business. The stuff that you're after was left, according to those in the know in Cairo and London, in a safe in the commandant's office at Heraklion airfield. That was, as you may recall, for a while, GHQ of Creforce in May '41.'

Woods nodded. 'Yes, that's what we were told. Hunter was

there with the Black Watch in '41 when the balloon went up. When I was down the road with Bob Laycock.'

Leigh Fermor glanced at Hunter with new respect. Woods carried on, 'How do we get to it?'

'Oh, the boys will get you there, no problem. And I have a map. Although perhaps Lieutenant Hunter might remember it. Hasn't changed much. And of course you've brought along your "special kit", haven't you?'

Hunter smiled. 'Yes, it's all safely stowed away and unopened.'

'Good. Well, that's key to the whole thing. I must say it's a damn clever plan, whoever came up with it.'

Hunter nodded. 'Damned risky. But damned clever, if it works.'

Leigh Fermor ignored his comment and produced from his waistcoat pocket a carefully folded piece of paper, which proved to be a hand-drawn plan of the aerodrome.

'Here you are. Now look at this. It's bang up to date. One of my chaps in the hills drew it – Julian's his name, a sapper. Got a real talent for maps. Gave me this one yesterday. There you see is the perimeter wire and that's where you go in. Once you're through that you just have to get across the area where the accommodation blocks are and then you turn left. Look familiar Hunter?'

'Yes, sir. I remember it well.'

'Good. So you take another right turn and then you're in among all the admin blocks. The commandant's office is located over here, to the right.' He pointed. 'Just there. Julian's marked it with a sort of an Iron Cross, d'you see. Frightfully witty fellow. So you can see, it's very simple really.'

Hunter took a closer look at the plan. Yes, it certainly

looked simple enough. All they had to do was to stroll across two hundred yards of open ground in full view of three hundred Germans, then break into the commandant's hut (making sure that he wasn't in there first) and crack open the safe. If the documents weren't there, they would have to go to the signals hut, which was the only other place they might have been placed.

Wherever they turned up they would simply have to grab the documents, along with anything else that happened to look interesting (that was their brief), and then leave all offices closed and relocked as if no one had been there. Then they would go back into the compound, stroll back across the square, get out through the wire (presuming their gap hadn't been discovered) and then climb back up into the hills and march the five hours back to the cave. It would, of course, be a piece of cake.

9

They had had no word from Wilson's raiding party since their two boats had parted company before reaching Crete, but that was all as it should have been. Now, though, the time was up and they were waiting for something when, on the fifth morning, one and a half days before they were due to head off on the operation, Andros appeared at the mouth of the cave with another partisan, having found him making his way up the path. He came, he said, from Wilson. 'Kapitan Wilson says to tell you that he is in place. His men are ready at the two other airfields and he and the others are hidden in the hills above Heraklion and is ready to go in shortly after you have taken what you need. He says to be sure to be out of the base by the agreed time. You must not be there after 2130 hours please.'

Then he added, 'Kapitan Wilson says to make sure of it.'

Woods frowned at the man's impertinence. 'You can tell Kapitan Wilson... Sorry, please will you tell Captain Wilson that we will do exactly that. We will be out of the base by the time he suggests. Tell him not to worry.'

He added, with more than a note of sarcasm, 'We wouldn't want him to get in a panic. Or to cause him any trouble.'

The Greek smiled, the sarcasm lost on him. 'Oh, is no trouble. And he will not panic. He just said, "Tell him to make sure".'

The man disappeared and Woods turned to Hunter. 'Bloody cheek. "Make sure of it"? Who the hell does Wilson think he is?'

'He's probably just nervous. Doesn't want anything to go wrong.'

'He doesn't trust us more like. It's simple. You go in there with your team and get the material and get out with no one the wiser. Then ten minutes later Wilson's men go in and blow the place to pieces. There's no need for him to get himself into a panic. It's all to do with timings.'

'He's not panicking, Peter. Besides we've got backup of our own if he bungles the job. I've got explosives and just the men to do it. Now you're worrying.'

'Of course I'm not. If you ask me we should just have done the bloody thing ourselves, without Wilson.'

'You know as much as I do that Fleming was told by the top brass that he had to have backup from the regular commandos. That was the only condition for our force to go ahead. For us to even exist. I know we can do it all. That we don't need them. But that's just the way it is. If it goes well then next time we can argue for our independence. Besides the real reason for Wilson being there is to make Jerry think it's just a regular raid. We don't want him to realise that we've got our own unit of intelligence commandos.'

'Yes, you're right. I know. I'm just over-reacting. It's just that boy upset me so much. Damn bloody Wilson.'

It wasn't the first time that Hunter had seen Woods in this

mood. He recalled the fiasco on Rhodes and his uncertainty then.

He was also concerned about a few elements of their plan. Surely it would have been better to have sent in a submarine to pick them all up after the operation rather than have Gorringe wait for them? As it was, only Wilson's men were to be collected by sub. That he understood. Once they had done their job and the two aerodromes were ablaze, the hills around Heraklion in the north and Kastelli over to the west, were sure to be crawling with the enemy. The idea was, of course that Hunter's smaller team would have accomplished their task long before that and would be halfway back to the cave where they could then hide up, before being taken off by Gorringe's caique.

The Germans wouldn't suspect that there were two teams and would use all their men hunting for Wilson's men who would be taken off further west. The mountain and hills around the cave and from Kastamonitsa, down to the southern coast would be about the safest place on the island. German garrisons in that part would certainly be dragged into the operation in the west, leaving him and his men to make their way down to the waiting boat, simply retracing their steps. It was, he supposed, a clever plan. But perhaps it was just too clever.

After briefing them, Leigh Fermor had gone to visit another partisan group, further to the west of the island. Hunter had to admit that he was not sorry to see him go. Oh he was pleasant enough. Friendly even. But Hunter was at a loss as to how someone in such a position as his – the key liaison officer between the Cretan resistance movement and the British and someone whose purpose in life was doing everything he could to help both British servicemen and Greek andartes and make life as difficult as possible for the enemy – could be quite so cool.

He just seemed to get on with the job. Whatever it might be. Whatever the danger. Not to worry at all. He certainly never showed it but Hunter could not help wondering if underneath it all there might not be some insecurity. Some vulnerability that he needed to cloak with bravado. Perhaps it was the same thing that Hunter knew to be there within himself.

Since their arrival at the cave, they had modified their routine while they were waiting for the operation and could now sleep at night at least for the coming forty-eight hours. There was an air of normality. As if they were taking part in an exercise or some sort of endurance test. And it was perhaps this that had urged a couple of the men to seek out more comfortable accommodation.

Russell and Fletcher had managed to make their way unnoticed into the upper floor of an old abandoned farmhouse that lay a hundred yards below the cave. Leigh Fermor had told them that it was too exposed to use as a permanent base, but some of the men had decided that it was a better place to sleep than under the trees. Of course a candle or any form of light was out of the question at night in an apparently deserted farmhouse and those who decided that staying under a roof and four walls was worth taking the trouble, just had to make sure they got down there while it was still light.

During the day the farmhouse was strictly off limits to everyone. On the evening before the operation though, Hunter had decided to change the rules. This evening the house was needed to serve a specific purpose. There were two vital pieces of kit that had still not been sorted out and, having left them till the final moment, their time had now finally come. And the one thing that had to be done must be done behind closed doors.

Ever since they had arrived here and had unloaded their equipment from the pack mules, Hunter had made sure that he had kept two large duffel bags crammed with kit close to his own quarters in the cave. Now the time had come to distribute their contents and, having been since his youth keen for any chance of donning fancy dress, he had to admit that he was looking forward to it. Hunter had told the others to meet him down at the house an hour before dusk, but he had set out deliberately early to make sure that he would get there himself a good half an hour before them. He waited until they were sitting beneath the trees, chatting to each other over a cigarette and a coffee and then, choosing his moment, slipped out of the cave, dragging both of the heavy bags of kit behind him.

Reaching the farmhouse, Hunter was surprised to find the door slightly ajar and to hear noises coming from the upper floor. He carefully placed both of the kitbags on the ground and, cautiously and silently, pushed open the door and pulled the narrow-bladed Fairbairn-Sykes fighting knife from its leather scabbard on his belt.

Entering the house, Hunter padded across the stone floor

to the white stone staircase on the far side of the kitchen and placed a foot on the bottom step. As he did so he heard a deep groan from the room above. Wasting no time, Hunter tiptoed up the remaining stairs and then flew into the room above, his knife at the ready.

There was no need for it. What greeted Hunter was a sight as comic as it was pathetic. Lying on a straw paillasse on the wooden floor of the bedroom was Bryn Fletcher. His trousers were around his ankles. And astride him, her skirts pulled up to her shoulders, her perfect, pearl-white bottom exposed to the world, sat one of the girls from the village. Fletcher looked at Hunter and grinned. 'Hello, sir. Didn't expect to see you here.'

'No, Fletcher. I dare say you didn't. I've got an "O" group scheduled here in half an hour. Can I suggest that you, er, smarten yourself up and help this young lady away from here. And for fuck's sake be discreet about it. You're bloody lucky Captain Woods didn't find you. And you know this place is out of bounds in daylight, anyway. Be quick about it.'

Fletcher's inescapable charm had had its way once again. The man was impossible. Hunter wondered where on earth he got his stamina from. He prayed that the girl's mother or father or brothers if she had any, would not find out before they all left the place. Even if they got away with it, the consequences would not exactly make it any easier for SOE to cement its relationship with the locals. And of course, the andartes would have Fletcher's balls for earrings.

Hunter replaced his knife in its scabbard and made his way quickly down the stairs, quickly followed by the girl and Fletcher. She smiled engagingly at Hunter, as if nothing had happened at all and, with a quick wave to Fletcher, left the house and hurried away down the hill. Fletcher looked at the ground. 'Sorry, sir.'

'You should be. That was fucking stupid, you idiot. You could have compromised the whole operation. Mind you, I don't blame you. Pretty young thing. And from her smile it looks as if you got away with it. Let's hope she tells no one about it. What I really don't know though is how, with your appalling command of the Greek language, you ever managed to get her into bed.' Fletcher opened his mouth to explain. But Hunter stopped him. 'Enough. Now get yourself back up to the cave and make yourself useful by making sure that none of my part of the team come down here for another half an hour. But tell Duffy that he needs to come down first. In twenty minutes' time. Oh and can you tell each of them that they need to bring a razor with them?'

'A razor?'

'You heard.'

'Righto, boss. Sorry.'

Fletcher went over to the door, followed by Hunter. 'Oh, Fletcher. Before you go there are two kitbags outside. Help me in with one of them.'

Fletcher walked outside and Hunter went after him. Between them they got the bags into the room and, after Fletcher had left, Hunter closed the door behind him. Hunter picked up the first of the bags and stood it on its end.

The two identical long canvas duffel bags, of the sort the navy used, were the only two unmarked pieces of kit they had brought with them in the boat. They had been sewn shut around the drawstring before leaving Athlit and sealed with a brass 'D' pattern duffel bag lock, fastened with a padlock.

The neck of each of them was marked with the stencilled words: 'Eyes only' and 'Lt Hunter'.

Hunter reached into his tunic and from a chain around his neck, took a small brass key, inserted it in the padlock, turned it and removed the lock. Then he again removed his fighting knife from its scabbard and carefully cut through the thick twine with which the openings had been secured. Then he repeated the process for the second bag. Once the locks were off, he opened out the mouth of the first bag and reached inside. Pulling out his arm, he produced a jacket. It was quickly followed by another.

One of them was in the unmistakable German *feldgrau* grey-green uniform of the Wehrmacht and the other, in the characteristic desert yellow used by the Afrika Korps. Both were nicely worn and faded and on closer inspection it was easy to see them for what they were: two original, identical German military tunics. Officers' tunics. Both bore a silver eagle on the right breast pocket and both also had silver flashes at the collar. One had the distinctive black and red medal ribbon of the Iron Cross, second class. He dug his hand further into the bag and produced two pairs of faded baggy trousers – one grey, one yellow – cut as riding breeches, followed by two pairs of high riding boots – one brown, one black.

Hunter moved over to the other bag and had a quick look inside before reaching in. His search yielded further riches. It contained four more tropical-issue German army tunics, minus the officers' markings but one with sergeant's stripes, along with four pairs of baggy trousers of the sort worn in the desert. All were again faded to the perfect hue to suggest long service.

Here then were six uniforms in all, for the four German speakers in the patrol: Hunter, Duffy, Martin and Russell, plus one more each for Jack Knox and Sid Phelps, both of whom as key specialists would have to go in with them. Hunter just prayed that neither of them would be asked any difficult questions by the guards. Bluff was everything and they had all been taught how to carry it off at Athlit. It was fine, providing their nerves held and, if the truth were to be told, Hunter was a little concerned. He brushed it off and quickly, started to strip off his clothes and try on his new, enemy uniform before the others appeared.

He had, of course tried all of his own German officer's kit on before, back in Cairo, to get the fit right. He had gone, as a matter of taste, for the desert yellow one, with the brown boots. The riding breeches were perfect and the boots of course, well weathered, had been selected from the many pairs held in the central quartermaster's stores in Cairo, taken from the feet of dead officers. Hunter had tried them on in Cairo, but he had forgotten quite how well they fitted. He found his chosen shirt and, equally happy with the fit, tucked it in to the waistband of the breeches, before pulling on the tunic. He had selected the one with the ribbon of the Iron Cross for himself.

It was a standing joke in the British Army that German uniforms were so much smarter and better cut than anything the British tailors could summon up, but here, thought Hunter, was the living proof of it. The moment he buttoned up the jacket, Hunter knew what the reason was. The Germans might be heartless bastards, that was a given. But you had to admit, they had style. Buckets of the stuff. The thing just fitted him so bloody well. It might have been tailored for him in Savile Row. But it was more than that. It was about the cut of the jacket. It oozed arrogance and power and fathomless self-confidence. No wonder the Blitzkrieg had worked. He fastened one of the belts around his waist and closed the buckle. '*Gott Mit Uns*' indeed. Then he placed one of the officer's caps squarely on his head and, with his hands clasped behind his back, feeling every inch the imperial Teuton, he waited.

The door handle turned and Duffy entered the room and, catching sight of Hunter, instantly froze, staring, wide-eyed. 'Good God. Is that you, sir?'

'Certainly is. What d'you think?'

'Well, it's good. Damned good. I'd forgotten how bloody good those uniforms were. You almost had me for a moment, sir. Think it'll fool the Nazis?'

'We can only hope, Duffy. Hope and pray. Want to try yours on?'

He pointed over to the pile of clothes in the corner. 'It's all there. Go ahead.'

Not waiting to be told twice, Duffy stripped of his own shirt and trousers and donned the other officer's uniform. Like Hunter's, it fitted him perfectly. He finished it off with the cap and belt and turned to Hunter. 'What d'you think, sir?'

'It's good. As you say. Bloody good. You definitely look the part. We make a right pair of Nazis.'

It was only natural that Hunter and Duffy should be playing the officers. Their German was nothing less than superb. But it was not just that. Both of them had that air of assured self-confidence, bordering on arrogance that was all too easy to assume when you had been through two of the country's finest public schools. Hunter had always suspected that his expensive education would come in useful somewhere.

Knox, Russell, Phelps and Martin would, of course, be playing the other ranks. Russell's German was passable and had an amusing origin. While he had been working as a barman in a certain nightclub in Soho, Russell had been befriended by a German countess named Olga, a refugee from Hitler's new regime, who, terrified that her mother's Jewish roots would condemn her in her homeland, had abandoned her riches and her schloss when she had fled the Third Reich. In London she had been reduced to working as a high-class tart, but even that did not supply the one thing she craved. Lovely Olga had an insatiable passion for Martinis. She craved a well-made Martini. And if there was one thing that Russell could do well, it was make one of the finest Martinis in London.

And so they came to an arrangement. He would give her Martinis and she would give him her ample favours. Only Russell didn't really enjoy sex with her. He wasn't of a different 'persuasion' it was just that she was so, well Teutonic. And so, instead, they would lie in her bed and she would teach him German. The arrangement lasted for six blissful months, in which he served her with hundreds of free drinks and she taught him rudimentary German, along with a bit of extra street language. She had told him he was a born linguist. Said he was a natural. All went well until the missing gin was discovered by the manager of the bar where Russell worked and he was fired. And that was that. So he had robbed the bar's safe, taken all that week's takings and scarpered. But he still had his command of German and here at last was a chance to use it.

Martin, with his fluent German, his tiny camera, his

photographic memory and his eye for detail, was an obvious choice, along with Phelps, the codebreaker. And Knox, well, he was just the safe-cracker.

As it so happened, Russell was the first of the main body of the raiding party to enter the room. Seeing Hunter and Duffy, he stopped dead. 'Shit. I mean Christ, it's you, sir. Blimey you had me going. Bloody hell, you really had me going. I didn't know whether to shoot you or shit myself.'

Knox and Martin appeared at the doorway, closely followed by Woods.

Knox let out a wolf whistle. 'Bloody hell, sir. You're a dead ringer for Rommel.'

Woods grinned. 'Well done, Jim. Bloody good effort.'

Hunter laughed. 'So, Herr Russell. And now perhaps you will put on your own uniform?'

One by one, the others got dressed, laughing at each other as they did so. The other ranks' tunics were most certainly not quite as flattering as the officers, but by the time they were dressed they all looked the part. Except of course for their beards. Hunter pointed at them, and put a hand to his own. 'They'll all have to go, I'm afraid.'

'Sir?'

'Your beards. Your moustaches, the lot. They'll all have to come off. We might allow it, but in the German army facial hair is most definitely "verboten". It's just not very, well, "Aryan".'

They all cast glances at one another. He was right, of course.

★ ★ ★

As if to answer his own order, Hunter took off his German tunic and filled a bowl with water from the little freshwater stream, which flowed from a spring, down the hillside outside the house. Then, with great care, he began to shave off the moustache and beard that he had grown in the past two weeks. It was not much, nothing when compared to the full growths sported by Leigh Fermor and Ffinch, not to mention most of the Greeks. But it had given him the necessary talisman of character and machismo that was needed to be able to mix with the andartes and gain their respect.

In a few strokes of the razor that was gone and he was suddenly the other side of the coin. A clean-shaven outsider. As un-Cretan and non-Greek as any of the strutting master race teeming over the island. He thought it somewhat ironic that, while none of his new Greek friends would now recognise him, his old friends in Cairo would not have known him with a beard.

The others were following suit now. Filling any bowl they could lay their hands on with water from the stream and shaving while there was still sufficient light to do so. There were a few stray cuts; a few oaths, but soon the job was done.

Woods had not shaved. It wasn't needed and he was pleased not to have to lose his beard. His Greek was good, but his German was not as strong as the other members of the party and so he would remain with the perimeter group. In any case, it also made sense not to send in two officers. Woods would keep two of the men with him, Fletcher and White, and an arsenal of weapons that could be deployed if things began to look a bit hairy.

Hunter and Duffy were going to walk into the camp carrying nothing more than a pistol each and the others of the raiding party were each taking one of the Schmeissers. They would take no grenades, no TNT. All that would either be back at the cave or with Woods and his men by the perimeter. Just in case.

One man would be needed to remain behind at the cave with the radio, an HMG and the bulk of the explosives. Miller got the job, albeit accompanied by the moody Andros.

'Miller, you know what to do if we don't show. Tell me again.'

'I'm to give you twenty-four hours from the time you go in. That's a full day after zero hour, which is 2000 hours tomorrow night. If none of you are back here by then, then I make for the boat, taking whatever I can. I radio Captain Gorringe on the caique and tell him the op was a washout…'

Hunter interrupted him, 'What's the code word for failure?'

'Medusa. It's Medusa, sir.'

'That's it. Quite right. Go on.'

'I tell Gorringe the op was a washout and to stand by. Then I destroy the radio set. I leave the explosives and any spare weapons with the Greeks. I get down to the boat and we offload four two-man folboats and leave them hidden in the cave down there with some field rations, water and extra ammo. Just in case any of you manage to get away…'

He went suddenly silent and looked at Hunter, his eyes filled with doubt. 'It will work, sir… Won't it?'

'Yes of course, Miller. Of course it'll work. We just have to make provision for the worst. You know that. Now carry on.'

'Then we push off and get back to Cairo.'

'Fine. So that's the emergency plan. But it's not going to come to that, is it?'

He looked at them. 'Is it?'

They all murmured a 'no' and shook their heads. Hunter carried on, 'Right. Good. So we leave this evening. There will be a poacher's moon tonight, so we should at least be able to move more quickly. Grigori tells me it'll take us nine hours or thereabouts to reach the place where we need to lie up. It's a little church. Very high up above Heraklion airfield. Very safe, he says. So we rest up there all day tomorrow and we go in at 2000 tomorrow night. We're in and we're out and then we scarper back. Almost the way we came, but a little lower, avoiding the church unless we need to go there. Means we can move faster. And then we leave the airfield to Captain Wilson and his mob. Right?'

The time had finally come for them to move off. They made a curious group. There were Hunter and Duffy, the two German officers, with their four men. Woods, in his characteristic battledress and service beret, topped off with a shepherd's scarf, and White and Fletcher, also in their variation of British uniform and with them, eyes and ears, Ffinch and Grigori.

They set off at nine o'clock that evening, moving off down the gorge that ran below the cave that had been their home for the last five days. Hunter felt somehow elated. More so than he had done since arriving there five days earlier. This was it. At last. The operation they had all been working towards. Months of training. Hard, painful, brutal training. All those miles of loaded runs across the hills, the assault training, the endless lectures in fieldcraft and espionage and everything from housebreaking to how to cut a man's arteries and where best it was to stab him with your fighting knife. And how many seconds he would take to die when you did. And, of course, that bloody interrogation. And now it was time.

And if they carried it off, then the way was open for them to do it again. But next time, if there was a next time, they would be on their own. They moved in single file, with Grigori and Ffinch leading the way, with Woods and Hunter next. Then Russell and Martin. Hunter had deliberately placed Phelps in the centre of the line, with Fletcher, White and Duffy behind him, the two big men carrying between them a case of ammunition and explosives. They couldn't afford to stop, for whatever reason. They would first of all have to come down out of the hills and then climb up again and then gradually down as they moved towards the north coast and the sea, until they reached the level of their new hideout. That, he knew, would be the hardest part and they would already have been going for five hours by then.

They continued their descent now, dropping down the hills, lined with olive groves and lemon trees, with increasing speed. More streams could be heard now to their right and left, babbling away noisily in the silent night, which was heavy with the scent of lemons and punctuated by the chirruping of the few nocturnal cicadas.

They had practised just this sort of cross-country mountain march more times than Hunter could recall, in the foothills of the Carmel Mountains, above the castle at Athlit and he thanked God for all that now. There was a method to it. You got into a rhythm, so that your legs were almost operating independently. And then you just carried on. After they had been marching in this way for some four hours Hunter began to realise that he was no longer actually thinking about it. That he had indeed gone into a sort of trance-like state. Grigori, who clearly had grown up walking the hills in just this way, would make them halt at regular intervals, almost every hour. But always it would be only for a few minutes. Just enough time to compose themselves and regain some of their strength, before starting again. And every time they began again Grigori would tell them, grinning, 'One more hour, sirs. Just one more hour, please.'

Their route had been designed specifically not to take them through any villages, which, while obviously necessary given their strange appearance, made the going all that harder as, from time to time Grigori would whisper, 'village', and they would have to detour off the path before rejoining it.

Typically, every third or fourth step someone would miss their footing and would be lucky to stay upright. The shale just fell away underfoot and it was pointless looking down as, despite the moonlight, the ground was far too dark to see your feet. The grass when encountered was slippery too. It was hell. But Grigori's exhortation had a clever purpose and sure enough, if you just thought to yourself that it might be only one more hour to go, it was possible to carry on.

Their hideout was to be in a church just to the north of Heraklion, about an hour's march away from the airfield. As they approached what Hunter had reckoned would be the last two hours of the march across the island, Ffinch found Woods and Hunter. 'Righto, chaps. I'm off to find the andartes. Good luck.'

They thanked him and watched him go. Ffinch turned and vanished into the night. Part of him wished that he was staying with them and taking part in the mission. But he knew that he was of more value to the bigger picture by doing what he did so well, liaising with the andartes and keeping them all sweet. It was not as he would have wished it, or indeed as he had planned it, when he had volunteered for SOE. His thoughts then had been to get into action, to put himself in danger. And, if he was to tell the truth, to get himself killed. For behind that polished, almost comical façade lay another, very different man. A man broken by loss and despair.

At the outbreak of war, Ffinch and his young French wife and their one child, a daughter, had been living in Normandy where he had worked as a writer and translator, making extra money as a farmhand. It had been all that he had ever wanted: to be surrounded by his books, by nature and by his family. But then the war had come. He had of course volunteered and was soon commissioned. He had been stationed at Aldershot, awaiting the arrival in England of Madeleine and little Sophie when the news had reached him of their death in a refugee column strafed by Stukas near Le Havre.

In that single instant everything had changed. It was not merely revenge that had motivated him to volunteer for the new unit, but a mix of a desperate need for vengeance, a need for something new and absorbing on which to focus his hopelessly damaged mind and a total disregard for his own safety, which had brought him to the War Department and ultimately here, to this beautiful island on which he knew he must surely, at some time, meet his own end.

But not before he had avenged the slaughter of his wife and child. And so, walking once again from another chance to do just that, Ffinch made his way through the darkness in search of the andartes and waited for his moment.

* * *

Back on the narrow path that led to their hideout, Woods and Hunter were still staring into the night after Ffinch when Grigori approached them. 'This now very dangerous part of march, sirs. We need to be very careful and also very, very fast. Please tell your men.'

They passed the word and with a superhuman effort, the little group managed to somehow increase their speed.

Woods and his party, White and Fletcher, were to remain in the church with the reserve of explosives and ammunition. Grigori was to go with Hunter and the others to show them the path down to the base. Once they were there, he would retreat back into the hills but remain watching and when they emerged would drop down and guide them up through the new escape route.

Gradually the land had changed from hillside with its slippery, loose rocks to a gentle terrain, with lush vegetation and olive groves. Nonetheless it still seemed barren and inhospitable. When at last their destination came into view, it was a revelation. And so it must have seemed to generations of all those travelling on this path, who had passed by here. This after all was the reason for its existence. The chapel of Agios Nikolaos had been built some one thousand years ago, in the ninth or perhaps even eighth century by a benevolent order of monks whose doctrine was the care of weary travellers. It might have been made with Hunter and his men in mind.

Seeing it, Grigori suddenly became very excited and began to point towards what to Woods and Hunter looked no more than a charming ruin, or perhaps just a pile of stones. But as they drew closer, he saw that it had a shape. A proper form. It was a single-storey, gabled building with just one low wall, made up of large stones, brown and purple mostly in colour. Above the doorway was a slightly ruinous bell tower, missing its cross. It was really just a rising flat wall topped with a pantiled roof and with a place for a bell, which of course was also long gone. The church was crowned to the rear with a circular dome with four tiny arched windows and a conical pantiled roof, part of which had fallen in.

'There. There it is, Kapitan. The church of Saint Nicholas. That is where we hide this morning. This very safe place. Very holy place.'

Hunter and Woods exchanged glances. It did not, for one thing, seem to Hunter at first sight to appear particularly safe. The little chapel stood on top of a shelf of rock among a number of olive groves and looked as if it might be open to view from a number of directions. He turned to Grigori. 'You are quite sure that it's safe?'

'Of course, sir. Quite sure. It is perfectly safe. It is almost not known to most of the Germans. They no longer patrol here. They believe all the local stories.'

Woods raised an eyebrow. 'Stories? What stories?'

'The stories that the chapel is haunted, Kapitan.'

Woods smiled. 'Oh, is that all. Got a few ghosts has it? The Jerries really lap it all up then?'

Grigori shook his head and gave Woods a knowing look. 'Do not be so doubting, Kapitan. The Germans started out by sending out patrols round here. Last year, when they first took the island. They were looking for escaping British and Aussies. But soon their men came back to camp with tales of strange noises and apparitions and floating mists and clouds and they were shaking with fear. So very soon the patrols began to make excuses to move around it and since then they have kept well clear. Very, very far away. They are very, very superstitious, the Germans.'

Woods smiled. 'Is that so? I'd never have guessed. Jolly useful for us though.'

Grigori looked at him. 'You don't believe in spirits, Kapitan?'

'No. Not really. Anyway, I'm more worried about the real threat. I don't want to get caught and if that means meeting a few old ghosts of monks then so be it.'

'Yes. I am like you. I am a realist. I believe in God and I believe in the devil, but most of all I believe in life and I do whatever I can to keep it. But even I. Even Grigori, I feel something here. There is something here.' He laughed. 'Come on please, sirs. Now we need to get on. Before the day comes.'

They moved faster now, with their goal in sight. And as they neared it, the path they trod became more regular and less overgrown. Clearly, at some point and quite probably over hundreds of years, it had been tended very carefully.

They reached the church and instantly Hunter realised that they were not in fact nearly as exposed as he had at first thought and saw how the church fitted into the surrounding landscape. There, perhaps half a mile away below it lay the open sea and beside it the flickering morning lights of Heraklion and spread out beside the town, to the north-east, the great open space and military dwellings that was the aerodrome. Their target for the mission. There were guards posted all around the airfield. Leigh Fermor's intelligence estimated perhaps three hundred men, housed in a number of old accommodation blocks. The layout had not been changed since the British had been there. Which was an added bonus as Hunter himself had been billeted there with the Black Watch before the Battle of Crete. He remembered it well.

But the main garrison was housed in the old Greek barracks which lay a mile directly to the west. The same buildings his own old mob had lived in. That German garrison now apparently stood at around three thousand men. In a way they were lucky. Until recently there had been sixty thousand Germans on Crete, three infantry regiments, an artillery regiment, a reconnaissance regiment and a tank destroyer regiment. But after Rommel's drive on Cairo had stalled, the garrison had been plundered for reinforcements. Two of the three infantry regiments had been sent to North Africa, along with the tank destroyers, leaving just one regiment of infantry and a fraction of the original artillery. In fact, the German garrison of the island had never been so weak. Leigh Fermor and Vickery were agreed on around fifteen to twenty thousand men. But it was the three thousand at Heraklion that concerned Hunter and more specifically those three hundred of the airfield garrison.

Hunter walked up to the door of the church, which lay open and, pushing against it gently, walked inside. At first it was hard to see in the dim light and as it was not quite yet dawn. But gradually his eyes grew accustomed to the gloom. The walls as he entered were whitewashed and, ensuring that its light would not be seen from outside, he struck a match. The interior appeared to be empty, save for a few simple wooden chairs, some of which lay on their side on the white stone floor.

Down beside the chancel and the plain altar stone, which was without the cloth that would in peacetime have been draped over it, the little church was decorated with frescoes. Well, at some point it had been although few seemed to have survived intact now. Those that had managed to escape the ruination of time and vandalism were simply stunning.

Hunter dumped his kit close to the door and looked around, scarcely believing his eyes. On one wall of the knave was a decorative pattern of lozenge shapes and diamonds in several different colours. The fresco in the dome of the chancel had clearly at one time been astonishing. All that was left now though was a glimpse of Christ in splendour above the saints. As he was looking at it his match went out. But outside the day was beginning to dawn and light had begun to filter through the three small windows at the top, in the dome. Illuminating exactly the spot at which he was looking.

Below the dome the real window at the end of the church – behind the altar stone – had been incorporated into a decorative scheme of false, painted windows to create an illusion. It was in every way, other-worldly. He turned to Grigori who had followed him into the church and was now standing close behind him. 'Fabulous.'

'You think so, sir? I too.'

'I mean it. This place is fabulous.'

Hunter looked around again and began to examine the frescoes. His father had known so much about archaeology but nothing about art and Hunter had tried to educate himself. In London he had always visited the public galleries when he could. The National Gallery and the British Museum had both become almost second homes to him when he had been working in Soho. But never had he seen anything quite so simple – at once so primitive and yet as sophisticated as these frescoes.

Woods and two of the others, Martin and Duffy, had also followed him inside now and stood staring. Woods ruminated, with his hand rubbing his bearded chin. They weren't really to his taste. He had been brought up surrounded by painted images of horse racing and partridge shooting, his father's twin passions. That was real art. This seemed somehow primitive, almost ugly and with a strange power about them that shook his soul in a most unpleasant way. Eventually, he delivered his judgement: 'They're good, I suppose. If you like that sort of thing. Prefer Stubbs and Herring myself. Just so damned good with horses. Can't really see what these are really meant to be here.'

Martin was open-mouthed. 'What a place. Blimey. Who'd have thought? Is this our gaff, sir?'

'Yes, Martin. This is our gaff. For one night only, I hope.'

There was certainly a sense of calm and serenity about the little chapel.

Grigori showed them around, as if he was the proud owner. He pointed to the altar stone, which had been carved from the rock on which the chapel stood and might have been older than the building itself.

'Here, look. This is where the altar stood and here...' He took them to the left. 'Here is a little chapel. This is most safe place on the whole of the island, sirs.'

There was a tiny doorway, just over two feet high, cut into the stone, stopped with a heavy oak door. It looked like a store cupboard. The sort of place where you might keep the altar silver. Woods stared at it. 'In there? In that cupboard? Are you serious?'

Grigori smiled, shook his head and scratched at his beard, knowingly. 'Sometimes, Kapitan, things are not what they seem. Not cupboard. I tell you, Kapitan. No, look. I show you.'

He bent down and undid the iron lock and opened the door. Then kneeling on the floor he began to crawl in. To their surprise, even his huge frame fitted quite easily through the doorway and within seconds, the big Greek had completely disappeared from sight. They heard him calling, 'Come. Come in. Come and see.'

Woods went first, uncertain as to whether he would fit. But soon, he too was gone. Hunter followed them. Through the tiny door was a short tunnel. The effect was slightly claustrophobic for a few moments, but then very quickly it was at an end and he emerged into a room, some six feet high, which extended to his left for what looked to be around twenty feet or more. It was dimly lit from small vents in the roof, which also provided a source of constant fresh air. Grigori lit a match and they saw that here too the walls had been decorated with frescoes. But here they were in black and white on the whitewashed rough-hewn walls. They depicted pastoral scenes: farming, grape and olive picking and men and women drinking. Hunter had no idea how old they were, but he supposed that they must date back to well before the Renaissance.

For a moment both officers were speechless. Woods spoke first: 'Good Lord. These are better, I'll say. I would never have guessed.'

Grigori smiled. 'They're good. No?'

'Good, yes. Very, very good. This is perfect. You're right. It must be the safest place on the island. Well done, Grigori.'

Hunter spoke: 'What do you suppose it was? Do you think it was always secret?'

Grigori nodded and led them down the room towards the end where, carved into the very rock of the building, there stood a tiny stone font. 'Look. This is what for. For baptism. Secret baptisms. Long time ago. It was difficult times here and this place was very, very secret.'

Hunter could only imagine what sort of people might have used the little church. A secret Christian sect, hiding from who or what? From the Ottomans in the 1820s? Or long before that from the old religion of the pagan Gods? Or more likely from the Greek Orthodox faith. Or Orthodox Christians hiding from the conquering Venetian clergy. East versus West. One form of Christianity murderously intent on destroying another. He imagined them here, all those centuries ago. Terrified men, women and children, crammed in, hiding in this tiny space. In constant fear of discovery and death. But always resolute in their faith. Determined to survive. It was not perhaps so different he thought, from today. A people, oppressed and terrorised. Unable to live in freedom, yet equally determined to survive and as they had done so many times before, to throw off the oppressor.

He looked at Grigori in the flickering matchlight. 'Very brave people were here, Grigori.'

'Yes, sir. Very brave people. Very, very brave.'

They crawled out one by one from the little room and Woods went to look at the outside of the church. The men were all inside the church now and, in ones and twos, Hunter took them to the little door and explained the room before taking them inside.

Straightening up, after crawling through, Duffy could

hardly believe it. 'I feel like Alice in Wonderland, sir. But no one's given me a potion. I just shrunk. How we got through that door, I don't know. It's magic, this place, sir. Pure bloody magic.'

They all managed to get through the door, even White, who almost didn't make it but scraped his huge shoulders against the stone roof of the entrance. Hunter was relieved though. If the worst came to the worst they could all fit into the secret chamber. He hoped, however, that it wouldn't have to come to that.

Woods, walking round the exterior of the building, had worked out why the little cell could not be seen from the outside. It reminded him of something he had seen when, as a boy, his family had toured the Loire region of his mother's native France, visiting friends and some of his mother's family who owned a number of chateaux. He enthused, 'It's rather clever actually. The room is designed as a sort of sleeve to the rest of the church. It runs down one of the walls, looking exactly like a solid piece of rock. Because the air and light holes are in the roof you can't see them from the ground. It's exactly mimicked by another sleeve on the other side. But that one really is solid rock. It's brilliant. Who would have thought that a simple rural people could ever have designed something so very clever?'

Hunter looked at him. Who indeed would ever have thought that a simple rural people could have created something so clever? That same simple rural people who had given the world so much, from medicine to philosophy, a legal system to mathematics and of course democracy. That precious democracy, which had been ripped away in so many countries across civilised Europe, in the name of Fascism.

This was where it had all begun. Of course it was. And it dawned on him that this, after all, was why he was here. He was defending civilisation. They all were.

But, he thought, with a smile, wasn't it also ironic that as well as those things that made us civilised, the ancient Greeks had given us the clue to inventing so many means of bloody mass destruction. From the missile catapult to some of the most unpleasant weapons today, in their own armoury and that of the enemy, from the hand grenade to the ghastly liquid fire of the flamethrower.

Although for none of them it held the boyhood connections that it did for Woods, or the ancient associations of Hunter's understanding, the men seemed happy enough with their new billet. Apart from anything else, most of them could now see just how hard it would be for the Germans to find them. Only Phelps had shown any sign of concern. When he had been in the hidden chapel, Hunter had watched him closely. He had seemed fine at first, but gradually Hunter could see him starting to panic. He saw the small beads of sweat break on his forehead and saw his eyes take on that same strange stare that he had noticed on the boat. It did not surprise him that Phelps should have quickly made an exit line for the little door and have been the first to get out. It was clear that within the little room's confined space, he alone had not just felt unsafe, but actually trapped.

Hunter began to worry. What if Phelps's unbalanced state should jeopardise the mission? For a moment he toyed with the idea of ordering him to return to the village, but quickly, he thought better of it. The man was surely merely nervous.

They all were. Phelps just showed it more evidently than the rest of them.

Putting unwelcoming imaginings from his mind, Hunter told himself that Phelps's nerves were nothing to be seriously concerned with and set about the more immediate business of making a plan for a defensive perimeter.

10

The dawn was just starting to come up, painting the skies above Crete with orange, amber and blue, as they settled in around the little church. Knowing that they would have to rest up here all day, Hunter issued orders to make the place as defensible as possible and his men somewhat less visible. The explosives he would place in the inner chapel and it would be best for Woods and White to remain in there as well, while the rest of them were away on the operation.

He made a quick reconnaissance trip around the building, inside and out, spotting the danger points and areas of best defence.

It was clear that if the enemy realised they were based here and a battle ensued then the building would not withstand a hit from a tank shell or artillery. However, with its thick stone walls, it would be a good place to defend against small arms fire. There were three arched windows in the chancel, in each of which he could place a man, along with a wall outside that would give cover to a machine-gun team. If they were to be trapped here it would be vital to have a few men away from the church to counter-attack and he drew up a plan in his mind that when they arrived back from the operation, if the enemy were in close pursuit, he would detail White and Fletcher, and he presumed Woods, to get out of the building and get themselves into good cover in one of the nearby olive groves and wait for their time before rushing any German attackers, with machine guns and grenades.

He wandered over to Woods and told him his plans, fully expecting a quick rebuff. But he was taken by surprise, as Woods nodded. 'Seems like a sound idea, Hunter. But if we are rumbled, then personally I think we should run for the boat rather than making a stand. This is no time for heroics.'

'I agree in a way. But just wanted to make sure that if we were cornered, I mean really and truly cut off, then we had a plan.'

'Well, I'm with you but I really don't think we'll need that sort of a plan, Jim. I don't intend to hang around here, if I can help it. You know what happened last time.'

Hunter had wondered how long it would take Woods to mention their last mission. To use it as some sort of justification. Well here it was. Hunter said nothing, but left Woods and wandered over to where Phelps was staring out of one of the windows across to the sea, as the rising sun began to throw out its light across the surface, changing the night's deep blue to the brilliant azure of day.

'Alright, Phelps?'

'Fine, sir. Never better.'

'You seemed to be a little tense when we were in the chapel. Were you? Tense, I mean?'

'No, sir. Not really. Just not that keen on small spaces. It's nothing. Won't happen again, sir.'

'You know, if you're worried about anything, Phelps, anything at all, you can talk to me. That's what I'm here for.'

'Thank you, sir. I'll be sure to remember that. If I need to.'
Hunter doubted it.

They spent the final day before the operation tucked into
their new base and taking turns to go on watch. For most
of the day the men were either lost in thought or busying
themselves with last-minute adjustments to their kit. In some
cases, Hunter knew these were utterly unnecessary, and were
only made to deflect the mind from brooding too much on
coming events. Some of the men chose to read instead, losing
their minds in some other world. Grigori had brought with
him a small piece of wood, which he was whittling into a
sculpture of a man – a goatherd – and he busied himself with
this, working carefully with the same razor-sharp knife that
he used to cut his food and pick his teeth.

Having helped each man check his weapon and webbing,
as morning turned into the sleepy warmth of early afternoon
Hunter pulled a tattered book from his bag and opened it at
random. Rouse's *Gods, Heroes and Men of Ancient Greece*
had been his constant companion for the last ten years,
offering him escape and advice, and it did not fail him now.
It fell open at the page in which Theseus offers to kill the
Minotaur on Crete, which was, thought Hunter, a remarkable
coincidence. He was even more taken aback when, looking at
the foot of the page he read:

> '...*Theseus ... like a true leader of men would never
> command one of his subjects to do anything which he was
> not ready to do himself.*'

So here he was, a modern-day Theseus, about to enter the Minotaur's lair on Crete. But where was his Ariadne and where was the ball of thread with which he was to get himself and his men out of the enemy maze? Turning the page and looking for an answer, his eye fell on another passage:

> '...*here was something new, which they did not understand; but it made them hope once more, for hope is always with us*'

It was true. However well they prepared and however good their intelligence, in the end, all that they really had was hope.

As Grigori had predicted, throughout the day, not a single German patrol came close to them. At around eleven they heard the sound of engines and Martin spotted a column of German half-tracked troop carriers about five miles away, on the road that ran close to the coast, from Heraklion to Chersonios. Binoculars revealed them to be crammed with infantry. But the vehicles were soon obscured in the cloud of dust put up by their tracks and they vanished as quickly as they had appeared, clearly intent on their purpose, whatever it might have been.

Then, a little later in the day, in the middle of the afternoon, Fletcher – whose turn it was on watch – gave a low whistle, like a bird, three times. Hearing the signal, Hunter moved out of the church and ran, as fast as he was able, half doubled up, across to the lookout position in the long grass to the north. Fletcher pointed towards an olive grove further down the hill, in the direction of Knossos. At first Hunter saw nothing, and then it came into view. Two German motorcyclists were standing together beside their motorbikes, chatting to each other and smoking.

It was soon obvious that they had not seen anything suspicious up in the direction of the chapel, but had merely encountered each other on the narrow goat track that ran below the hills. Fletcher had been right to alert him, though, and Hunter put them all on a heightened state of readiness until the two men had parted and ridden off in different directions. Hunter stood the men down and they all went back to what they had been doing. But the episode was enough to remind them all of their purpose and to jerk them back to reality.

Zero hour crept ever closer and soon the atmosphere was noticeably charged with nervous agitation. At this point Hunter decided to play his trump card. They were all in the church, save Phelps, who was on sentry duty. He looked at his watch. It was two minutes away from 1800. An hour before they would have to leave. He stood up and walked to the altar. It seemed appropriate. 'Listen up, all of you. I have an important announcement to make.'

The men looked up and gathered round him. Woods looked quizzical. 'Hunter?'

'It's alright, Peter, this is my shout.' He paused, for effect. 'Right, there are two bottles of white wine in my valise. At Waterloo the men had gin, on the Somme it was rum. Well, we can go one better. And it's the good stuff. Enough for a good mug each. Shall we, gentlemen?'

There was a restrained, ragged cheer from the men, as

Hunter unbuckled the canvas valise and brought out two bottles that he had specifically asked Grigori to find for him. There were also three bars of Greek chocolate. He looked at Woods, who was shaking his head and smiling.

The men, Grigori among them, found their mugs and gathered round Hunter, who dispensed the wine as if he were a priest serving at communion. It was just enough. Too little to get anyone drunk, but sufficient to cheer you on your way and make the world seem somehow better. Hunter called Fletcher over to him. 'Bryn, go and stand in for Phelps, will you. Mustn't leave him out of it.'

'Sir.'

Fletcher left, clutching the mug with the remains of his own wine. This, thought Hunter, this was the way it should be. Comrades, together. Soldiers, united against a barbarian enemy and united in friendship. This was an unbreakable bond. Truly, he thought, they were a band of brothers. Phelps entered the church and stopped, looking at the others, gathered about the altar. Hunter saw him.

'Ah, Sid, there you are. Well done. There's wine. We saved you some. Find your mug. It's really very good.'

Phelps fumbled in his kitbag and drew out the tin mug, which, hesitantly, he handed to Hunter. 'I'm… I'm not sure, sir. Might blunt the senses. Wouldn't want to cock anything up. You know.'

'For heaven's sake, man. I'm not trying to get you rotten. It's just a mug of wine. Something before we go. And we don't go for another hour. And no one's going to cock anything up. Alright? Here.'

He pressed the mug of warm white wine into Phelps's hand and noticed that it was trembling. 'You alright?'

Phelps pulled away. 'Yes, sir. I'm fine. No problem. Just got a bit, cold out there.'

'Well. Get that down your neck. It'll warm you up. And stop bloody worrying.'

Phelps sipped at the wine and smiled. 'Thank you, sir. I... I didn't want to seem ungrateful.'

'No matter, Phelps. Don't worry. And remember what I said before. I'm here. I'm always here.'

The others had finished their wine and were chatting among themselves. Woods wandered over to Hunter. 'I saw that. That was a very clever thing you did just now.'

Hunter was surprised at the praise. Given their strained relationship, it had been the last thing he had been expecting from Woods. He played it down. 'Clever? Really, Peter? I wouldn't call it clever. It just sort of felt, well, right. The right thing to do.'

'Are you really worried about Phelps?'

'A little, yes. But he's just a bit windy. That's all. He'll be fine.'

'Really? Will he be fine? Are you quite sure? Not better to send White or Fletcher in his place?' Woods's tone had changed now. There was no doubt in his voice that he was the superior officer.

Hunter responded with equal candour, 'Wouldn't work. The others don't have his skills. And besides they don't even speak German.'

'Neither does Martin.'

'Yes, but he's the codebreaker. No. I think we have to take Phelps but we just have to keep a very close watch on him.'

Woods shook his head. 'Well, it's a mistake, if you ask me. You'll regret it. And if I could, I'd order him to stand down.'

Hunter shook his head, thinking to himself, *But you can't, can you. You may be my superior officer, but this is my show, and you know it.*

Woods seemed to sense his mood. He turned away and left Hunter to check his weapons.

And so they remained for the following hour, chatting and snoozing, until at length, Hunter looked at his watch and got to his feet.

'Righto. That's it. Time to go. Come on, chaps.'

The others rose and found their few pieces of equipment, strapping on webbing and belts.

Slowly, they left the church and bade adieu (not goodbye) to Woods, White and Fletcher who watched them go. They moved off down the hill, Hunter at the front, just behind Grigori, with behind him Russell, Phelps, Martin, Knox and Duffy, in a loose single file, which made them harder to see against the landscape.

They continued downhill, through the olive groves, skirting the small villages and farms on their way until after they arrived at a small hill just beyond the southern perimeter of the airfield. Grigori looked at Hunter. 'Alright, sir?'

Hunter nodded. Said nothing. For the briefest of moments he froze.

He was experiencing a strange feeling of déjà vu. Hunter had been here before, of course. That was one of the reasons he had been sent. But what he hadn't counted on was the fact that he had been to exactly this place before. Their approach to the airfield was precisely what had been his own route in and out of the camp in those halcyon days before the German airborne invasion. Here he had strolled down the track from this hill, sometimes arm in arm with one of the local girls, more than often after a few glasses of raki, dodging around the huts to reach the camp unnoticed.

And now here he was again, once again attempting to remain concealed. But the difference was that before there had been no real danger, other than a reprimand from the RSM and possibly a punishment. Now the odds were very different. Now they were all risking captivity, torture and death.

Snapping out of his musing, Hunter looked around. The Greek was talking: 'Alright, sir. I must go now.'

'Eh? Yes, Grigori. Sorry. Yes, of course.'

Grigori slipped away, back the way they had come, and vanished quickly into the night. Hunter tapped Russell on the shoulder and, needing no second command, the man crawled forward towards the wire.

Then Russell stopped and watched. For a good ten minutes he sat there in cover, some way forward from the others and at a little distance from the camp, with his eyes firmly fixed on their objective. 'Casing the joint', as he always put it, until the time was good. They had learnt of the guards' regular movements from Leigh Fermor's close briefing, but, like any good burglar, Russell just wanted to make sure of it.

Eventually, as satisfied as he would ever be, and moving nimble-footed, with all the ferret-like agility of a seasoned housebreaker, relishing every second, he insinuated himself further and further down the hill, right up to the perimeter wire and then, choosing his moment with care, he half stood up and cut a slit in the perimeter wire, six foot high. In width it was barely more than a few inches. Just enough to fold back with gloved hands. Just wide enough for a man to squeeze through, without snagging his clothing on the barbs. Having created their entrance, Russell then lay down as flat as he could, hugged the ground and waited.

For five minutes the wire lay open and Russell felt horribly exposed, knowing that if it were to be seen by a single passing sentry then the whole game would be up.

Never before had he felt so vulnerable. He began to imagine it unfolding in his mind. The sentry spotting the cut wire. The flashlight blinding him, shining on his face. The shout in German and then the burst of semi-automatic fire and the sickening pain as the bullets ripped open his abdomen. He was sweating hard now. He tried to move his mind away from it. But the image kept coming to him. He clasped his hands together and thought of home. Of Soho. Of the old time. Of Olga and the girls. He looked at the wire again. How could they miss it? How could they?

But no one saw it and, before Russell knew it, at the given time, the others were down there with him.

Hunter was first to arrive and Russell heard him padding down the hillside, and felt a sudden wave of relief sweep over him. Quickly, he turned to see him. Neither man spoke. Hunter nodded, pointed to the gap in the wire and gave him a thumbs up.

The others were close behind him. Hunter motioned them, silently to follow him through the gap, and this they now did. One by one, with Hunter leading the way, followed by Duffy and then the three privates – Russell, Phelps and Martin – along with Sergeant Knox. Once the last man was through, still watching for anyone who might have seen them, they carefully folded the wire behind them and walked nonchalantly towards one of the accommodation blocks.

Once again, Hunter led the way, walking with Duffy and talking quite clearly in his finest German, so as to be fully audible to anyone they passed. This he knew was the most audacious of all moments. His heart was thumping in his chest as they approached an area where several of the German garrison were chatting to each other and handing round cigarettes. One of them looked round and raised an eyebrow before giving them a curious stare.

For a moment, Hunter was unsure as to what to do. Then it happened. The man looking at him, a grizzled private, wearing an Afrika Korps uniform suddenly realised that Hunter was an officer and snapped to attention, throwing his cigarette to the ground, his arms rigid at his sides, before his right hand snapped up in the traditional Wehrmacht salute. The others, seeing him, followed suit. Hunter returned their salute, hand to head, in the old style and breathed an inward sigh of relief as Duffy did exactly the same. He was thankful too that the man hadn't used the Nazi stiff-arm salute. No SS here, perhaps, he thought.

The Germans remained rigid until the two 'officers' had passed and then relaxed, offering each other more cigarettes and not noticing the other saboteurs following on behind Hunter and Duffy.

As they neared the group, Hunter and Duffy split from the others, who now acted as if they had a task to carry out and moved off with purpose towards the administration block.

Hunter and Duffy meanwhile began a rehearsed conversation, in full sight of the group of German soldiers.

It was of course all quite intentional. For one thing, the two 'officers' spoke the best German and for another, if they were ever to be suspected then they would have to disassociate themselves from the others. There was also of course the obvious bluff in the fact that the men were carrying out the actual mission while their superiors were providing the diversion.

However it was intended to work, it seemed to do the trick, for soon the Germans who had been looking over at them returned to their own jokes and chatter. Hunter and Duffy slowly walked on, heading in the direction of the accommodation blocks where they knew the officers' mess to be located. This was the dangerous stuff. The last thing that they wanted to do was to get into a conversation with genuine enemy officers. Nevertheless, if they were to look like the real thing, they had to behave as if they were. Leigh Fermor, with his intense SOE training in deception, had stressed the importance of this moment when explaining the layout of the camp to them.

It had been agreed that once sufficiently far inside the camp, the team would split into two. While there was a ninety per cent chance of the file being in the commandant's office, as Leigh Fermor's source had suggested, there was still an outside possibility that it might still be in the signals office, part of which had apparently been heavily repaired with a new internal wall, having suffered badly in last year's fighting. It was located in an adjacent block to the commandant's and so, while four of the men would search the commandant's hut, the others would take the other option. If the file was in the signals office it would not be in a safe, so Knox as safe-cracker, was detailed to the commandant's hut, along with Phelps and Martin. Russell headed for the signals office, knowing that he would soon be followed by Duffy.

For the present time though, Hunter and Duffy continued their bogus conversation. Then, just a few moments later, Hunter glimpsed out of the corner of his eye, the welcome sight of Phelps, Martin and Knox, now on their own, heading for their target. He looked at Duffy and spoke in a barely audible whisper: 'Right. Looks like we're on. They've split up. Which means they weren't rumbled. You go and find Russell and get to the signals office. I'm off to help the others in the CO's hut.'

Duffy nodded, still in character, as if he might be smiling at a make-believe joke. Then he threw down his cigarette, ground it beneath the heel of his jackboot and walked slowly away from Hunter, looking at once terribly alone.

Hunter too felt isolated. This was another critical time, when the group was as fragmented as it ever would be. Being careful not to look behind or act at all suspiciously, he began to walk slowly towards the commandant's office.

As he approached the doorway, which was illuminated by a single bulb hanging in the porch, he was alarmed to hear voices. They were coming from inside the hut and they were emphatically German. His first thought was of Phelps, Martin and Knox. He wondered, with horror, if the three men were already inside. Had they been discovered? He tried to detect whether the German voices might be going in or coming out.

His second question was answered first as into the lamplight stepped two genuine German officers. One was wearing the uniform of the Wehrmacht, with a feldmutz and baggy riding breeches over boots. The other man though was dressed in black from head to foot, his uniform highlighted by silver trimmings and topped off with a peaked officer's service cap. He wore the ribbon of a Knight's Cross and on his collar he bore two distinctive silver lightning flashes. The central badge on his cap was a silver death's head. Good God, he was SS. Hunter hadn't been told by anyone about the possibility of an SS presence on the island, although he had suspected that there surely might be one. They knew that apart from the German garrison of fifteen to twenty thousand, there were also as many Italian troops on the island, who were entrusted with menial tasks and unimportant garrison duties.

Of the German presence though, they had been assured that the elite alpine troops who had taken the island had been replaced entirely with the sort of Wehrmacht infantrymen he had just encountered and a number of Luftwaffe ground troops who manned the large number of anti-aircraft guns that had made the island so impregnable to air attack. But SS? Surely Leigh Fermor would have known about them? He wondered how many there might be. A battalion? A brigade? He prayed not. Or could this officer be on his own? On a solitary mission, whatever that might be?

Hunter stayed as much as he could in the shadows, determined to avoid being seen by either officer. He decided that to back away would be conspicuous and so slowly turned round and started to stroll towards another of the huts. He could hear the two officers laughing behind him and presumed that he must have got away with it when from his right he heard a voice: 'Sir. Over here.'

Moving just his eyes, he caught sight of three familiar figures – Martin, Phelps and Knox. They were standing in a narrow gap between two huts. And were completely hidden in shadow.

Hunter winked at them, and signalling them with his hand to wait it out, continued to walk past them, retracing his steps until he reached the end of a hut and turned left. He stopped and breathed freely again, recovering his composure. There was no one around him now and he took the opportunity to quickly evaluate the situation. He could still hear the two German officers talking and laughing, back from the way he had just come. They must, he thought have left the commandant's office by now, as their voices were becoming distinctly more faint. And if they were gone then the coast must surely almost now be clear for Martin, Phelps and Knox. There would be just one man to come and join the commandant and that would be his aide-de-camp a Captain Finck, so their intelligence briefing had informed them.

Leigh Fermor's detailed intelligence had also stated that once the commandant had left his office at this same time every night, and headed for the mess and his customary pre-dinner cocktails, the door of the office would be closed behind him and only reopened after half an hour, when his ADC would return there, having had a single drink with his boss in the mess, and tidy away the affairs of the day, before locking the office for the night. This half hour was to be their only window of opportunity. They had just half an hour in which to get into the office, open the safe, find the file, wherever it was hidden, and anything else of use. They would then photograph anything extra of value, take the vital document and then close the safe, leaving it apparently just as it had been, beforehand, ready for the arrival of the ADC.

What happened after then would be up to Wilson and his men. When 8 Commando got here the whole place could be blown to blazes. What was vital was that, when he arrived, the commandant's ADC would not suspect that anything was missing or that anything had been tampered with. The idea being that in the likelihood of his surviving the raid, he would not report that a previous commando team had broken in and removed any intelligence. They had to leave the office exactly as it had been.

Hunter waited in the shadows, just to the left of the commandant's hut and a couple of minutes later saw a figure emerge and close the door behind him. Hunter watched carefully. He did not lock it. A German captain stepped into the light of the porch. That would be Finck. Having brushed himself down and straightened his service cap, the ADC walked away in the direction taken by the commandant, towards the officers' mess. Waiting until the man was almost out of sight, Hunter walked back towards where the three men were hiding and motioned to them to follow him. Then, one by one the four of them made their way to the door of the commandant's office. Martin went first, opening it slowly before moving quickly inside. The others waited.

After a few moments Martin reappeared and signalled the all-clear. Phelps and Knox entered and Hunter remained outside and lit a cigarette. There was little movement in the camp. A few guards were walking the perimeter and others were still in the mess while, from the sound of it, it seemed some were attending a movie show in one of the huts. From further away, towards the airstrips, Hunter could hear the sound of engines and presumed that ground crew were working on servicing the fighter-bombers.

It was, in all, a far calmer scene than he recalled when he had last been standing here, some sixteen months ago. He could still see the frantic attempts of the radar unit to destroy their equipment, as officers ran in all directions trying to restore order and to affect an orderly retreat as it became clear the Germans were about to surround them. The German bullets thudding into men around him, some of them his friends. He recalled talking to one of them one minute – Jock Thompson, a plasterer from Fife – and the next minute he had dropped to his knees, a sniper's bullet clean through his forehead. That couldn't have been more than thirty yards from where he was now. And he remembered the mortar rounds crashing in and throwing men into the air and the occasional whiz and crump of a huge 88 shell, fired horizontally, taking out an entire building or transforming a group of soldiers into a pile of bloody body parts and mutilated wounded, shrieking for their mothers or pleading for death.

Hunter lit another cigarette and as he did so, he realised that his hand was shaking. He thought of Phelps and how very fragile they all were. Then he tried to forget his own ghosts and to concentrate on the job in hand.

With Knox stationed in the narrow corridor leading from the front door, his Schmeisser at the ready, Martin and Phelps were now standing at the doorway of the commandant's personal office. Martin looked closely at the room from the doorway and then, very slowly entered. As he did so he looked around himself, taking in every detail he could. He walked to one wall and then back to the door, before walking to the opposite wall. Finally he walked to the window, opposite the doorway and then turned around. He moved to the commandant's desk and scanned every item on it with his eyes.

Phelps stood in the doorway and watched, looking

towards where Knox was standing on guard, all the time listening for the slightest footstep or warning noise of anyone approaching. There were none. But Phelps was sweating heavily now. Wishing that Martin would hurry up. But there was no hurrying him. This was a vital moment. Martin's extraordinary mind was assimilating the visual information before him and banking it in his brain so that when they left, everything could be set back just as it appeared now.

At last it appeared that Martin had finished. He turned to Phelps. 'Right, Sid. Come on. Look sharp. Go and fetch the sergeant.'

Phelps stared at him. Martin stared back. 'Sid. Snap out of it. Go and get Sergeant Knox.'

Phelps suddenly realised what was happening. 'Yes, thanks, mate.'

He turned and walked to the door and found Knox who saw his staring eyes and sweaty brow. 'You took your time. You alright, lad?'

'Yes, Sergeant. I'm fine. Martin wants you.'

'Righto. You stay here, lad, and listen out.'

Knox hurried past Phelps and into the office, where he found Martin. 'You'd better swap places with Phelps, Martin. Get him back in here. He's all over the place. No use to us, like that. You stand guard. Send him to me. Where the hell's Mister Hunter?'

Martin nodded and left the room. He found Phelps leaning against the wall of the corridor. He was breathing heavily.

'Come on, Sid. The sergeant wants you back with him. I'll take over here. Well, go on then.'

Phelps smiled at him and pushed past, hurrying back down the corridor to the office, where Knox was waiting.

The sergeant was kneeling on the ground in front of the safe, which stood in the far corner of the room. In one hand he held a stethoscope, which he had placed against the door of the safe, close to the combination lock. He was listening intently as Phelps entered. He looked up. 'Sshh. Not a sound.'

Phelps froze. Knox moved his other hand to the dial of the lock and very, very slowly and gently, began to rotate it. Phelps could hear it click as Knox moved it round from number to number, each click to him sounding louder and louder. Bound to bring the enemy crashing in on them.

Martin, standing on guard in the corridor, looked at his wristwatch. It was almost time. He listened at the front door of the hut and heard what he thought sounded like a footstep. Then another. A single man was approaching the hut. This was it. Martin slung his Schmeisser on his shoulder and drew his fighting knife, then, as quietly as possible, he moved to a position in the space where he knew the door would open and from where he could take the intruder by surprise. The handle of the front door began to turn and Martin got ready to move. As it opened, he tightened his grip on the cross-hatched hilt of the razor-sharp, double-edged dagger. The door was opening more fully now and a figure stepped inside, wearing the uniform of an officer in the Afrika Korps. Martin sighed with relief.

'Mister Hunter. Thank God it's you.'

Hunter quickly closed the door behind him. 'Martin. Where's Phelps? I thought he was on stag.'

'He was, sir. Change of plan. I've done what I had to do, first off. Sergeant Knox is busy with the safe – and Sid... Well, he just didn't look too good, sir. If you know what I mean.'

'Yes, I do know what you mean. Damn it. I should have

got here sooner. Right. You go and help them. Reckon they'll need you in a mo'. Once Sarn't Knox has done his stuff. I'll stand guard here. Give me your machine gun.'

Martin handed him the Schmeisser and went to find the others.

He walked in just as Knox managed to open the door of the safe. The sergeant looked jubilant. 'That's it. Got the bastard. There you go. Over to you, Harry.'

Martin smiled. 'My pleasure.'

He looked at Phelps. 'Right, Sid. Come on. Sooner it's done, sooner we're out.'

Knox, rummaging around in the safe, began to hand out documents. Sid Phelps had knelt down beside him now and took each of the documents as Knox handed them to him. He looked at them and in silence sifted through them, discarding the majority in a pile on the floor and passing the rest up to Martin.

The accountant was clinically methodical, analysing each piece as it appeared. He had produced the tiny camera from his pocket and was dutifully snapping every item, even though in Martin's case, of course, a camera wasn't really necessary.

While Knox and Phelps worked in silence, Martin had begun jabbering away quietly to himself, becoming increasingly excited by the sheer quality and quantity of all the material Phelps was handing to him.

'*Geheim. Geheim. Geheim.* It's all bloody secret, boys.' He showed one of the documents to Phelps. 'There you are, that one's for you, Sid. Blimey another one. Looks to me like a cipher code. Not my thing, thank God. You'd know more about that, Sid, wouldn't you. Bloody hell, this place is a right treasure trove. A regular Aladdin's cave, this is.'

Then he stopped. 'Oh, hang about a minute. What have we got here then? *Geheime Kommandosache*, this is. Top secret, brass hats only.'

He looked at it again and used the camera.

Knox pushed another bundle of papers at Phelps. ''Ere, lad. You cop these. This is the last lot. That's it. Where is the bloody thing? Sod it. Look, Sid, I'd just take the whole lot if I were you. Here. What do you say?'

Phelps took the bundle and began to sort through it, but then he felt the bottom of the pile and, realising that the paper there was somehow different, pulled it out and looked at it. It was a piece of blotting paper, stained with blue ink spatters. He was about to discard it when, on looking more closely, he realised that it was not one piece of blotting paper but two, which had somehow become stuck together. Intrigued he began to peel them apart and found between them another thin bundle of documents, typed on brown tracing paper. He ripped the blotting sheets apart and freed up the papers inside. He handed them to Martin.

Martin looked at them and suddenly froze. They were in English. He read the heading:

MOST SECRET   EYES ONLY   BIGOT
OPERATION GYMNAST
ALLIED INVASION OF NORTH AFRICA AND SICILY

For a moment Martin was lost for words. Then he found his voice: 'Christ, boys, this is it. Bigot. Gymnast. We've only gone and found the bloody thing. Sid, go and find Mister Hunter while we finish off here. Bloody hell, Sarge, we've done it. Sid, go on, get Mister Hunter.'

But Sid Phelps didn't move. Sid did nothing. Said nothing. Sid Phelps couldn't speak. Sid Phelps had panicked. Because Sid Phelps was afraid. Very afraid. Fear had gripped him early on and now it wouldn't let him go. He felt immobile. Lifeless. Unable to move at all. Sid Phelps was lost, drowning in fear.

It seemed to Phelps that he was thinking in slow motion. He felt calmer now. Just thinking. Someone, somewhere seemed to be calling out his name, but it didn't matter right now. Sid was thinking. He was thinking how it took him like this sometimes. About how he had always been prone to it. How as a boy he had suffered from dreadful nightmares and had woken up screaming. How the dogs had helped. His greyhounds. When he was with his dogs, his boys and girls, his greyhounds, everything had seemed alright. They had become his world. Had helped him with the endless, echoing emptiness.

Then he had met his Mary and everything had changed. And when they had had Robbie and little Daisy, life had been complete. Wonderful, wonderful Mary and his little ones. They seemed a million miles away. Another life, and another world. And so it was. For he knew that those days would never come again and after that Phelps's nightmares had returned and they were worse than he had ever known as a boy. And sometimes like now, they wouldn't just be in his sleep. He would be in a living nightmare. Would see their faces. The faces of Mary and the kids. There in front of him. Calling out to him for help. And when that happened, well then he just froze. He had told no one about it. The MO would have had him kicked out of the regiment. And that was the last thing he wanted. To feel useless.

He had volunteered for the commandos. Partly to try to

get involved and get rid of the nightmares, partly to avenge the deaths the bloody Jerries had caused. The deaths of his world. Mainly he wanted to kill them. He wanted them to feel his pain. But it hadn't worked. He had had a moment on the caique when they were getting ready to attack the German boat.

He had tried to conceal his fear behind a veneer of bravado. But it had crumbled all too quickly under pressure. He was sure that Hunter had seen it and that worried him. But Hunter had said nothing. The action had jolted him back to reality and in fact he had enjoyed the killing. Perversely, taking the life of one of the enemy made him feel human again. But now this. Phelps stared at the wall and said nothing.

It was Harry Martin who was the first to realise that something was badly wrong. 'Sid? Sid, mate, you alright?'

Phelps still said nothing. He was now staring at a photograph on the desk beside the safe. It showed an officer in a neat Nazi uniform sitting in a meadow in the lee of a mountain. Beside him was a pretty girl and between them a small blonde-haired child, a girl. She was wearing a white dress and had flowers in her hair.

Martin tried again: 'Sid. What's wrong, mate? You're as white as a sheet. Come on, snap out of it. We've done it. Now we've got to scarper, mate. Got to get out of here. Our time's almost up. Oh fuck it.'

Knox took charge. 'Martin, you go and get Mister Hunter.'

Martin ran out into the corridor, searching for Hunter.

Knox stood up and put a hand on Phelps's shoulder. 'Now, lad. Come on.'

Without warning, Phelps lashed out and brought the framed photograph crashing to the ground, smashing the glass. At that moment Hunter and Martin entered the room. Instantly Hunter bent over Phelps and picked him up, dragging him out of the room. Phelps made no attempt to resist, but hung limp and wide-eyed in Hunter's arms. From the doorway, Hunter turned to Martin and Knox.

'Martin, make sure you bring whatever it was you found. Too bad, when they see this mess but there's nothing we can do. Just make sure you've taken snaps of everything of any use and then stick it back in the safe. We've only got a few minutes before the ADC comes back. I'll get Phelps out and try to keep him out of sight. Just do whatever you can and get the hell out of here.'

Hunter left them, half-carrying Phelps, and as he left, Knox and Martin were already busy refilling the safe with papers. Martin folded the brown tracing sheets and tucked them into his pocket as Knox shut the safe door and turned the dial to lock it. Martin stared at the desk. The picture frame had knocked over a number of other objects and he delved into his memory to find their original positions. He straightened four pencils and moved a lead paperweight in the form of a swastika two inches to the right before slightly shifting the position of a crystal water glass. Knox watched Martin with fascination and moved towards the office door.

'Right, Harry, son. That's enough. Let's go.'

'But what about the picture and all that glass?'

'Too bad, mate. Perhaps they'll think they've got a ghost. Anyway by the time Captain Wilson and his crew have finished with this place it'll all be blown to atoms. Come on, let's get out of here.'

They left the office, crunching across shards of broken

picture glass and the shattered wooden frame. Their boots leaving dirty imprints on the photograph of the idyllic mountain scene. Mud and sand and broken glass had scarred the smiling faces of the perfect Nazi family.

On the other side of the compound, Duffy and Russell were lost. Duffy had found Russell some minutes ago and they had headed towards the signals hut that had been indicated on Leigh Fermor's plan. The plan had shown that the building was two blocks away and to the right of the commandant's office. But when they had got there it had turned out to be just another accommodation hut. Unsure as to what to do, they had turned around and walked straight into a group of Germans, who had offered Duffy a cigarette, which he had accepted. The man had wanted to chat. Had asked them their unit and Duffy had bluffed it out quite well, he thought. He had even spoken to him about his (bogus) hometown of Essen and they had discussed the local baker.

But the encounter had taken time and had also put them off course again and now they were desperately trying to find the line of huts they had been in before, at the same time as not arousing any suspicions. At last Russell found it and they strolled along the line of buildings, but none bore the slightest resemblance to a signals hut. Then, as they came to the end of the row, Duffy pointed. There, on top of the last building in the next row of huts was a radio aerial.

'That's it. There. We were in the wrong bloody row. Come on.'

They walked towards the hut but stopped dead as an SS colonel emerged from it. He turned back towards the building, clearly talking to someone inside. Duffy whispered, 'Bloody SS. That's not right. What the hell is he here for?'

Russell shook his head. 'Not a bloody clue.'

'Damn it. We'll never get in there now. They should all be shovelling scoff in their mess hall. What a balls-up.'

'Well, he's obviously got them on extra duties, hasn't he. Too bad, Bill. We had a go. Can't be helped.'

'We'd better get out of here a bit sharpish. Wonder if Mister Hunter's had better luck.'

'Well, I bloody hope so. Or all of this has been for nothing.'

11

Hauptman Eric Finck was in his element. He was having the most wonderful of evenings. As the recently appointed aide-de-camp to General Kellner, he had been singled out that day by his new CO for particular praise and had been invited by him to join not only the Herr General but his distinguished visitor, a highly decorated colonel in the Waffen-SS. They were to have cocktails in the mess, prior to dinner. Annoyingly, Finck's only chore now was that which he enjoyed the least. He had to leave the officers' mess and return to the commandant's office to tidy up. But, immediately that had been done he would go back and rejoin the general and his guest. He felt that he had been accepted as one of their number. Truly one of the elite.

All in all it promised to be one of the best nights Eric had ever known. How his dear mother would have loved to see him with them. She would be so very proud. And his father. His poor, dear father. Eric had never really known his father. Johannes Finck had lost a leg in the Great War, fighting the British on the Somme and on his return from the military hospital had eked out a hard living in Potsdam as a cobbler. A one-legged cobbler, for God's sake. Life had been unbelievably hard for them all under the outrageous terms of the Allied reparations and his father had cursed them all. First the French and the British, then the Americans and then all capitalists. Then his venom had been turned against the Communists and finally, and with most hatred in his eyes, against the Jews. And they all knew now of course that it was the Jews who were really to blame. For everything.

It had come as no surprise that his father had gone to an early grave. Still cursing. And then the Weimar Republic had come. Republic? How he had hated it. Democracy was the last thing that Germany had needed back then. The Führer had so clearly been the answer. Had brought them salvation. The Führer had saved the German people and given them back their honour.

And Eric, who like so many had suffered for so long, had suddenly thrived. And now here he was, a friend of the general. A friend of a distinguished SS colonel. A man of substance. A man with a golden future.

Eric entered the commandant's office and suddenly stopped. He stood in the doorway for a moment. Then he saw the smashed picture on the ground. And in a moment Eric's wonderful evening was as shattered as the broken picture glass.

It didn't take him that long to form some sort of idea of what had happened. Someone had been here. Someone had broken into the commandant's office. But who? Who could possibly have done this thing and, more importantly, why? And what exactly was missing? At first sight, he thought, not much. In fact, bizarrely, apart from the smashed picture, everything else appeared to be in precisely the place in which it had been put by the general himself. It was all very strange. He simply couldn't understand what had happened.

Finck ran out into the night, saw a guard, and then an officer, an Afrika Korps captain he didn't recognise. He shouted to him, 'Hauptman. Run to the officers' mess. Find General Kellner immediately. Tell him his office has been broken into. But nothing's missing.'

The officer nodded and ran off towards the officers' mess block.

Finck turned away and walked back inside the commandant's office and as he did so, unseen by Finck, the DAK officer he had ordered to tell the general to come at once, changed direction and ducked down a gap between two of the blocks, followed by one of the guards.

Martin smiled at Knox and Hunter, 'Blimey. That was good, sir. That Jerry captain thought you were the real thing.'

'Yes, but now the game's up and we're only playing for time. And we're bloody lucky he didn't rumble me. Phelps, you alright?'

'Yes, sir, better now.'

'Good.'

He turned to Martin. 'Keep an eye on him, Harry. Right all of you. Come on.'

He left the passage and carried on walking, followed by the three men, trying to make for the direction of the area of the wire where they had got in. Several of Finck's words kept resounding in his mind, most notably: 'Nothing's missing.' Thus far they hadn't clicked that the safe had been opened. That at least was reassuring. More of a problem was that the element of surprise had been blown. Wilson and his men would arrive soon, at the appointed time, and the camp would be crawling with guards, all of them on the alert. And what then?

At that moment, just as Hunter and the others were trying to make their way to freedom, Eric Finck had turned and gone back into the commandant's office. He looked again at the scene. Tried to work it out. What was there in here that would have justified such a break-in? Had the intruders planted a bomb? Finck bent down and scanned the floor for trip wires. Nothing. He felt gingerly under the desk and then ran his hand along the tops of the desk drawers. Nothing appeared to have been tampered with.

He looked around the safe and then stopped. The safe. Of course. That was it. Someone might have broken into the safe and ransacked their files. Even, he supposed, the ones they hadn't yet deciphered. British commandos. It must have been them. It was obvious. But they had been clumsy. One of them had knocked over the picture and surely the noise must have alerted the guards? And why hadn't they blown the place up when they had gone? Nothing made sense. Perhaps the general would have an answer.

But it took another ten minutes before Finck realised that the general wasn't coming back. And a moment after he did realise, all hell broke loose.

Finck began to yell. They had been attacked by commandos. By damned British commandos. Gangsters the Führer called them. Not soldiers at all. Not honourable men. They came by night and fought dirty. If caught they were to be shot. And it looked as if at least one of these bastards was dishonouring the German uniform. Had had the gall to dress as a DAK officer.

Finck alerted the guards to stop any officer of the Afrika Korps. He had no idea what they wanted or what they had done. But he knew that they were somewhere in the camp. And he knew too that he had to do all he could to find them. And to kill them.

Hunter was walking as slowly as he could now. Which was almost impossible, as he was at the same time trying to stop himself from shaking with fear.

The night was still relatively quiet. Perhaps his ruse had worked. Perhaps the general was still at dinner and the ADC hadn't been believed. Perhaps they had got away with it. Perhaps...

At that moment a siren went off, wailing into the night. It was followed by another, and another. And with their wailing, Hunter's hopes vanished. This was it. The ADC had raised the alarm. It was now of no matter what General Kellner thought. The SS man, whoever he was, would of course relish all this. Hunter carried on walking. That was the only way they would get out. Bluff it out.

Everywhere around him were German guards, running in all directions, looking for orders. Thankfully, as yet, they seemed to be taking no notice of him. To his left were Martin and Phelps. Somewhere over to his right was Sergeant Knox. But God knew what had happened to Duffy and Russell. He looked again across to Martin and Phelps. Wondered if Phelps was in trouble again. His reason conquered by fear. At least he was moving alongside Martin. Propelled by the other man's momentum. Hunter knew that he would snap out of his funk eventually. But when? All that he could hope was that when his mood did change, Phelps wouldn't panic and run. He had to act as calm as possible. For now, more than ever, was the time when they had to behave as if they were really part of the garrison.

Hunter carried on walking. Saw over on his right, Russell emerge from behind a building, walking, just as he was, as if he was a part of the place and knew exactly where he was going. Trying desperately to look as if he had been given an order to carry out. Walking with a purpose. That was the trick they had all been taught at Athilt. *Get a brass neck*. Bluff it out. He kept on repeating the four words to himself, over and over in his head.

Where, he wondered was Duffy? Hunter had now seen all of the others. So why then was Duffy nowhere to be seen? He was dressed as a German officer. If that bloody ADC had realised that Hunter was a fake, and had spread the word, the guards would also think that Duffy was an imposter. Everyone would be looking for any officer wearing a feldmutz and riding boots. Hunter felt suddenly utterly exposed. He was naked.

Quickly, he removed his headdress and, rolling it up, pushed it into one of the pockets of his tunic. Less conspicuous now, he thought. Better without the hat. Much better. Still moving in the general direction of the gap in the wire, he began to look again for the others. Realised that Knox was suddenly beside him. The sergeant spoke quietly, 'Sir. We've got to get away from here, before it's too late.'

'Sarn't Knox. Thank God. Any sign of the others?'

'I lost track of Martin and Phelps a little while back down that line.' He pointed. 'Haven't seen Russell at all, not since the off. Duffy's over there.'

Hunter looked and saw Duffy coming towards them. He was running and mouthing something initially inaudible. At last Hunter caught it. Breathless: 'Did you hear what I said, sir? There are three SS officers going around, telling the guards to arrest any man in Wehrmacht or Afrika Korps officers uniform. Looks like you and me are their prime targets, sir.'

Hunter put a hand on Duffy's shoulder. 'Don't panic, man. There are three thousand men around this bloody airbase. How many officers is that? About a hundred and fifty, I should think. You just can't arrest that many officers.'

'Sir?'

Hunter smiled. 'The men wouldn't like it.'

Duffy managed a grin. Hunter went on, 'It's just the SS flexing their muscles.'

Knox cut in, 'But what about just this compound, sir? There must only be about twenty officers in here. Twenty-five at the most. I reckon Duffy's right. We really are in the shite, sir. Aren't we?'

Hunter looked at him. 'We're not dead yet, Sarn't.'

He looked back at Duffy. 'Anything in the signals hut?'

'Couldn't get into it, sir. Wasn't where it was marked on the bloody plan. And then when we did find it a bloody SS colonel was using it. Sir, what are SS doing here? We weren't told about that, were we?'

'No, Duffy, we weren't.'

Why, thought Hunter, was he not surprised either about the plan or the SS colonel? Much of their intelligence had proved wonky. He carried on, 'No matter. We've found what we came for. Where's Russell?'

'Don't know, sir. He just vanished.'

'Damn. Right. Everyone head for the gap in the wire. Right. Go.'

No sooner had he uttered the words than they were gone. Hunter followed them, carrying on straight towards their entry point, trying all the time to stick to the shadows and hug the walls of the huts.

They had been walking for a while now and at last Hunter could see the tiny gap in the wire where they had entered the camp. Finck had turned on the emergency searchlights and the base was now lit up as bright as midday. Incredibly though, while the rest of the compound was bathed in light, the area of ground to the south, behind the accommodation blocks, had remained almost pitch-black. It was the devil's own luck. Thank God he was on their side.

Hunter motioned quietly to Knox. 'Look, there. That's where we came in. And it's as black as pitch.'

Knox peered into the night. 'That's a stroke of luck, sir.'

'I'll say. We've not had much luck tonight.'

'We found the intel, sir. I'd call that a bit of luck.'

'You're right, Sarn't. Of course.'

As usual Knox looked on the positive side. Even at times like these the couthy Glaswegian was an optimist.

They began to walk closer to the gap in the wire. But, not wanting to give the game away, Hunter whispered, 'No. Not all together. Best to peel off, get away from it and then go out one by one. I'll lead the way.'

He used his fingers to signal the timings. 'Five, ten, fifteen. Right.'

The men nodded and all began to walk in different

directions, more quickly now, as if they were themselves intent on catching the saboteurs. Hunter looked at his watch. It was 2135 hours. Five minutes beyond the agreed time for Wilson's force to go in. He could only presume that Wilson had arrived at his laying-up place and, seeing the mayhem in the camp, had decided to call it off. It would, Hunter knew, have been his own reaction. A small group of commandos had no chance at all against a camp that was on full alert. What a bloody cock-up. Woods had been right. They should have left Phelps at the church. He should have known himself that the man was wobbly the minute he had spotted him with the shakes on the boat. It was all his own fault. At least they had come away with the documents and now they had to get them back to GHQ.

Hunter began to retrace his steps, walking a little more slowly until he found a chance to slip into the shadow behind one of the blocks closest to the perimeter wire. He looked at his watch again and watched the hand move closer, then at precisely 2140 he moved to the gap and pulling it open, managed to squeeze through.

Hunter dropped to the ground and lay flat for a few moments, before crawling slowly through the grass and up the incline, making sure all the time that he was as much as possible in cover. He managed at length to find a rock and curled himself up behind it and waited for the others.

From the blackness behind him he heard a sudden noise and turned, gun at the ready. There was another rustling and then a voice spoke in a whisper, 'Hello, sir.'

Grigori peered at him through the night, his line of cracked teeth a gleaming line of white.

'Grigori. I could have killed you.'

'No, sir. But you are late. Very late. I was here before. I saw the Germans running. Something's wrong?'

'Yes, something's wrong. Very wrong.'

'And the other British soldiers? Captain Wilson's men? They are not coming? No bombs?'

'No, Grigori. I'm sorry, no bombs. Not tonight. We've had… a few problems.'

The two men peered through the darkness towards the base and after a few more minutes Hunter saw a shape in the shadows pass through the gap.

They waited and a few moments later, Knox was at his side.

'Sir.' He spotted Grigori and smiled. 'Good to see you again.'

They watched again and after a short time another shape appeared at the wire. Two shapes and then one again. It was hard to make out what was happening. Before they knew it though, Martin was crawling towards them.

Hunter looked at him, narrowing his eyes. 'Hold on, where are the others. Where's Duffy? Martin, I thought Phelps was with you?'

'He was, sir. Isn't he with you? I took him right up to the wire and pushed him through the gap. Then I went off back inside, like you said and then I came back and up here. The bloody fool must have gone back in there just after I did.'

Hunter shook his head. 'I don't bloody well believe it. What the devil was he thinking? Christ almighty.'

'What shall we do, sir?'

'Well we can't just leave the poor bugger in there. The man's lost his nerve. Either they'll kill him or they'll torture him and if he cracks, we've all had it.' He thought for a moment.

'There's only one thing we can do. I'll have to go back and get him out. And Duffy's gone AWOL too. And where the hell's Russell?'

Hunter had faith in Russell to somehow find his way out. He was naturally resourceful. And he was wearing an 'other ranks' uniform. Duffy, on the other hand, was a very different sort altogether. Not nearly as wily or street-wise as the ex-burglar and with a tendency to hesitate that might, thought Hunter, just cost him his life. Plus he had the added disadvantage of wearing an officer's uniform.

Hunter turned to Martin. 'Harry, you've still got it, haven't you? The document?'

Martin tapped his breast pocket. 'Yes, sir. Safe and sound. And I've got the camera, with the snaps.'

'Good. Right, well you'd better scarper. The pair of you. And Grigori. Get back to Captain Woods at the church as quick as you can and tell him what's happened. And make sure you tell him that the bloody SS has turned up. And that as far as we know, Captain Wilson's decided to hold off his raid.'

Knox protested, 'Sir, don't you think it would be better if we were to stay here with you? One of us at least, sir?'

'No Knox, I don't. The important thing is to get that intelligence back safely.' He paused, hoping that they would understand. 'Right. I meant it. Get going and don't look back. Anyway, I'll be better on my own. And make bloody sure that Captain Woods knows not to wait for me beyond the agreed time. It's absolutely vital that we get that document back to Cairo.'

Reluctantly, led by Grigori, they turned away and Hunter watched briefly as the three men crawled uphill through the long grass before they broke into a crouching trot and disappeared over the first ridge. Then he turned back towards the camp. Somewhere down there were three more of his men and he meant to get them out.

As far as he could see, not much had changed in the last fifteen minutes. Which, he thought, could only be a good thing. The place was still in mayhem. He spotted a group of five Wehrmacht officers being held at gunpoint and realised that the SS were thoroughly enjoying attempting to fulfil their commander's order of rounding up every suspect Wehrmacht and Afrika Korps officer in the place. It suddenly occurred to him that he should have asked one of the two men he had just sent off to swap tunics with him. But then of course that would have put one of them in greater danger and in any case he doubted whether either of their tunics would have fitted him.

Moving slowly and hardly making a sound, Hunter slid back down the hillside to the gap in the wire and, hardly believing what he was doing, held it aside and pushed himself back into the compound, into the very jaws of danger.

Once inside, he straightened up, staying in the shadows, and moved behind the closest building. He felt horribly conspicuous and wondered if there was anything he might do to disguise the officer's uniform. He had seen a few of the guards in greatcoats and it occurred to him that if he could find one that would solve his most pressing problem. He stayed for a few minutes in the shadows, watching until a man in a greatcoat approached his hiding place, which he realised was adjacent to a latrine block. Hunter waited until the man went inside and then readied himself. Gently, he placed his Schmeisser on the ground in the space between two huts and then moved slowly and silently to the back of the latrine hut. He walked up the two steps and closed the door behind him, before drawing his fighting knife from its scabbard on his belt. The man was nowhere to be seen, but one of the latrine stalls was clearly occupied and its door shut.

Hunter stood inside the other stall and waited. After a couple of minutes the sound of an overhead flush came from the neighbouring stall and the door began to open. The man emerged and, as he did so, reached to pick up his greatcoat from the top of the door. Hunter moved quickly. In the briefest of moments he was behind the German and plunged his blade into his neck at the base of his skull, where the head joined the neck. It cut the brain stem. Death was instantaneous and the man slumped almost silently to the floor of the cubicle. Hunter reached over the body for the coat, before moving fast to the door, quickly donning the coat and making his exit.

Outside he closed the door and stood there calmly for a little less than a minute, before stepping down on to the gravel and walking away. Already he felt less conspicuous. He took out his feldmutz and placed it on his head. It was of the same design as an 'other ranks' cap and, with it worn in combination with his newly acquired greatcoat, he knew that he would blend in more effectively.

Now all that he had to do was to find Phelps, Duffy and Russell. He walked from the latrine block towards the accommodation huts, in the hope that his men might have again taken refuge in the dead space between them, but wherever he looked he saw no one. Where the devil were they? It was impossible for three men to simply disappear. In particular, he was concerned about Sid Phelps, who in his occasionally catatonic state might be capable of anything.

He decided to make circuits of the camp in ever-decreasing circles, thinking that this might somehow bring him into contact with one of them and was just starting in on the second of these loops when he heard from directly to his rear, a sudden, abrupt shout, in German: '*Halte*.'

Afraid and partly convinced that the command must have been intended for him, Hunter swung round to look and saw immediately that it was not. Some thirty yards away, across the compound, two black-uniformed SS soldiers were standing with their Schmeissers poised, both aiming at the figure of a lone German Wehrmacht officer. But it was no German. It was Duffy. And he looked utterly terrified.

In that same moment Duffy caught sight of Hunter and as soon as he did, he looked away from him, afraid that his line of sight might reveal the lieutenant's position. Hunter stared at him, powerless to act. The two SS men approached Duffy and motioned with their guns that he should raise his hands while at the same time telling him to do so, in German. Duffy did as they asked and they closed in on him as around them in the camp, similar isolated scenes were being played out with genuine German officers being arrested. Close to Duffy, a number of guards stopped to watch. One of the SS, a sergeant, went up to Duffy and it looked to Hunter as if he must be asking for his papers. Duffy reached into his top pocket and produced the counterfeit *ausweis* and other bogus identification documents, with which they had all been issued.

The sergeant looked at them and then passed them to his colleague who examined them and shrugged before passing them back. The sergeant took the papers and then, rather than returning them to Duffy, put them in his own pocket. Now Hunter was really beginning to worry.

Shouting further sharp commands in German, the SS sergeant motioned to Duffy to move forward before him and at the same time to keep his hands in the air. Duffy walked away, in front of the two men, whose guns were now levelled with his back. It was horribly clear to Hunter what was going on. They were taking him off for interrogation and they both knew exactly what that meant. For a moment it crossed Hunter's mind to open fire and even perhaps to shoot Duffy. But he did nothing. Even if Duffy was dead, and unable to be tortured into giving away secrets, he himself was still a problem. And what of Phelps and Russell?

Then Hunter saw Phelps. He was standing beside one of the accommodation blocks, close to a group of Wehrmacht soldiers, and he too was staring straight at Duffy. Phelps's face was a white mask of terror. Slowly, Hunter edged towards him. Most of the troops around them were now watching the unfolding drama with Duffy and for a moment the figure of a single man in a greatcoat moving among them caused no comment. Hunter was getting closer to Phelps now, almost beside him. He tried to catch his eye, but his gaze was fixated on Duffy as he was marched away. Finally, Hunter moved next to Phelps and touched him lightly on the arm. Phelps looked round and seeing the lieutenant's face, froze. For an instant the two men stared at each other and then a voice broke the silence around them. And it spoke in perfect English: 'Halt. Do not attempt to move. If you move, I will shoot you both.'

Turning towards the speaker, Hunter found himself staring into the eyes of a young German officer. It was the aide-de-camp.

Hauptman Eric Finck spoke again: 'It's you. You are the

one. You are the one who did not tell my general. You are the damned British commando.' He looked at Phelps. 'You too. You are his accomplice. And you are both in German uniform. You will be shot. It is the Führer's order.'

Instantly, the men standing next to Phelps moved in. There was nothing to be done.

Forty yards away, directly in front of Hunter and Phelps, Duffy's captors had stopped momentarily and turned to see what was happening behind them. It was the chance that Duffy needed. Without hesitation, he turned and dealt the SS sergeant a huge, swinging uppercut that connected with his chin and, amplified as it was by the sharpened solid brass knuckleduster that Duffy had just attached to his hand, it smashed through the bone and ground into the man's jaw, sending teeth and blood flying from his mouth. The sergeant crumpled to the ground and as he did so, the other SS man swung round towards Duffy and gently squeezed the trigger of his Schmeisser.

It was only a half burst. Duffy didn't know what hit him. His body was raked diagonally by twenty rounds from the lethal semi-automatic, which, at point-blank range, almost cut him in half. His eyes staring wide in shocked disbelief, Duffy collapsed in his own blood and died in moments. Across the yard, Finck turned instinctively to see what was going on and for a brief second Hunter was almost on him. But it was too late. Even as his right hand reached out to level his own gun, two of the Germans standing beside him had ripped his weapon from his hands and pinned his arms behind him.

As the SS man who had shot Duffy bent down to help his wounded sergeant, Finck spun round to face Hunter. He was smiling. 'You see. So shall die all commandos. You're vermin.

Gangsters. Not fit to wear any uniform, far less than our own that you now dishonour. Take off your coat!'

The soldiers released Hunter's arms and he unbuttoned the greatcoat and removed it. Finck laughed and nodded. 'I knew it. You're a spy. You pass yourself off as an officer of the DAK. Who are you? What is your name?'

Hunter said nothing.

'No matter. Soon you will tell us everything we need to know.'

He nodded to the men around Hunter to restrain him and looked at Phelps. 'You too. You are one of them.'

Phelps was silent. Unable to speak.

Finck struck him across the face with the back of his hand. 'You dare to look at me in defiance. We shall see how long you remain defiant.' He turned to a sergeant who was among the men holding Hunter and Phelps. 'Take them to the colonel. I will follow. I need to clear up this mess.'

He nodded in the direction of Duffy's body.

Each of them escorted by four German guards, Hunter and Phelps were frog-marched away. Their route, either deliberately or by chance, took them past Duffy's body and Hunter cast a last, regretful glance down at his dead comrade. Finck was kneeling beside Duffy. He had pulled open the dead man's tunic and, his hands covered in blood, was rifling through anything he could find inside. He wasn't going to have much joy, thought Hunter. All of them had absorbed the lessons of the training school and had taken care not to bring any genuine personal documents. All that Finck was going to find were whatever of Duffy's fake papers hadn't already been taken by the sergeant, a map of the island, a book of Greek phrases, a bar of chocolate, a purse of twenty gold sovereigns and a 500,000-drachma note, both of which he presumed the young captain would be quick to pocket for himself.

He saw that he had already appropriated Duffy's fighting knife, the coveted commando dagger, which was lying beside his body and also his beret, which he had, like all of them, hidden in one of his pockets as the only means of identifying himself as British, when the moment came. For Duffy that moment would never come.

Hunter hoped that Phelps would not look at Duffy's mangled body, but knew that he would be drawn to it regardless and that the sight of it was bound to have a profound effect upon the man's already shredded nerves. He could only imagine now what Finck had in mind for the two of them and dared not contemplate their fate at the hands of the SS colonel. How, he wondered, would Phelps possibly cope with what was coming?

Russell had seen and heard everything. He was standing in the narrow space between two of the huts just to the left of where Duffy had been shot. When Duffy had gone to punch the SS sergeant, Russell had had to stop himself from shouting out to him. Had been desperate to tell him not to try anything. But he had known what would happen. So he had managed to hold his silence and keep absolutely still as it all happened before him. Now Duffy was dead and as he watched from his cramped hideout, he saw Hunter and Phelps being marched away, taken prisoner. He hadn't seen either of the others and hoped to God that they at least had managed to get away. As for the mission, it was anyone's guess what had happened.

He knew that Wilson's commandos should have attacked the base by now, but guessed that they too must have seen events unfold and had decided to call it off. The question now was what should he do himself?

It occurred to him that, given the fact that he was still well armed and had not yet been wounded, his duty might be to attempt to help Hunter and Phelps get away. His only problem with this was that, given the fact he was wearing enemy uniform, were he too to be caught, he would almost certainly be tortured and shot, as they were now sure to be.

Russell weighed up all the options and after a few minutes came to his decision. Then, taking great care not to be observed, he left the narrow hiding place and quickly leant against the rear wall of one of the buildings, where he reached into his hand and pulled out a packet of German cigarettes. He flipped open the lid and lit one, then took a long drag and looked around. Waiting. Sure enough, it was only a few moments before a senior sergeant appeared and seeing Russell shouted at him, in German, 'Hey there. You. Put that cigarette out and get over here, on the double. We're still looking for the others you know.'

Russell, his German perfect, muttered a hasty '*ja*' and stubbed the cigarette out on the ground, before picking up his weapon and hurrying over to the sergeant major. As Russell drew closer, the man took a closer look at him.

'Who are you? Where are you from? I don't remember you.'

Russell replied, taking care not to use the cultivated German that he had originally been taught by the contessa, but the more provincial dialect that Hunter had told him about. 'Private Wulpert, sergeant major. I'm with the new bunch, sir. We only arrived this morning. From the mainland. To replace 322 regiment.'

The sergeant nodded. Seemed happy enough with the answer. After all, it was true. Just that morning 322 had been posted to join Rommel in North Africa and to replace them a few dribs and drabs had arrived on the island. This man must be one of them. No enemy commando would know the exact date and details of such an irrelevant troop movement, would he? God knew, he hadn't heard about it himself until this morning. Communications here were less than useless. Nobody gave a damn. They'd all got too sloppy. No wonder they'd been taken by surprise. He addressed Russell, his accent that of a manual labourer from industrial north Germany.

'Right then, Private Wulpert. Get yourself along to the perimeter gate. There's a search party going out in ten minutes and you've just volunteered for it. Right? We've got to find those bloody commandos. Can't let them get away. The captain's in a filthy mood and I can't see the CO being too happy about it all, neither.'

He paused and looked again at Russell's appearance, moving his gaze from top to bottom and back again. For a moment Russell thought that the game might be up. He needn't have worried. After some consideration, the sergeant spoke. 'Christ you lot are a bloody shower, aren't you. I'll smarten you up, my lad. Just you wait. I'll tell you something, Sergeant Franz Neuer won't tolerate sloppiness in his unit. See? Can't abide it. Right, what are you waiting for? Get moving.'

Russell could hardly believe his luck. Firstly to have been taken as a genuine German soldier by a senior sergeant-major and then for the same man to actually have sent him to go to the perimeter and out through the gate was more than he might have hoped for. The man had even given Russell his name! He hurried over to the gate and found two squads getting ready to leave in pursuit of the commandos. Noticing that while one was made up of ten men and the other of just nine, Russell went towards the second and found the sergeant. 'Private Wulpert, sir. Sergeant Neuer sent me. I'm from the new intake. Arrived this morning.'

The sergeant looked at him. 'Are you? I've never seen you before.'

Russell didn't move. Perhaps he had gone too far. Perhaps he'd muddled his accent. The sergeant spoke again. 'Neuer sent you, did he? Really? Is he having a laugh? Well, too bad. If Neuer says to take you, then we'll just have to take you. Right then, fall in with the rest of them. We're going to fan out and all of you, keep your eyes peeled. They're a shifty lot these bloody commandos. You never know when they'll pop up behind you and slit your throat. Keep on your guard. Alright?'

Russell joined the rear of the squad and they filed out through the gate. None of the men spoke. He could see why. Then one of them whispered to him, 'You know, this whole thing was bloody inconvenient. I mean there we were. Just eaten, there's a great film showing in the hut, *Anuschka*. Really, a great movie. And then, bang, out of nowhere, a load of bloody British commandos drop in and mess up your evening. I tell you, my friend, it's just bloody irritating. Bloody gangsters. What does a man have to do? I've been looking forward to that movie for weeks. She's gorgeous, that Hilde Krahl. The real thing.'

Russell nodded. 'Yes. You said it. She's a real piece of skirt.'

The soldier offered him a cigarette. 'Turkish. Very good.'

Russell accepted with a well-spoken '*Danke*' and tucked it behind his ear.

Slowly, the squad to the right, and then the other, including Russell, to the left, they climbed the path that led either side of the road into the aerodrome and headed into the hills. After a few yards as the sergeant had directed, they fanned out until there was a long line of twenty men, five metres from each other, trudging through the rocks and scrub, weapons levelled, at the ready. Ready, thought Russell, with an ironic smirk, to shoot the 'bloody gangsters'.

12

The night was at its darkest now and out on the hill above the searchlight-bright airfield, the men of the German search parties were all finding it heavy going, as they advanced steadily in extended line, further and further into the unpredictable, rocky terrain countryside. Moving with them, Lennie Russell had been trying for the last twenty minutes to work out a plan that would allow him to slip away from his squad when the man to his right gave a cry.

'Damn. Help me.'

Russell moved across to find him in the darkness and saw the figure of the German guard who had spoken to him earlier, rolling on his back and clutching his right foot.

'Ahh, Christ. I think I've broken it. My ankle.'

Russell bent down to look and carefully felt around the man's right ankle. The German let out another anguished cry.

Russell spoke to him in perfect German. 'Hard to tell. It might just be a sprain. Can you walk?'

'No, not without help. No, I can't.'

'Right. There's only one thing for it. I'll have to help you back. You can't go on like this.'

The squad leader was nearing them. 'What's wrong?'

Russell spoke: 'It's his ankle. Probably just a sprain. But I think it might be broken. Either way he can't go on, Sergeant. Shall I take him back and rejoin you?'

'Alright. That would be best. But be quick and bring another man with you. We can't afford to lose these bloody gangsters. Anyway, there should be two more squads moving up the hill behind us. Why don't you just hand him to one of them and then catch us up?'

Russell nodded. 'Yes, Sergeant. That's what I'll do. I'd better get a move on.'

The German sergeant gave Russell a pat on the back. 'Right, lad. Good thinking, well done.'

Russell bent over the injured man and gently helped him to his feet, allowing his weight to fall on his left-hand side. Russell couldn't believe his luck. Here was the ideal opportunity and it had been handed to him on a plate. Slowly he helped the man away from the squad, back down the hill, in the general direction of the airfield. It was hard going in the dark and twice he almost lost his own foothold. Gradually though, he managed to steer the man over to the right, away from both the squad and the camp. The German was in too much pain to notice at first, until they had lost sight of the squad. He muttered, 'Are you sure we are going in the right direction? The lights of the camp. They look smaller to me, I think.'

Russell calmed him. 'No, no, it's an illusion, my friend. We're getting closer now. It's just the pain doing it. Don't worry.'

They carried on and, at length, Russell managed to steer them on to a level contour, so that they were no longer going steeply downhill. But the German was becoming increasingly agitated. 'Where are we going? Where are you taking me? I can hardly see the camp now. Where are we going?'

Russell whispered to him through the darkness, 'I think we need to stop.'

Russell gently lowered the German to the ground and placed his head against a rock. There was hardly any moonlight and what there was, was obscured by the towering forms of several tall cypress trees. The man looked down at his ankle. Tried to see it. 'It's so sore. Christ, it hurts so badly. I can't see it. Can you see it? It's so dark here. Have you a light?'

Russell said nothing. He readied himself to make his move and as he did so his heart began to beat hard in his chest, so hard that it seemed to pound in his head. Adrenalin pumping, he began to move. Everything, every action, seemed to happen in slow motion as he silently slipped his fighting knife from its scabbard with his right hand. Trying to recall in detail everything he had been taught in the fighting school at Athilt, Russell moved fast, slipping swiftly behind the supine German, very quickly and with great dexterity. His whole body was horribly tense as, trembling, he knelt down behind the man and plunged the knife into his neck. The cut made, he started to recall everything and pushed it hard in for what he thought must be about an inch and a half. Then, quickly, he cut the man's throat from left to right, severing the carotid artery. There was a sudden rush of thick, dark blood, followed by the gurgling of air escaping the severed trachea. Sounding almost like a cry for help, it lasted for a few ghastly moments and was followed by more blood, thinner but in a powerful spray. Then there was silence.

Russell's pumping heart was slowing down and his hands

no longer trembled. He wiped the blood from them and from his knife. The German lost consciousness in five seconds and was dead within twelve. And Russell knew that he had got it right.

Just as Russell was finishing off covering the German's body with branches and brushwood, down in the airfield camp the situation had begun to develop and things were not looking any more promising for Hunter and Phelps. In fact, Hunter had to admit it to himself, it was hard to remember a time when things had looked bleaker.

He and Phelps had been marched through the compound, to the commandant's hut, and back into the very room where they had broken into the safe, what now seemed an age ago. The floor was still covered with the broken picture glass, although someone had picked up the photograph and placed it against the swastika paperweight on the commandant's desk. The commandant himself was not yet there and they were being held in a small anteroom by two armed guards who had made them stand against opposite walls with their hands behind their heads.

Hunter turned his head to look at Phelps. 'Phelps, you alright?'

There was no reply.

He tried again: 'Phelps?'

One of the guards pushed Hunter in the small of the back, painfully. 'Shut up. No talking.'

Phelps spoke: 'Fine, sir. I'm fine.'

The guards struck Phelps on the shoulders, making him groan. 'I said no talking. Bastard.'

Neither man spoke again as they stood there for the next ten minutes. Their position against the wall was by now becoming quite uncomfortable and Hunter had begun to wish that what he knew to be the inevitable would come sooner rather than later. As if in answer to his prayer, at that moment the door opened and the commandant entered. Both of the guards snapped to attention. Colonel Hans Kellner walked towards Hunter and stood directly behind him.

'So. What have we here? English commandos in the uniforms of the Third Reich. This is not something we see every day, is it, Hauptman Finck?'

The ADC had also entered the room. 'No, Herr Colonel. Most unusual.'

'You. You are an officer. Perhaps you are. What is your name?'

Hunter said nothing. Kellner asked again, 'Your name, Englishman. Even by the Geneva Convention, you must give me your name. And your rank.'

'Lieutenant James Hunter, Herr Colonel.'

'Ah. You are a polite man, Lieutenant Hunter. And also a clever man, I think.'

He moved across to Phelps. 'And you? Are you an officer, or just the ordinary man you pretend to be?'

Phelps said nothing. Kellner spoke again: 'Please. Don't make this difficult.'

Hunter said, 'His name is Phelps, Herr Colonel. Private Sidney Phelps.'

'Is he dumb? Can't speak?'

'No. He's just in shock.'

'In shock, eh? I'm not surprised. I would be in shock too, if I were in your position. I am puzzled, Lieutenant. Very puzzled indeed. You see, I am at a loss to see why you should risk your lives. In fact condemn yourself and your men to certain death, for no apparent reason.'

Kellner's English was very polished and his accent smooth and cultured. What the Germans called '*gepflegt*'.

'You break into the camp and into my office. You smash a picture of my son and his family and then you leave, without doing anything else. You do not destroy anything, no planes, no ammunition dumps, no fuel dumps, as I would have expected. In fact you do not blow anything up at all. You do not set any charges. So why are you here? That is what intrigues me. That is what I need to know. That is what you will tell me.'

He paused for a moment and stared at the floor, before looking Hunter in the eyes. 'What were you doing here?'

Hunter said nothing.

Kellner bit his lip and closed his eyes. After a few moments he reopened them. 'I advise you to tell me.'

He looked at one of the guards, a large, well-built man, and motioned him to put down his gun. Kellner called him over. 'Corporal, show the lieutenant why he needs to talk to me.'

Saying nothing, the man turned his back on Hunter and took a pace away, then turned and delivered a running uppercut to the right side of Hunter's face. Hunter reeled away and staggered, then clutched at his jaw, checking that it wasn't broken. It felt intact but his hands came away covered in blood.

But the guard hadn't finished. He followed up before Hunter could avoid him and dealt him a blow to the solar plexus that sent him to the floor.

Finck watched with interest and turned to Kellner. 'Sir, would you mind?'

'No, please, go ahead.'

Finck walked over to Hunter who was kneeling on the floor spitting out blood and kicked him hard in the small of the back with his heavy jackboot. Taken completely by surprise, Hunter fell forward, his head hitting the floor. Blood began to pool around him and for a moment, Finck thought that he might have gone too far. That he had broken the man's skull. But Hunter started to push himself up on his hands and Finck could see that the gash in his head was not that big. It always surprised him that any head wound could produce quite so much blood.

Hunter was kneeling again and felt his head, sizing up the scale of the damage as he peered through the blood and wiped it away from his right eye. Kellner spoke: 'That's enough. Enough for now. So, Lieutenant, are you ready to talk to me?'

Hunter, both unable and unwilling to speak, simply shook his head.

'Oh dear. That is such a pity. We will have to continue our conversation at a later time.'

He turned to Finck. 'Eric, I think we might need to find a dressing for the lieutenant's head. He appears to have slipped on the floor and cut it open. See to it please.'

Finck detailed the corporal to find someone attend to the first aid. They couldn't have a prisoner bleeding everywhere. It was so very, messy. He knew though that it would take a lot more than their level of questioning to make these men talk. Eric Finck loved his work. But he really didn't like the sight of blood. He realised, however, that there was a simple way around this. He turned to Kellner. 'Herr Oberst, I think that this might be the time for us to hand them over to Oberst Hilmann. Don't you, sir?'

Kellner mused for a moment. 'Yes, Eric. Yes, I think you might be right. I don't think I will be able to get anything more out of these two using my simple methods. I think it is time for someone who has more persuasive ways to ask them questions.'

Hunter grimaced. This was what he had feared. They were going to be handed over to the SS colonel.

In the low-lying hills to the south-west of Heraklion airfield, Captain Sandy Wilson lay and watched in disbelief. For two hours he had waited here. His two other teams had hit Tymbaki and Kastelli at the appointed hour, shortly after 2200. That was half an hour after Hunter's men were meant to have come out of Heraklion allowing Wilson's men to go in. But something had clearly gone wrong. From the intelligence he had received on his field radio, the other raids had gone well, with blazing planes, numerous enemy dead and wholesale carnage. But just as he had been about to get his team into Heraklion airfield, the place had come alive. Sirens had sounded and searchlights had suddenly come on, lighting the place up like bloody Blackpool Illuminations. It could only mean one thing. Hunter had been discovered. The game was up.

A career soldier who had commissioned into the Coldstream Guards in '38, Wilson had been through Dunkirk and survived. Just. A stomach wound had very nearly finished him. But Wilson was a fighter. In every way. The moment he had been passed fit, he had volunteered and in the year since he had joined the newly formed special forces, Wilson had seen much and learnt a great deal and one of the major lessons was that there was always a way out. You didn't wait for opportunities to come to you, you had to create them yourself. You had to see the moment when it came and act on your own initiative. And now was one of those moments. Wilson had a down-to-earth attitude perfectly suited to an officer who commanded men whose role was destruction. Raiding was what he was good at and he had absorbed the lessons of Dieppe, Vaagso and all the other commando failures. Wilson was good at his job. The best some said. And he knew it. But above all he was a pragmatist.

Wilson remained in position for ten minutes, watching the enemy running in all directions. Knowing that soon they would send out patrols to hunt for any other raiders. Such was the delay that the Germans would have had reports of the other attacks by now.

There was nothing to do but call off the mission. Wilson's initial frustration had turned to fury. He not only felt let down by Hunter, he also felt compromised. Exposed. And all for the sake of some documents.

The priority now was to get off the island. He wondered if any of them had managed to escape capture and get back to Woods. Whether Woods would even be aware of what had happened. He was about to set off for the church when one of his men came running up. It was signaller Maggs, the radio operator. He looked terrified. 'Sir. Message from the boat, sir. It's under attack. The Jerries must have hooked on to Sarn't Dobbie's team. Followed them back. They've all been shot up, sir. What the hell are we going to do?'

'Have you still got them on the 38?'

'Yes, sir. I think so.'

He knelt down beside Wilson and spoke into the mike: 'Hello, Ocean One, this is Sunray. Over.'

There was a pause. He tried again: 'Ocean One. This is Sunray. Come in.'

Suddenly the headset crackled into life. 'Got them, sir.'

Maggs gave the headset to Wilson, along with the mike. Holding one of the phones next to his ear, Wilson spoke into the mike: 'Hello, Bertie. Sandy here. What the hell's going on?'

A faint, panicked voice came on the headset. 'Sandy. Thank God. No use here. All fucked up.'

In the background Wilson could hear the sound of submachine gun fire and explosions. The voice spoke again: 'Get yourselves out of it. Get back to the other boat. Get off the bloody island. We're goners.'

There was a crackle, then silence. Wilson handed the headset and mike back to Maggs. 'Anything?'

The signaller held one of the headphones to his ear. 'No, sir. It's gone dead.'

'Damn. Well, right then. We'll have to make for the other boat. Woods's caique. It's our only hope. Where's that Greek, the guide fella? Find him, quick. We need to get to Captain Woods.'

The cell block lay on the north side of Heraklion airfield, close to the sea. Inside there were six small cells, each one measuring just six by five feet, and with a single barred window to the rear. A wooden bed and a bucket that served as a latrine were all the furniture and it was in one of these spartan rooms that Hunter and Phelps now found themselves. They were sitting on two wooden chairs, which had been placed against one of the walls, opposite the bed and set about four feet apart from each other. They had been here for the last half an hour and during that time had come to know the SS Colonel who they had first seen earlier that evening.

He had entered, accompanied by two black-uniformed SS guards, both carrying Schmeissers. Oberst Gustav Hilmann had introduced himself to them as if they had all been at a cocktail party and the false friendliness made the encounter all the more terrifying. He had begun with the usual simple questions: name, rank and unit. Unit had proved a sticking point. Both men had given their original regiment, Black Watch and Royal Corps of Signals. But Hilmann wasn't having any of it.

'You are commandos. That much we know. You no longer belong to those units. Do you think we are stupid? We know all about you commandos. How they hand-pick their men from your traditional regiments. You know very well that what I want to know is what your new unit is called and what is its purpose.'

Hunter spoke: 'I told you, we're reconnaissance. Our unit has no name.'

Hilmann nodded to the guards. Both of them approached Hunter and Phelps and each dealt one of them a hard slap across the face. Phelps was knocked from his chair and hit his head on the floor. For a moment Hunter thought he might have knocked himself out, but he crawled to his feet and sat down on the chair.

Suddenly, Hunter was back in the cell in Athlit with the two 'Nazis', naked and bleeding. He had survived that and he would damn well survive this. And so would Phelps. Hilmann was speaking again. 'You see, it really would be much easier to cooperate. And so much less painful.'

Neither man said anything.

Hilmann tried again: 'Let's try another question. What did you come for? Why were you in the office?'

Silence. Again Hilmann nodded at the guards and again they stepped forward. This time though only one of them acted, kicking over Hunter's chair so that he fell sprawling on the floor while the man stamped hard down upon the fingers of his left hand. Hunter screamed in agony as the German ground the heel of his jackboot against his knuckles, pushing them hard into the stone floor until they bled. Hunter writhed in agony but managed to control his voice to produce rather than a scream, merely a whimper. Phelps watched him, his eyes staring wide.

Hilmann walked across to him. 'So, what have you to say now? Your lieutenant is in pain now. Next time my man will make sure to stamp upon the same wound. Again and again and again until his fingers have become a pulp and he has no hand. Have you anything to say?'

But Phelps said nothing. Hunter was trying to get to his feet now, holding his bleeding hand and managed to sit back down in the chair. Hilmann nodded to the other guard. The man walked up to Phelps and kicked the chair from beneath him. Phelps had hardly hit the floor when the same guard dealt him a savage blow with his boot, high in the pelvis. Phelps howled with animal agony that hit Hunter worse than any blow. He watched, nursing his fingers, as Phelps contorted his body on the ground, doubling up with the searing, unthinkable pain.

Phelps spoke, the words gushing from his mouth as fast as

he could get them out. 'Alright, Colonel. I'll tell you what you need to know. Only don't hurt us any more. Please. You can shoot us, but don't hurt us. Please!'

Hunter looked at him, unsure as to what to think. Either Sid Phelps had at last recovered his senses and this was part of a great act, or he was being genuine and was about to give the whole game away. Everything.

Colonel Hilmann looked at Hunter. 'Lieutenant, your man here is being very, very sensible. He knows how a man should die. Not in the sort of horrid, slow and painful ways we might have had planned for you both. But swiftly and cleanly. With a single shot. He is very clever.'

He walked over to Phelps. 'Right. You may begin. Tell me firstly, who you are.'

Phelps spoke quickly, nervously, desperately. 'We're not spies. And we're not commandos. They're coming later. We're just reconnaissance. We're scouts, not spies. That's what we are. Recce. Our orders were to come in and find out how many men were here and the layout of the field. Everything. And then one of us went too far. But he's dead now. Private Duffy. You shot him. He went too far and broke into the commandant's office and wanted to steal some papers, but he couldn't break into your safe. And then we heard someone and we rushed out and Duffy knocked over the picture. That's it. That's all.'

The colonel looked Phelps hard in the face. Then he walked away across to the other side of the room. After a while, he spoke: 'I have no reason to doubt what you say. But somehow I don't think that you have told me the whole truth. There is still something not right here. Something smells bad. You're lying.'

Phelps sounded panicked. 'No, you're wrong, sir. That's it. That's all, sir. I've told you everything. That's why we're here. You've got to believe me.'

Hunter, still nursing his battered hand, snarled at Phelps, his face a mask of anger. 'Oh, shut up, you snivelling little coward. Can't you see you've told him what he wants to know. You told him the commandos are coming. Now they'll be waiting for them. It'll be a bloody massacre.'

Hilmann looked at Hunter. Then he looked away and said nothing. Hunter spoke again: 'My God, Phelps, if I could get my hands on you I'd beat you to a bloody pulp. You're a coward and a traitor and you deserve to die. You know what you've done? You've condemned twenty good men to death. Here. Our men. How could you do it, man?'

The colonel had still said nothing. Now he turned back to Hunter. 'Lieutenant, you seem genuinely upset. I'm touched. But you speak of good men. These are not good men who are going to die. They're commandos. The men our dear Führer calls gangsters and has classified as criminals, to be shot on sight.'

Hunter said nothing. Hilmann continued, 'I think in fact that your friend here may not be lying. I am inclined to believe him.'

He moved over to Phelps. 'How will they come? Are they here on the island already? Where are they?'

Phelps shook his head frantically. 'No, sir. They're not here yet. Only our party. They're coming tomorrow night. By plane. By parachute. They'll land a few miles away. There's a dropping zone and then they walk in here with a Greek guide.'

The colonel smiled at him. 'You're certainly very obliging.

Thank you. So we shall be waiting for your friends when they come tomorrow. Waiting with all our might. We will let them get very near to the camp. Let them think that we have no idea that they are coming. And then...'

Moving fast, he punched Phelps hard in the pelvis. 'We strike.'

Phelps folded up and screamed at the unbelievable pain, as the blow had hit him just above the genitals, exactly where he had been kicked by one of the guards, just a few minutes earlier.

Hunter snarled, 'You bastard. They'll never fall for it.'

Hilmann shook his head. 'Oh but they will, Lieutenant. That's where you're wrong. They'll fall for it because you're going to tell them that the coast is clear. You're going to radio to them and tell them what our strengths are and our weaknesses. You are going to tell them everything about the camp that you have discovered and it will all be false.'

'I won't do it.'

'Oh, I think you will, Lieutenant. When you hear your friend cry out in agony and see what we do to him to make him cry. When he begs us to stop and begs us to kill him. You will do whatever we ask of you.'

'You're a monster.'

'No, Lieutenant. I am not a monster and you are not a hero. And your friend here is a coward and he will suffer. Very, very much. And now I will give you both a little time to rest and to think about what I have said. And then I will return.'

He turned sharply and one of the guards opened the door of the cell for him, closing it behind him. Hunter looked at Phelps, who was clutching his abdomen. 'You alright, Sid?'

'I, I think so, sir. Hurts like hell though.'

'Don't talk to me. I'm sorry, Sid. But if we're going to live, this has got to look right.'

Gently, Hunter guided Phelps to the bed and helped him lie down.

'Get some rest. We're sure to need all our strength.'

Hunter walked across to one of the chairs and sat down. He paused and breathed slow and deep, trying to assimilate all that had just happened and to come up with some sort of plan. But nothing came. The mission was compromised and their covers blown. To say that their prospects looked bleak was an understatement. There was nothing else for it but to help Hilmann. But to do so would go against everything in which he believed and all the principles that had been drilled into him over the past months.

No, he could not do it. Phelps would have to suffer in order that others might live. One man's pain in exchange for so much more. That was life. That, he thought, was war. Bloody, brutal, uncompromising and as so often, giving one man a terrible moral dilemma. And to his growing horror, Hunter knew that this time that man was him. He looked at Phelps. He was sleeping, his eyelids flickering and his face twitching. Dreaming. In anguish.

Hunter closed his own eyes and thought of sleep. But it would not come. Over and over again he retraced the argument in his mind and still there was no solution. He could not give in. Phelps would suffer. And then they would both die. It was not what he had had in mind for his life and he wondered for a moment what the years might have brought him and then stopped himself. No point. This was the end.

It was nearing one in the morning when Colonel Hilmann reappeared. He was smiling. He spoke to one of the guards: 'Tie them both. Bind their hands. They're coming with us.'

Within minutes Hunter and Phelps were on the move, being marched from the cells and out of the block, surrounded by four SS guards and preceded by the colonel. They walked through the almost deserted compound and stopped outside the signals office.

Hilmann turned to them. 'You will be aware, Lieutenant, of what has happened.'

Hunter looked at him. 'I'm sorry. I don't know what you mean.'

'Don't pretend, Lieutenant. You know exactly what I mean. You know that last night, while you were here "gathering your information", your friends attacked two other bases on the island. They destroyed sixteen aircraft and killed dozens of men. Don't tell me that you didn't know that, Lieutenant. It won't make things any easier. Yours was to be the third attack, was it not? But you lied to me.'

He paused for a moment and Hunter wondered if he had somehow discovered the truth about their mission.

'Your friends are not going to drop by parachute, are they? They are already here. And now you are going to contact them, as arranged and you are going to let them know that everything is ready for their third attack, tonight. You are going to send a message to your friends and tell them exactly what I tell you to. And if you do not, well, we shall see what happens to this man. And so will you.'

They were pushed inside the building and entered the radio office where two Wehrmacht signals soldiers were seated, one at a radio transmitter.

Hilmann spoke: 'Sit down. Just you, Lieutenant. Your friend will remain standing. You know how to use this thing?'

'Yes, of course, it's a simple transmitter.'

The German radio operator stood up and Hunter took his seat.

'As a matter of fact you're right. It is one of yours. It was left behind here last May when we captured the island. Apparently it has proved most useful in sending out false messages. Your Morse code is very distinctive. But of course it is no longer secure. We have many signals operators who are able to understand it. I presume you know the call sign for your friends?'

'Yes. Of course.'

'Then we shall have no problems. It's a good start, Lieutenant. Begin.'

Hunter sat facing the transmitter and turned one of the dials. Then another. The German signaller pulled up a chair and sat watching him. The colonel spoke again: 'And just in case you do not transmit what I tell you, Corporal Schmidt here will be watching you. He understands Morse code and he speaks very, very good English. Now listen to me very carefully and tap out only exactly what I say.'

Slowly, and with great attention to detail, the colonel gave Hunter the information. It differed in almost every aspect from the details of the defence and routine of the camp that Leigh Fermor had given to Hunter and his men. Hunter tapped away at the transmitter, watched dutifully all the time by the signaller. Twice the colonel stopped and nodded to Schmidt to ensure that Hunter was sending the right messages. Schmidt nodded back to him and he carried on.

Suddenly Hunter stopped and put down the transmitter. 'No. I won't do it. I can't.'

Without warning, Hilmann struck him a blow to the head, which sent him crashing against the desk. Hunter straightened up as the colonel spoke: 'Don't be a fool. It was going so well.'

'No. I won't do it.'

Hilmann nodded to one of the guards, who was standing next to Phelps and then barked an order. Instantly, the man smashed the butt of his machine pistol with sickening force, hard against Phelps's back, aiming at his kidneys. Phelps screamed and collapsed to the floor. The guard stood over him and dealt him a full, jackbooted kick in the face, which connected with his nose, cracking it. Phelps clutched at his bleeding face and as he did so, the guard again brought down the butt of his gun, this time on Phelps's shoulder. Phelps screamed again and the guard raised his weapon, ready to smash it into his head. Hunter rose from his chair, only to be pushed back by the other guard just as the colonel shouted to the guard to stop.

As the man returned his weapon to rest, Hilmann spoke again: 'You see, Lieutenant. This is how it will be now. But this is only the beginning. This is the clumsy part. Next things will become – how do you say it? – so much more intimate. So much more delicate. Pain is an extraordinary thing. You think you cannot feel any more and then suddenly it can start all over again in such a new and interesting way. I have other men who have a way with knives. Such a way. They really can't wait to introduce themselves to your friend.'

Hunter watched as Phelps writhed on the floor. After a few moments he picked up the transmitter and began to tap again.

Hilmann applauded. 'There we are. You see? So easy. So very sensible. Now where were we?'

For the next half an hour, Hunter tapped out messages to the commandos. Messages that were sure to lure them in just far enough. Just close enough to the airfield so that they would be completely surrounded by the colonel's men. They had put Phelps on a chair now and he was holding a cloth to his broken nose, which was still bleeding intermittently. A few nasty bruises and a smashed nose were one thing, thought Hunter. An encounter with Colonel Hilmann's 'men with knives' was quite another and he was certainly not prepared to sacrifice Phelps in the name of deception. So he carried on tapping away; sending out the colonel's messages into the night.

And as he did so, miles away, on the south side of the island, a Morse receiving unit had sprung into life. Now it had been receiving strangely worded messages for almost half an hour. They detailed the troops strengths, routines and details of the layout of the airfield at Heraklion.

The man who was receiving them was not sure what to make of them. He had no idea why the messages had been sent to him, or indeed what they might mean, but the call sign attached to them had been 'Scotsman' and if there was one thing that Dick Gorringe, aboard the *Rosetta*, where she lay under her camouflage covers, had imprinted on his mind, it was that word. *Scotsman*. It meant only one thing. Wherever he was and for whatever reason he was sending these strange messages, Jim Hunter was still alive.

Sandy Wilson's men had done well to move so far and so fast in the darkness. Well, it was partly down to the skill of their guide. In the last half an hour, they had moved south-east, in what Wilson would have thought must have been cross-country, but which proved to be a series of tiny paths, which took them safely through the hills. Now they were climbing again and the terrain was becoming more and more difficult. Wilson spoke to the Greek: 'Much further, Andrea?'

The man shrugged and grinned at him. 'Less than an hour, sir.'

That, though was what they always said. Every time you asked them how far it was it was always: 'Less than an hour, boss.'

The six men, all that was left now of Wilson's command, carried on behind him, climbing steadily until they were able to see, on a ridge, partly hidden by an olive grove, what looked like a small chapel. Andrea turned to Wilson. 'This is it. Here is the church. Here is Kapitan Woods.'

'Thank you Andrea. Let's get up there.'

As they approached the little church Wilson held up his hand to halt and they all sank to one knee. Andrea cupped his hands together and made the sound of an owl hooting. Three times, with a gap between each. He was answered by a low whistle. Wilson got to his feet and the men followed, before advancing towards the building. Fletcher was standing behind the low wall, waiting for them. Woods appeared at the doorway. 'Wilson? What's happened. What's gone wrong?'

Wilson turned on him. 'Wrong? Just about anything that possibly could have. I've lost twelve good men and the crew of the caique. Dead or captured. All of them.'

'How did it happen? Did they get to the airfields?'

'Oh, they got to their objectives alright. Carried out their jobs perfectly. Planes destroyed, dozens of enemy dead and wounded. But they were sloppy. Someone slipped up and a guard managed to track them. The Germans found them at the boat. I heard it all on the radio.'

'God, that's awful. Poor buggers.'

'That's not all.'

'What?'

'Your man Hunter's in trouble. Big trouble. I've no idea of the details, but he didn't make it out of the camp by H Hour. I had to call off my op.'

'What's happened to them?'

'Like I said, I've no idea. But when I left the place was alive with guards. The searchlights were all over it and we could see two patrols setting out up the hill.'

Woods shook his head. It was unbelievable. How on earth had Hunter and his men been caught? Everything had been planned in such meticulous detail. But no sooner had he asked himself the question, than he came up with an answer.

It was, after all, just typical of a mission in which Hunter was involved that something should have gone badly wrong. The man was a jinx. A Jonah. It seemed clear to Woods now that everything in which Hunter had been involved had ended in some sort of cock-up. For God's sake, the man had even scuppered his own love life. Wilson was a professional. A proper soldier. A real commando. Hunter was an amateur. By anyone's standards. They'd been doomed even before they had started.

He looked back at Wilson. 'I'm sorry. I had a bad feeling about this one.'

'I reckon he's dead. That or he's a POW. They might all be, for all I know.'

Woods thought for a moment. And then he was gripped by a strange feeling of certainty. 'But perhaps they're not dead. Or captured. Not if there are patrols going out. Not if the Jerries are mounting a search of the area.'

'I wouldn't count on it.'

Noticing the half-full bottle of retsina sitting on a low table by the door, Wilson pointed to it. 'Christ, I could murder a drop of that.' He walked over to the bottle and removing the cork, held it to his lips and took a glug. 'What a bloody night, Woods. What a bloody night.'

'What will you do now?'

'We need to get away. We all do. You too. This place will be crawling with Jerries in no time.'

'They don't dare come in here the locals say. They think its haunted.'

'Ghosts or no ghosts, I reckon they'll come here just the same. They'll be out for revenge. I'm taking my men down to your boat.'

'You can't do that.'

'Watch me. And you'll come with us, if you're sensible. We've no other choice. The only radio set is on that boat and there's no other way of getting off, unless we call up a sub.'

For a moment, Woods was tempted. If Hunter really was

a jinx, then why not just leave him here? But then he thought of the others. Who knew how many might still be alive and on the run. He couldn't leave them. Their blood would be on his conscience.

'What about Hunter's lot?'

'Hunter's gone, Woods. Forget him. They're all gone. Your caique will take you three and me and all of my men and we can slip off before Jerry has time to catch up.'

Woods said nothing for a while. White watched him in silence, while Wilson's men sat around, exhausted, resting against the walls of the church. He weighed up the situation again. In a sense Wilson was right. With the mission a failure, there was little point in sacrificing men who might get away for the sake of others who could not. That was the commando's way. And it was the squadron's way. But, he thought, it was not his way. He had a code of honour. A code instilled by his father and backed up by everything he believed in as a British officer.

'I don't like it. I can't believe that they're all dead or POWs.'

'Face it, man. They're gone. Your man Hunter messed up and it cost him his life and cost us the operation. The ball's in your court. What a cock-up.'

Woods stared at him, his perspective suddenly altered. This was a more serious accusation. 'You're actually blaming my officer for aborting your mission? Blaming me?'

'That's what I said, isn't it? He was meant to get in there, get what you wanted and get out. Well he didn't. He cocked up, didn't he? They caught him. So now nobody wins. You and your bloody spook bosses in Cairo don't get whatever it was you wanted. I don't get what I was ordered to do. And Hunter and his men? Well, they just don't get to live.'

'You're just bitter because of your men at the other airfields. There's no point in taking out your anger on us.'

'Isn't there? I intend to file a full report when we get back to Cairo. Then we'll see who's right and who's wrong. What matters right now is getting off this bloody island. You'd be best to come away with us. You're a fool if you don't. Chasing after dead men.' He turned to his men. 'Right, lads. Up you get. We've got a march ahead and we'd better make use of the night. Andrea, we need to get down to the other boat. Yes?'

'Yes, sir. I will show you the way. It is a most pretty part of the island.'

There was suddenly a noise from outside the chapel and Woods heard Fletcher giving a whistle. The reply to the owl call. The password. Thinking that it must be Hunter, Woods dashed to the doorway. Fletcher was there, staring into the darkness. Listening.

'Someone out there, sir. Not sure who yet.'

'Mister Hunter?'

'Don't know, sir. Hard to tell. It's one of us, though.'

A figure came towards them out of the night. It had the gathered outline of a German Army tunic and baggy trousers and for an instant both men froze and instinctively levelled their weapons. It drew closer. Woods called out, 'Who are you, there? Identify yourself.'

A distinctive, Scottish voice spoke: 'Sergeant Knox, sir.'

Another voice: 'And Private Martin, sir.'

Both men walked towards the chapel and in the dim light, Woods recognised them. 'Thank God. We thought you'd had it.'

Knox spoke: 'Not us, sir. Not yet. They've got Mister

Hunter, though, and Phelps. And I reckon Duffy and Russell too.'

'What happened?'

Sergeant Knox told the story. 'It was all going well, sir. We got in. Managed to pull off the whole thing. Mister Hunter was bloody brilliant, sir. A right, proper Jerry officer. And Duffy too.'

'Go on.'

'So we get into the office and I'm right into it. Get right into the safe, nae bother and there's mountains of papers in there. So I hand them to Phelpsy and he goes through them and anything that looks tasty, he passes to Harry who looks at them and takes a snap. And then we get to the bottom of the pile and we've no found the bloody thing we're after. But then Phelpsy finds it, stuck tae some blotting paper. We got it, sir.' Martin reached into his tunic pocket and produced the brown papers.

Woods grabbed them, grinning. 'You did it. You got the bloody thing. Well done, boys. Bloody marvellous. What about the others? What happened?'

'Well, that's it, sir. It was Phelpsy. Hadn't been himself for a while. But then you knew that. And he's in the office and doing his stuff and we put it all back and I close the safe and it all looks tickety-boo. Like nothing's ever happened. And we get ready to scarper. And then he just flips. He sort of loses it. He lashes out at a photo that's sitting on the desk. Some Jerry family it was. And it flies off and lands on the floor and the glass breaks and goes everywhere. Well at first we think someone's heard it, but no one comes so we just brass it out and leave the place and Mister Hunter's looking after Phelpsy. But Russell and Duffy have gone off to the signals hut and we can't see them. So Mister Hunter arranges for us all to get out and he guides us through the wire. And Martin and me and Phelpsy all get out and find Mister Hunter. But then we lose Phelpsy. Seems he's gone back in. So Mister Hunter tells us to leg it and says that he'll go back in, find Duffy and Russell and he'll look after Phelpsy. And that's about it. And somehow we managed to get back here.'

'Well, you did bloody well, both of you. And bloody well too to find your way here. We've had a bit of a night too. Captain Wilson's men at the other two airfields did their job. And well too. But they were run down by the enemy and badly shot up. Their boat's gone too. The captain's going to take our boat and he wants us all to go with him.'

Knox spoke up: 'We canny do that, sir. What about Mister Hunter and the others? We canny just leave them.'

'No, Knox. I think you're right. We can't just leave them. I'm going to stay on the island and see if we can't get them out. There must still be a chance.'

Martin spoke: 'Then we'll stay too, sir.'

Woods shook his head. He had already made up his mind. 'Sorry, Harry. Not you. I'm sending you off with Captain Wilson. You and your document and your camera and that head of yours, with all its memories. You're off to Cairo. And you'd better get out of those Jerry togs. Sarn't Knox, if you wouldn't mind, I'd rather like to have you here with me. And the same goes for you. Get your own battledress back on.'

Knox smiled and nodded. 'Of course, sir. I've never been happier tae obey an order.'

13

Woods and Knox watched Wilson and his men, and Martin with them, as they made their way down the hillside and into the gloom. It was shortly after 3am when they left and the dawn would soon be ready to rise, over in the east, away to their left. The birds would not start their chorus for another hour, but the morning insects were already replacing those of the night with their own distinctive chirruping and clicking.

Woods counted them lucky so far. Whether it was to do with the fact that the successful attacks had come in the west of the island, or whether there really was truth in the belief that the Germans avoided the chapel because it was haunted, there had been no sign of any patrols from Heraklion in their vicinity as yet and whatever the reason, by Woods's reckoning, they might have an hour or so to get closer to the base and see if there was any evidence of what on earth had happened to Hunter, Duffy, Phelps and Russell. It would be damn dangerous, as by the time they got there it would almost be light and their journey away would make them horribly visible. But Woods could not think of any alternative. They simply had to get closer to the camp.

He had asked Wilson to hold on for one day, when he

arrived at the caique and, reluctantly, he had agreed. Although Woods realised that he might change his mind at any time and they might all be left marooned with no transport and no means of communication with which to effect any form of rescue.

Knox spoke: 'Think Martin will make it back, sir?'

'He'll have a bloody good try, Sarn't. And he's got more chance with Captain Wilson than he has with us. That's for sure.'

He walked with Knox back into the church, where Fletcher and White were busy in the darkness, checking their weapons and packing their haversacks.

Woods spoke in a whisper: 'White, you almost done?'

'Yes, sir. Pretty much, I think.'

'Right, get yourself out there on stag. We'll be leaving in fifteen, but I don't want any unwelcome surprises at this stage.'

'Roger that, sir.'

White, Sten gun in his hand, made his way outside and Knox made the last checks to his own weapons and the straps on his kit.

As he was doing so he spoke to Woods, who was standing nearby: 'Sir, can I ask you a question?'

'Go ahead, Sarn't. I'm all ears.'

'Would you have left Mr Hunter?'

'Sorry? No, of course not.'

'It's just that, well, me and the lads, we knew that the two of you didn't see eye to eye over something and we didn't think that there was any... well, any love lost between you.'

Woods looked at him. Shook his head. 'Sarn't Knox. If you think I'm fool enough to allow some petty differences come between me and the life of a brother officer and a man I count as a friend, then you're very much mistaken. That is not what I do. I intend to do whatever I can to save Mister Hunter, if it's not too late already. But we don't have much time.'

Knox was about to say something when there was a noise from White. A softly whispered cry of: 'Sir, sir. Quick.'

Woods and Knox, followed closely by Fletcher, moved to the door and what they saw there made them stop in their tracks.

Lennie Russell looked terrible. His face was covered in dust that had caked into the blood from the cuts he had taken, falling more times than he could remember in the darkness in the olive groves on his climb from the airbase to the church. How he had accomplished the distance, not even he knew, but Russell had simply followed his nose and now here he was. Among friends.

Instantly, Woods abandoned his timings and after taking Russell inside, sat him down and in the growing light of dawn, gave him a few sips of the retsina that Woods had left in the bottle. Russell coughed and then drank, gratefully. After a few minutes he regained some sort of composure.

Woods placed a hand on his back. 'Well done, Russell. Jolly well done. Were you followed?'

'Not as far as I could tell, sir. They all seemed to be going off towards the west.'

'That's very good news. Very good news indeed. But how on earth did you get out?'

'You won't believe this, sir, but they took me for a Jerry and put me in a patrol. We all went out and I was dead lucky. The bloke next to me twisted his ankle so I volunteered to take him back and then I got him off in the other direction and, er, just got shot of him. Then I legged it back here.'

'Good man.'

Russell looked at him in the eyes. 'Duffy's dead, sir. Shot by the Jerries. Almost cut in two he was. Point-blank. It was horrible.'

'Poor devil.'

'But Mister Hunter's still alive, sir. And Phelpsy. At least they were when I left. God knows now, though. Bloody SS have got them both.'

Woods started, 'The SS? In Heraklion? Good God.'

'Yes, sir. We weren't told anything about that, were we? But they're here alright. There's this colonel. Big bloke. Didn't get his name. And I suppose he might have about a company strength with him. Bastards. It was them that shot poor Duffy. He was already a prisoner. Unarmed. Evil bloody bastards.'

'They shot him in cold blood?'

'He went for one of them. One of the SS. Punches his lights out, sir. But then the other one just swings round and lets him have it with his machine gun. Point-blank, like I said, sir.'

Woods shook his head. 'We've got to try to get them out.'

'But how, sir? What can we do? There's hundreds of bloody Jerries in there. SS and all.'

'Well, we can at least try. Will you come with us, Russell? You know the lie of the land. We could really use your help.'

'Well, I don't see how but, you just try to stop me.'

'Good man. Well, you'd better get your kit changed pretty sharpish. We need to leave here just as soon as we can. And we'll have to be damned careful. It's almost light and we can't wait for nightfall. Time is everything now. We might be too late.'

Fletcher shook his head. 'Sir. If I may, I've got to say something. I know I shouldn't. This is madness. What chance do we have?'

Woods looked at him and nodded. 'You're right of course, Fletcher. But I was forced to leave a man behind before. Not so long ago. And I'm not prepared to do it again.'

Fletcher nodded, but said nothing more.

Russell swapped his German tunic for his own battledress top and the kepi for his regimental beret and was ready within a few minutes.

'Good riddance to all that. I never felt happy in it.'

Fletcher quipped, 'Oh I don't know, Squirrel. I think it sort of suited you. After all you can speak the lingo.'

White joined in, 'Course he can. Learnt it off a Jerry countess. Didn't you, Squirrel? Your lady friend taught you how to spick Deutsch pretty well, didn't she? What else did she teach you? A few of her old tricks, eh?'

Russell smiled at him sarcastically. 'More than you'll ever know, Chalky.'

Fletcher grinned. 'Don't need any tricks, me, see. That's what all the ladies say. It's all in the quality of the equipment see. All about the gear.'

They yelled abuse at him. Woods spoke: 'That's enough. Pipe down all of you and let's get a move on.'

They set off in the direction of Heraklion airfield, with Russell leading the way down the rough path up which he had come, and, as it was now daylight, they stopped to take cover every hundred yards. It was very slow progress and Woods began to wonder if he had made the right decision. They had just made one of their pauses reconnoitring around them for any sign of the enemy, when, from a dense group of olive trees over to their left, Grigori suddenly appeared. He was running, bent over and as he neared Woods they could see that he was in a state of great agitation, and signalling for them to wait. They didn't move, and when he did reach them they could see that he was smiling.

He spoke to Woods: 'Sir, sir. I have news. Very, very important news.'

'Yes?'

'They are still alive. Your two men.'

'Hunter and Phelps? What? You're sure?'

'Yes, sir. I am sure. Very sure and now the Germans are moving them. Moving your men.'

'Moving them? Where to?'

'To Hania. To the general commandant. The SS colonel wants glory for himself. Then…' He wiped his fingers across his throat. 'Then, kaput.'

Woods understood. 'So what you're saying is that we have one chance. One opportunity to rescue the two of them before they're killed and that chance is when they're moved from the camp.' He paused. 'Well, one chance is better than none at all. This is great news. Thank you, Grigori. Our next problem is how the hell four men are going to ambush a heavily armed prisoner escort?'

Grigori smiled again. 'Oh we have thought of that. We can help you. We have already thought of it.'

'We? Who's we? The andartes?'

Grigori nodded. 'Yes, boss. Yes. The andartes and Kapitan Ffinch.'

Ffinch. That was a stroke of luck. Woods had wondered if two Effs would be involved.

'Where is Captain Ffinch? I need to talk to him.'

'Yes, sir. He's coming to talk to you. He has made a plan.'

'He has?'

'Yes. A most clever plan.'

Ffinch arrived half an hour later, looking very pleased with himself.

'It's true, Woods. The Germans are going to move your friends in two days' time, in the evening. So now there's no need for you to go down to the base. We're going to ambush the convoy and get them out. We've already found a spot. It's a narrow stretch of the road near a place called Anoyeia.'

He pulled a battered map from his pocket and spread it out on the ground before them, pointing his finger to where a group of buildings was indicated. 'You see, it's here. Where the road is cut into the side of a ridge, following the contours of the hill. Above the road there's a sheer bluff, and the whole thing's packed full of trees. You still have the explosives you brought with you, don't you?'

'Yes, we've got tons of the stuff. Its back at your cave, with Miller. Too much of all that kit really, if you ask me. Bloody annoying. I could never really see why we brought it all.'

Ffinch smiled at him. 'Well now we really do need it and that's no lie. I'll send a runner right now to fetch the TNT. They can bring it up by mule, with your man Miller. It'll take a full day, so if you give the say-so, I'll get it started now.'

Woods nodded. 'Go ahead. Sounds like the best plan anyone's come up with so far. There's only one thing. Our explosives man's dead. Caught and killed down there in the camp.'

'I say. That is bad news. Poor chap. But don't worry. I can

manage the detonators, timings and all that myself. My stock in trade, don't you know? What we have to do now is move west and sit up for a bit in the hills below Anoyeia. We don't have a great deal of time.'

He called over Grigori and spoke to him in Greek. The partisan nodded then looked across at Woods and waved farewell before darting away into the hills, heading south. Ffinch explained, 'We have a system of runners d'you see? To communicate messages more quickly. Word will get back to Paddy's cave by nightfall and they will come tomorrow. It's about fifteen miles.'

'What about us? My men. Where do we go now?'

'Well may you ask, Captain. We need to head west, towards Anoyeia, but on a lower track. It's cross-country but not quite in the high mountains. About ten miles. The best thing is that we'll be on a system of goat tracks that the Germans never use. Quite close to where we plan to attack the column there are a number of caves. We can hide up there.'

'It must be jolly useful, having all these caves.'

'Yes, I'll say it is. Island could have been made for fighting a guerrilla war. So, once we've done the job and rescued your men, well it's really a straight walk south from the caves to the sea. To where your boat is. Of course, you have to go high first. Up into the real mountains. But you'll all manage that. You're all fit. Anyway. There's no time to lose. We should get going west. Come on.'

Ffinch stood up, folded up his map and tucking it away, began to walk away from the track they had been following. Woods signalled to the others and, turning, they followed his lead, as he went after Ffinch.

As Woods was trying to assimilate all the information with

which Ffinch had just bombarded him, it occurred to him that there was one piece of the complex jigsaw puzzle that did not fit. Their boat. Their only means of escape. If they were to have to wait for two days until the attack and then march across the White Mountains down to the sea, they would most likely not reach the *Rosetta* for at least four days. And Wilson was headed there right now with instructions to wait for them for just one day.

The only thing that he could do would be to somehow get word to Gorringe letting him know about the planned attack and giving him their schedule. Then surely he would wait. And Wilson would wait, wouldn't he?

Hunter and Phelps were waiting for the end. They had been left in the cells for the best part of a day and neither man now expected that he would see another dawn. Hunter's fingers were still throbbing with pain, and he wondered whether one or more might have been broken by the guard. His head wound had sealed itself up, but he was now nursing a dreadful headache. His back too felt badly bruised and was horribly sore.

Phelps looked dreadful. It wasn't just the physical injuries he had suffered: the mental trauma seemed to have no respite. Perhaps death would be a happy release for the poor bugger, thought Hunter, lost as he was in his own inner nightmare world.

The sound of marching, jackbooted footsteps came from down the hall and stopped abruptly outside their cell. Then the door opened and Hilmann entered. 'Ah. How are you both? I hope you slept well.'

He sounded more like the genial host of a country house party than a sadistic Nazi. Hunter glared at him but said nothing.

'We are going to get you cleaned up and try to address those nasty wounds.'

Hunter looked at Phelps and shook his head in despair and disbelief. He turned to Hilmann. 'May I ask why you would want to bother to do that? Why not just kill us now? That's what you're going to do anyway, isn't it?'

Hilmann laughed. 'Of course it is, Lieutenant. But first we have something else to do with you.'

Oh good God, thought Hunter, what fresh torture was this?

Hilmann continued, 'The general commandant of the island, General Müller has expressed a desire to meet the men responsible for the murder of so many of his own men and so much destruction. He has asked that we take you to see him in his headquarters at Hania.'

'You must be joking.'

Hilmann shook his head and laughed. 'No, Lieutenant. This is no joke. I am deadly serious. But the general cannot see you in this state. He does not want to meet men covered in blood, looking like savages. So I have instructed my medical orderlies to treat your wounds and make you look somewhat more respectable than the criminals you truly are.

'We will take you there by truck. In two days' time. That will give you plenty of time to look better. It's only a shame that we can't let you have your own uniforms back. If only you had brought them with you. Nonetheless, I will introduce you personally to the general and when he has spoken to you enough and learnt anything else he wants to know, then we will truly have a great day. The world and the Cretan population will see exactly how we deal with so called "commandos".' He spat the word out.

'A public execution in fact,' Hunter commented.

'Yes. And what an occasion. What a celebration. It's just a pity that you won't be able to take part in the festivities.'

'You're obscene.'

'Oh, I doubt it very much. At least I wouldn't describe myself as such. But I'd rather be "obscene" than dead, Lieutenant. I'll send the medical orderlies in soon. Please do your best to cooperate with them. I'd hate to have to hurt you again.'

It took Woods and his men four hours' hard marching to reach the caves above Anoyeia. Ffinch led the way and every hundred yards or so he would turn and make sure that the others were alright and still following. They arrived as the evening was coming in and Woods was surprised to see that they were far from alone. An entire platoon of andartes had arrived at the caves earlier that day to take part in the attack. Their commander was a surly, thick-set man in his forties named Yanni. He seemed to have unquestioning respect of every man in his platoon.

Ffinch introduced them and they shared a glass of raki together. Then Ffinch took Woods aside and explained what they intended to do. 'The plan is to isolate the column. It's how the andartes like to do things and this is really their show.' He had drawn a sketch plan of the area and made a copy, which he gave to Woods.

'We've found this stretch of the road, as I said, which looks ideal. In terms of firepower, what we have are two heavy machine guns and some lighter MGs. There's a small hillock on the east side of the bluff, which will make the perfect position for one of the machine guns, a captured MG34. It can cut off any attempt at retreat.'

Woods nodded his head. 'Thanks for this. Let's hope it works. That we can get them out.'

'Well I would say we don't have any other chance, old chap. Wouldn't you?'

Ffinch said goodbye and rushed off to a rendezvous with one of his scouts.

Woods joined the men, who had found common ground with the andartes in a liking for raki. He shared half a bottle of the stuff and then settled down to try to sleep. But an hour later, Ffinch arrived back at the camp.

He was out of breath but wore a huge grin. He went straight to Woods. 'I say, you'll never guess what's happened. It's almost beyond belief.'

Woods struggled with waking out of a sound sleep. 'What are you talking about?'

'Such a stroke of luck.'

'What is? Spit it out, man. For God's sake, tell me.'

'Guess who's coming along for the ride when they take your men to the general.'

'No idea. Adolf? Rommel?'

'No. Really. None other than our SS colonel. Oberst Hilmann himself. I have it on good authority from the andartes. We can either kill him or take him prisoner. What d'you think?'

It took a few moments for the news to sink in with Woods. 'That's tremendous. We'll take him prisoner and get him off the island and back to Cairo.'

'Yes, I thought you might say that. Don't think it's going to be popular with some of my chaps. If you ask me most of them would rather see him dead.'

'I would have thought it would be better for them if we were to spirit him away. Either way, they'll have reprisals. But if he's seen to be killed, well, that might be much worse.'

'That's what I said.'

'Still. This is very good news. Either way it's a bonus. But I really think we have to insist on taking him.'

'Up to you, Woods. I'm only the bearer of news.'

'How on earth did you get all the intelligence?'

'We have our means. There's a girl. Pretty thing. Works in the camp. A Greek girl. Eleni. She's not from the island. Came here from Athens. Very proper family. But relations over here. So when Athens fell to the Nazis she came here and settled in with her family. First she got a job in a café in the village. Now she works in the officers' mess at the camp. She's one of our best agents.'

Woods looked up. 'Really?'

'Well, when I say she works in the officers' mess, I mean she has had to make certain… um, sacrifices. If you understand what I mean by that. There are many officers in the mess and they all need to be looked after.'

Woods understood only too well. Everyone made sacrifices during a war like this and this was her way. He hoped it was worth it.

Ffinch continued, 'It's her way of getting justice. Revenge. She was married when she first came here. Her husband was a lovely man – an Athenian doctor – and when one of the Germans was killed a year ago, and the bastards took reprisals they murdered ten men in exchange. And her husband was one of them. Two months later she took the job at the café of the garrison in Heraklion and a few months after that the andartes began to receive extremely useful information. It wasn't difficult to work out where it was coming from. Men are at their most vulnerable when they're in bed. Particularly when they're in bed with a very attractive young woman.

'Eleni's grateful officer clients were soon giving her more information than she could handle. The most important thing, though, is that Jerries still don't seem to have a clue, but they must be starting to wonder how on earth we seem to know their every move. She's brilliant, Woods. One of our finest assets. Bright, resourceful, incredibly brave, and utterly devoted to her one goal. And she has the finest of motives. She just wants to kill Germans.'

Sandy Wilson led the party down the track from the hills towards the cove where the *Rosetta* lay at anchor beneath its ingenious camouflage coverings. It had taken them almost three days to get here and Wilson was hugely relieved. They had made it back to Leigh Fermor's cave with relative ease and he had been worried that they would not be able to find their way down to the cove. He need not have worried. They had found Ffinch there who had provided them with a Greek guide to lead the way.

Of course Wilson had tried to persuade Miller to go with them. But the man was not to be persuaded. He said that he would rather see if Hunter and Woods were still alive and, if they weren't, well he would just stay on the island and do what he could to help the andartes.

And so they had gone. Down the hill towards the coast, boulder by boulder and tree by tree.

As they approached where Martin remembered the caique to be anchored a voice hailed them from the shadows, 'Right. Stop where you are. Drop your weapons and hands up.'

To a man they complied, and the next moment three men stepped out into the light. Martin recognised Gorringe and the two seamen. Fortunately the recognition was mutual. Gorringe lowered his weapon and addressed Martin: 'Thank God, we wondered what had happened. Where are the others?'

'That's it. We're all that's coming, Captain.'

'They're dead? All of them?'

'No. Captain Woods has taken his men to try to rescue the lieutenant and Phelpsy. Private Miller's waiting for them. This is Captain Wilson. Half his men are dead.'

Gorringe nodded to Wilson. 'Good to meet you, Wilson. Yes, I heard on the radio. I'm sorry. So what are we to do now?'

Wilson spoke: 'We need to get this man to Cairo with whatever he is carrying. That's paramount. And we'd also be immensely grateful if we could use your boat.'

Martin interrupted, 'Remember what Captain Woods said, sir. We need to wait.'

'I know what Captain Woods said, Martin.'

He turned to his men. 'Go below, boys, and get your kit stowed. You too, Martin.'

Wilson waited until Martin was safely out of earshot, below decks and then took Gorringe aside. 'Captain, we need to get off the island as soon as possible.'

'What about the others?'

'Others? There are no others. They're all dead or taken prisoner.'

'Well, I spoke to your man Dobbie at the same time that he was under attack.'

'Yes. Sarn't Dobbie. The poor bugger.'

'So I know for certain that he is dead and probably all of his men. But I also had a message from Lieutenant Hunter. It was sent in Morse code, with his call sign. Scotsman. No one knows that call sign. Well, very few people. It must mean he's still alive, Captain. Lieutenant Hunter is still alive.'

Wilson paused. 'When did you receive the message?'

'Two days ago.'

Wilson thought for a moment. 'It's a fake, Gorringe. We know that Hunter had been taken prisoner by then. They've clearly tortured him. And he's talked. He's given up his call sign to them. They're trying to make you stay here on the island while they hunt you down. Don't you see, Captain? You've been tricked.'

'Well what about Woods and the others in his team?'

'They're all goners, I tell you. Woods is on a suicide mission. He's going to go into the camp and try and get Hunter and Phelps out. But he'll never do it. It's utter madness. Suicide. The important thing is to get Martin away with the intelligence. That was his mission. We've achieved most of our objectives. We've got to ensure that he achieves theirs.'

Gorringe thought about it for a moment. In his heart, he was convinced that Hunter was still alive. He knew though that what Wilson was saying made sense. To attempt a rescue mission was futile. Once the Jerries had you, you were as good as dead.

After a while, he nodded. 'Very well, Captain. We'll sail this evening. For Alex. Until then I'm keeping her under covers. We go at nightfall.'

The caique slipped away under cover of darkness and sailed on until daybreak. The *Rosetta* had been running on her engines at full throttle for far too long and rather than have them overheat and seize up and also to save fuel, Gorringe had decided to revert to sail power. But the wind had died down and now the boat was sitting momentarily becalmed in the middle of the Libyan Sea. Gorringe called to one of his men, a naval rating with a real knack for running the engine room.

'Cook, we'll need to get the engines up and running again. Soon as you can, please. Wind's gone down and we badly need to move.'

Below decks, Harry Martin was wondering what had happened and why the boat wasn't moving. He was feeling agitated and concerned about what was going to happen to them all. In particular though he was wondering where on earth he and Wilson's men were to be set down, while Gorringe went back to collect Woods and the others. That at least was what Wilson had told him was happening before they had sailed. At length, Martin could wait no longer. He pulled himself out of the small bunk and, after pushing open the little door, climbed up on deck. The sea was as glassy flat as a mirror and there was not a breath of wind. From below there was a sudden thudding followed by a crunch as Cook brought the engine into life.

Martin walked over to where Gorringe was standing at the

wheel. 'Captain. Could you possibly tell me where you intend to set us off?'

Gorringe turned to him. 'Sorry, Martin? Set you off?'

'Yes, as the captain said. When you return to Crete to get the others.'

'But I'm not going back, sonny. That's it. We're bound for Alex.'

'No. That's not right. We can't just abandon them. They're not dead.'

Wilson had been listening. 'They're as good as dead, Martin. You know that as well as I do.'

'I won't have it.' He looked back at Gorringe. 'Captain. You have to turn the boat around.'

Gorringe shook his head.

Wilson yelled at Martin, 'That's enough, Martin. Saving the intel and getting you back is what we need to do now.'

Gorringe spoke again: 'I'm sorry, Martin, but the captain's right. But I have an idea. Captain Wilson, how long did it take you to reach us?'

'Best part of three days.'

Gorringe pondered the answer, before replying, 'I don't see why we shouldn't alert Cairo by radio. My set's still working. We can see if they can't send a motor launch to the cove in, say, four days' time. That would be big enough to pick them all up. Then, if any of the others have managed to get away, they will have reached the coast by then. It's not much and I dare say the timings probably won't work, but I want to try something and that's all that we can do.'

14

The following morning the explosives arrived at the camp in the caves. Ffinch opened box after box of them as Woods watched him. The man was like a child, he thought, unwrapping Christmas presents with evident glee, until at length he seemed content that he had found what he was looking for. 'Look at this, Woods. This is the good stuff.'

He held out a lump of green plastic to Woods. It smelt strongly of almonds.

Woods smiled. 'Very nice. Lovely.'

'Nobel 808. Beautiful stuff. Just the ticket.'

Together they made piles of everything that would be needed for the attack on the convoy, as Ffinch went through a litany of combustion: 'Exploder, cable, electric detonators, detonator cord... It's all here. This is really first class. Absolutely splendid.' He paused to look at it. 'I'd better make a start. No time to lose.'

As Ffinch scurried off to his cave to create the bombs Woods settled down with a glass of raki to look again at the small, hand-drawn plan detailing their attack. It was hardly the most complex of ideas, but there again, greater battles had, he supposed, been won by plans sketched out on cigarette packets.

In a couple of hours Ffinch announced that he was ready, and the Greeks loaded up six heavy parcels on to three mules and led them off down the hill towards the spot selected for the ambush. Woods and the other commandos went with them, each of them carrying a Sten gun, along with spare ammo, a pistol, a fighting knife and two hand grenades.

As soon as they reached the appointed place, the andartes began to unload the explosives and detonators from the backs of the mules and put them safely in an irrigation ditch at the side of the road. The rough stone road cut its way through the tree-lined slopes of the hill, snaking away tortuously with a meander that would ensure the slowness of the column when it came. The Greeks were first going to dig a shallow gully diagonally across the road and then set the bombs in it before covering it over with the spoil. The plan was to set the whole lot off at once. There was the Nobel 808 explosive and to it Ffinch had added six linked anti-tank mines. It was going to make a hell of a bang.

The Greeks began to dig the trench in the road that would take the explosives. Woods and his men and two of the Greeks remained on the road, ready to deter anyone from proceeding along the road. But no one came.

Then they moved back up the hill and sat and waited. The early evening was growing colder now. Other men of the andartes platoon began to arrive from the caves, bringing with them the two heavy machine guns and boxes of ammunition. They set up the guns and camouflaged them cleverly with brushwood, before disappearing into the landscape where they too sat down to wait.

Down the hill, five miles away from where the andartes lay in the woods, Hunter and Phelps were beginning their fourth evening of captivity. They had eaten in their cell – sauerkraut, thick black bread and porridge – and were preparing for the move to Hania to meet the general commandant.

Neither man said much. There was not much to say and both of them knew all too well what awaited them.

There was a commotion outside and the door swung open to reveal two of Hilmann's SS. They walked into the cell and grabbed Hunter and Phelps, leading them out of the cell block and into the compound. Both men were downcast, but Hunter had become increasingly determined, as hope had abandoned him, not to allow the inevitability of their fate rob him of the one thing he had left: his pride. He walked out wearing as military a bearing as he could muster.

They were marched in the gloomy twilight from the cells to the parade ground, where three lorries stood waiting. Beside them were two open-topped, Kübelwagen staff cars and an armoured car. And standing beside them, though hardly in parade order, was an under-strength platoon of some twenty black-coated SS soldiers, commanded by a senior sergeant. They were relaxing: chatting and flicking through copies of *Signal* magazine. This, he presumed was to be their escort to the general commandant, and to the gallows. He felt strangely honoured by the high level of security. He smiled at Phelps. 'Looks like this might be our honour guard, Sid. Quite a turnout. Quite a send-off.'

Phelps looked back and smiled and nodded. He hadn't said much for a while now. He seemed to Hunter to be merely an empty husk.

The Germans looked at the two men indifferently and carried on chatting and smoking until, a few minutes later, a command rang out across the square. Instantly all cigarettes were extinguished and all chatter ceased. The men snapped to attention in two neat ranks.

Oberst Hilmann walked across the parade ground, accompanied on his right by his aide-de-camp and on his left by a woman. Hunter looked at her. She was young and captivatingly pretty. Aged perhaps twenty, she was dressed immaculately in a well-fitting grey linen skirt, a white blouse and a little cotton jacket. A double string of pearls hung around her neck and she was carrying a smart little handbag.

Her presence was utterly bizarre, here in this military convoy taking Hunter and Phelps to be paraded before a high-ranking enemy officer before being executed in a public display of barbarity sanctioned by a madman. He wondered what on earth she could be doing here. Was she the colonel's wife? Or his mistress, perhaps? He certainly seemed to be treating her with the sort of politeness that either such position might demand. Hilmann made no show of her before the men but called forward the sergeant, who escorted her discreetly towards one of the command vehicles. Then Hilmann cast a look at Hunter and Phelps and he and the ADC entered the other staff car, joined by their driver and the guards.

Hunter and Phelps were pushed with rifle butts towards their own vehicle, a standard Opel Blitz truck. Their handcuffs were momentarily removed to allow them to clamber aboard, before being replaced once they were inside. As Hunter was climbing aboard he overheard a conversation in German between two of the guards.

'That's her. See that? That's the colonel's bit of skirt.'

'She's not the colonel's, she's anyone's.'

'Any officer you mean.'

'Well, I wouldn't say no.'

'She's out of your league, mate, and anyway, since when were you an officer?'

'So why's she coming with us?'

'I heard the colonel talking to his ADC saying that he was going to "lend her to the general". What about that? She's a present for him.'

'They'll do anything for promotion. Bloody officers.'

'The general commandant is a personal friend of the Führer.'

'Makes sense then, doesn't it. Some present.'

Hunter was not surprised. The same sort of thing must be happening right now all over the great Reich. Women, selling themselves to get on in life, or merely to save their own skins. War wasn't just about killing and maiming. It was about ruining lives, in every way possible. Things just got out of hand. There were no winners in a war. People did stupid things and they did what had to be done to survive.

He felt suddenly sorry for her, this pretty Greek girl, and wondered how she had come to this. Still thinking about her, he moved along the wooden bed of the Opel Blitz truck and sat down on the hard wooden bench. The engine roared into life and, as the little convoy moved off through the airfield gate and into the night, Hunter stared across at Phelps who stared back at him and to his surprise gave him a huge, beaming smile. The man looked relieved and somehow at peace with himself. And Hunter saw that, through the smile, there were tears coursing down his face. Finally there was something certain in Phelps's life. He was going to die and in death, Hunter realised, he would finally find release.

Up above the camp, the moon shone bright above the olive groves and the tall, waving cypresses, and cast its white light upon masses of purple carlina flowers.

Woods was struck by the beauty around him and the stillness. The road was now eerily quiet, save for the clicking of the insects in the undergrowth and the occasional howl of a distant village dog. From their high vantage point, looking down into the valley to their right, it was possible to see the lights of any vehicles. A few came into view but they did not seem to be moving in any particular direction and Woods presumed they were not yet the lights of their target. He looked away and tried for a moment to get things into focus in his mind. To gain an overview of all that had happened.

Fletcher trotted up to Woods. 'They're here sir. They're coming.'

Woods waved him down. 'Get down, man, and get in position.'

Around the bend at the bottom of the low hillock, just where they had reckoned they needed to secure the road, came a German armoured car, with a heavy machine gun mounted on the turret, manned by an SS gunner. It was followed by a lorry, an Opel Blitz, its back covered with a tarpaulin and presumably filled with armed guards. Then came another lorry. They had been informed by Eleni's smuggled message that it was the second truck that would contain Hunter and Phelps and that they would be shackled and guarded. After this second truck came an open-topped Kübelwagen staff car containing the distinctive, black-clad figure of Oberst Hilmann and his ADC, along with a driver and an SS guard.

Woods watched them come and then, behind Hilmann's staff car, saw a second open-topped Kübelwagen, which had not been mentioned in the intelligence. This took him somewhat by surprise, for, apart from its driver, it contained a girl in her twenties, and two more SS guards. The girl was remarkably pretty and she was clearly not a prisoner. She was not shackled or cuffed and was dressed in the manner of a respectable middle-class woman.

As the lead vehicle approached their position, Ffinch pushed down with all his might on the plunger. There was a huge sheet of flame, which, lighting up the night, seemed to leap from the road, followed by an enormous, ear-shattering explosion, and then black smoke and dust everywhere. The armoured car was hit hardest. It was thrown into the air with the full force of the blast and toppled over the edge of the cliff. As it hit the ground upside down the gunner in the turret was decapitated and the vehicle went on tumbling down the hill, with the headless body still in place, eventually catching fire as it went and incinerating everyone inside who had not been killed by blast or crash. The lorry behind it was also lifted up and crashed down on its side across the road, trapping the men inside. Within seconds those closest to the road had begun to scream in pain.

The second lorry, with Hunter and Phelps sitting opposite each other in the rear, crashed into the back of the first, which was now lying on its side and swerved right, straight into the bluff. The driver was thrown into the window and killed outright.

The first staff car careered into the side of the now diagonal second lorry, throwing forward its inhabitants with such force that two of them, the driver and an SS guard, were knocked out at once. The others, Hilmann and his young ADC, seated in the rear, were thrown forward against the backs of the front seats with massive impact and were both badly winded, the ADC breaking two of his ribs.

The driver of the second staff car, which contained Eleni and two more black-uniformed guards, managed somehow to swerve to the right and, skidding along the road, in a mountain of dust, crashed screaming into the rear of the first Kübelwagen side on, injuring all of the inhabitants. The driver came off worst, being crushed against the other car, breaking his arm and wrenching his neck. One of the guards on his side was knocked out by the impact. The other guard was luckier, smashing against the driver's right side but the gear stick caught him hard in the knee and he screamed in pain. Eleni, sitting behind him, was the least injured, but sat in shock, unable to move.

The four guards in the back of the lorry containing Hunter had now dropped the tailboard and began to dismount, pushing Hunter and Phelps out with them so that, their hands still cuffed, they both toppled to the ground and tried to get up. Two of the guards started to run away from the convoy, down the road, only to be met by a hail of fire from the heavy machine gun that had been covering their escape route. They fell, dead to the ground.

The other two, mere boys in SS uniform, looked terrified and uncertain. They raised their weapons and for one moment Hunter thought they might shoot him and Phelps where they were, crouching in the dust, still trying to stand up. But then he caught the eye of one of them and, as he finally made it to his feet, just shook his head, nodding so that the boy would notice the numbers of andartes who were now descending the hillside to swarm around them. One of the boys dropped his gun and raised his hands. The other just stared at him. In that instant Hunter spoke to the first, in German, holding up his hands: 'The keys and you live.'

Not needing to be told twice, the boy fumbled at a ring on his belt for the key to Hunter's handcuffs and finding it, undid the lock, freeing him. Hunter grabbed the Schmeisser he had dropped and, turning to the other guard, who was still trying to understand what was going on, gently squeezed the trigger. The man stared at him for a moment and then dropped dead. Hunter turned back to the boy and pointed to Phelps. 'The key. Undo him.'

Quickly the German, fumbling in his fear, undid Phelps's handcuffs and as Phelps was soothing his cut wrists, Hunter dealt the German a hard blow on the back of the neck with the butt of the gun, which knocked him unconscious.

With the guard lying at his feet, Hunter pushed the Schmeisser into Phelps's hands and grabbed the other man's gun from his dead grasp. He turned to Phelps, who was looking around himself, still a little bemused.

'Phelps. Stay here. Stay on watch. They're all friends. Greeks. Andartes. Go with them and they'll look after you.'

Phelps nodded. Then, without a word, aware that time was everything, Hunter dashed forward to the second staff car.

As he did so, the final lorry screeched to a halt behind the second staff car and, quicker than the Greeks had expected, the tailboard dropped and six Germans began to drop from inside on to the road. However, no sooner had their boots begun to hit the ground, than the rear machine gun on the hillside opened up, spraying them with a belt of bullets. The men danced and fell, writhing and jumping in the contortions of death, like so many black-clad puppets.

Woods had been watching the whole thing unfold with great care, keeping his eye on Hilmann's staff car in particular. As it smashed into the rear of the lorry, he raced down the slope and, hitting the road, dashed towards it, his right hand firmly on the trigger guard of his Sten. He was determined to make sure that no trigger-happy Greek would shoot Hilmann before they could take him prisoner.

As Woods got to within about ten yards of the car, he was able to see that the driver had come round. Seeing Woods, the man began to fumble at his belt for a pistol. Woods squeezed the trigger of the Schmeisser and shot him in the chest. The guard beside him was still a little groggy, but he started to raise his gun and Woods gave him a short burst from the Schmeisser.

Hilmann meanwhile had managed to force open the door at his side of the vehicle and had climbed out. Now he too went for his gun. His holster was open and in seconds he had it out and pointed at Woods as he dealt with the second guard. He was about to shoot when there was a shot that knocked it clean from his hand. Woods looked round to see Andrea smiling at him. The colonel yelled and grabbed at his fingers, one of which had been shot clean off. Woods shouted to Andrea and another of the Greeks, 'Don't kill him. We need to take him alive.'

The colonel's young ADC had finally managed to get out of the car and was leaning against it, holding his side in pain. Woods decided he was no threat and was beginning to wonder whether it might not be worth saving him too, when Yanni walked up behind the boy and shot him once with a Webley revolver in the base of the skull, spattering the upholstery with blood and brain tissue. Woods walked over to Hilmann, who was staring with horror at the body of the ADC.

'Herr Oberst. Now it seems you are my prisoner.'

The German scowled at him. 'Maybe, Captain. But not for long. My men in Heraklion will soon be on your tail. And we will take reprisals for every man you kill or hold prisoner. For that poor boy. There was no need for that.'

'Really? I don't think you quite understand, Colonel, do you? Should I tell my friends about your reprisal plan? They might be inclined to kill you now rather than wait. Come to think of it, perhaps that would be the best thing.'

Hilmann said nothing.

One of the andartes approached Woods. 'This the German you want, Kapitan?'

'Yes, this is the one.'

'So now we can kill all the others?'

'Well, let's just see who is alive and who isn't, shall we?'

Hunter could see the injured passengers of the second car now. It was protected from the forward machine gun's fire by the two crashed lorries in front of it and from behind by what had been his own truck, but as he watched, a group of andartes came down the slope, making straight for it. Hunter ran across to Eleni and yelled at the men on the slope, 'Don't shoot. Hold your fire.'

Eleni had come out of shock and was now moving, trying to get out of the car, but her door was jammed. Hunter spoke to her in Greek: 'It's alright. We're friends. You're safe now.'

As he said it the guard who had been in the front turned to him and levelled a Luger pistol at him. Reacting fast, Hunter raised his Schmeisser and opened up, hitting the German and shooting him dead before he had time to fire. Then, looking away to his left he glimpsed Hilmann. The colonel was holding his hand, which was bleeding, and was talking animatedly to Woods. For a moment Hunter was tempted to shoot the German dead. But in that same moment the injured guard from the second car came round and instinctively grabbed for his gun. But Hunter moved faster and again fired first, hitting the man in the head.

Eleni, still trapped in the car, sat, white-faced and shaking, just staring blankly at the two dead men. Hunter grabbed her and pulled her through the door of the Kübelwagen. Then, holding tight to her arm, he moved with her towards the hill. As he did so the place exploded in a hail of bullets, as the andartes struck the column in earnest, killing any of the enemy they could find.

Hunter walked a little distance up the hill and found White, who was leaning against an olive tree changing the magazine of his smoking Sten gun. He handed Eleni to him. 'Look after her. She's been through a bit of a hard time. And she's in shock. Just stay with her.'

The big man smiled at him. 'Will do, sir. Come here miss. Best you sit down.'

Hunter left her with him and returned to the road where chaos now reigned.

The guard and the driver of the first staff car had now regained consciousness and were staggering about the road like drunks. One of the andartes, a wiry villager from Kastamonitsa named Vardas, walked straight up behind one of them and shot him at close range with his Sten gun, then turned it on the other man and did the same.

And then, as suddenly as it had started, it was over. The noise, which up until that moment had been intense and interminable, suddenly ceased, save for the moaning of the remaining wounded and the crack of pistol shots, as the andartes walked around finishing them off with a single shot to the head.

Ffinch came up to Hunter, who was standing with Hilmann, whose arms were being held in the firm grip of two of the andartes. The German said nothing and had long since stopped struggling.

'Good show, Hunter. Well done. Glad we got you out.'

'Not as glad as I am, sir. Thank you.'

Ffinch turned to Hilmann. 'Herr Oberst. I'm most terribly sorry to have interrupted your evening. Frightfully sorry and all that. Now what we're going to do is go for a little walk and then… Well, then we're going to get you on a boat to our friends in Cairo. And if you attempt to escape. Well, then, I'm afraid we're just going to have to kill you.'

Still Hilmann said nothing. Merely glared and smiled. Ffinch turned back to Woods. 'Right, Lieutenant, we'd better get a move on. Up the hillside and I'll guide you on from there. These chaps all know the way. I'll find Captain Woods. Take it easy as you go. It's a little treacherous.'

They made their way away from the carnage of the road where a score of Germans lay dead, amid the wreckage of the toppled trucks and the twisted staff cars. The ghastly tomb that was the armoured car was still burning at the foot of the hill. Tomorrow, thought Hunter, there would be hell to pay.

They moved away up the hill, an extended party, Hilmann under escort and Eleni being helped by White. Phelps was back with Hunter now, where he felt at his safest, while Ffinch was gabbling away to Yanni about what a great success it had all been. Not only had they captured the general, rescued Hunter and Phelps and saved the girl, the andartes, said Yanni had picked up several briefcases from the staff cars containing not only some papers they couldn't read, but more importantly packs of sugar, sweet biscuits and Viennese cake. Not to mention the cigarettes. Yanni was a very happy man.

Woods walked over to Hunter and Phelps, who were surrounded by the others. Fletcher was speaking to Hunter. 'Bloody hell, sir. We really thought we'd seen the last of you.' He turned to Woods. 'Didn't we, sir?'

'Indeed we did. We'd almost given you up for dead.'

White spoke: 'But the captain here insisted on going back for you, sir. In fact, truth to tell, he was leading us all down to the airfield when we heard you was being moved.'

Hunter smiled at Woods. 'Is that so, Peter? Thank you. That was good of you. Bloody good.'

Woods looked at him. 'You'd have done the same, wouldn't you? Can't give up a man without at least having a go, Jim.'

He smiled. 'You know that as well as I do. Can't leave a man behind.'

Hunter smiled back and nodded. They had both learnt a hard lesson on Rhodes and it had forged a bond between them that they now knew nothing could break.

They came to a halt and Ffinch told them to take a brief rest.

Dawn was coming up but none of the Greeks seemed perturbed that they might be spotted by the enemy.

Ffinch explained, 'Jerry doesn't really come up here. Far too dangerous for him.'

Yanni moved among them, handing out some of the German chocolate and the Viennese cake that he had liberated from the staff car. As they were eating it Woods turned to Hunter. 'You saved the girl, Jim. Well done. That was bloody clever of you.'

'Well I presumed we might want to save her. She looked a little out of place, sitting there. Was I right?'

'Were you right? I should say so. Of course we wanted to save her.'

'Why? Who is she? She's Greek, isn't she? Is she a quisling? A Nazi? She was at the camp. We saw her being taken to the car. But she was no prisoner. She went of her own accord. I overheard the guards talking. Something about a present for the general?'

'Yes. Her name's Eleni. She works... worked in the officers' mess at the camp. They were taking her as a "present" for the general commandant.'

'That's what I thought they said.'

'She, well, she looks after the officers' needs.'

'Oh. I get it. I see. She's a high-class soldiers' whore. That's what I've bloody well saved.'

'No. There's more. She's also our intelligence source. It's

only through Eleni that we knew they were moving you. Otherwise, you'd still be on your way to Hania.'

Hunter whistled. 'Christ, that's good. I had her all wrong, didn't I? Perhaps I should thank her then?'

'Yes, Jim. Perhaps you should. God knows what we're going to do with her now though. I doubt she can go back undercover.'

'Well, surely, we get her out. Get her back to Cairo if we can. She might well be of use.'

'Really? In what way?'

Hunter smiled. 'Well, if she's prepared to go to those lengths for her country, who knows what else she might do for the war effort.'

'Are you sure that's such a good idea. She might compromise the whole thing.'

'Oh, I don't think so. Anyway, we're more than a little compromised already.'

Changing the subject Woods pointed to Hunter's bandaged head and hand. 'I say, are you alright?'

'Bit of an argument with an SS guard and the stone floor of a cell. But I reckon I'll survive.'

'How about Phelps?'

'Hard to say really. His nerve's totally gone. He just sort of folded up. In the camp, I mean, on the op. Just when we were right in the thick of it. He cracks. Then they beat us up quite badly. But it was really not knowing what they were going to do to us... with us, next. It was bad enough for me, but God knows what it did to him. He's no use to us now. Or to anyone, poor bugger.' He looked at Woods. 'Thank you, Peter. Thanks for getting us both out.'

'It was nothing. It was two Effs' doing, really, and the andartes. Oh, and Eleni.'

'So what's the plan?'

'Now we have to walk. Into the mountains apparently, and down the other side to the coast. It's about twenty-five miles. Might take us two days.'

'And what about the boat? Is Gorringe still there? I sent a message.'

Woods shrugged. 'That's just it. Obviously I sent Martin off with the papers and Wilson and his men with him, what was left of them. I told them to wait for a day when they got to the boat. But by the time we get there we'll be two days late. I doubt if even Gorringe will have waited.'

'Well, I suppose that we'll just have to see how it plays out, won't we? This place will be crawling with Jerries soon. Hadn't we better go?'

'Yes, I think that's in Ffinch's plan.'

And together, they began to walk up the hill.

15

Their escape route lay on a direct route to the south coast and Cape Kochinoxos, where they had landed with Gorringe, what seemed to Hunter like weeks ago. But it was not a simple matter of retracing their steps. They had gone too far west for that. First, as Hunter was only too aware, they would have to get across the formidable natural obstacle of the snow-capped Lasithi Mountains. They had started by heading for Anoyeia, the largest village on the island, Ffinch had told him, and the key to the mountains. It lay four miles uphill from their ambush spot and the going from the start was hard.

Every time they paused, which, given the fact that it was now night, was often, Hunter looked to his right and every time what met his gaze was the huge, imposing mass of Mount Ida, its summit capped with snow. If their war was to be lived in caves then there was the cave to outdo them all. The Idaean cave had hidden the infant Zeus from his father Cronos, its entrance and the baby's crying concealed by the mad war dances of a band of warriors. Hunter was struck by the parallels to his own situation. Although rather than Cronos, they were being pursued by hundreds of Germans who, he was horribly aware, were even now hot on their trail.

There was no real path to speak of and as they climbed the undergrowth grew thicker and more thorny. The journey was made easier though by the moon, which lit their way allowing them to avoid the sides of the ravines along which their path had taken them. A constant chorus of cicadas and croaking frogs provided an almost musical accompaniment to their steps.

At last, after three hours of climbing, they saw ahead the white houses of a village. Yanni drew alongside Hunter. He whispered with pride, 'Look there. There she is. My village. Anoyeia.'

Hunter looked at his watch. It was one in the morning.

They entered the village in silence, a curious little column. A real mixed bag, thought Hunter, with the Greeks in front with Ffinch, followed by Hunter and Woods and, with them, Eleni and Yanni, and then Hilmann, his hands bound with the same pair of German handcuffs so recently worn by Hunter himself. The colonel was flanked by Fletcher and White. Then came the rest of the commandos: Russell carefully helping Phelps, Miller and Sergeant Knox in their rear, keeping a watchful eye. And finally six more of the andartes.

They did not wake the village as they entered and walked its cobbled streets. Yanni knew exactly where they were headed and took them there immediately. When the door opened it was on to an unexpected sight. The kitchen table was crammed with food and drink.

Knox gasped. 'Bloody hell, sir. They've pushed the boat out for us and no mistake.'

Hunter turned to Yanni and thanked him profusely in Greek. The house belonged to Yanni's cousin's wife who greeted him with open arms.

Soon all of them were standing around the kitchen eating their fill of eggs, cheese, bread and olives.

Hunter walked over to Ffinch who was standing by Woods eating goat's cheese and soaked rock bread. 'So, where do we head from here? They'll be after us now. That's for sure.'

Ffinch spoke between mouthfuls: 'Oh, across the mountains. It's the only way.'

Woods looked at Ffinch. 'You're not thinking of climbing Mount Ida?'

Ffinch shook his head and laughed. 'No, of course not. Why ever would I want to do that? We'll sacrifice concealment to speed. Head further east and skirt the highest mountains to get down to Tymbaki. There's a five-mile climb, but then we drop down and carry on going down all the way to the coast.'

'But surely the Germans will follow us on that route?'

'We're sending a decoy party into the hills. One of them will be wearing the black uniform of the SS and two of them will have your German uniforms. Sorry. But we need to use them. We stripped many of the SS bodies on the road. I'll also need the colonel's service cap. But that's all.'

'You really have thought of everything, it seems. Think it will work?'

'I certainly hope so. Anyway, it's the best we can manage. Oh and, incidentally, the colonel needs a change of clothes too. Here you are.'

Ffinch handed Hunter a pile of clothes. He took them across to where Hilmann was sitting eating a piece of cheese, still with his hands in handcuffs. 'Colonel, we need you to change your clothes. These will probably fit you.'

Hilmann looked at him in disbelief. 'Don't joke with me, Lieutenant. I am a German officer. An officer in the SS. I am not like you. I will not give up my uniform so easily.'

'Well I'm afraid you're just going to have to. Or we're going to have to help you. Please don't give me an excuse.'

Hilmann picked up the garments with distaste and looked at them, holding them up, one by one. There was a typical Cretan waistcoat, a pair of baggy trousers and a blue shirt without a collar, along with a crimson scarf.

He stared at Hunter. 'Really? You expect me to dress as a clown?'

'There wouldn't be much of a difference, would there?'

Hilmann ignored the jibe and looked again at the clothes. 'The jacket yes, and perhaps the shirt. But I am keeping my own trousers and my boots.'

Hunter nodded. 'Quick as you can please. Your friends can't be far behind. We're moving off.'

He left Hilmann with the clothes, watched over by Fletcher and White, who unlocked one of the handcuffs to allow him to put them on.

A few minutes later Hunter walked back to them and was amused to see the colonel clad in what could easily have been taken for the typical dress of a Cretan peasant. Even his riding breeches and jackboots seemed to fit the bill. All that was missing was facial hair.

Hunter reached out for the black, silver-trimmed SS officer's tunic that Hilmann was holding. Reluctantly, the colonel surrendered it to him.

'Thank you, Colonel. I assure you your tunic will be returned to you before you meet my own general, in Cairo. We wouldn't want you to make the wrong first impression, would we? Oh, and I'll need your cap, please.'

Hilmann handed over the peaked officer's cap. 'I'm sure that you will have a clever plan. A decoy. Someone dressed as me? It's so obvious, Lieutenant. Not even the most idiotic of my men would fall for it. Not even an imbecile. You underestimate the Germans, Lieutenant. You always have done. You are a very arrogant people, Lieutenant. We will prevail. In the end, we will win.'

Hunter walked up to him so that their faces were almost touching. He spat out the words: 'You'll never win. And d'you know why? Because you're evil. Pure evil. Just like your master. Now shut up, you Nazi bastard, or I'll change my mind and kill you myself. Got it?'

He turned and walked away, leaving not just Hilmann, but also Fletcher and White, speechless.

Hunter stood and fumed. He had not intended to do that, but the man was insufferable. Grabbing his glass of raki, he looked up and his eye caught that of the girl, Eleni. For the first time since they had met, she smiled at him. And in that smile he thought for an instant that he saw a glimmer of real affection. And that was something he had not seen for a very long time.

He smiled back and then quickly looked away at his watch, which now read 0230. They had spent over an hour at Anoyeia and needed to make up ground. He could almost feel the enemy upon them now, could sense their presence, growing closer by the minute. Ever since the ambush he had been aware that there was nothing now to hold the Germans back. The inevitability of their arrival hung over Hunter like some ominous black spectre that grew in intensity with every step they took.

Ffinch led the way, with Yanni now as they moved off through the streets of the village to its southern side and then moved quickly from the cobblestones back on to the stony surface of the hillside. Soon they had begun to climb again.

Before they did so, Ffinch sent off a group of the andartes away to the west. Three of them were dressed in German uniform. One as the colonel, complete with his cap and the two others in Hunter's and Phelps's tunics, which they had swapped for their original battledress tops. Their kepis, sadly, had disappeared in the airfield. Nevertheless the group made an impressive impersonation of their own. Soon, said Ffinch, the Germans would see them and start to pursue them and providing they were not caught, they would lead the enemy through the White Mountains off to the west and as far away as possible from the real evaders, as they made their way south.

But Hunter was not completely convinced. Every step he took now he knew was being matched by their pursuers. Every snap underfoot of a twig or a branch, every small stone that stumbled away down the hillside, made him feel more vulnerable. More exposed. At any moment he expected to hear a rifle crack ring out across the hillside.

They walked through the night and at around 5am, just as the dawn was breaking over Mount Ida, Ffinch signalled them all to stop. He pointed to a shallow ridge about twelve feet above them and said simply, 'Up there.'

Hunter looked for a means of climbing and saw, half hidden in the stone of the rock face, what could have been carved steps. He approached them and saw that that was exactly what they were, but that a trick of perspective had concealed them. Gradually they climbed up and on the ridge at the top found the entrance to a concealed cave. A man stood in the entrance, an elderly andarte with a fine beard and white hair, his shoulders draped in ammunition belts. Ffinch gave him a huge hug.

'Michalis.' He turned. 'Everyone, this is Michalis. He will guide us down the other side of the mountains. This is his home. Now let's rest. It will take us another day and a half.'

During that day, Hunter wasn't certain at what time, two young andartes arrived at the cave and sought out Ffinch. They brought news, which he delivered to Woods and Hunter: 'So, the Germans seem to have fallen for our ruse. The plain west of Heraklion is teeming with them and they've sent more troops up into the White Mountains.'

Woods and Hunter both grinned. Ffinch continued, 'But that doesn't mean we're off the hook. We've no room for complacency. It could all go belly-up at any moment. We must start again just as soon as it begins to get dark.'

So they waited again, and gradually the evening light crept up on them. Woods had not slept well and at intervals during the day he had wandered in and out of the cave, listening to the chat of the andartes.

Late in the afternoon he found Ffinch. 'They're not happy.'

'You noticed it too?'

'Yes, we both did. Hunter's been listening to them. They're

not very happy about the colonel. The general feeling seems to be that we should have killed him. That while that might have brought reprisals down on their people, it would have given them a focus for the fight. As it is they're now condemned to shuffle around the hills with a man whom they hate, while their band is split up and chased by the enemy. They're not happy at all.'

'Which makes it all the more important that we get you to the coast as quickly as possible.'

Woods nodded. 'I'm going to talk to Yanni. To apologise. To explain.'

Ffinch shrugged. 'It might help. But in reality nothing's going to please them unless the colonel dies or we get him away as soon as we can.'

Woods sought out Yanni. The big man was sitting in a corner of the cave cracking his knuckles and sipping raki. 'Kapitan Yanni.'

It was best to address him formally. To flatter him. Yanni looked up.

'Kapitan Woods. Please sit with me. A glass?'

He poured another raki and handed it to Hunter, who began, 'Kapitan, I have to say, I am very sorry for the position we are in. The last thing I want to do is compromise your men.'

Yanni smiled at him. 'Kapitan, please. My men do as I say.'

'Yes, of course, but that's not really the point. They're not happy. I can tell. And I know why. If I could kill the colonel, believe me I would. And believe me I really do want to.'

'Oh I believe you, Kapitan. I know what he did to you and to your friends. He must die. But he must die by British methods not by ours. And that is why you need to get him off this island.'

'Yes, you're right. Thank you for your help.'

'Kapitan, you are a great man. Truly, I mean what I say. I know that you will go on to do great things in this war. But first we need to get you away to safety. And that is why God has given me this challenge and this great chance. So now we drink and then we rest and then we must start to walk again.'

He raised his glass and drank to Woods's health and Woods did the same to him and when he got up and walked back to Ffinch and Hunter, he felt that something had changed. That they had somehow at last become accepted by the andartes.

Ffinch saw him coming. 'How did he take it?'

'Well. Very well. He treated me as if I was his own son.'

'Then he must like you. Believe me, I've been practically adopted by several of the local leaders. And I'm godfather to two of their children.'

They rose at dusk and began to make their way once again in the direction of the coast. At one point Eleni, who, even though she had been kitted out with a pair of walking boots and a pair of oversized battledress trousers, seemed to be finding the going more difficult, fell back and walked alongside Phelps and Miller. Knox, walking just behind them, saw her and slowly made his way to where Hunter was in the line. 'Sir, it's the girl. Reckon she's getting tired, sir. She's fallen back a fair bit down the line. Might be good to have a word, sir. See if we can help?'

'Good idea, Sarn't Knox. You stay here with the captain; I'll go and see what's up.'

Hunter turned and fell back to where Eleni was now walking with Miller, falling in with her in the line. 'Are you alright? Not too tired?'

She shook her head. 'Of course not. I'm a Greek. We don't get tired.'

'I just wondered. You seemed to fall back a little.'

'No, no. I just wanted a change of scenery.'

They walked on together for a while before she spoke again: 'Kapitan Ffinch told me. Told me what you did.'

'What do you mean?'

'Your captain wanted to leave me here, on the island. I can understand why. I am a hindrance. Another person to carry. Another possibility for being discovered. But if you had left me, I would have been killed by the Germans. Worse. It was bad enough already, but once they had found out what I had done and how many of their soldiers' deaths I had caused, I would have been no more than a piece of meat. Female meat, to be used and then killed.'

Hunter winced. 'Yes. I guessed at that. That's why I had to get you out.'

'You care that much?'

'I do. Of course I do.'

She smiled at him again. That same smile.

He went on, 'I'd do the same for anyone in your position.'

It wasn't what he had meant to say, but something inside Hunter's mind was making him take back what he had said before. She had stopped smiling and was staring at the ground.

They carried on walking, desperately trying to make ground, and Hunter became aware that they were now descending quickly. They started to slither down over loose rock and found themselves among vineyards and olive groves on the lower slopes. The rest of the night passed as slowly as those before but thankfully without event and before they knew it they had left the foothills of the mountain range. Within another hour they had emerged on to a wide plain and there in the distance, Hunter was at last able to see the moonlit enormity of the sea.

Moving across the fields with their goal in sight their steps seemed somehow lighter and as he walked with them Hunter noticed that the mood of the andartes had become lighter and that they were laughing and chattering as they grew ever closer to the sea and the prospect of returning to their villages.

The cove had not changed since they had landed. But now that moment seemed an eternity away. He found the cave where they had stowed the folboats and to his relief they were still there. The enemy had not discovered their anchorage and it was clear to him and Woods that Gorringe had sailed and they could presume that Martin was on his way to safety.

Ffinch decided that the best thing to do would be for him to leave, along with the andartes.

Woods was not so sure. 'But, we'll be hopelessly outgunned.'

'We would be anyway, old man. This way, if we split our forces then there's a fighting chance that the Jerries might do the same. Or they might even all follow us. And in the unhappy event of you being taken prisoner, we won't end up in the bag too.'

Woods had to admit he was right. Hunter also saw the logic of it and so as soon as they were ready, Ffinch said a final goodbye and the andartes slipped away into the night.

Yanni gave Hunter a huge bear hug. 'Kapitan. I am sure we will meet again, my good friend.'

Hunter returned the hug as best he could. 'Yes, Yanni. I truly hope so.'

There were two more hours left of darkness and they posted Miller and Fletcher as sentries, lying on top of the gullies above the beach. Hunter sat in one of the smaller caves among the pebbles and, for the first time in days, lit a cigarette. No one on the land could see him now and it didn't seem to matter if anyone at sea saw his light. He inhaled deeply and enjoyed the novelty. As he blew out the smoke, a figure appeared at the mouth of the cave, outlined against the night sky and instantly recognisable: Eleni.

'Can I come in? Do you have another of those?'

Hunter took another cigarette from his pocket and lit it in his own mouth, before handing it to her. She sat down beside him and, blowing a smoke ring, spoke quietly: 'Do you think we'll get away? Really?'

'It's anyone's guess. If I was the captain of our boat. Well, what was our boat, I'd have sent a signal to Cairo by now asking for a sub or a launch. Just in case we had made it out alive. But I'm not Captain Gorringe and I really don't know what he'd do.'

'I wanted to say thank you.'

'You already have.'

'No, I really wanted to say thank you for saving me. I don't know what I would have done.'

Stubbing out her cigarette, she quickly reached around Hunter's neck and, pulling him towards her, kissed him hard on the lips. Taken completely by surprise, he didn't respond, but pulled back. 'What was that?'

'Thank you. I want to say thank you.'

She unbuttoned her coat and took it off then started on the buttons of her shirt. Hunter put his hand over hers. 'Eleni. This is a lovely idea, but not here, and not now.'

'But I owe it to you. You saved my life.'

Hunter cursed himself. He had almost been taken in. But he realised that this for her was payment. She was giving herself to him to thank him for her life. That was all. A transaction. This was nothing to do with the expression he thought he had seen on her face in the village. If there was really anything more to that look, then the last thing he wanted was the girl here to sleep with him as a form of payment. He whispered to her, 'I'm sorry. I just don't think it's the right moment.'

She was already buttoning her shirt. 'You know the real reason why I fell back on the march, two days ago. Behind the others?'

'Tell me.'

'I wanted to be able to see that bastard.'

'Colonel Hilmann?'

'Hilmann. I wanted to work out just how I would be able to kill him while we were walking. To see if I could possibly push him off the mountain, or if I would need to stab him first.'

'You have a knife?'

'I have a knife.'

She drew from her coat pocket a knife with a blade around twelve inches long. It had a black-lacquered handle and a distinctive nickel pommel and as she drew it from its scabbard, it glinted in the moonlight and Hunter was able to make out the motto – '*Meine Ehre heißt Treue*' – that ran along the axis of the blade.

Hunter looked at it. 'That's an SS dagger. Where did you get it?'

'I took it from one of the bodies at the ambush. I wanted that pig to feel what it was like to be killed by one of his own knives.'

Hunter shook his head. 'Killing him isn't the answer, Eleni. Getting him back to Cairo is. He'll be useful to us there; he might even save lives.'

She shook her head. 'He deserves to die. Slowly and painfully. In return for all the pain he has caused to so many.'

'Yes, I'm sure you're right.'

'I know that I'm right. That man is a monster.'

She raised the front of her shirt and showed him a long scar on her right breast, which almost reached the nipple. 'There. There is an example of his sort of lovemaking. Nice, eh?'

Twisting round she pulled up her shirt at her back. Hunter was horrified to see more scars. Evidence that she had been flogged.

'He likes to play games that one. Nasty little games.'

'How revolting.'

'Now you see why he must die.'

'If you give that sort of evidence, in Cairo, he probably will be shot. But not before he has told our chaps there everything they need to know.'

'I couldn't care less about what they need to know. I need to know that he is dead.'

'Believe me, Eleni. What he knows could save hundreds, thousands of lives.'

She had put her coat back on now, but he noticed she was still shivering.

'You're cold?'

'Yes.'

He touched her shoulder and pulled her towards him and then they slept. And when they woke the new day dawned and they watched the sun rise in the east, further round the coast, and Hunter wondered what new horrors or new miracles it might bring.

They sat in the cove. And they waited. Every moment was filled with apprehension. What, Hunter wondered, would come first? The sound of German troops as they swarmed down the gullies leading to the beach? The noise of an enemy torpedo boat as it moved slowly along the coastline, its searchlight seeking out their hiding place, which would then be raked with fire from machine guns and ack-ack guns? He realised that, having done his best to remain so positive for so long, having led his men into the very heart of the enemy and through unimagined adversity, here at last, on this beach, he was starting to lose any hope that they would be rescued.

He was still musing on this when there was a commotion in the gully and Russell came running down from the dunes and into the cove. 'Jerries, sir. Dozens of them.'

Hunter ran over to him. 'Where? How close?'

'They're not close. Not yet. But they're coming. That's for sure.'

Hunter followed Russell back to the gulley and, joined by Woods, they reached the top. Then, without showing himself, he put his field glasses to his eyes. It was as he had feared.

Russell was right. Off in the distance, on the road that led to the fields beyond the beach, he could pick out three half-tracks. They would be packed with enemy troops. And he had no doubt they were heading for the cove.

He passed the binoculars to Woods. 'How long do we have, do you think?'

'How far away are they? Five, six miles?'

'About that. I reckon it might take them about twenty minutes to get here.'

'Yes, you're probably right.'

Together they dropped back down through the gulley, leaving Russell to man the post. Woods called the men together. 'We've got company. There's a platoon, perhaps a company of Jerries in half-tracks heading this way. They'll be here in twenty minutes. That's what we've got. Fletcher, White, find that case of grenades. What else do we have?'

Knox answered, 'Two Brens, the 34, ten Sten guns and two Schmeissers, but there's not much ammo for them.'

Hunter spoke: 'Right, we're going to forget the sea for now. I want all eyes on those half-tracks. Our best bet is to wait until they're almost on us and then use the grenades. If we can get them when they're still in the vehicles we've got a chance. If they dismount further out and walk in, well then we'll just have to use the machine guns.'

Following the others as they made their way up through the gulley to the higher ground, White and Fletcher carried the box of grenades that they had brought from the cave. They could see the enemy in the distance. Three vehicles moving across the flat plain below the mountains. Fifteen minutes or so, thought Hunter. They might just have a chance.

Russell, who had been down on the beach bringing up

ammunition for the Bren was the first to hear the new noise. He came running up the gulley to where Hunter and Woods were lying. 'Listen, sir, can you hear it? That noise?'

Both men were silent. Listening.

Russell was right. There was a noise. Distant but distinct. A sort of chugging. Knox appeared. 'What's that?'

They could all hear the engines now. Some sort of boat was coming towards them, hugging the coast as it came. But there was no way of their knowing what it might be, or whether it was friend or foe. Hunter yelled to the men, 'That's a boat. Enemy boat. All of you, get back down to the beach. And take some grenades with you.'

There was a frantic scramble as they switched the focus of their defence from land to sea. Hunter did his best to post the men. 'Fletcher, White, both of you get behind those rocks, take a Bren. Sarn't Knox, climb up there with the '34 and see if you can get a clear line of sight. Miller, you watch the colonel. Gag him and keep him covered. Then try to find some cover and keep him down. Phelps, you stay with Eleni in the cave. Take your Sten. Russell, stay with me and Captain Woods. We're the mobile reserve.'

The engines were creeping closer now, as the boat neared the edge of the cliff that masked it from their sight and also hid them from its crew. Hunter whispered to Russell, 'Hold your fire. Wait for my signal, pass it on.'

And in seconds the order had filtered through to all of them. They waited, poised, every finger on a trigger guard. Every eye on the edge of the cliff.

Then, with a burst of her throttle, the prow of the boat broke round the cliff and it came into sight. Not a man fired and Hunter waited to give the command, until he was absolutely sure. It was a motor torpedo boat by the look of it, but whose? In an instant the wheelhouse came into sight and instantly, Hunter knew.

'Hold your fire! Hold your fire! Don't shoot.'

As the words left his mouth, the main deck came into view, along with the white ensign, fluttering proudly on the mast of His Majesty's Motor Torpedo Boat 309.

16

Hunter was not entirely sure how long it would take him to readjust to what passed for normal life or to reassemble his frayed nerves and raw emotions.

But he did know that after two days he had not yet begun to come anywhere near to it. He looked at the faces of the men and women, civilian and military, on the crowded Cairo streets and wondered if they noticed anything strange or remarkable about the man in khaki who was walking past them. Hunter felt that he must somehow look different.

He knew, too, he had left a part of him behind somewhere on a hillside in Crete. He felt empty, emotionless. With every corner he turned in the dusty street he expected to meet a patrol of German soldiers or SS. Of course after every mission you were relieved and also deflated, as the thrill of ever-present danger evaporated. But this was unlike any homecoming Hunter had experienced before.

After so long sleeping rough and living in the field, and being among so much violence, suffering and death, what he had seen before as the filthy streets of the bustling city seemed now remarkably clean and fresh. What troubled him were the sheer numbers of people who pushed and jostled around him and increased the sense of claustrophobia that came with the way in which the tall buildings left just a small patch of blue sky above your head. It was about as different a view of the world as you imagine from the broad expanse of the heavens that soared above the Cretan hills.

It was nearing eleven in the morning and, summoned to a long-expected debrief, Hunter had left his temporary quarter in the officers' mess at Citadel barracks up on the hill overlooking the city deliberately early and walked into the centre of Cairo. He desperately needed more time. Time to think. Time to rehearse his report on all that had happened in the week since he had been away. But he knew it was too late for all that.

He had headed down the boulevard Muhammad Ali, to the Opera House and as he passed Groppi's he thought for a moment of Lara and wondered what she might be doing at that moment. And then he thought of Eleni and he was back in the cave on Crete, staring at her scars and holding her sleeping form close to his as he watched for the dawn and waited.

He turned on to Suliman Pasha street and knew that in less than five minutes he would arrive at his destination at Rustum Buildings. Faces flashed into his mind. Eleni's smile, Hilmann's scowl, Yanni's huge, generous grin and the faces of the other andartes, Phelps's hollow eyes and then Duffy's dying stare. Feeling suddenly drained, he slowed his pace and wondered if perhaps he could delay this moment. It was all too fresh, too raw. But then it really was too late.

In the distance Hunter caught sight of a familiar figure. Woods was waiting for him outside SOE Headquarters in Rustum Buildings. As Hunter drew closer he smiled and held out his hand. Hunter took it: 'Peter, how are you?'

'I'm not sure yet. You?'

'Oh, about the same. Just feel a bit, displaced.'

'Yes. Good word. Shall we?'

They walked in to the building, returning the smart salute from the two redcaps as they went. Inside nothing seemed any different from their last visit. Together they climbed the iron staircase to the first floor and walked along the corridor to flat 7. Woods knocked and the door was opened by the same pretty young WRN.

'Oh, hello again.' She looked at the clock on the wall. 'You're dead on time. That's lucky. He'll be pleased.'

She walked across the office, followed by the two of them, and knocked on the inner door. There was a grunt from within and she opened the door.

Both men were somewhat surprised to be met, not by Vickery, but by Commander Fleming. He held a half-smoked Sullivan Powell oval Turkish cigarette in his hand and was seated in the leather chair, behind the same antique desk. He was alone.

'Welcome back gentlemen. Cigarette?'

He held out the silver box and opened the lid. Both men took a cigarette and Hunter flicked open a Zippo and lit them.

Fleming spoke again: 'Well, what can I say? I'm pleased. And so, I hear, is Winston. In his opinion the operation was ninety-five per cent successful. He's really very pleased indeed.'

Woods stared at Fleming. 'Churchill's pleased? It went that high?'

Fleming smiled and nodded. 'Of course. It was your first outing. Naturally, Winnie was in on it. He sanctioned your existence.'

Hunter shook his head and looked at the commander.

'Sorry, sir. We lost one man and have another who's lost his mind. Captain Wilson lost two-thirds of his command and a caique. Two of us were very nearly executed and we just managed to make it off the island by the skin of our teeth. And you tell us that Churchill's pleased?'

'Yes indeed. Very pleased. Normally of course you'd both get a gong. But you know how it is with us. It's all hush-hush. And I'm sorry too about your man who was shot. Duffy, wasn't it? And the other fellow, Phelps. Our chaps are with him now, seeing what they can do to help.'

Hunter spoke again: 'If you ask me, he's beyond help, sir. And I'd just like to say that we need to make sure that sort of thing never happens again. The training needs to be able to sort out those sort of problems before it's too late.'

'Yes, believe me Hunter, we are looking into that as well. Won't happen again.'

Woods spoke up. 'What about Wilson, sir? Has he been debriefed yet?'

'Yes, we've spoken to him. He's pretty shaken. Losing so many of his men like that. Not an easy thing for anyone to take.'

He paused before continuing. 'He was a bit miffed that you apparently compromised his mission at Heraklion. In fact he was very angry.'

Hunter shook his head. 'If you want the truth, sir, he over-reacted. There was nothing we could do – Phelps just broke and that was that. We just had to get out of there. After that there was never going to be any hope that his boys would get in there and do their bit. I will say that Captain Wilson didn't really seem to understand the importance of our mission compared to his.'

Fleming nodded and lit another cigarette. 'Yes, well I'm afraid that's how it's always going to be for us. The demolition boys just don't get the more sensitive side of our work.'

He paused again. 'Captain Wilson even went so far as to suggest that in the grand design of the operation, his own mission might have been merely a diversion and that you had been given the priority. You wouldn't agree with that would you, Lieutenant?'

He smiled. 'Not my place to agree or disagree, sir.'

'That was exactly the answer I wanted, Hunter. Thank you. Anyway, I've had a quiet word with Wilson's CO. I'm sure it will all be smoothed over.'

'I'm not sure that I agree with that, sir. Wilson will always hold a grudge against us, won't he?'

'I very much doubt it now. He's been warned off, you see. And in no uncertain manner. Certain things, Hunter, are just more important than others in this business and I think Captain Wilson might have had his eyes opened. The good thing was that he managed to get Martin off the island.'

Woods spoke: 'And Wilson managed to save himself and his men at the same time.'

'That sounds like resentment, Captain. Is it?'

'No, sir. No resentment at all. I'm just suggesting that Captain Wilson seemed to me to be more concerned with getting off the island than he was with either getting Martin and the intelligence out or saving the lives of my men.'

Fleming nodded. 'Point taken, Captain. Let's leave it there, shall we?'

Hunter cut in, 'What about Colonel Hilmann, sir?'

'Ah yes, the good colonel. Well that really was an extra bonus. Well done both of you. An inspired move. Just the sort of initiative that we were hoping for when we invited you to join our merry band of brothers.'

'Can I ask, sir, what you intend to do about him?'

'Yes, of course. Well we've actually started already. He's really being most co-operative and we've managed to come to an agreement.'

Hunter stared at him, 'An agreement, sir? With that monster? Surely not.'

'Yes. An agreement. Hilmann has agreed to tell us whatever he knows about the Nazis' plans, secrets, positions, whatever we want really.'

Woods spoke: 'But will he? Can he? He's a Nazi, through and through. Committed to his Führer. He's an idealist, isn't he?'

'Oh, I don't think so, Woods. It's really just a lot of pompous posturing. He's like all the rest of his kind. Just in it for his own ends. Out for whatever he can get and for sale to the highest bidder. Gangsters in uniforms. That's all they are.'

Hunter smiled. 'And that's what they call us, sir, isn't it. The regulars. Our own side. Gangsters. Criminals.'

Fleming ignored the comment and continued, 'So, as I said, he's proving to be very helpful. And in return we've agreed... not to kill him.'

'You're not going to kill him?'

'No. Not for the present at least. He's far too useful to us alive. Wasn't that, after all, why you brought him out of Crete?'

'Sir, at this very moment on Crete there are men, women and children being lined up against walls and shot. Burned to death in their own homes, thrown down wells, hung from olive trees. You name it, sir, and the Jerries are killing them in any number of barbaric ways. And do you know why? Because of that man. Because of Hilmann. Reprisals, sir. That's what's happening.'

Fleming smiled again and stubbed out his cigarette before reaching for another from the silver box. 'Yes, Hunter. We're well aware of just what the Nazis are capable of. Of all the foul methods they employ. But even if you'd killed him on the island this would have happened. It happens every time a single German soldier is killed. Ten Greeks are arrested and shot. We know all this. And that is why you brought him out isn't it? You told the girl that didn't you?'

'How do you know that?'

'Lieutenant, I can't believe that you are so naïve to suppose that we would not already have interrogated Eleni Evangelou. She has been most helpful and illuminating about her time with the andartes and with your commandos. And I get the impression that she rather likes you.'

Hunter bit his lip. Fleming continued, 'And we rather like Miss Evangelou. In fact we like her so much that we're thinking of asking her to join us. She's got guts that girl. To go undercover, on her own and to do everything she's done. She's clever too. She'll do well with us.'

Hunter shook his head. Commander Fleming was nothing if not a fast worker.

'You've recruited Eleni? I didn't even think you would have questioned her before you spoke to us.'

'There is an order to our ways, Lieutenant. It's just how we do things and how we make things work. So that is how I know that you told the girl that the colonel was of use and that keeping him alive would save...' He looked at a pile of notes on his desk. 'How did you put it? "Hundreds, no thousands of lives".'

Hunter shook his head. 'She really did tell you everything, didn't she? Did she show you her scars too, sir. Where the bastard beat her and where he cut her while he was raping her?'

'No, she didn't. But she did tell me about them.'

'I've seen them. I know that man for what he is, sir. He deserves to be shot. Won't you at least sentence him?'

'Not now, Lieutenant. I'd like to, but I can't. You know that's not how it works. That will all come later when we've won this bloody war. He's told us a great deal already and I'm quite sure that there's more to come. In fact one of the things he's told us about is the fact that there's a German raiding flotilla ranging around the islands, Naxos, Iraklia, others and terrorising the population. We'd heard something about it but he's given us actual names and numbers. Well now of course, we need someone to go and see if he's telling the truth. If we can trust him on this one, then perhaps we can trust him on other, bigger stuff.'

Woods spoke: 'You're asking us, to go back. To go in and recce Naxos? In what might be a trap?'

'Yes, of course I am. But not now. All in good time, Captain. All in good time. Now why don't you two go and get some rest. You look as if you might need it. We'll be in touch. We know where to find you. And, Hunter, remember, you're one of us now. There's no going back.'

Author's Note and Glossary

Although this book is a novel, it is based on historical fact. While the basic timeline is accurate, I have moved some individual events to allow the plot to work and to drive the action.

The SBS of the title stands not for Special Boat Service but Special Boat Section and later Squadron, that unique unit which had operated since June 1941 in the operation which inspires my opening chapter. It was also known as Folboat Section and was attached to 8 Commando. It was not a naval unit, despite its name, but contained mostly marines and army, all of whom were expert canoeists. By April 1941 it had been transformed into 1st Special Boat Section working with 1st Submarine Flotilla but not under the jurisdiction of either army or navy.

Its main operations by this time had been in the summer of 1942, including a July raid on Sicily. It was then attached to David Stirling's infant SAS in October 1942, and consisted at that time of fifteen officers and forty other ranks. At the same time a second unit of SBS was formed.

In the spring of 1943, after the capture of David Stirling by the Germans, the Special Boat Section (1st SBS) was transferred to the command of Royal Navy Captain the Earl

Jellicoe (who had been David Stirling's second in command) and the unit was thus now under naval command.

Legend has it that it was on 1st April 1943 that the Special Boat Section became Special Boat Squadron. In fact it was on 19th March when the SAS regiment was reorganised into two parts, the SAS Raiding Forces (under the notorious Paddy Mayne) and the SBS (under Jellicoe).

The new unit's first operation was in Crete in June 1943 and it is this which provides part of the inspiration for Hunter's mission.

Ian Fleming did indeed create a specialist unit of intelligence gathering commandos, later 30 Assault Unit, modelled on the German unit raised by Otto Skorzeny. Its mission was to feed enemy intelligence back to London. Apart from its work in Greece and Italy, it was key in destroying the V1 and V2 rocket programmes.

Fleming was in Naval Intelligence and a serving naval officer. The unit was thus a naval unit but was split into three sections of navy, marines and army, so it had a mixture of army and navy personnel, not unlike Hunter's unit, which is essentially fictitious, a hybrid of 30 AU and the SBS, attached to 8 Commando.

Throughout the book I have employed numerous military acronyms. A glossary is given below:

EDES   The Greek Centralist/Nationalist resistance
         movement.

EKKA	The Greek 'National and Social Liberation' resistance group. National Socialists.
ELAS	The military wing of the Greek Communist resistance movement EAM.
ENSA	Entertainments National Service Association. Organisation providing entertainment for the British armed forces during WWII.
SIS	Secret Intelligence Service (MI6) (UK).
SOE	Special Operations Executive (UK).
TA	Territorial Army (UK).
WRNS	Women's Royal Naval Service (UK).
WAAS	South African Women's Auxiliary Army Service.

About the Author

IAIN GALE is the author of twelve military historical novels and two works of military history. Iain was for many years a member of the Scottish Committee of Combat Stress, the armed forces' PTSD charity. He also sat on the Royal Scots Dragoon Guards Waterloo Committee at Edinburgh Castle and was privileged to be invited by the regiment to take a major part in its bicentenary commemorations. He is a recognised authority on the Battle of Waterloo, and has taken numerous tours there, including leading a tactical military exercise of thirty-two serving US Army officers. Iain also guides regular small battlefield tours to the Somme, Arnhem, Dunkirk and Normandy and presents military history lectures. He is married with six children and lives in Fife and Edinburgh.